Lynda Page was born and brought up in Leicester. The eldest of four daughters, she left home at seventeen and has had a wide variety of office jobs. She lives in a village near Leicester. Her previous novels are also available from Headline, and have been highly praised:

'In Lynda Page, we have an author who writes with skill and style; her characters are strongly drawn and thoroughly believable and her settings are just that little bit different . . . it keeps the reader enthralled from start to finish. Mark my words, on this showing Leicester's Lynda Page is destined to share the limelight – and bestseller lists – with the likes of Catherine Cookson'
Hull Daily Mail

'You'll be hooked from page one' *Woman's Realm*

'Lynda Page creates strong characters and is a clever and careful storyteller . . . She has the stamina not to alienate you as a reader and to keep the story going on a constant flow of purpose and energy . . . A great writer who gives an authentic voice to Leicester . . . A formidable talent' *LEI*

'A terrific author' *Bookseller*

Also by Lynda Page

Out With
The Old

Lynda Page

headline

First published in 2003
by HEADLINE BOOK PUBLISHING

First published in paperback in 2004
by HEADLINE BOOK PUBLISHING

10 9 8 7 6 5 4 3 2 1

ISBN 0 7553 0110 2

Typeset in Times New Roman by
Letterpart Limited, Reigate, Surrey

Printed and bound in Great Britain by
Mackays of Chatham plc, Chatham, Kent

Papers and cover board used by Headline are natural, recyclable
products made from wood grown in sustainable forests. The
manufacturing processes conform to the environmental
regulations of the country of origin.

HEADLINE BOOK PUBLISHING
A division of Hodder Headline
338 Euston Road
London NW1 3BH

www.headline.co.uk
www.hodderheadline.com

For my beloved daughter, Lynsey Ann Page.

All mothers want to shout to the world about their children's achievements. I'm no exception.

Many congratulations on your 2:1 LLB honours degree in Law. My admiration for the dedication you've shown and the hard work you've put in is immeasurable. But then, from the moment you were born I knew without doubt that not only were you going to grow into a delightful, beautiful woman but that you were also destined for greatness. Mothers are always right!

Acknowledgements

Sherise Hobbs at Headline – my 'little treasure'. Thank you for your unwavering 'listening ear' and willingness to help me no matter what. You are indeed a credit and I know without doubt that your boss appreciates what she has in you!

Jean and Len Matthews – a wonderful lady and a great gentleman.
I am in awe of you and so proud to be part of the family.

Chapter One

Sitting rigidly at the table, hands clenched so tightly her knuckles bulged like stepping stones, Lavinia Deakin stared transfixed at the suitcase by the door. There was nothing special about the case. It was a plain brown box-type bought cheap twenty-two years ago from the market. It was battered now after its long years of service in many different guises. Its clasps had ceased to function and it was now secured by two fraying leather belts. Vinnie likened the suitcase to an old family friend: strong, dependable, always there when she needed it. A sickening sensation gnawed her stomach. She was about to lose her old friend, but far more importantly the person taking it away, the person whose belongings it now held, would be lost to her also.

Her eyes went straight to him as he walked into the room. Thomas Henry Deakin. Despite his forty-odd years he was still breathtakingly handsome, easily passing for a man several years his junior. Over six foot in height with broad shoulders; no age lines as yet marring his smooth light-olive skin; no jowls hanging from a masculine square jawline. He had eyes of a deep velvet brown, and his full head of immaculately groomed dark hair showed hardly a trace of grey.

Pulling on an overcoat above his smart navy suit, he strode across to his wife and placed something before her. His house keys. She couldn't swallow for the lump in her throat.

'I'll be off then.'

His tone was brusque, barely recognisable. She raised bewildered, grief-stricken eyes to him and, bottom lip trembling, murmured, 'Why, Tommy, why?'

He looked and sounded agitated. 'Don't start, Vinnie, we've already been through this.'

She scraped her fingers despairingly through her fashionably styled flaxen hair, not caring that she was leaving it wildly dishevelled. 'But you've told me nothing, Tommy, just that you're leaving me. I don't understand,' she implored. 'Up until a few minutes ago when you dropped this bombshell, I thought we were happy.'

With a set face he told her, 'Maybe *you* were, Vinnie.'

She gazed at him, mortified. 'But you *weren't*, is that what you're saying?' She gasped. 'For how long, Tommy? How long have you not wanted to be with me and said nothing?'

He gave a shrug. 'I dunno. Does it matter?'

She leaped up from her chair to face him. 'Yes, it does,' she cried. 'I want to know, Tommy. I want to know what I did that made you fall out of love with me. I want to know why you never said anything. I want to

2

know why you won't give us another chance.' She grabbed at his arm, gripping it tightly, pleading with him. 'It's not too late, Tommy. All couples go through bad times. We can sort out whatever is wrong and put things right between us, I know we can.' She stared at him wide-eyed. 'You can't seriously be prepared to throw away twenty-two years of marriage just like that?'

Wrenching his arm free, he stared at her crossly. 'Just accept that it's over, Vinnie.' He waved one hand. 'Look, this isn't easy for me and I really don't want a fuss . . .'

'*You* don't want a fuss,' she interjected, her face twisting in utter disbelief. 'How dare you, Thomas Deakin? How dare you announce so matter-of-factly that you're leaving me, giving me no warning whatsoever, and expect me to sit quietly and not say a word? Did you think I'd help you pack and wish you well, tell you to pop by for a cup of tea for old times' sake any time you felt like it? Well, did you?'

He looked at her darkly. 'Don't be sarky, Vinnie, it doesn't suit you.'

She wrung her hands. 'It seems to me that I don't suit you at all anymore, sarky or not,' she whispered.

He stared at her for several long moments before saying, 'Life changes, Vinnie. Things just happen that we ain't prepared for and we can't control.'

She frowned, puzzled. 'What do you mean by that?'

She looked at him searchingly. The man standing before her was suddenly a stranger. At this moment hardly anything about him reminded her of the husband she had lived with for what seemed an eternity, whose arms had held her close less than an hour ago as they had danced to the 'Anniversary Waltz' at the end of their daughter's wedding. He was staring back at her unblinkingly and she strongly suspected he was desperately searching for a more valid reason for what he was doing than the limp excuse he just didn't love her anymore. What he came out with made her gasp in shock.

'Let's face it, Vinnie, you've let yourself go.' Immediately his mouth clamped shut, a remorseful expression momentarily appearing. 'Look, sorry, I didn't mean to say that and I didn't mean for our marriage to end like this. But I can't help me feelings. I loved you once. Now I just don't anymore and I can't go on living this lie.'

She automatically stepped backwards as though physically struck. 'You made love to me last night,' she uttered, bereft. 'How could you do that if you don't have feelings for me?'

'It was a duty, Vinnie, that was all. I did what was expected of me.'

Mortified, she slumped back down on her chair and cradled her head in her hands. How she wished he had spared her that last admission. But even so his account of last night was nothing like the way she remembered it. He had been the one to approach her and she had responded willingly as she usually did, thoroughly enjoying their lovemaking which she had always believed got better and better as the years passed.

Afterwards they had fallen asleep nestled against each other. If Tommy had merely been performing a duty then Vinnie had never realised before what a good actor he was.

Her eyes caught sight of the hat she had taken off when she had arrived home less than an hour ago: wide-brimmed, draped in cream chiffon, tastefully decorated in two-tone blue fabric flowers. The events of the day flooded back to her. She lifted her head and looked at him. 'Why of all days did you pick today to leave me, Tommy? The day our youngest daughter got married. It's been such a wonderful occasion. Now all I'll remember of it is that it was the day you left me. Could you not have waited until tomorrow or the next day even, left me with *this* day as a good memory instead of . . . of . . . one I'd sooner forget?'

His face contorted in anger. 'As far as I'm concerned our youngest daughter is our *only* daughter.' This shocking admission and the venom in his tone made her gasp. 'The other selfish madam has brought both of us n'ote but heartache. She may as well be dead as far as I'm concerned. She might be for all we know. We've heard nothing from her since the day she walked out of this house nearly five years ago. I don't suppose she's ever given a thought to the worry she's caused us. All I can say is that if she's any sense she'll never come back.'

'Oh, Tommy, how can you say that! Why Janie walked out without a word or hasn't contacted us since when she knows we'll be worried sick is beyond me, but she's still our daughter. It doesn't change the fact that you've two children, not one. You might have wiped Janie out of your life but I haven't. She must have left for a reason and until we know that reason, neither of us has the right to judge her harshly.'

A flicker of shame crossed his face which was quickly replaced by a look of frustration. 'Look, this is getting us nowhere, Vinnie. Marriages fall apart. Can't you just accept that ours has?'

'No, I cannot,' she cried. 'Yes, marriages do break up, but not just like that, Tommy,' she said, clicking her fingers. 'Are you trying to tell me I'm that blind I haven't noticed ours has been in trouble?' She gave a bewildered shake of her head. 'And even if it is, after the length of time we've been together usually the one wanting to leave affords the other a last chance to put things right, or at the very least gives them a bit of warning. Don't I deserve any consideration, Tommy?'

His silence gave her her answer.

Out of the corner of her eye she caught a glimpse of the case over by the door and pain overwhelmed her. She wanted to use any means she could to get Tommy to stay so they could talk and try and reason this awful situation out, but she knew from his whole manner that whatever had brought on his mystifying behaviour, Tommy would be resolute in his decision and any further pleading on her part would be futile and only result in further humiliation for her. She could only hope that this was a temporary aberration, that he'd quickly realise what a terrible mistake he had made and come back begging her forgiveness. She swallowed a choking sob and falteringly asked, 'Where . . . where will you go?'

He averted his gaze, shuffling uncomfortably on his feet. 'I've . . . er . . . arranged to stay with a mate 'til I get a place. I'd best be off, I'm expected.'

She froze in horror, her heart thumping painfully. Tommy *had* planned this then. It was no momentary madness on his part, as she had hoped.

Out of habit he made to step forward and kiss her cheek. When he saw her flinch he turned from her, picked up the case, and without a backward glance walked out of the house.

It seemed to Vinnie that no sooner had the front door clicked shut than the back door shot open and her next-door neighbour of twenty-two years, Noreen Adler, was pulling out a chair at the table opposite her.

Just a few months apart in age, Noreen and Vinnie, both newly weds, had moved into adjoining rented two-bedroomed terraced houses on the same day, and much to Vinnie's dismay it had immediately become apparent that her new neighbour was the loud, bossy sort with no regard for anyone's opinion but her own. As their respective husbands had helped each other manoeuvre in their heavy furniture, and while Vinnie herself unpacked her bare minimum of possessions, Noreen had settled herself at Vinnie's well-worn gate-legged kitchen table. It was obvious she was expecting to be plied with tea or preferably something stronger as she proceeded to instruct Vinnie on how she should arrange her new home. She had been passing judgement on every aspect of Vinnie's life ever since, from the way she raised her children and tended her husband, to how she decorated her home – which showed what a nerve she had considering how badly Noreen kept her own house and that she certainly didn't act in the way Vinnie felt a wife and mother should to her husband and son.

Vinnie had lost count of the number of possible good friends she had lost through Noreen's rudeness and tactlessness; of how many unnecessary rows had been caused with other neighbours in the street by her friend's volatile streak which would erupt without warning – when angry, Noreen was known to use language so foul she could make a grown man blush. However much Vinnie tried to dissuade the constant intrusions into her life, Noreen never took the hint and, to avoid causing bad feeling between the two adjoining households, Vinnie had no choice but to suffer her presence.

Once girlishly pretty with voluptuous curves, the passing years had not been kind to Noreen. But then, she had no one to blame for it but herself. Her greediness for food, regular consumption of Mackeson stout, and twenty-cigarettes-a-day habit were clearly visible on the thirty-nine-year-old woman. She tried to hide the deepening age lines on her face with thick makeup, and mistakenly nursing the illusion that her figure was the same now as it had been at eighteen, crammed her increasing girth into gaudy, tarty clothes several sizes too small for her, thinking she looked classy and alluring. Under the impression she was every man's dream woman, she would flirt outrageously whenever she got the chance, heedless of the embarrassment she was causing her victim.

In private Tommy was forever telling Vinnie how much he detested their neighbour. He thought her a brassy, vulgar slapper whose figure and features reminded him of a heavily pregnant sow and whose constant unprovoked flirtation with him made his stomach churn. The only reason he tolerated her was because of his friendship with her husband Eric, though he could never understand how such a pleasant man had come to saddle himself with the likes of his wife.

Eric Adler was an unremarkable-looking man with an easygoing nature. Of medium stature, his youthful slimness had now given way to rotund proportions. Like his wife he adored food. Eric's expectations were simple. He had been born in these streets and was quite happy to see out his days in them. To him happiness was returning home each night from his day's work to find his slippers warming by a roaring fire, his dinner plate piled high ready on the table. He liked to relax watching favourite programmes on his treasured black and white television; looked forward to his pay packet at the end of the week so he could settle his bills and afford his wife a night out down the local on a Saturday evening, where she'd play bingo while he supped at the bar or played a game of dominoes with his life-long cronies.

But as far as Noreen was concerned, if Eric expected her to warm his slippers and do soppy things like that then he was a fool to himself. Her approach to house-keeping was to do as little of it as she could get away with. In her favour it had to be said she did cook good meals but only because she herself adored food. And she'd readily join her husband down at the pub as in her opinion a man should pay for his wife's drinks and games of bingo, though she never shared her winnings. She had won them, so in her opinion they were hers to spend on herself.

Twenty-year-old Barry Adler, Eric and Noreen's only child, was a good-looking, long-haired youth typical of his generation, content only when he was listening to his latest records or dressed up in the latest fashions to go dancing in one of the many discothèques springing up in Leicester in 1966. His pride and joy was his Vespa GS 160, customised in his own individual style with extra spotlights, two extended aerials protruding from the back of the pillion seat, the whole vehicle smoth-ered in fox tails and strips of fur. Feeling like the bee's knees in his parka, he would cruise the streets with a friend on the pillion, hoping to attract the attention of potential conquests he'd then arrange to meet inside a club on Saturday night. Weekdays he worked as a plumber's mate for a local firm.

A visit from Noreen was the very last thing Vinnie felt like at the moment. She didn't want to see anyone. Still numb with shock from Tommy's bombshell and subsequent departure, she desperately wanted to tell her neighbour to go and leave her in peace so she could try and take in what had just transpired, make sense of it all. It seemed she was in the middle of a nightmare, that soon she would wake up and find Tommy snoring beside her, but the excruciating physical pain building within her was telling her otherwise. This was no dream. The man she'd loved without reserve, taken care of, borne two children by, had thought she would grow old with, the man who all those years ago had promised before God to cherish her until the day she died, had just bluntly told her he didn't love her anymore, packed up all his belongings and left.

Vinnie needed to digest this terrible development herself before she could share it with anyone. To arouse any suspicion in Noreen was the last thing she wanted to do. One inkling of trouble and Noreen would demand an explanation then immediately offer her advice on how to retaliate which she would expect to see taken. But it was too late for Vinnie to make an excuse and ask Noreen to leave, she had already settled herself. There was no alternative but to endure the visit, hope her neighbour noticed nothing amiss, pray she didn't stay long.

Noreen glanced around her. 'Tommy out?'

Vinnie looked at her blankly. 'Er . . . yes . . . er . . .'

'Oh, gone ter catch last orders, has he? Eric stopped off at the pub on the way home. I was sorely tempted meself to have one for the road, round the day off so to speak, but the need to get off me stilettos which were pinching me bunions summat terrible was greater. I expect the men are all at the bar now, toasting the happy couple for the umpteenth time. Any excuse, eh? I dread ter think what state Eric'll be in when he does manage to come home as he was having a job walking straight when we left the reception. He missed his footing and fell in the gutter more than once.' Noreen gave a loud guffaw. 'The last time he did it I just left him to get on with it.'

Completely oblivious to the fact that the person she was chatting away to had her mind fixed firmly on other matters, Noreen pulled her faded well-worn quilted dressing gown tighter around her thickening body, folded her plump arms and leaned on the table, her eyes glazing over.

'I've gotta give yer yer due, Vin, that were a grand wedding. The best I've ever been to. Mind you, it should have bin, the money I know it cost yer. Can't say as I liked all the music that band you hired played, though. You should have hired the one I suggested. Still, fair dos, they did play lots us older ones could dance to.' She screwed up her face scornfully. 'I can't be doing with this new-fangled stuff the kids listen ter these days. And the names these bands use! Well, fancy calling yerselves the Rolling Rocks or the Cockroaches . . . Bugs . . . summat ter do with creepy crawlies anyway. And the length of their hair and the fancy clothes they wear! Well, they all look like nancies ter me. I keep telling our Barry if he doesn't get his hair cut like a man's should be then I'll personally stick a basin on his head and chop it off meself. Mind you, I might as well be talking to a brick wall for all the notice he teks of me. But these rock group chappies all seem dirty-looking tykes. If it were up ter me they'd be thrown in the bath and given a good scrub with carbolic. Yer can call me old-fashioned but gimme Dickie Valentine or the Dallas Boys any day. At least they look like men and yer can understand the words they sing.'

She gave a rasping smoker's cough and swallowed back phlegm. 'I've not danced as much as I did terday since I was a youngster down the local youth club. My Eric has never been what yer could call a dancer. He just looks a right prat clodhopping around on his two left feet. But your Tommy can certainly cut a swathe on the floor, can't he? Did yer see him swirl me under his legs when we were jiving? I hope I didn't show me knickers but I was more worried about busting open me corset.

'Talking of corsets, I tell yer, Vinnie, I was bleddy glad to get that contraption off. I was forced to fork out good money on that thing 'specially for the occasion. Well, I had no choice as that gel in C&A's sold me the wrong size dress or else the factory stitched on the wrong label. I kicked up a right stink but they insisted it was a 16. Said they'd swap it for an 18 but that's all they were prepared to do.' Her face screwed up in disgust. 'Bleddy 18! In truth I'm a size 12 and always have bin, it's them that's got their sizings wrong. But no matter, they wouldn't tek it back so I had no choice but to buy that corset as I was adamant I was going to wear the dress. I've a good mind to go down and stand in the middle of the shop waving that corset around until they offer ter pay for it. D'yer know, I think I just might. That'll bleddy teach 'em fer trying to get the better of me.'

Noreen paused for breath and licked her lips. 'Oh, the food was outta this world! I really got a taste for those vontevoll thingies. What were in 'em? Chicken or mushroom, wannit, in some sorta sauce? Tasty they were anyway.' She giggled. 'I hope nobody noticed I ate a whole plateful. Still, food's ter be eaten, ain't it?' she said by way of excusing her greediness. She extracted a cigarette from a packet of Park Drive kept in her dressing-gown pocket, lit it with a Blue Bell match, and noisily blew a plume of smoke in the air. 'I expect yer glad it's all over now, you having worked like a Trojan these past months to mek Julie's day perfect, though it's my opinion you could have saved yerself a lot of money by holding the reception in the Mission Hall instead of that hotel.'

She tapped her cigarette over an ashtray and muttered under her breath, 'I just hope your daughter appreciates what yer did, but knowing her as I do I somehow think she'll find summat to complain about.' Then her face lit up and she beamed at Vinnie broadly. 'But just think, eh, yer've done yer bit fer yer kids and now it's time fer you and Tommy to sort yerselves out.'

Vinnie had hardly heard a word of Noreen's prattle but that last statement brought her up sharp. 'What do you mean by that?'

'Eh?' She gave a nonchalant shrug. 'I don't mean

14

n'ote in particular. Just . . . well, for the first time in twenty-odd years you and Tommy will have the house to yerselves, and yer can please yerselves what you do in it now, can't yer?' She gave Vinnie a suggestive wink. 'Be like newly weds, you two. I shall have ter put earplugs in tonight. Yer know how thin these walls are.' She stopped her flow of talk, scrutinising her neighbour. 'What's up with yer face? If I didn't know better I'd say you look like you've just returned from a funeral rather than yer daughter's wedding.' She glanced Vinnie over. 'You ain't even bothered to get yerself out of that outfit yer paid a small fortune for from Joseph Johnson's.' She smirked sarcastically. 'C&A weren't good enough ter you, was it? So what *is* up with yer then?'

'Oh, I'm, er . . . just tired. It's been a long day. You're right, I ought to go and change before I ruin my good suit.'

Extremely grateful for a chance to escape Noreen for a moment, Vinnie practically ran from the room. Upstairs, she stood in the bedroom where only a matter of minutes ago Tommy had packed up his belongings while she sat below, frozen in shock at his announcement, secretly praying her husband had not meant what he'd just said; that it was all some sort of macabre joke.

There was an empty space on the dressing table where Tommy's personal bits and pieces used to be and the wardrobe door was still open, showing a gaping void where his clothes used to hang. The empty hangers seemed to leap out at her mockingly, reinforcing the fact that he had really gone. Running across to the wardrobe she put her hand on the door, meaning to shut out what it represented, and as she did so caught sight of herself in the long mirror fixed inside. She stood and stared at her reflection. She was not a person to heap praise on herself; nevertheless the woman staring back at her didn't look to her like someone who had let herself go, as Tommy had so bluntly accused her of doing.

Vinnie traced slender fingers over one cheek. The flush of youth had long gone but in its place was an attractive maturity. Her creamy white skin, on which she was careful to use Pond's Cream every night, was as yet hardly touched by age lines, just a few around her large blue eyes. She wasn't quite as slim as she had been when young, but her curvy figure was still good for a woman of forty who had borne two children and whose life had not been without its worries and strain.

She ran her hands slowly down the front of her outfit. Having taken great trouble to choose this suit, she looked lovely in it, she knew she did, its pale blue offsetting her blondness and pale skin, bringing out the violet flecks in her eyes. The cut of the heavy satin fitted jacket showed off her trim waist and the pencil-style skirt flattered her shapely legs. Vinnie had turned a blind eye to its cost, spending far more on it than she'd dared admit because she had wanted to look every inch the gracious mother of the bride, make Tommy feel proud to have her on his arm as they walked out of the church. And hadn't she received numerous compliments today? Even from her daughter, who was usually slow to give anyone praise of any sort. Besides today, she always took care with her appearance, mindful of her advancing years while wanting to keep fashionable.

But obviously her efforts had been wasted on her husband.

Her fight to keep her composure broke then. Like a dam bursting its banks, fat tears of devastation flowed down her face and intense pain filled her whole being. Collapsing onto her knees, she wrapped her arms tightly around herself, rocking backwards and forwards, sobbing hysterically.

'My God, gel, what on earth's wrong?' Noreen demanded as she arrived breathlessly in the bedroom. She looked hard at Vinnie then shook her head knowingly. 'Come on, gel, pull yerself together. We all lose our kids some time. Well, hopefully. Despite the fact my Barry is hardly at home, I worry he'll never leave permanently. Your Julie's nicely settled, Gary seems a decent sort. Much too good for her in my opinion. I bet once she realises marriage ain't all it's cracked up ter be, that gel will never be off yer doorstep. Mind you, do yer really want her constantly mithering yer with her hoity-toity ways? Still, I suppose she's your daughter and it's you that has ter put up with her, not me. Anyway, I'd give me right arm ter be in your position, so I would.'

Shivering violently, Vinnie choked, 'No, you wouldn't.'

Noreen reared back her head and looked at her as though she had completely lost her mind. ''Ave you gone crackers in yer old age, Vinnie? I bloody would,' she returned with conviction. 'The way my Barry's carrying on, it seems ter me I'll never be rid of him. Let's face it, both your two gels have ran yer ragged in their own ways. I know it broke yer heart when your Janie went off without a word but she was never the best-natured of kids, was she? Always a surly sod. As fer Julie . . . well, I think she's under the impression you were both put on this earth just to do her bidding, especially her dad who she's got wrapped around her little finger. You should be happy, gel, rejoicing that you've got yer life back to do exactly what yer please with.'

Sniffing hard, Vinnie raised her head and looked at Noreen through blurred, swollen eyes. Her face wreathed in utter misery, she replied, 'Rejoicing? That's the very last thing I feel like doing, Noreen. I've lost everything in my life today. Everything.' Then, unable to stop herself, she blurted, 'Tommy's left me.'

Noreen's jaw dropped, her face a picture of surprise. Blindly, she went over to Vinnie and took her arm. 'Tommy's left yer?' she uttered, astounded.

Shuddering violently, Vinnie gulped for breath and nodded. 'Just now. Packed all his belongings and went.'

Not much struck Noreen speechless but this news stopped her in her tracks. 'Gone?' she said, finally finding her voice. 'Tommy's gone? Oh!' She stared at Vinnie for several long moments before demanding, 'Where? Where's he gone?'

She gave a helpless shrug. 'To a mate's, he said, until he gets himself sorted.' Then a great well of fresh tears bubbled up to gush down her face, and racking sobs shook her. 'Oh, Noreen, this is so awful,' she blubbered. 'What am I going to do?'

Her neighbour looked blankly at her for several long moments before saying, 'I know what I'm gonna do.' Grabbing Vinnie's arm, she pulled her unceremoniously upright. 'Get you downstairs so you can tell me proper what's gone off. And I need a fag. This news has fair knocked the stuffing outta me. Never in a million years did I expect to hear this. No, I certainly didn't!'

The cup of tea Noreen thrust before Vinnie several minutes later was scalding hot and burned her lips when she took a sip.

'It's summat alcoholic we need, gel,' Noreen said, disgruntled, as she plonked herself down in a chair at the table opposite Vinnie. 'After raking yer cupboards I couldn't find a drop of anything stronger than Ovaltine, and as I can't abide the stuff we'll have ter mek do with tea. Drink it down, it'll do yer good.' She lit a cigarette and drew deeply on it, then settling back in her chair, eyed Vinnie searchingly. 'You ain't having a joke with me, are yer?'

Vinnie stared at her incredulously, noticing a look on Noreen's face she couldn't fathom. 'Joke!' she exclaimed. 'Are you honestly asking me that question about something so serious, Noreen Adler?'

Noreen shuffled uncomfortably on her seat. 'Well, yer've gotta admit this is so out of the blue it took me by surprise, that's all.'

So that was the expression she had read on Noreen's

face? Surprise. Vinnie frowned. 'Took you by surprise? That sounds to me like you expected him to do something like this, just not right now.'

Noreen threw back her head, scowling fiercely. 'By God, you're touchy, gel, but I expect that's understandable in the circumstances.' She took a breath and her features softened. 'It was a daft choice of words. I meant ter say shocked. I'm shocked by this news, really I am.' She looked hard at Vinnie. 'He's definitely gone? Yer sure about that?' she urged. 'I mean, for all you know Tommy was just drunk and . . .'

'He wasn't drunk,' Vinnie cut in, her voice resolute. 'I've never seen him like this before but I know he wasn't drunk. He acts soppy when he's had a few too many. He was acting far from that tonight.' She took a deep breath and sighed despairingly. 'I haven't checked around yet but Tommy told me he took everything personal with him, so if that's not definite then I don't know what is.'

For several long moments the two women sat contemplating their own private thoughts. The long silence was broken by another flood of tears down Vinnie's parchment, pain-etched face.

'I can't understand it, Noreen,' she sobbed, wiping her face with an already sodden handkerchief. 'I thought we were happy. Our marriage hasn't been without its up and downs, but then whose has? We've had our disagreements but most of those were over something to do with the girls. Nothing marriage-threatening as far as I'm concerned. Obviously Tommy thought otherwise. But why didn't he say something, Noreen? Why? Why?'

She pursed lips still stained red from the remnants of the lipstick she'd worn earlier and shook her head. 'I dunno, gel. Maybe he just couldn't find the right time to raise the subject. Men ain't very good at that kinda thing. Just bury their heads in the sand when problems arise and rely on us women to sort them out, else hope they'll just fizzle away.' She eyed Vinnie intently. 'So what reasons did he give for leaving?'

Renewed pain jolted through her and a sickening bile rose up to burn the back of her throat. 'If you don't mind, Noreen,' she croaked, 'I don't really want to talk about this anymore. I just . . . well, I just want to curl up and die if you want the truth. At this moment in time I feel my whole life has ended.'

Noreen leaned over and patted her hand. 'Well, yer bound ter feel like that, gel, but you'll be better in the morning when yer get this all into perspective. It's a good idea to sleep on things.'

'Sleep?' Vinnie exclaimed. 'Some hope I have tonight, or ever again.' She looked at her friend quizzically. 'Since when have you ever slept on anything? Knowing you as I do, I'm surprised you're not threatening to find Tommy and knock his block off for what he's done to me.' She searched Noreen's face. 'Are you sure you didn't know anything about what he had in mind?'

Noreen flashed her an angry glare. 'And how the blazes would I know what your Tommy was up to? You lived with the man, and if you didn't know what was in his mind then how the hell would I? I hope you ain't accusing me of aiding and abetting your husband, Lavinia Deakin? 'Cos I ain't. I've already told yer, I'm as shocked at this as you are.'

Vinnie looked at her, mortified. 'No, no, I'm not accusing you at all,' she insisted apologetically. 'If I sounded as though I was, I'm sorry, Noreen. All I meant was . . . well . . . have you noticed anything different about Tommy lately? What about today? Was he acting . . . I dunno . . . strangely at all?'

She gave a shrug. 'Apart from when I grabbed him up to dance, I was too busy enjoying meself to notice what kinda mood he was in.' She scraped back her chair, stood up and demanded, 'Tell me the address of the mate he's gone to and I'll go and see him and find out what the hell is going on.'

'I don't have an address. I don't have any idea what mate he's staying with either.'

'Yer must have a clue?'

'For God's sake, Noreen, I don't. He didn't give me any details. Anyway, even if he had, I don't want you to go round and cause trouble. It'll only make matters worse.'

She sat back down again, face screwed up in annoyance. 'Yer didn't say that when your Janie disappeared. Yer begged me to help yer look for her then.'

'You can't compare my Janie going off to this. Janie was my child, my baby, out there somewhere trying to fend for herself amongst God knows what kind of people. Even now she's on my mind constantly. I'm always worrying what's happened to her, trying to work out why she did what she did. The passing years haven't made it any easier on me, Noreen, you know that. Tommy going off . . . well, it's different. For a start he told me he was going and . . .' Her voice faded as a lump formed in her throat.

Noreen's eyes sparkled inquisitively, 'And what, Vinnie?'

'And . . . and . . . he told me why he was leaving, which is something Janie never did.'

'And that was?' Noreen probed.

Vinnie slumped despairingly. 'That he didn't love me and hadn't for a long time,' she choked.

'Oh . . . oh, I see. And that was all the reason he gave yer?'

Vinnie raised her head and flashed her an angry glare. 'You really are the limit, Noreen. You'll not be happy until I give you a blow by blow account, will you?' Her face crumpled and she gave a mournful groan. 'I'm sorry, I didn't mean to snap at you. I know you're just trying to be helpful. Yes, that was all Tommy told me, and to be honest that was enough, I don't think I could have stood any more home truths tonight.'

Noreen looked at her sympathetically. 'No, I suppose that one was bad enough.'

Just then a loud thud reverberated through the thin walls.

Noreen snorted in disgust. 'Jesus Christ, Eric's obviously home and bust down the front door by the sound of it.'

'You'd best get off and see to him, Noreen.'

'Yes, I'd best do that,' she said. 'I'll pop in in the morning and see how yer are. If Tommy really has gone then you've ter mek plans, gel.'

Vinnie eyed her blankly. 'Plans? What sort of plans?'

'Well, yer've ter work out what yer gonna tell your Julie when she gets back from her honeymoon fer a start. I wouldn't like to be in your shoes when yer do. Idolises her dad, don't she? Can't see past him. Then there's work to consider. You and Tommy work at the same place and you'll need to prepare yerself for how yer gonna handle that situation. And there's other things, but they'll keep fer now.'

As the back door slammed shut Vinnie issued a loud groan of anguish and rubbed her hands despairingly over her face. She had been so taken aback by the shock of Tommy's unexpected departure that she hadn't considered the aftermath. And Noreen seemed in an awful hurry to get home when she usually overstayed her welcome, on numerous occasions over the years having to be turfed out so Vinnie and Tommy could go to bed. Still, Vinnie couldn't blame the woman for wanting to get away from her. Not the best end to a wonderful day, having to listen to her terrible tale of woe.

Slowly rising, she made her way to the window at the back of the room, pulled the curtain aside and peered out. It was pitch dark with no moon and she could barely make out the outline of her back wall. At the other side of it ran the jetty, a narrow alleyway giving on to the back yards which was used as a shortcut to adjoining streets. During daylight hours it was usually filled with children playing games, disgruntled pedestrians weaving between them, but darkness saw it occupied by groups of youths, their transistor radios blaring out the latest pop music transmitted by Radio Luxembourg, who were constantly being herded off by local residents, as were courting couples seeking the privacy of the shadows.

Vinnie's attention was caught by the sudden illumination of a bedroom light being switched on in a house opposite. Silhouetted against the thin curtains she could see a couple readying themselves for bed. A sob caught in her throat and her heart sank. That was what she and Tommy should have been doing now. Instead he was gone and she was alone.

From next door the noise of a commotion building could be heard as Noreen cursed loudly in her struggle to get an inebriated Eric up the stairs to bed. Normally Vinnie would have laughed, picturing the comical scene, but tonight nothing would have raised a smile.

Suddenly it all became too much for her and she sagged in desolation. She had endured a long day; it had started off joyfully and ended in heartbreak and bewilderment. She wrung her hands. Going over it all, trying to fathom sense or reason in Tommy's behaviour, she felt like a hamster on a wheel. Round and round and round and round she went, never coming to a conclusion. It was all so raw, so painful. She felt an overwhelming need to blot it all out, sink into an oblivion only deep sleep allowed. How she wished she had something to induce that state miraculously, but she hadn't, as Noreen had grumbled, even a bottle of alcohol at her disposal, let alone a sleeping pill.

All she could vehemently hope was that the Good Lord would see fit to help her in her time of great need.

Chapter Two

A loud hammering on the back door jolted Vinnie unceremoniously awake. Forcing her eyes open and struggling upright, her body aching from the uncomfortable position she had lain in, she fought to remember how she had come to spend the night on the settee. Then like a thunderbolt it all came racing back. Tommy had left her. The terrible emotions she had experienced the previous evening rushed back.

The persistent knocking suddenly registered and a great rush of hope flowed through her. Had Tommy come back? He would have to knock to gain entry as he had left behind his house keys. Practically wrenching the door off its hinges in her urgency to get it open, she then had to fight with all her might to control her terrible disappointment on finding not Tommy but an irritated Noreen on her doorstep.

'My God, gel,' she grumbled, pushing past Vinnie and on into the back room, 'I was beginning ter think yer'd died in the night. Me knuckles are red raw from knocking.' She turned and glanced critically at her neighbour. 'You look like yer've been dragged through a hedge back'ards, gel, then had a bus run over yer. Don't tell me you slept in yer good clothes?'

Vinnie looked at Noreen in disbelief. Her neighbour's hair all tousled, face streaked with the last of yesterday's makeup which she hadn't bothered to remove. Wrapped in her ancient nylon quilted dressing gown, a well-worn winceyette nightdress underneath, pair of holey slippers on her feet, Vinnie felt Noreen was hardly in a position to make derogatory comments. Feeling as wretched as she did, though, she hadn't the energy to respond. She ran her hand through her matted hair. 'I'll put the kettle on,' she said, going back into the kitchen.

When Vinnie returned with the tea things, Noreen had settled herself at the table. 'The kettle won't be long,' Vinnie said, setting out the cups. 'How's Eric this morning?' she asked in an attempt to talk about anything unconnected with her own dire situation. 'I expect he's not feeling too good.'

'Never mind him,' Noreen snapped gruffly. 'Whatever he's suffering this morning he's brought on himself. You look terrible, gel, and I gather by that blanket you spent the night on the settee?'

Vinnie sighed. 'I couldn't face our bed with Tommy gone.'

Noreen pulled a face. 'Well, if he has gone fer good then you'll have to get used ter it. I tek it you've heard n'ote from him as yet?'

She shook her head. 'No. That's the kettle, excuse me for a minute.'

'It's no good me asking if yer got any sleep,' Noreen commented as she spooned several sugars into the cup of tea Vinnie pushed across the table towards her a moment later. 'I can see not by looking at yer.'

Vinnie rubbed her hands wearily over her face. 'I dozed in fits and starts but that was about it. I've never spent the night on my own since Tommy and I got married and I found it quite frightening.' She declined to add lonely too.

Noreen eyed her gravely. 'Well, as I said before, gel, if Tommy really has gone fer good then you'll have ter get used to that.' She took a sip of her tea, lit a cigarette then asked, 'Did you think any more about where he might be?'

Vinnie heaved a despondent sigh. 'That was one of the things that kept me awake. I can't fathom out where, though. He knows lots of people – neighbours, his pals down the pub, and his workmates. He could have gone to stay with any one of those. People like Tommy, you know that, Noreen. He's very popular.'

'Mmm. So what yer gonna do?'

Vinnie sighed a mite irritatedly, wishing the woman would stop urging her to make plans. It was far too soon for her to start doing that, she hadn't even come to terms with it all yet, and besides, she wouldn't have to make plans at all if . . . when . . . her husband came back. 'I don't know what I'm going to do yet, Noreen. I've hardly had time for this to sink in, let alone to make any decisions. Anyway, it's too early for me to make any. This is . . .' she gave a bewildered shake of her head '. . . I dunno, just madness on Tommy's part, it's got to be, can't be anything else. Wherever he stayed last night, I bet he mulled things over and realised how silly he's being. He'll come back, I know he will.'

Noreen pursed her lips. 'But what if he doesn't, Vin? For all you know, Tommy might have found someone else and just couldn't bring himself to tell yer.'

Vinnie's jaw dropped in utter disbelief. 'Someone else!' she exclaimed.

'Well, it's just a thought yer should consider, that's all I'm saying.'

'Tommy would never do that to me, Noreen, never,' she exclaimed. 'I don't know how you can even be suggesting such a thing.'

She gave a haughty sniff. 'Evelyn McCrae still swears to this day that her old man is in Ireland trying to get together the boat fare after he went back home to bury his mam, but we all know he's really living across town with that brassy blonde he met when he tarmacked her drive.'

Vinnie's face was grey with fear. 'Are you trying to tell me . . .'

'I'm not trying ter tell yer anything, Vinnie. But for yer own good I'm getting yer ter start facing facts. I mean, like you, I'm hoping Tommy turns up suitably sorry fer what he's done, but I've a feeling on me that he ain't going to or he'd have done so before now.'

Her face crumpled, bereft. 'Oh, Noreen, please don't

talk like this, please don't. Look,' she cried, standing up, 'I think you'd better go. I know you mean well but I can't take this kind of talk right now. I . . . I . . . think it best I try and act normal. I'm going to get myself washed and changed and make a start on the dinner. Tommy'll be famished when he comes home and if I don't make too much of a big deal of this . . . well, the last thing I want is to make matters worse by having a go at him as soon as he comes in. Best to let things calm down first then we can talk about it properly and sort out whatever the problem is so it doesn't happen again.'

Folding her arms under her ample chest, Noreen pursed her lips. 'I think yer living in a fool's paradise, gel, and the sooner yer come to terms with the fact that your husband has gone for good, the sooner you can get on with yer life.'

A sudden anger erupted inside Vinnie and she slammed her fist down hard on the table which made Noreen jump. 'Why are you so adamant that Tommy's not coming back? Are you sure you don't know anything?'

Noreen slammed her fist down too, glowering with indignation. 'I've told yer, I know as much as you and I'm getting bloody annoyed you keep implying I know more than I say.'

Vinnie felt ashamed. It was very unlikely Noreen could know anything of Tommy's movements, unless she had found out by accident. He couldn't abide the woman so was unlikely to confide in her. 'I'm sorry, Noreen, I didn't mean to snap at you.'

'Huh,' she grunted, folding her arms again. 'All I'm doing is trying to get yer to prepare yerself for the worst, that's all. I know you think I'm being harsh but it's an awful blow yer've had and you're gonna make it worse fer yerself if you don't start being realistic. By all means mek the man his dinner but don't rule out having ter throw it all in the dustbin when he doesn't turn up to eat it. I'm trying ter be your friend, Vinnie, but it's obvious you ain't gonna tek any notice of what I've got to say.' She scraped back her chair and stood up to go. 'I'll leave yer to it. You know where I am if yer need me for 'ote.'

As she heard the back door slam, Vinnie let out a deep groan of despair. The last thing she wanted was to upset her neighbour but she couldn't bring herself to listen to Noreen's warning. This wasn't the end of Tommy and her, it couldn't be. The thought was just too unbearable to comprehend.

She suddenly realised the state of her appearance. It wouldn't do for Tommy to return home and find her in this dishevelled condition. Spinning on her heel, she rushed upstairs to ready herself for his return.

Vinnie pulled aside the net curtain and tentatively peeked out of the front window. Darkness had fallen and already the signs of a heavy frost were shimmering on the pavements in the deserted street outside. Letting the curtain fall back into place, she despondently retraced her steps into the back room and stared disheartened at the table she had prepared so carefully in an effort to welcome her husband back home. What a waste of time that had been as had preparing the roast dinner now shrivelled in the oven. Noreen had tried to warn her she was wasting her efforts and to her own cost she had chosen to ignore her neighbour's good advice. It was looking increasingly likely that Tommy wasn't coming back today.

Oh, Tommy, her mind silently screamed. Where are you? Come home. Please come home.

A cold shiver ran through her and automatically she moved over to the fire to warm herself. As she did so an assortment of family photographs displayed on top of the walnut china cabinet by the fireplace drew her attention. Absently she picked up a silver-framed photograph of her late mother and stared at the image. Oh, Mum, she thought sadly. I wonder what you would have made of this turn of events?

Milly Perkins, a widow since the age of thirty, had been a kind-hearted woman, liked by all who knew her, and a loving, caring mother to Vinnie and her two brothers Reggie and Arthur – both sadly lost in the early days of the war. Vinnie knew her mother would have been devastated by this rift between her daughter and son-in-law of whom she had always approved. She'd believed her daughter's choice was an extremely sound one, the union had had her blessing and she'd had no doubt it would last for life. Tommy was from a poor but solid background, both his parents hardworking, law-abiding citizens, and their only son seemed stamped out of their mould. Although she missed her mother greatly, as she did her now deceased in-laws, Vinnie was glad at this moment in time that none of them was alive to witness this bewildering situation. Both sets of parents had held old-fashioned principles, one of which was that upon marriage couples were bound together for life.

Vinnie had met the then sixteen-year-old Thomas Henry Deakin at her first works' Christmas dance. It was held in the company's social hall and was the highlight of the workers' year. She had spotted the handsome apprentice dye man on several occasions before in the canteen at lunchtime. Despite being very pretty herself with many admirers, she'd noticed how the other young girls, many she felt to be much more attractive than herself, swarmed like bees around him and she'd thought he'd be too occupied with their attentions to take notice of her, thus dismissing him as a potential boyfriend.

She had been full of excitement at attending her first grown-up function and had looked extremely attractive in a pale green, boat-necklined, full-skirted dress made from yards of shiny satin filled out underneath with several layers of stiff sugared netting underskirting. The material had cost her a good slice of her wages from Lewis's department store and with the help of her mother she had spent hours making up the creation on their ancient treadle sewing machine. Accompanied by several other young girls she had become friendly with from her own department, she entered the hall determined to have a good time.

Vinnie had barely had time to deposit her coat when the tall, handsome youth she had thought hadn't even an idea she existed was at her side, asking her to dance. From that moment on the pair had been inseparable.

Until now, that was.

A vision of her own wedding day rose vividly to mind. It was as if it was yesterday. Much to the young courting couple's dismay Tommy had been called up at the age of eighteen to do his bit during the last two years of the war and had served as a gunner. This time apart was torture to them both, the two years he was away seeming endless. Thankfully Tommy returned home unscathed and the pair, so madly in love, planned their wedding immediately on his return, to be apart any longer unthinkable to them both.

On the big day, Tommy dressed smartly in his blue demob suit. Vinnie wore a borrowed off-white satin dress made from parachute material, tucked and pinned to make it fit. Her mother's veil of floating white muslin had been kept wrapped carefully in tissue paper for just this occasion along with its silver-gilt tiara edged in dainty fake drop pearls. The young couple, proudly and with deep sincerity, proclaimed their vows. As the vicar announced them to be man and wife, much to the congregation's delight Tommy swept Vinnie in his arms and kissed her long and passionately. Throughout the reception he was nervy, on edge, and Vinnie had known instinctively that it was because he was having great difficulty controlling his urgent need to whisk her off to the privacy of their bedroom and consummate the marriage. Hadn't she herself felt the same? Only she had been able to disguise her feelings better than he.

Vinnie felt a choking sob catch in the back of her throat as she remembered the day they had moved into this little terraced house, the deposit and first month's rent funded by money she had managed to save from her meagre wages at the factory during Tommy's service years. How deliriously happy they had both been, excited at the prospect of moving into their first home together.

They had been extremely fortunate to secure a house. One hundred years old, and with antiquated amenities, it was only just habitable, but after a thorough scrub through, and by cleverly arranging the assortment of shabby furniture they had acquired from second-hand shops and generous donations from members of their family, they managed to make their home look present-able. Over the years they had transformed the miserable old property by tasteful decoration and saving hard for better quality furnishings, the high point of their achievements being a fitted carpet in both the front and back rooms, to the envy of all their neighbours.

At the end of the 1950s they had seriously consid-ered the idea of applying to be added to the list for a new council house as several estates were being built on the edge of the city, but then the landlord, aided substantially by grants given by the local council, modernised the kitchen and installed a bathroom by converting the adjoining outhouse, so they decided to stay put. Of course the rent was raised but that was something most tenants were willing to pay in return for modern conveniences.

The arrival of Jane Louise just nine months after their wedding day thrilled them both, and Julie Rose's arrival twelve months later completed their little family. Their marriage hadn't all been plain sailing, though. Neither of them earned enough for luxuries after the bills were paid and periods of hardship had been endured when the girls were babies, with only Tommy's wage coming in. And over the years the factory where they worked had gone on several strikes lasting weeks over grievances against the owner's outdated work practices and pay structures.

Raising the girls, neither of them the easiest of children, had caused Vinnie many a heartache, the worst being the bewilderingly sudden departure of Janie at the age of fifteen. Neither the police, themselves, family nor friends had subsequently been able to uncover her whereabouts. Regardless, through it all Tommy and Vinnie had stood side by side and overcome these obstacles, their love and regard for each other never waning.

Or so she had thought.

Shutting her eyes tightly, she let out a deep sigh of despair. Where had her husband gone? The man confronting her yesterday evening as soon as they had entered the house after their daughter's wedding in no way resembled the kind, thoughtful one she had married in a blaze of love, the one who had given her not a single reason throughout their twenty-two years together, despite their ups and downs, to question her total belief that he was happy with the life he shared with her.

Replacing the photograph of her mother, she bent down and put a couple of lumps of coal on the fire. It was turning extremely cold and in her upset state she was feeling it more. As she straightened up, a picture of her daughters as young teenagers caught her eye. It had been taken with an ancient Box Brownie bought for a couple of shillings from a jumble sale. Standing in the back yard, the girls looked so pretty in their flowery summer frocks. At the time Vinnie had congratulated herself on having managed to get her daughters to pose together at all, and with smiles on their faces.

Her eyes lingered on the picture of Janie. Such a beautiful, sunny-natured baby she had been, growing into an inquisitive, delightful toddler. But at around seven years old and seemingly overnight she had undergone a complete personality change, becoming quiet and withdrawn, and the close relationship she had had with her father prior to this completely disintegrated, to the stage where they were barely polite to each other.

Vinnie had been at a loss to understand this sudden alteration in her daughter's attitude but put it down to a stage in her growing up and begged Tommy to make an extra special effort with her. Despite his assurances that he would, it didn't appear to Vinnie that he tried at all. He simply devoted his attention to his youngest daughter, making it painfully obvious where his preference lay. It had been very hard for Vinnie to witness this estrangement between them and she prayed that things would eventually revert to the way they had been before. Meanwhile she endeavoured to ensure they still acted as a family unit, doing all the things other families did together.

But nothing changed regarding Janie's altered personality, nor did the situation between herself and her father improve. Equally as worrying was the antagonistic relationship that developed between the sisters. At times Vinnie felt she was in the middle of a war zone, the constant keeper of the peace.

Then out of the blue, at the age of fifteen, barely having settled into her job as an apprentice machinist in the same factory where her mother and father worked, Janie vanished. Vinnie arrived home one night to find her eldest daughter and her belongings gone, with no word of explanation for the sudden departure.

Vinnie sighed in distress now and asked herself the question she'd asked herself hundreds of times since her daughter had left. Why had she suddenly gone like that, without so much as a word of warning? Would her mother ever find out what had made her do something so bewildering? Where was she now? Was she all right? How she ached to hold her daughter in her arms again, tell her that she loved her unconditionally, and that despite the pain and heartache she had caused, Vinnie bore her beloved child no grudges.

Suddenly the memory of her husband's verbal attack on his elder daughter the previous evening registered full force and Vinnie frowned, deeply confused. She had always believed that Tommy was as upset about Janie's going off as she herself was, and that he had longed for her return as much as Vinnie did. But last night he had spoken as if she had committed a cardinal sin, done something so bad it was unforgivable and irredeemable in his eyes, felt so strongly about it he never wanted to clap eyes on her again. Face grim, Vinnie shook her head. She must be wrong, have misconstrued him in her own confusion, blowing out of proportion everything he had said and the way he had put it. Tommy had been deeply hurt by his daughter's actions but he loved her, of course he did, she was his own flesh and blood. He wanted as much as she did to know that Janie was safe and sound, and would welcome her back into the fold as readily as her mother.

It suddenly struck Vinnie then, and with a shock, that two people very close to her had abruptly left her side. Was it because of her – a kink in her own personality that she was unaware of? But what? As far as she knew she had been a good wife and mother. Nurtured her children, kept nourishing, tasty food on the table, the house warm, inviting and happy, been a supportive and loving wife. But then something had caused Janie to go, and there had to be a reason why Tommy had followed suit, something more than his excuse that he had fallen out of love with her. People didn't just fall out of love for no reason, Mother Nature didn't work in such a cut and dried way.

As her mind whirled, trying to think of a plausible explanation for Tommy and Janie's behaviour, Vinnie's eyes settled on the photograph of Julie standing beside Janie and she froze. If Tommy had indeed gone for good then telling her younger daughter would be the thing she most dreaded. Vinnie didn't usually agree with Noreen's blunt opinions of people but in this case she did. Julie was horribly self-centred, and Vinnie knew deep down that Tommy was responsible for the development of this trait in her. Like her elder sister, Julie had been a sweet, happy child but suddenly, at the age of six, had found herself the focus of her father's affections. She had quickly realised that by acting in a certain way she could always get what she wanted. She became wilful, prone to throwing temper tantrums, and began to side with her father against her mother, seeming to enjoy the arguments that she caused between them. Much against her better nature, Vinnie would find herself giving in to the child just to keep the peace.

Age hadn't improved Julie either. She developed into an uncompromising woman, at times still throwing childish tantrums to achieve her aims. Vinnie often marvelled at the way the easygoing, likeable Gary put up with her. Regardless, though, she did love her daughter and sincerely hoped that one day Julie would take a long hard look at herself and see herself as others saw her, change her attitude, and in doing so make the lives of those around her so much happier.

Her eyes then settled on a snap of Tommy. He was leaning against the back gate, smiling charmingly at the camera – at her, because she had taken it. She had worried she'd cut his head off and ruin the shot. Her eyes became distant as she remembered the day it had been taken, about seventeen years ago, just before Janie's behaviour began to change.

It had been a glorious day and for once the family had managed to escape without Noreen finding out and inviting herself along. They had taken the children for a walk in the Abbey Park, spent several hours there fishing in the large pond for tiddlers with homemade nets then playing on the swings, slide and roundabout. The girls, aged around five and four, had both been in high spirits. As Vinnie and Tommy strolled arm-in-arm across the expanses of freshly cut grass, the children ran around giggling, chubby arms outstretched, pretending to be aeroplanes and fairies. The family finally arrived home and ate a picnic tea in the back yard, a fitting end to their wonderful day out.

Other such memories came flooding back then, happy family occasions that Vinnie had planned. Hope rose within her. Tommy couldn't have left for good. All they had gone through and meant to each other bound them together, surely it did. Whatever had caused him to act so uncharacteristically had to be something trivial brought on by the momentous occasion of his beloved daughter's wedding. Hadn't she herself felt almost overcome as she had stood and watched Julie take her vows, a playback of her own life from baby to young woman flashing before her? Vinnie had suddenly felt redundant, her daily role of mother stripped cruelly from her. She had thought it was only herself experiencing these emotions but obviously Tommy had been too, enough to cause him to act as he had. Then a profound realisation struck her. Wherever he was now, maybe Tommy was regretting his actions, feeling foolish, but couldn't bring himself to admit to his own stupidity and was waiting for his wife to ask him back and save his pride. A warm glow rushed through her. Yes, that was it, it was as simple as that. Tomorrow at work she would go and see him in his department and resolve this awful situation once and for all.

She heard a noise nearby and jumped, startled out of her thoughts. 'Oh, Noreen, I never heard you come in,' she said, clutching her chest.

Her neighbour gave a disagreeable sniff. 'Well, I knocked loud enough.' She cast a critical eye over the table. 'I told yer yer were wasting yer time. He never put in an appearance then?'

Vinnie shook her head. 'No.'

Noreen pulled a knowing face. 'Well, I think . . .'

'I know what you think, Noreen,' Vinnie cut in. 'That Tommy's not coming back.'

'That's exactly what I think,' she erupted. 'It's as plain as daylight or he'd have been here by now. Keep yer pride, Vinnie, let him go 'cos that's obviously what he wants. No point in dragging all this out. It ain't like the old days when yer had to stay together through thick and thin, both on yer as miserable as sin. Ways are more liberal now. There ain't so much stigma attached ter being divorced. Yer young enough ter find someone else.'

Vinnie was gawping at her. 'Someone else? I can't believe you're speaking like this, Noreen. I'm shocked at you. Our marriage is a good one. We're going through a bit of a rough patch, that's all. Lots of couples experience that.'

'Bit more than a rough patch if yer ask me.'

'But I didn't ask you, Noreen,' she snapped crossly. Her features softened. 'Please, don't let's fall out too, I've enough on my plate as it is. Look, I've been going over things and I started to think that maybe it's something about me that caused both Janie and Tommy to leave. But I can't think of anything I've done or any way I've acted that would make them both do such a thing, can you?'

Noreen gave an indifferent shrug. 'Nothing in particular.'

'Precisely. So I've come to the conclusion that Janie's leaving, regardless of the cause, was just something simple that got out of hand. Kids of that age make mountains out of molehills, don't they? She probably didn't like her job or something, and didn't know how to tell us, and felt that leaving home was the only answer. It's pride that's stopping her from coming back. But I pray one day she will. I don't care if she never explains why she left as long as she comes home eventually so I can tell her how much we love her and have missed her. Then I'll make sure she never feels the need to leave again.

'As for Tommy, well, I feel it's something to do with Julie getting married. It hits men in strange ways does growing older, suddenly realising that life's passing them by. They get all sorts of fanciful ideas. I know he didn't mean what he said about not loving me anymore. You don't have a good marriage like we've had and suddenly stop loving the other person without something major happening to cause it. Well, nothing major has happened to us, so I have to be right, don't I? Like Janie, I know it's just his pride that's stopping him from coming back. Tommy must feel foolish for the way he's acted and doesn't know what to say to me to put things right between us, that's all. So it's got to be me that does it. I shall sort it out with him at work tomorrow and by night we'll be back to normal.'

Noreen looked unconvinced. 'Mmm, we'll see. So yer've no idea where he's stopping then?'

Vinnie issued an irritated sigh and snapped crossly, 'How could I, Noreen? I've told you, I haven't seen him. I know you mean well but, as I said last night, if it's on your mind to go and give him a tongue lashing and drag him back home that's not what I want. Please leave well alone. This situation is delicate enough without you making it worse. And when you next see Tommy, please don't mention anything about this. I want to sort it out and put it behind us as quickly as possible.'

Noreen's face set. 'Right, I'll be off. I hope termorrow goes as well for yer as you hope it does.'

Vinnie could tell by Noreen's tone that she thought her stupid to believe this situation was going to be resolved so easily but decided not to comment. Instead she gave her neighbour a quick smile and wished her goodnight.

Chapter Three

Vinnie slept no better that night than she had the previous one, still unable to bring herself to occupy the marital bed without Tommy beside her. She couldn't sleep as she meticulously planned tomorrow's approach to him, endeavouring to make absolutely sure no words she said could possibly be misconstrued at the risk of prolonging this insane situation unnecessarily. At all costs Vinnie desperately wanted her husband home where he belonged. Two nights estranged from the man she loved with every ounce of her being was to Vinnie two nights too many. She meant to succeed in her quest as soon as humanly possible.

The next morning she hesitated outside the large iron gates before W. Brewin & Sons, Hosiery Manufacturers, where she had earned a living since leaving school at the age of fourteen.

Brewin's wasn't the largest hosiery manufacturer in Leicester but it was one of the oldest, having started as a cottage industry in the early 1850s in the front room of a small terraced house on Leamington Street in the

West End of the city. The business now operated from a three-storey Victorian red-brick factory, a huddle of smaller outbuildings adjoining it. The firm's expansion over the years to its present workforce of over a thousand and healthy turnover had been gradual. From small beginnings Brewin's now enjoyed a reputation for high quality and supplied both large and small outlets all over Great Britain and abroad with adults' and children's socks, underwear, and a selection of women's dresses, blouses and skirts.

Vinnie had started as an apprentice cutter, progressing to overlocking then machining before taking several years off work while she raised her children. Not fancying the prospect of labouring over a machine all day on her return to full-time work when both her children were of school age, she'd accepted a job in the inspection department as an interim measure while she took her time deciding which department in the factory interested her the most and hoped a suitable vacancy arose. But nothing better had presented itself. She liked her present job well enough and the women she worked with were a good bunch. Comradeship in the department was very high.

Taking a deep breath, she squared her shoulders, praying none of her workmates noticed her preoccupied state, and joined the rest of the throng making their way inside.

'Bloody 'ell, Vinnie gel, you look washed out. Your Julie's wedding was that good, eh, you ain't recovered from it yet?'

'Pardon?' Vinnie stared blankly at Betty Trubshaw, a matronly woman of sixty-one who had worked alongside her for the past twelve years. 'Oh, yes . . . yes, it was a very good do,' she said lightly. 'I'm just a bit tired after the excitement of it all.'

She extracted her card from the clocking-in machine and slotted it in its place in the clock-card rack, then made her way upstairs to the inspection department workers' locker room to deposit her belongings, conscious that her attempt to conceal her pale complexion and puffy, dark-circled eyes under a layer of skilfully applied makeup hadn't been as successful as she had thought.

'How did it go then?' twenty-four-year-old Ruby Dolman asked as she joined Vinnie, giving her a hefty nudge in the ribs as they made their way into the large room where they all worked. She was a big girl, several stone overweight, whose facial features were likened by some unkind people to the back end of a bus. Ruby was forced to dress very conservatively by her aged, overbearingly strict parents and had yet to acquire her first boyfriend. Her only distraction outside the factory was reading her *Tit Bits* weekly, which she did secretly under her bedclothes aided by a torch, and the Saturday night game of whist in her parents' parlour with several of their dour cronies, a ritual she dreaded but had no choice but to endure else suffer her parents' displeasure. Anything outside her own mundane existence was exciting to Ruby.

'Yeah, we're all dying ter 'ear,' several other work

colleagues urged enthusiastically.

'Any fall outs or fights?' one of them asked eagerly.

'Now, now, ladies,' a male voice boomed. 'Let's keep the gossip until breaktime, please. We've orders to get out.'

They all turned and silently looked across the cluttered room to where Keith Hamlin, the department manager, stood in the doorway of his office, stern-faced.

'Yes, come on, ladies,' Cynthia Dodds, the department forelady, shouted, clapping her hands. 'Let's get to it.'

All of them scurried off to their individual workplace.

'He's a miserable old bugger,' Betty grumbled as she heaved across a huge basket filled with bundles of garments for inspection. 'Well, I suppose not so old . . . about forty-odd, I reckon, but he'd be quite handsome if he smiled once in a while. I pity his poor wife. If he's as grumpy at home as he is at work then it's a wonder she hasn't left him. Archie Pegg might have drove us all daft with his old wifey ways but at least he'd a sense of humour and yer could have a laugh with him. Pity he had to retire. Don't you agree with me, Vinnie? Vinnie?'

'Pardon? Oh, er . . . I can't compare them really. Mr Hamlin has never said more than two words to me in all the five years he's been my boss, so I've no idea what he's like really. I get the impression he doesn't like me, though,' she said matter-of-factly.

Betty frowned at her. 'Whatever meks yer say that?'

When Vinnie didn't reply, she scowled at her crossly. 'Vinnie, fer God's sake, what is wrong with you today? Yer in a world of yer own. I asked what meks yer think Happy Hamlin don't like yer?'

'Eh? Oh . . .' She gave a shrug. 'Just a feeling I get. I catch him looking at me strangely sometimes. I must have done something to him but for the life of me I can't think what. Anyway, it doesn't really matter as we deal direct with Doddsie, so as long as I do my job well he can't get rid of me, can he?'

'I think yer imagining things, Vinnie. I can't imagine anyone not liking you. Oh, bugger,' Betty exclaimed, 'it's them fancy lacy knickers we've on terday. Though how the hell they've the cheek ter call 'em knickers I'll never know, there's not enough material on 'em to cover a stick insect's modesty. Gimme winceyette drawers to check over anytime. Now *they're* what yer call drawers. At least they keep yer bum warm and yer personal bits hidden, which is what knickers are really intended ter do.'

'You only like doing them big sort so yer can hopefully nick a few pairs for yerself,' piped up Ruby. 'I like doing these,' she said, holding a pair of the flimsy ones up admiringly. 'They're so pretty.' Then she gave a wistful sigh. 'Yer gotta be like a clothes prop to wear 'em, though, ain't yer?'

'Yeah, yer have,' Betty bantered back. 'And you wouldn't even get one of your ankles inside the waist of the largest size.'

Ruby flashed her a hurt look as she flung the pants

down on the work counter in front of her. 'I might be fat but I've got feelings, yer know, Betty Trubshaw. I'm going on a diet, then I'll show yer.'

'You, diet? That'll be the day! You like yer chips and Pukka pies too much ever to diet, Ruby Dolman. You're the only person I know that can eat three pies at one sitting.'

Ruby looked at her. Then, slowly, a proud smile lit up her round face. 'Am I, Betty? The only one, really? Eh up, that means I'm special, dunnit? The only one that can eat three Pukka pies in one go.'

Betty tutted disdainfully, then her better nature took over and she smiled kindly at the girl. At times she was openly rude to Ruby but, deep down, had a soft spot for the workmate she knew didn't have an easy home life, forever at the beck and call of her aged, demanding, narrow-minded parents. She felt mortally sorry for the fact that Ruby had been dealt a cruel hand in the looks and figure department, although the size of her was not entirely Mother Nature's fault. Ruby ate for comfort, the huge amounts of food she consumed providing the emotional support that was otherwise lacking in her life.

Betty knew Ruby's parents had encouraged her vast appetite. From her very early childhood, they'd piled her plate high and forced her to eat every morsel, whether she wanted to or not. Betty suspected their secret agenda was that a grotesquely fat daughter was unlikely ever to succeed in finding a man who would take her away from them, and they would then have

their own personal nursemaid to care for them throughout their dotage. Betty thought them thoroughly selfish
rotters.

'Yeah, you are special, me duck, and don't let no one
else tell yer otherwise or they'll have me ter deal with. If
you're gonna diet then yer can count on me to help yer
all I can.' Her eye caught the large clock on the wall
opposite and her good intentions faded as hunger
rumbled in her own stomach. 'Oh, it's not far off the
time for you to fetch the breakfast cobs, Ruby ducky.
Mek mine a bacon and tomato and don't dally on the
way back, I'm starvin'.' She pulled a face. 'Anyway, I
think we're gonna have ter change cob shops. That one
I had last Friday tasted peculiar,' she grumbled.

Ruby lowered her head, feeling a tide of guilt burn
her cheeks. She wasn't surprised the cob had tasted
funny. Trying to balance the dozen or so individual
orders she had fetched while ramming a Mars Bar into
her mouth, to her horror Betty's had toppled off the
top of the pile, to hit the pavement and burst its bag,
contents scattering. Not having the money or the time
to buy another, Ruby had hastily scooped it up,
brushed off all the grit and dirt she could see, and put it
back together, praying Betty would notice nothing
amiss. She might have known she would, Betty missed
nothing. 'It's 'cos that woman serving never washes her
hands,' Ruby said, trying to make an excuse. 'It's a
wonder we ain't all had dysentery.'

'Well, you tell that slouch from me that from now on
she'd better wash her hands, 'cos if I go down with 'ote

nasty after eating summat from her shop then I'll personally rub her nose in anything I bring up.'

Ruby cringed at the vision Betty's remarks conjured up, feeling awful for blaming the poor assistant for something that wasn't her fault in order to escape a severe reprimand herself. 'I . . . er . . . will, Betty,' she said, despite having no intention of ever doing such a thing. As Ruby worked away inspecting a batch of the lacy knickers for flaws she hummed along to Sonny and Cher's 'I Got You Babe', which was being played over the factory wireless system. A faraway look came into her eyes and absently she said, 'I happen to think he's handsome, a bit like Burt Lancaster. Has he gorra wife, do yer reckon?'

Betty frowned at her, bemused. 'How the hell would I know if Burt Lancaster's gorra wife? You read *Tit Bits* from cover to cover so you'd know that better than me.'

Ruby stared at her, non-plussed. 'Eh! Oh, no, I meant Mr Hamlin.'

Betty grimaced. 'I expect so. Some poor women are that desperate they'll take anything wearing trousers.'

'Oh, yer are unkind, Betty,' Ruby replied.

'Speak as I find, me, yer know that,' Betty retorted. She gave Ruby the once over. 'Fancy Happy Hamlin do yer then, our Ruby?'

The girl blushed scarlet. 'I might,' she said cagily.

Betty ruefully shook her head. 'It's as I said, some women are that desperate they'd fancy 'ote in trousers. He's far too old fer you, ducky. Warrabout that new lad that's started in the stores? He's more your age.'

Ruby looked at her thoughtfully. 'He's not bad, I suppose. His acne is really offputting and he's a bit on the thin side but a few good meals 'ud soon sort that out. He's got a funny eye though, ain't he? When he's talking to yer, yer think he's looking at someone behind yer, only there's no one there. Anyway, there's no point in discussing this, he wouldn't fancy me,' she added matter-of-factly.

'Yer never know. Let's face it, Ruby, he's not exactly in a position ter be choosy. I think you two would mek a nice pair meself. I'll put in a good word for yer when I next see him. If he ever does asks yer out, take my advice and go. He just might turn out to be your Prince Charming, bad acne, thin, wonky eye or not.' Betty glanced at Vinnie beavering away beside her. 'You're quiet, gel. Cat got yer tongue?'

Vinnie's mind was full of her own terrible situation and she didn't hear Betty.

'Oi, Vinnie, have you gone deaf? I said, you're quiet, gel,' she repeated, raising her voice several decibels to be heard over Tony Blackburn announcing the next record.

'Pardon? Oh . . . well, it's difficult to get a word in with you two,' said Vinnie, forcing herself to be jocular.

'Well, we're all ears now, ain't we, Ruby? So come on, gel, let's hear all the gory details about the wedding of the year.' Betty had made no secret of the fact that she was disgruntled not to receive an invitation, despite knowing that due to Julie's insistence on the best of everything guest numbers had had to be cut down.

Vinnie had been sorry and ashamed to have to tell her close workmates they weren't on the list.

'No gory details, Betty, it all went very well. You know I'm sorry about not being able to ask you and Ruby to come.'

'Yeah, I'm sorry an' all,' her friend said gruffly. 'Not often I get the opportunity ter wear a hat and I'd me eye on just the one I was gonna wear. In Lewis's it was, reduced in the sale an' all, down to four and six. Still, never mind. Your Julie had to have the best, didn't she?' she added sarcastically. 'I suppose I shall just have ter content meself with a bit of cake. Yer did bring us a bit of cake in?'

Vinnie's face fell. Because of what had happened after the reception she had forgotten to cut up pieces of the wedding cake and bring them in for her work colleagues to enjoy. 'I'm sorry, I was in such a rush this morning I forgot all about it. I'll bring some in tomorrow.'

'Huh! Well, I suppose that'll have ter do.' She eyed Vinnie inquisitively. 'Are yer seriously telling me that there were no mishaps at this wedding at all?' she asked, pulling a disbelieving face.

'None,' Vinnie said, more sharply than she'd intended. 'It all went very smoothly.'

'Oh!' Betty grimaced, disappointed. 'I ain't never been to a wedding where no fight broke out or some miserable sod ain't complained the music's too loud. You sure you were at this wedding, Vinnie?' she asked, guffawing with laughter. Her attention was suddenly diverted to the large double entrance doors across the room. 'Huh, here's the factory bike come ter pay us a visit. Wonder what that little madam wants? And just look at the length of that skirt she's wearing. I've seen more fabric on a curtain pelmet! And if she shows any more chest she might as well not wear that top.'

'I'd wanna show off what I'd got if I had her figure,' said Ruby enviously.

'And if I were yer mam, I'd scalp yer arse and yer wouldn't get past the doorstep in a get up like that, especially fer work,' Betty shot back at her.

As she already had a mother who was worse than that, Ruby declined to comment.

As they worked away, out of the corner of their eye they all watched as Maxine Upton, a clerical assistant in the General Office, made her way around the individual work benches, handing out Xeroxed notices to all the workers. Maxine was fully aware of how attractive she was to the opposite sex and was unashamedly flirtatious with any man she came into contact with, much to the rage of the other female employees. Whether it was true or not, she had earned herself a reputation for offering sexual favours to any man willing, hence her nickname of 'the factory bike'.

Maxine eventually made her way around to Vinnie, Betty and Ruby's work counter. 'Hello, ladies,' she chirped breezily with a flick of her shoulder-length auburn tresses. 'A notice from management,' she announced, thrusting three pieces of paper towards them. 'The canteen is shutting from tomorrow for the rest of the week for its yearly overhaul.' She gave Ruby a malicious smirk. 'Better warn the local chippy to order an extra ton of spuds in to accommodate you, hadn't I?'

Without waiting for a response she stepped over to Vinnie and, tilting her head, a sly smile on her lips, asked: 'How did the wedding go then, Mrs Deakin?' She gave Vinnie the once over, her eyes glinting wickedly. 'You look worn out, it must have been so tiring for you. You should have took a sicky today. Well, at your age yer gotta look after yerself, ain't yer? I saw your husband earlier. He didn't look at all tired. Extremely pleased with himself, I'd say. In fact, I ain't never seen him so happy.' She leaned towards Vinnie, thrusting her voluptuous chest in her direction, and, smirking slyly, said in hushed tones, 'Like he'd had his every wish granted.' She straightened up, flicked back her hair and said cheerily, 'Well, can't stand chatting to you lot all day.' And giving a dismissive wave of her hand, she called out, ''Bye, ladies,' as she flounced off on her fashionable high heels.

'Don't you take no notice of that nasty cow,' Betty was saying to Ruby. 'You mark my words, that gel will come to a sticky end one of these days when someone puts their fist in that big gob of hers. I'd 'a' done it meself if Happy Hamlin hadn't been in his office and I'd risked the sack. Now dry yer eyes and get back ter yer work before Doddsie catches us slacking.' She turned to face Vinnie. 'And just what did that trashy piece say ter you?' she demanded.

'Eh? Oh, I . . . I didn't catch what she said, Betty.'

She had, though. Every word of what Maxine had said had struck home. Tommy was looking extremely pleased with himself. Happy. Like he'd just had all his heart's desires granted. That was the very last description of him Vinnie had expected to hear. Upset, miserable, distracted, subdued . . . definitely not pleased with himself. Maxine must be lying. But then, why would she?

Suddenly sorting out her marital problems was paramount for Vinnie. She couldn't wait until lunchtime, she had to see Tommy now.

She spun round to face Betty. 'I've got an errand to do. I'll clear it with Doddsie. Won't be long.'

'But . . .'

Vinnie was already halfway across the room.

Cynthia Dodds was a diminutive woman in her early-forties with a frizzy perm and features reminiscent of a gnome. What she lacked in size, though, was made up for by her gigantic ego. She felt she was better than all the other women in this room because she had been singled out and put in charge of them, and never let any of them forget it. Now she craned her skinny neck, glaring up at Vinnie in shocked surprise at her audacity. To ask to be excused during working hours! 'I can't give you permission to leave the floor just because you feel the need, Mrs Deakin. Surely whatever you have to speak to your husband about can't be that urgent it can't wait until breaktime? Those orders you're working on are due for shipment on Wednesday and we're already cutting it fine to manage that.'

'But it can't wait, Mrs Dodds. I have to see my husband, now.'

Giving a superior sniff, the forelady folded her arms and took a stance. 'I'm sorry . . .' she began.

'So am I, Mrs Dodds,' Vinnie erupted, 'but I *have* to go. I won't be long. I'll make up the time.'

And much to her forelady's surprise and indignation, Vinnie kicked up her heels and ran from the room.

The dying shed, as it was nicknamed, the place huge quantities of raw fabric were permanently coloured before being sent on their travels through the factory to end up as finished garments, was a large building situated furthest from the main factory at the back of Brewin's premises, a good five-minute walk from where Vinnie worked. She took a deep breath before she entered through a side door, fully aware that the stinking fumes emitted from the various dyeing sessions in progress would hit her full force. She often marvelled at the way Tommy could spend at least nine hours a day in this awful atmosphere as he had done for the last twenty-six years. He said it was something you got used to, and besides he liked his job as foreman over his shift. Because of its inhospitable environment and the three-shift system in force – which, unlike most men, Tommy didn't seem to mind having to abide by – the wages paid here were marginally higher than in other departments. Tommy was on day shift this week so she knew he would be around somewhere.

Fully intent on achieving her purpose Vinnie hurriedly weaved around several large vats in urgent pursuit of her husband. She spotted George Collins, one of the workers she knew. He was halfway up a ladder propped against a vat, mixing dye solution into it with a huge wooden spatula. 'George,' she called up to him, 'I'm sorry to bother you but do you know where Tommy is, please? I need to speak to him urgently.'

He shook his head. 'Ain't seen him this morning, Mrs D. Sorry.'

She flashed him a quick thank you smile and continued her search. But she could find no trace of Tommy whatsoever. Then suddenly it crossed her mind that he could be in the manager's office.

Ralf Kimble, Tommy's boss, was a kindly, family man, but despite being extremely fair towards his workers he still expected certain departmental and company rules to be strictly adhered to or the culprit risked facing disciplinary action. One of these rules forbade carrying out personal business in company time, and certainly not in such a dangerous area as the dye house, a place that held many hazards to the lay person as Vinnie herself was.

Suddenly a terrible thought struck her and she stopped in her tracks. She had been so consumed with her need to resolve matters between herself and Tommy that she had completely forgotten that should Ralf Kimble catch her in the dye house, not only would she be in severe trouble herself, but she risked heaping the same trouble on her husband. She had been thoughtless in the extreme doing what she had. Sorting this matter out with Tommy would have to wait until dinner break. An urgent desire to get out of the dye house before she was detected rushed through her and she turned to make her escape, almost fainting with shock to find herself face to face with Mr Kimble himself.

'It's all right, Mrs Deakin, I know,' he said, laying a reassuring hand on her arm. 'Though you really shouldn't be in here, you know that, don't you?' he added, wagging a warning finger. 'In the circumstances I'll let it pass this time, but please don't do it again. I really wouldn't like you to suffer the consequences.'

She breathed a great sigh of relief. 'Thank you, Mr Kimble.' She was just about to hurry away when a thought struck her and she eyed him enquiringly. 'You said you already know, Mr Kimble. Er . . . know what?'

He looked at her blankly. 'That your husband has been signed off by the doctor for a few days with a pulled muscle in his back. I understand it's so bad he's bedridden. Too much jigging about at the wedding, I expect. Tell him to hurry up and get better, I need him back here.'

'Oh! Er . . . yes . . . yes, I will. Er . . . Mr Kimble . . . just who exactly told you about Tommy?'

'Eh? Oh, I can't remember now. I've had a couple of things to deal with since then.' He scratched his head. 'Er . . . oh, yes, I got a telephone call from someone in the General Office. I take it you'd informed them to tell me?' He looked at her strangely. 'Is that not what you did?'

'Er . . . yes, that's exactly what I did.'

He frowned at her, bothered. 'Are you all right, Mrs Deakin?'

'Yes, yes, I'm fine. Just a bit brain-fuddled after the wedding, that's all.'

'Well, I expect seeing yer kids married does that to most parents. I've got it all to look forward to when my three daughters take the plunge and I can't say as I'm looking forward to it. The thought of the cost alone is frightening me ter death.' He eyed her quizzically. 'So why exactly are you here then?'

'Why am I here?' Her mind thrashed wildly. 'Oh, er . . . just checking you got the message, Mr Kimble, that's all. You can't always trust those girls in the General Office to pass messages on, and I wanted to make sure you'd got it in case you thought Tommy just hadn't bothered to turn up.'

'I'd never think that of your husband, Mrs Deakin. I've not had cause to grumble about his work in all the years I've been his manager. In fact, I can't remember the last time he was off through sickness. Can't say the same of all of my other workers.' He gave Vinnie a friendly smile. 'Best get off back to your own department before you risk a reprimand yourself. Don't forget to give Tommy my best and tell him I need him here as soon as possible.'

All the way back to her department Vinnie's thoughts raced wildly. Her husband lay ill somewhere and because of his actions she wasn't there to take care of him. But above and beyond that were other bewildering questions to which she had no answers. Who had telephoned the General Office to inform them of Tommy's incapacity? Who was caring for him? It had to be whoever was putting him up. And when had he suffered this injury? He was in perfect health when he had picked up his suitcase and left the house on Saturday night. As matters stood Maxine couldn't possibly have seen Tommy this morning so why had she told those terrible lies? But then, Vinnie reasoned, Maxine was renowned as a vicious trouble-maker amongst the women workers so this morning's panto-mime was probably just an opportunity she'd taken to cause animosity between Vinnie and Tommy. Betty was right, one of these days Maxine would do it to some-one who wouldn't stand for her nonsense and then she'd regret the consequences.

'Doddsie's got a face like thunder and she's breathing hell fire,' Betty whispered to Vinnie as she slipped back behind her work bench. 'What you did has put us all in the dog house. I hope it was worth the trouble you've got us all into,' she snapped.

Vinnie eyed her, ashamed. 'I'm sorry but it was something I just had to do,' she said evasively.

'Huh! So . . . what was so important it couldn't wait?' Betty demanded, irritated.

'If you don't mind, Betty, that's private between me and Tommy,' she answered, grabbing up a batch of garments from the basket by her side and proceeding to work on them.

'Oh, private, is it? I see.' Betty flung back her head. 'Well, when yer are ready ter talk about it, don't expect me to lend a sympathetic ear.' She glared across at Ruby. 'You gonna fetch them cobs or does a woman have ter keel over in starvation before you move yer fat arse?'

Cynthia Dodds, her gnome-like features wreathed in indignation, approached Vinnie. 'You've worked in this department long enough to know that conduct like you displayed this morning, Mrs Deakin, will not be tolerated. Mrs Gilders, the last forelady, might have let you all away with murder but I will not. Between the hours of eight and five you're here to work, not socialise. You were away exactly twenty-four minutes so I will expect you to make that time up during your dinner break. Do anything like this again and I'll report you to Mr Hamlin. I can assure you he won't take such matters lightly. Understood?'

Vinnie felt like telling Cynthia Dodds exactly what she could do with her job but she had enough to contend with at the moment without adding looking for work to her list. She just nodded her reply.

The day dragged by slowly, each second seeming to last an hour to Vinnie. The only thought that kept her going was the hope that lying in his sick bed would have given Tommy a chance to reason out his silly behaviour, and that he would send round whoever he had parked himself on to inform her what was going on, hoping Vinnie would be forgiving. Tommy knew her well enough to realise she would welcome him back with open arms. Though if his back was that bad how they were going to get him home was another problem, but one she was determined to solve.

It was a mortally relieved Vinnie who gathered her belongings and clocked herself out when the five o'clock hooter blew.

One amongst hundreds of other workers desperate to be on the other side of the large iron gates, she suddenly stopped short, grimacing in pain from a piece of gravel which had worked its way inside her shoe. She hobbled through the throng in the gateway to lean against the iron railings outside while she removed the offending article. Job done, she straightened up and prepared to resume her journey, and as she did so caught sight of a woman several feet away. With her back to Vinnie the woman was pressed up against a brick gate post. She had her face pushed against the railings, peering intently through them, obviously searching for someone. What surprised Vinnie was that the woman was Noreen. She frowned, perplexed. None of the Adlers worked at Brewin's. Noreen was a machinist for Lady's Pride, a factory in the other direction, and normally at this time of night would be making her way home to prepare her family's evening meal. So what was she doing here and who was she looking for?

Vinnie went over and tapped her on her shoulder. 'Noreen, are you all right?'

A screech of shock rang out as Noreen, face wreathed in stunned surprise, spun around to face her. 'Oh . . . Oh, Vinnie, there you are!' she cried, clutching at her chest through her winter coat.

'I'm sorry, I didn't mean to scare you. Why are you here?'

'I, er . . . I, er . . .' Her eyes darted frantically as she shuffled on her feet. Vinnie wondered why she was acting so guiltily, like a child who'd been caught red-handed stealing a sweet. Before she could ask again, Noreen flung back her head and looked Vinnie in the eye. 'I was looking out for you. I left work early, said I'd a bad headache 'cos I wanted ter check you were okay. I was worried about yer, that's all.'

Vinnie stared at her, taken aback by this uncharacteristic display of thoughtfulness in Noreen. Despite her wretchedness she smiled, warmed by the thought of her neighbour's concern for her welfare. 'I appreciate that, Noreen. Apart from a terrible headache and a cut on my toe from a piece of grit in my shoe, I'm all right. I'll be glad to get home, though. It's been a long day.'

Noreen eyed her warily. 'So what happened? Did you see Tommy and sort anything out? Did you find out where he's staying?'

She sighed despondently. 'No. Tommy wasn't in work so I wasn't able to do anything. He's laid up wherever he is with a bad back. Pulled a muscle. How on earth he did it I've no idea but he'll obviously be in terrible pain.' She looked at Noreen, aggrieved. 'He should be at home, Noreen, with me there to care for him.' Her shoulders sagged from the sheer weight of her emotional burden. 'Oh, this situation is so awful! It's like a nightmare that just keeps getting worse. When will it end, Noreen? When will it end?'

Her neighbour eyed her knowingly. 'As soon as you accept he's not coming back. I can't understand why yer feel such concern for him. He's left you, Vinnie, and doesn't seem to be bothered how much suffering he's causing you.' She stared straight at Vinnie. 'In all the time I've known Tommy I ain't never known him to have a bad back before so it seems strange to me he should have one now. It's just an excuse not to be at work, to avoid facing you. He's letting the dust settle, that's what Tommy's doing. You see if I ain't right. You've gotta pull yerself together, gel, and accept facts. If Tommy had any regrets he'd have crawled back to sort it out with you before now, bad back or not.'

Vinnie looked at her, astounded. 'No, Noreen, none of what you're saying is true. I know Tommy better than anyone and I'm sure he didn't mean this to go on for so long. It's his back that's stopping him from coming home now. I'm sure whoever is putting him up will have popped a note through my door telling me all about it, or if not will be around tonight in person. Now, if you'll excuse me, I need to get home.'

There was no note through Vinnie's door when she arrived home and no one called. By nine o'clock she had practically worn a trench in the carpet from pacing backwards and forwards, listening for a knock on her door – willing it to come. As the clock on the fireplace struck the hour her heart plummeted, hardly beating. She had to admit to herself that no one was going to call on her tonight. As time passed it was looking increasingly likely that Noreen's interpretation of events was more accurate than her own. But she couldn't accept that Tommy had gone for good, she just couldn't. The idea was just too unbearable.

If only she knew where he was staying. How could she find out? Her only option she'd let pass her by. As soon as she'd found out that Tommy was laid up with a bad back, she should have swallowed her pride and asked his work colleagues if they had any idea of his whereabouts. But it was too late for her to do that now as she'd already lied to Ralf Kimble, Tommy's boss, and explaining herself to him would be so humiliating and only make her look bad. And besides that was the knowledge that should she come clean, she would have to face her marital problems becoming common knowledge, gossiped about throughout the factory. That prospect made her shudder in dread, as did the thought that Tommy, when he found out what she had done, would be far from pleased, further aggravating the situation. That she must avoid at all costs.

The conversation she'd had with Noreen earlier outside the factory gates came flooding back and Vinnie felt a surge of guilt wash over her. Noreen's show of caring had come as a real shock. There'd been a faint suspicion in Vinnie's mind – although she felt terrible for thinking it – that Noreen was secretly enjoying this situation between herself and Tommy, an underlying excitement always bubbling deep within her. Regardless of that, Vinnie felt that she herself had been out of order to have responded as sharply as she had. She ought to apologise to her neighbour for her bad conduct and do it now or risk incurring Noreen's displeasure which Vinnie knew from previous experiences could last for weeks even after something far less trivial than this. Life was miserable enough at the moment without adding to it. Despite her misery, Vinnie collected her coat and made her way around to Noreen's back door.

As she made to knock, to her surprise the door burst open and Barry stood on the threshold. He jumped in shock to find Vinnie standing there.

'Bloody hell, Mrs D, what a scare yer gave me! After Mam, a' yer? She's upstairs. Ain't a clue what's she's doing but she's meking enough noise about it. I don't know what's up with her but since she got up Sunday morning she's bin like a rocket about to blast off.' He pulled a face. 'You as well as most, Mrs D, know me mam's not exactly the easiest of people, but I've never seen her quite like this before. Me dad's fed up pussy-footing around her, he's escaped down the pub. That's what I'm gonna do too.' A cheeky grin suddenly split his face. 'Not the same pub as me dad, though, 'cos I don't want him cramping me style. See yerself in, won't yer, Mrs D?'

Oh, dear, Vinnie thought. Her own problems were affecting her neighbour badly. She hadn't realised before how much Noreen cared about her. She felt shocked by this knowledge but glad she had made the effort to come and make amends after her earlier behaviour. She flashed Barry a quick smile.

'Enjoy yourself.'

'Oh, I will, no danger. Tarra.'

Vinnie stood in Noreen and Eric's bedroom doorway and stared bemused at the scene before her. Noreen was never the tidiest of housekeepers; nevertheless Vinnie was surprised to see the chaos in the room beyond. Wardrobe doors were flung wide, drawers in the tall chest hanging open, items spilling out of both, and clothes were heaped all over the place. There was a large open suitcase on the bed, three-quarters filled with Noreen's possessions. So engrossed was she in sorting through a mound of clothes, she hadn't heard Vinnie enter.

'Are you going somewhere, Noreen?' Vinnie asked, advancing inside.

Noreen jerked upright, spinning around to face her. 'Eh? Oh, no . . . er . . .' She flashed a glance at the case, then back to Vinnie. 'Well . . . I might be. Seems me sister Bren's not very well.'

Momentarily forgetting her own dire situation, Vinnie frowned in concern. 'The one that lives in Blackpool?'

Noreen nodded. 'I had a letter from her today.' She patted her apron pocket. 'I'd let yer read it only I seem to have put it down somewhere. Anyway, never mind. Seems Bren's not bin well for a while. It's my opinion she's poisoned herself with that muck she serves up to the boarders in her guest house. Anyway, the doctor's told her that if she gets any worse then it's bed rest, and she's asked if there's any chance of me going up for a week or so to give her a hand. I checked with work and under the circumstances they haven't a problem. I

71

haven't told Eric or Barry in case it doesn't come to it. Yer know what men are like. If I said 'ote about me going away for a bit they'd be panicking about their dinners and what not. But I thought I'd pack a case just in case she gets any worse and I have ter leave in a hurry.'

'Oh, Noreen, I am sorry,' said Vinnie sincerely. 'If you do have to go, I'll keep an eye on Eric and Barry for you, that goes without saying.'

'Ta, I appreciate that. Well, if yer don't mind, I'd like to get on.'

It was most apparent to Vinnie that Noreen wanted rid of her and this fact hurt. She took a deep breath and fixed her eyes on her. 'Noreen, I know you're upset with me for how I was with you earlier so I came to apologise. It was rude of me, storming off like that, and after you took the trouble to come and meet me from work to see how I was.'

Lips tight, Noreen folded her arms and glanced slowly around the room before bringing her eyes back to Vinnie. 'I suppose it's hard to accept what's happened and the last thing you want is to hear me spell it out for yer.' She looked at Vinnie for several long moments before flashing a quick smile. 'Apology accepted. Now, if you'll excuse me, I really must get on.'

Vinnie eyed her in surprise. 'You haven't asked me if Tommy's back or if I've heard anything from him?'

Noreen looked at her knowingly. 'Well, I know he's not or I'd have heard the door go, and if you'd received a note or anything then you'd have bin round ter tell me earlier.'

'Oh, yes, I suppose.' There was a long silence. 'Well . . . I'll . . . er . . . leave you to it.' She made to leave but suddenly the thought of returning home to an empty house held no appeal whatsoever. 'Would you like a hand with your packing or I could make you a cuppa?' she offered.

'I'm almost done and I had a cuppa only minutes ago,' Noreen flatly responded. 'But thanks fer asking.'

It seemed that despite her acceptance of the apology Vinnie still wasn't completely forgiven. 'Oh! Oh, all right. Er . . . I'll see myself out then.'

As she reluctantly made her way back home annoyance grew within her. Noreen's attitude was out of order considering the terrible situation Vinnie was in. She must be very worried about her sister but nevertheless could show Vinnie a little more compassion instead of adding to her problems by being so off-hand.

She let herself back into her house. The emptiness immediately hit home and sadness at Tommy's mystifying actions consumed her again. Slumping down on to a kitchen chair, she cradled her head despairingly in her hands and wept.

Chapter Four

'Vinnie, a' yer listening ter me? D'yer want chips with yours or what?'

She rubbed her hands wearily over her face. 'No, thanks, Betty. In fact, I really don't want anything. Would you please cancel my order?'

'I'll have Vinnie's chips if she don't want 'em.'

Betty looked at Ruby scornfully. 'You've already ordered a double helping with yer Saveloy, *and* two rounds of bread and butter, *and* four pickled onions. What happened to yer diet?'

'I'm starting it next Monday.'

'That's what yer said last week.'

'Yeah, I know, but I kinda forgot.'

'Well, yer can start it today then.'

'Yer can't start yer diet on a Thursday.'

'Why not?'

Ruby gave a shrug. ''Cos yer can't, that's why.'

Betty tutted loudly. 'I give up with you.' She turned to face Vinnie. 'What d'yer mean, yer don't want 'ote? Yer can't go all af'noon with n'ote in yer stomach, gel.

You'll be keeling over yer work bench. You never had a breakfast cob neither. In fact, I ain't seen you eat all week. What's going on, Vinnie?'

'Will yer gerra bleddy move on?' a loud voice bellowed.

Betty shot a murderous glare at the woman responsible, standing further down the long queue in the chip shop opposite the factory. 'You can shut yer gob, Jessie Hibbert. Just wait yer turn like everyone else.' She turned her attention back to Vinnie. 'Well?'

She sighed, conscious that the chip shop owner was becoming impatient and the rest of the queue agitated, conscious their dinner hour was passing rapidly. 'I'm just not hungry, Betty,' she replied firmly. 'Now, please, can you get yours and Ruby's order and let's get out of here?'

'I'll be flipping glad when next week comes and the canteen is open again,' Betty grumbled loudly. 'Chips, chips and more bleddy chips for me dinner is getting on me nerves. Not that the food dished up in the canteen is much better but at least yer have more choice.' She gave a shudder. 'And I'm all for picnics, but not in the middle of bleddy November. The management should have found us somewhere ter sit and eat while the canteen gets its overhaul. Leaning against a bleddy wall is bleddy ridiculous at my age.'

'They do it every year, Betty, so it's not as though it's unusual,' Vinnie said, hoping to calm her mood a little.

'Yeah, but why pick winter? Why not summer when we could sit on the grass and enjoy the sun? Bloody management, no brains. It's the same when they do a fire drill, always when it's throwing it down with rain. Sure you don't want a chip, Vinnie?'

'Sure, but thanks for asking.'

'I'll have what yer don't want, Betty,' Ruby piped up, screwing her empty wrapper into a ball and lobbing it behind her.

'You got flipping worms, Ruby? I fear one of these days you're gonna burst like a balloon if yer carry on eating the amounts yer do. Anyway, can yer nip to the Co-op and get me a loaf?'

'Eh?'

'You heard,' Betty said, thrusting a shilling at Ruby which she had taken from her coat pocket. 'It won't hurt yer. The exercise'll do yer good. Mother's Pride, thick slice. Off yer go then.'

Ruby knew she was being given no choice. She grabbed the shilling and lumbered off.

As soon as she was out of earshot Betty looked at Vinnie hard before asking, 'What's going on, gel? And don't try and tell me there's nothing 'cos I'd call yer a liar. You ain't been right since yer daughter's wedding, and as the days have gone past yer getting steadily worse.' She glanced Vinnie over critically. 'You look dreadful, like you ain't slept fer weeks, and I know for a fact yer work's beginning to suffer. You let a batch of underslips go through this morning with a flaw in the fabric. Don't worry, I salvaged the situation before Doddsie got to hear of it. And you still ain't brought our wedding cake in despite me reminding yer every night on leaving time.' She took a deep breath. 'Now I know it's summat ter do with you and Tommy.'

'Me and Tommy are fine, Betty,' Vinnie said sharply. 'He's laid up with a bad back and I'm worried about him, that's all. It's natural for a wife, isn't it, to be concerned for her husband's health? Thank you for covering for me, I hadn't realised I'd been slipshod, and I promise I'll bring the cake in tomorrow. Now, if you don't mind, I'm going back to the factory.'

Vinnie made to head off but Betty stopped her by pushing her back down into a sitting position on the low wall. 'It's *where* Tommy's laid up that's concerning me.'

Vinnie frowned. 'Where? What do you mean? He's . . . he's at home where he should be.'

Betty snorted disdainfully. 'Now look here, I ain't took the trouble of getting Ruby out of the way to hear a load of clap-trap come out of your mouth. Wherever Tommy is laid up it's my guess he's not at home. Now call me nosey, whatever yer like, but I've a high regard for you, Vinnie. I couldn't care tuppence for most of the gels I work alongside but for you and Ruby I do, especially you. You were bloody good to me when my Alfie died. In fact, I wouldn't have got through that time without your support, and many other times too yer've helped me out – which is more than I can say for even me own bloody kids who seem to have a knack for disappearing whenever I need 'em. I know what people think of me, that I'm a nosey old widow woman. Well, I might be, but I never forget a kindness and under here,' she said, poking at her chest, 'beats a heart of gold, though I keep that part of me especially for the people that mean summat to me. As I've already said, you mean a lot, Vinnie. Now I wasn't gonna say anything but . . . well . . . there's rumours going around and I don't like the sound of them, especially when it looks like that little trollop is behind 'em.'

Vinnie gulped. 'Rumours?' she uttered, her face paling alarmingly. 'What rumours?' she demanded. 'And what little trollop are you talking about, Betty?'

'Maxine, that's who. Jeanie Shaw collared me in the lavvies this morning and asked if I'd heard what the little madam has been spreading. 'Course, she couldn't wait ter tell me more. I told her it was a load of balderdash but then on me way back I overheard a couple of the gels from packing gossiping about the same subject with a bloke from Tommy's own department who was delivering a load of dyed fabric to the stores. And I got to wondering if there's any fire to this smoke Maxine seems to be fanning, considering the way you've been acting all week. So, Vinnie, is there?'

'No, there's not,' she insisted. Then gnawed her bottom lip anxiously. 'Just . . . just *what* is being said, Betty?'

'That Tommy's left yer and moved in with Maxine.'

Vinnie's jaw dropped, face draining to a deathly white. 'What?'

'That's what's being said, gel. Now I don't for a minute believe it's true. Your Tommy would be mad to get himself involved with the likes of her, especially having a lovely wife like he's got in you. I just felt it'd be better you hearing from me what's going around than from someone else.'

Vinnie was staring at her wildly. 'It's not true, Betty. Of course it's not true.'

'So Maxine is up to her usual tricks and Tommy's laid in his *own* home with a bad back?'

Vinnie stared at her then swallowed hard, averting her eyes. As much as she wanted to walk away from this probing, tell Betty to mind her own business, she also felt a great need to unburden herself upon someone she knew without a doubt cared for her and was not just confronting her in order to confirm some juicy gossip.

Getting through the last few days, desperate for news of Tommy and hearing not one word from him, had almost destroyed her. She had no idea where to make a start looking for him. Neither had she anyone close enough to her to discuss such a personal situation with. Since Monday evening Vinnie had not seen hide nor hair of Noreen, despite calling round twice. Each time she had been told by a very embarrassed Eric that his wife wasn't at home, when Vinnie knew she was. From past experience it was obvious to her that Noreen was in one of her moods and milking this situation for all it was worth, wanting the satisfaction of making Vinnie get down on bended knees before she would be willing to revert to their former relations. Vinnie felt such pettiness to be unforgivable in the circumstances, and with all that was going on hadn't the energy to play

Noreen's game. As far as Vinnie was concerned she had made her apology and if Noreen was bloody-mindedly continuing this feud then she could get on with it. Regardless, though, Vinnie missed her friendship greatly, especially now when she really needed support.

For the last three nights she had sat inside her four walls brooding alone, willing Tommy or his representative to call. Even if her husband was too incapacitated to be brought home, just knowing his whereabouts would have put her mind at rest. So consumed was she with thoughts of getting him back, she hadn't given any attention to gossip circulating at work and certainly not the terrible lies Maxine appeared to have instigated.

She knew she couldn't go on trying to cover this up anymore, tell any more lies, and certainly not to Betty who was offering her the hand of friendship. She needed a friend just now, desperately. She took a shuddering breath, and when she spoke her voice was low and filled with emotion. 'Someone called into work on Monday to say Tommy's laid up with a bad back but it wasn't me, and you're right, he's not at home, Betty. I don't know where he is. He's . . . he's left me.' She lowered her head and wrung her hands, distraught. 'He informed me of his intentions as soon as we got home after Julie's wedding reception on Saturday night. He packed his bags then and where he's gone I've no idea.' Her eyes filled with tears and she sniffed hard to try and stem their flow. 'I'm so confused. I'd no idea whatsoever, no inkling at all, he was going to do something like this.'

Betty sighed heavily and patted her arm affectionately. 'The wives are the last ones ever to know, ducky. Hearing what you've been through, it's all credit to you that you've managed to get to work this week, let alone 'ote else.' She paused for a moment while she pondered her thoughts. 'Mmm, God knows how but it looks to me like Maxine has got hold of the fact that Tommy's left yer and is laid up somewhere with a bad back, then the scheming little bitch has added her poundsworth by saying he's moved in with her just to cause you humiliation at work. 'Course, she'll deny it's anything to do with her if you tackle her with it. Born liar if ever there was one.' A thought struck her. 'Oh, I've got it. She more than likely knows the person Tommy's staying with, and in that case it's gotta be a man. More than likely Maxine's giving this man Tommy's staying with her favours, and that's how she found out. Makes sense, dunnit? Pillow talk they call it, don't they? Mark my words, one day someone will land Maxine one, and if she's not careful that someone will be me.'

Vinnie groaned in despair. 'How do I find out where Tommy is, Betty?'

'You could ask his workmates. Someone is bound to know. It's probably someone from the factory putting him up being's Maxine seems to know all about it.'

'I couldn't do that. I've already lied to Ralf Kimble on Monday, making out Tommy was sick at home. If I start asking questions my lies will come out and it could make matters worse between me and Tommy when he gets to hear that all and sundry know our business.

From what you're telling me it seems there's enough rumours spreading already, which I'm sure Tommy's not going to be pleased about when he does return to work. Someone is bound to tell him, aren't they?'

Her friend nodded, then eyed Vinnie searchingly. 'Tell me the truth now, Vinnie. Was Tommy acting strangely? Late home from work? Been rowing with you? Anything at all different about him lately?'

She shook her head. 'No. I know I've been busy concentrating on Julie's wedding but I'd still have noticed if something was wrong with him.'

'Well, in that case it's my opinion he did what he did on a whim, and if he hadn't hurt his back he would have been home by now.' She eyed Vinnie sorrowfully. 'Oh, Vinnie lovey, you don't deserve this. You're a good woman, so you are. As fer Tommy, well, he needs a good shaking. What man in his right mind walks away from everything he's got? What on earth is he playing at, I wonder?'

'I don't know, Betty. I only wish I did.'

'I bet you feel like killing him?'

'I just want him home, Betty. That's what I want.'

She patted Vinnie's arm again. 'Yes, 'course yer do, ducky. 'Course yer do.'

'And I need to put a stop to these rumours it seems Maxine is putting about.'

'Best way to tackle them is to ignore 'em, Vinnie. If you start denying them people will automatically think you're doing that because there's truth in 'em, if yer see what I mean.'

Vinnie looked at her, surprised. 'Yes, I do. It'll be hard to ignore them but I will.'

Betty grinned. 'That's my girl. Now as fer getting Tommy back where he belongs, tek my advice and sit tight. Wait for him to come to you.'

She frowned questioningly. 'Don't do anything, you mean?'

'That's right. Hard to do, I know, but best in the long run. Drag him back and there's a chance he'll do it again. Leave him to come home in his own time and of his own free will and there's a good chance he won't do anything like this again. Some men do strange things at your Tommy's age, it's n'ote unusual, gel. They suddenly get it into their heads that the grass is greener on the other side and act before they've put their brain in gear. Your youngest has just got married. It probably hit Tommy like thunder that he was the father of the bride and not the bridegroom. Next stop grandfather. It's all down to getting older and life passing yer by. Women cope with this sorta thing much better than men.'

Vinnie gave her a hopeful look. 'I must admit those were the lines I was thinking along, Betty. I've racked my brains and can't think of any other reason for his leaving like he did.'

'Well, we can't both be wrong, can we? Not that I have had any experience of that kinda behaviour. My Alfie, God rest his soul, never gave me a minute's worry from the day we met until the day he died, but I hear the gels talking in the canteen and every other one of 'em has had problems with their man at some time or another. You must have heard 'em yourself? Well, they bleddy talk loud enough for all to hear. No shame or pride.' Vinnie nodded in agreement. 'Yer never think summat like that will upset your own home but no one knows what's around the corner. I'd advise you not to act as most of them have done and that's set about things kicking and screaming, causing as much trouble as they can, which only humiliates the men into relenting whether they want to or not. Don't mek a fool of yerself, Vinnie, like most other wives around here would. You keep yer pride intact, gel. Let Tommy see in no uncertain terms that you're more than just the woman he married. Some men don't realise what they've got until they ain't got it no more.'

She paused and eyed the woman before her with deep sincerity. 'Listen, ducky, not many marriages never suffer an upset at some time or other, so this with yours is n'ote out of the ordinary. And let's say the worst should happen and Tommy decides not to come home. Well, I know yer might love him and think yer life's ended with him not around but, believe me, he ain't worth having if he can put you through all this pain without so much as a sorry.'

Vinnie could see the wisdom in her words and looked at her, startled. She had worked alongside this woman for years and never realised before now how astute she was. 'You're a wise old owl, aren't you, Betty?'

She smiled and said tongue in cheek, 'I have me uses. You've never had reason to need me like this before, so that's why yer didn't know I had these qualities. I should have been one of them Agony Aunts in the women's magazines. I missed me calling, didn't I? Oh, here's Ruby,' she said, spotting the girl waddling back across the road towards them. 'There's one person I'd like to help get a decent life for herself, but for me to help her she's first got to find the courage to deal with her parents. Now, Vinnie, I'll be back to me normal bolshie self when we get back to the factory, but bear in mind what I've said and if yer need help or even just a listening ear then I'm always here for yer, gel. And let's look on the bright side. Hopefully, wherever Tommy is laid up, he'll have had time to think and to realise how stupid he's acted. Come the weekend his back should be better enough for him to get himself home.' Her eyes twinkled mischievously. 'I bet he ain't half missed his home comforts, if yer get me drift.'

Vinnie smiled warmly, then threw her arms around her and gave her a hug. 'That's what I'm hoping. Thanks, Betty.'

'Ged off, yer daft sod,' was her brusque response.

Vinnie set to work that afternoon with a lighter heart. She dearly hoped that Betty was right and come the weekend Tommy would be home, all would be back to normal and this awful situation over. In the meantime Vinnie was going to follow her advice and wait it out, let Tommy return of his own accord.

Hopefully this would all happen before Julie's expected visit to her parents after her return from honeymoon. Vinnie dreaded the thought of having to explain to her what her father had done. She knew Julie would automatically accuse her mother of being the reason for his actions, wouldn't listen to a word of her side of events. But, God willing, Tommy would be home by then and Julie need never know anything about this.

It was just approaching four-thirty that afternoon when the double doors to the inspection department burst open and Maxine waltzed through as usual, like she owned the place. As she had on the previous Monday she began to hand out printed notices to each worker in turn.

Betty spotted her first and stepped to Vinnie's side, giving her a nudge. 'Remember, act normal, gel. Don't let that little tart know she's got to yer. Okay?'

'I'll do my best,' Vinnie whispered back.

Moments after that Maxine arrived before their work bench and thrust three pieces of paper at them.

'Canteen's back in operation from Monday, ladies.' She fixed her eyes firmly on Ruby. 'Did you just hear Jimmy Young announce on the radio that a hippopotamus has died at London Zoo and they're looking for a replacement? Shall I put your name forward?' Before the girl could respond, Maxine had moved over in front of Vinnie. She glanced her over critically, then fixed malicious eyes on hers. 'Hello, Mrs Deakin. Still not recovered from your daughter's wedding, I see. My goodness, you do look dreadful. Mind you, big events take it out on older people, don't they? Maybe a spell in one of them rest homes for the aged 'ud do yer good.' She leaned over the counter, thrusting her face closer to Vinnie. 'Or could it be that you're upset 'cos you've found out your precious husband is now living with me?' Her mouth twisted into a wicked smirk. 'And he's never been happier. A man like him needs looking after in *every way*, I'm sure you understand what I mean by that, and that's exactly what *I'm* doing.'

Vinnie was staring at Maxine, dumb-struck. The room seemed to sway, the walls closed in on her. Then suddenly all hell seemed to break loose around her. Someone was screaming, someone else bellowing at the top of their voice. Then there was lots of shouting accompanied by the pounding of feet across the wooden floor.

Vinnie couldn't stand it. She had to get out of this nightmare. Without a backward glance she fled.

Chapter Five

Panting heavily, heart thumping rapidly inside her chest, Vinnie pressed her back against her closed front door and stared blindly down the gloomy hall. She couldn't remember the journey home, running all the way, not even collecting her belongings from her factory locker. All she knew was that she had been consumed with a need to get out of the factory – get away from Maxine.

She felt a sudden lurch in her stomach and knew she was going to be sick. Dashing through to the kitchen she just managed to reach the sink before she expelled a spurt of yellow bile – not having eaten for days it was all her stomach contained. After swilling out her mouth, she slumped back against the sink, her whole body sagging. What Maxine had told her couldn't possibly be true. It just couldn't. The thought of Tommy living with anyone but herself was unthinkable to Vinnie, but the thought of that woman being someone like Maxine, a woman young enough to be his daughter and one possessing such a malicious nature, a woman whose reputation for being a slut extended far beyond the factory walls . . . it was just too unbearable to comprehend. But why would Maxine have so blatantly announced it, and loud enough for others to hear, if it wasn't true?

A loud hammering on the front door made her jump and she heard her name being called through the letter box. It was Ruby. 'Let me in, Vinnie,' she was bellowing. 'I know yer in there. If yer don't let me in, I'll bust the door down.'

Ruby's threat was no idle one. She certainly had the build to knock the door off its hinges. As much as she didn't want to see anyone, Vinnie knew she had no choice but to obey.

As they faced each other in the back room, Vinnie took a breath and asked Ruby lightly, 'Why are you here?'

'I was sent to check on yer after yer ran off like that.'

'Oh! Oh, well, thanks for coming but you can see that I'm fine. I . . . er . . . suddenly had the most dreadful headache. I don't know what came over me but I just wanted to come home. I expect I'm in trouble for what I've done, I'll just have to face that.' She forced a smile to her face. 'Anyway, you'll be wanting to get off yourself?'

Ruby was looking at her worriedly. 'Well, I do need ter pop and see Betty too but . . .'

Momentarily forgetting her own problems, Vinnie looked at her in concern. 'Betty?' she cut in. 'What's wrong with her?'

Ruby eyed her, taken aback. 'Don't you remember what happened, Vinnie?'

'Happened?' She frowned. All she remembered was Maxine's leering grin, her face coming uncomfortably close as she spewed forth her venom, and her own great need to get away. Vinnie shook her head. 'I don't know what you're talking about.'

Ruby's face lit up. 'Oh, Vinnie, it was like summat outta a film. If it wasn't so serious I'd have found it all exciting. I've never known 'ote like this happen at work before.'

'Ruby, just get on with it,' Vinnie urged, irritated.

'Oh, yeah, sure. Well, we all heard what Maxine said to yer. I mean, she said it that loud yer'd have had to have bin deaf not to. I've never seen Betty move so quick. Before I knows what's happening meself, Betty was around the bench and had grabbed Maxine around her throat, threatening to throttle her. Maxine was screaming blue murder. All the women ran across then, shouting and goading Betty into giving her a good thumping. Then Doddsie charged through the doors like a tornado. Her face was the colour of beetroot and she was screaming her head off, telling Betty to stop it. When Betty took no notice of her, Doddsie flew into such a temper she punched Betty on the chin. So Betty let go of Maxine and punched Doddsie back, sending her sprawling. You should have heard the gobful Betty gave her. I knew she could swear but even I didn't know she knew words like that. Anyway, then Betty got hold of Maxine again and was shaking the life out of her. It was Mr Hamlin who finally broke it all up.'

Face ashen, Vinnie was staring at her astounded. 'Oh, God! Oh, God!' she uttered, mortified. 'Betty will be sacked for certain for what she did and it's all my fault. Did Mr Hamlin sack her, Ruby?' she urgently cried.

The girl gave a helpless shrug. 'Dunno. He told us all ter get back ter work and ordered Betty, Maxine and Doddsie into his office. Minutes later he came out and ordered me to finish early and come and check on you. Then he went back in his office to finish dealing with them. Sorry, Vinnie, that's all I know. Anyway, even if Mr Hamlin hadn't told me ter, I was gonna come to see you off me own bat. I was worried about yer, see.'

Vinnie flashed her a wan smile of gratitude then rubbed her hands over her face. 'I'll come with you to see Betty.'

Ruby held up a warning hand. 'You ain't in no fit state to go and see anyone, Vinnie. Yer shaking like a leaf and I've seen more colour on a corpse. Not that I've ever seen a dead body,' she added, 'but yer know what I mean. I'm gonna mek yer a cuppa, then I'll go and see her.' Her face screwed up angrily. 'It's my opinion Maxine got what she deserved. I'm only sorry I never had the guts ter do what Betty did after all the times she took the mickey out of me.' She looked at Vinnie gravely. 'Your Tommy ain't gonna like it when he hears Maxine's lies, is he? I wouldn't like ter be in her shoes when he goes to sort her out.' She paused in thought. 'I wonder what made her say it? Been on the booze at lunchtime, do yer reckon?' Ruby saw the frozen look on Vinnie's face and, her own clouding quizzically, asked, 'It is lies Maxine's telling, ain't it, Vinnie? Vinnie?'

'Eh? Er . . . yes, yes, of course. Look, I really appreciate your coming, Ruby, but I'd like to be on my own now. Please tell Betty I'll see her . . . I'll see her . . .'

Ruby patted her shoulder. 'Don't you worry, Vinnie, I'll tell Betty you'll see her at work termorrow.' She didn't want to say that was providing Betty hadn't been sacked, which she sincerely hoped hadn't happened but which she suspected was the case. No matter what the reason, it was considered very serious misconduct to attack another work colleague. 'Well, that's providing yer feel up ter coming in yerself termorrow. Tongues'll be wagging but you'll have ter face 'em sometime, Vinnie. Anyway, all of us in our department are behind yer. We all know what a spiteful mouth Maxine's got on her and to be honest I bet most people are glad she's finally got her comeuppance. Maybe in future she'll think twice before she does 'ote like this again. And maybc Betty won't be sacked, not when Mr Hamlin knows the truth of it all.'

The thought of having to cope with the gossip this terrible incident was bound to have created around the factory made Vinnie shudder in dread but at this moment she had a far more serious matter to think about: whether Maxine was telling the truth or not. 'I hope you're right, Ruby,' she whispered distractedly.

As she heard the door click shut after Ruby saw herself out, Vinnie sank down on a chair at the table and stared blindly at the wall. She needed to find Tommy and demand some explanations. She knew there was no alternative for her but to traipse the streets visiting all those she knew of who might be harbouring him and hope one of them turned up trumps. After what had happened today she couldn't sit here and wait for him eventually to come to her. She'd go mad if she did that.

Determined to achieve her aim, she stood up. As she did so a thunderous knocking on the back door froze her rigid. Oh, no, her mind screamed. Not Noreen. She couldn't face her just now. Her neighbour had obviously realised that Vinnie wasn't going to play her childish game and she herself was going to have to be the one to make the next move towards restoring their relationship. Of all the times to do that, she had to pick now. Noreen would take one look at Vinnie's face and immediately know another catastrophe had befallen her and not be satisfied until she had all the gory details. Then she would insist on coming with her to find Tommy and Vinnie didn't want that. She wanted to speak to him by herself, get to the truth of this matter in a dignified manner. It was Noreen's nature to create trouble, she couldn't help herself.

The door was banged on again and Vinnie hurriedly decided to plant a smile on her face and tell Noreen she was glad to see her but that she was on her way to catch the shops before they shut and would call round later.

Steeling herself, prepared to play out her part, she

opened the door and nearly fainted in shock to find Tommy standing there.

He looked at her sheepishly. 'Can I come in, Vinnie?'

She was so stunned to see him, she automatically stepped aside to allow him entry. She stood looking at him, standing awkwardly by the dining table. So many questions she needed answers to but they all seemed frozen in her throat. What she did say was, 'I'm glad to see your back seems to be better.'

He looked at her blankly then gave a sudden grin. 'Oh, God, yeah. It's been awful. The pain was terrible. I couldn't walk.'

The relief on her face was clear to see. 'Oh, so you really *have* been laid up then?'

He gave her a look that said he was hurt she doubted his story. 'All week, Vinnie. It only eased up today. I'd have been home sooner otherwise.' He frowned at her quizzically. 'You don't think I'd lie about a thing like that, do you?'

'No, it's just that you've never had a bad back before.'

'And I never want another.' Taking a deep breath, he looked at her apologetically. 'This is such a mess, Vinnie, and it's all my fault. Saying sorry doesn't seem enough for what I've put you through. I can only say I don't know what came over me on Saturday night.' He blew out his cheeks and held up his arms in a helpless gesture. 'I suddenly felt so old. I'm over forty and I couldn't remember living through that time, like it had just flashed by in the wink of an eye. I was young then suddenly middle-aged and before I knew it I would be an old man. It frightened the wits out of me, Vinnie. I just wanted to run away, it was all I could think of.' He sighed heavily, a look of shame filling his face. 'I never meant what I said to you. Not one word. Regretted everything as soon as I walked out of the house. It was pride that stopped me coming back. I felt such a fool. I was on my way back to you, hoping you'd forgive me. Sunday morning it was. I bent down to pick up my case. Next thing I knew, I was writhing in agony on the floor. The emergency doctor said I'd pulled a muscle in my back and only rest would cure it.'

'You never thought to let me know?'

His face clouded in remorse. 'I should have, I'm sorry.'

'Yes, you should have. I've been frantic all week not knowing if you really meant what you said, feeling terrible because you were ill and I wasn't around to care for you.'

'Oh, Vinnie, please forgive me,' he begged.

She looked at him for several long moments. She desperately wanted to throw her arms around him, let him know how glad and relieved she was to see him home, but there was still the question of Maxine and her involvement in all this. She suddenly felt a dreadful feeling of foreboding in the pit of her stomach and realised she didn't really want to know the truth, she was afraid of it. But if their marriage was going to return to the happy, trusting relationship it had been then she had to ask the question. She prepared herself to hear the worst, not sure how she would handle it.

Taking several deep breaths, before she lost her nerve she asked him, 'Does Maxine know you've come here?'

He looked at her, non-plussed. 'Maxine?'

'Maxine Upton?'

He gave a bewildered shrug. 'The young girl that works in the General Office? What has she to do with anything?'

'She seems to think she has everything to do with this, Tommy. She's been putting it about that you've moved in with her. Took great delight in telling me herself this afternoon, in fact.'

His jaw dropped open in shock. 'What? You're having me on?'

'I'm not.'

'But she's lying, Vinnie. I hardly know the girl.' He screwed up his face scornfully. 'Anyway, even if I wasn't happily married to you, I wouldn't touch the likes of her with a bargepole. There's hardly a man in the factory hasn't been with her, besides the rest. I might have just acted the fool, Vinnie, but I'm not a complete idiot.'

Her heart soared. 'So everything she said about you two was lies?'

'Believe me, Vinnie. As I said, I wouldn't go near the girl.' He looked at her hard, then sighed. 'I think I know why she did this.'

'You do?'

He nodded. 'Revenge.'

'For what?'

'I never told you because to me it wasn't important,

not worth causing trouble between us anyway. A few months ago Maxine started coming on strong to me. I laughed it off at first, then she became persistent and I eventually told in her no uncertain terms where to go. She turned ugly. Warned me I'd regret turning her down. I laughed, said there was nothing she could do about it. I never gave it another thought. That's the truth, Vinnie. But it's obvious now she was biding her time until the right chance came up.'

'But how did she find out you'd temporarily left home and was stopping with . . . Who were you stopping with, Tommy?'

'George Collins from work. I fibbed to you. I hadn't arranged anything beforehand. I just turned up on his doorstep hoping he'd take me in. Since his wife died the other year I think he's been lonely and was quite glad of my company.'

She looked up at him, confused. 'But I spoke to George last Monday at work when I went to find you in the hope of sorting this out. He said he hadn't seen you.'

'Did he? Oh. He never told me he'd seen you either.' Tommy gave a shrug. 'I dunno . . . Maybe he thought it best not to interfere in our problems. He's a good sort is George.'

'He certainly is! Good enough to disguise his voice and pretend to be me when he called into the office to inform them you were ill.'

Tommy looked at her for a moment before saying, 'Well, someone had to tell them, Vinnie, else I risked losing me job. But please don't say anything to George when you see him, he was only doing me a favour. Anyway, how the hell Maxine found out what was going on between me and you is beyond me. As far as I know George is the only one who knew about this. She obviously knows him through work but he wouldn't have said anything to her, he'd no reason to. Mind you, after hearing all this, nothing would surprise me about Maxine. Rest assured though, Vinnie, she won't dare do anything like this again after I've finished with her.'

'And you, Tommy? Will you ever do anything like this again?'

'Oh, dear God, Vinnie, no, definitely not.'

Her whole body sagged in sheer relief. 'Oh, Tommy,' she uttered, tears of happiness spurting from her eyes. 'I thought I'd lost you.'

The next thing she knew she was in his arms and he was hugging her tightly. 'So we're all right, are we?' he asked, tenderly kissing her forehead.

Smiling up at him lovingly, she nodded.

'Shall I go and fetch my case or have I to spend another night in George's lumpy spare bed?'

'You'll be spending no more nights in any other bed than the one you belong in, Tommy. That's the one you share with me. I'll get your house keys for you.'

He kissed her lips. 'Don't worry about that now, I'll get them later.'

As he reached the door, he stopped and turned to look at her. 'I won't be long,' he said, smiling at her seductively.

She stood for several moments staring at the closed door. A broad smile of happiness split her face. Her nightmare had ended. Tommy was back home where he belonged. Maxine's malicious actions had stemmed from feelings of vengeance because Tommy wouldn't have anything to do with her. Vinnie felt a rush of pity for the young woman, feeling her life must be very empty for her to sink to such depths in order to fill the void of her own loneliness. What a shame, she was such a pretty girl too. The love of a good man was all she needed, something she would never find if she carried on fuelling her own bad reputation. It did men's ego the power of good to spend a night with women like Maxine but as long-term girlfriend or wife material the likes of her were not even considered.

Vinnie worried for a moment about how she was going to deal with Maxine the next time she saw her, then decided she wouldn't think about that now. She had things to do before Tommy returned. She wanted to cook him a nice meal as a welcome home and hadn't much time to prepare it or make herself presentable as she knew she looked a terrible mess. She needed to hurry if she was to achieve all that before he came back.

Just then she heard the Adlers' front door knocker slap against the wood as it was being shut and for a moment worried again that Noreen was about to pay her a visit. She wanted to make up with her neighbour, get their relationship back to normal, but not right now. She and Tommy needed time on their own. Vinnie made to switch the lights off, pretend she wasn't at home, when it struck her it wouldn't be Noreen coming to call as it would have been the Adlers' back door she would have heard go and not their front. Obviously it was Eric or Barry she'd heard going out for the evening or maybe all three.

Humming happily to herself, she set to work.

The clock struck nine and Vinnie frowned. Tommy had left to collect his case just after six-thirty, saying he wouldn't be long. She had no idea where George Collins actually lived but it couldn't be that far away. Worry began to nag at her. Could something have happened to him? Had he done his back in again? Then another thought struck her and her worries faded. More than likely he had taken George for a drink by way of saying thank you for putting him up.

She rose and went to check the meat pie she had hastily put together, thinking then she hadn't much time. It was beginning to dry up, and the roast potatoes too. She turned the oven down, hoping Tommy wouldn't be much longer or she feared the meal would be completely ruined. She wanted this evening to go well, give Tommy no reason to regret his return home, for them both to forge ahead with the rest of their lives together.

She settled down to wait.

The clock struck ten, then eleven, and still he hadn't returned. Vinnie began to feel annoyed. A thank you drink was one thing, but considering the circumstances

Tommy could have opted for a night in the pub another time.

She heard the Adlers' front door bang shut. Obviously they had come home. She wished Tommy had too. A moment later there was a knock on her own front door and, heart racing excitedly, she leaped up to open it.

She tried to hide her dismay to find Eric not Tommy standing on the pavement.

'Sorry to bother yer, Vinnie, but is Noreen with yer?'

She shook her head. 'No, sorry, I haven't seen her.'

His face fell. 'Oh!' he scratched his bald head, perplexed. 'I had to work late and I've just got home. There's no sign of her. She never said she was going anywhere.'

'Doesn't Barry know where she's gone?' Vinnie asked.

'He's gone ter stop with his mate for a few days.' Eric sighed forlornly.

A memory struck Vinnie. 'Oh, has her case gone, Eric?'

He frowned, bewildered. 'Case? What case?'

'The one she'd packed last Sunday. Sorry, I'd better explain. It's her sister, Eric. The one in Blackpool. She's been ill for a while apparently and the doctor told her that if she doesn't improve then it's bed rest. She sent Noreen a letter asking if that happened, would she go and help run the guest house. Noreen told me she'd squared it with work and they were quite all right about it. If the case has gone then I expect she got called to Blackpool urgently. I heard your door go just after six-thirty. Someone must have got a message to her and Noreen left in a hurry.'

'Oh,' he uttered, relieved. 'Is that why she's been in such a mood, 'cos she's been worried about her sister? I never knew she cared about her that much. Never said a good word about her that I can remember. Still, she should have said what was bothering her. Saved me and Barry a lot of bother if she had.'

'She told me she wasn't going to tell you unless it came to it in case you worried how you'd manage while she was away.'

He snorted disdainfully. 'Daft bugger, she is. I'm quite capable of meking meself beans on toast. And I can wash a shirt. Not too hot on ironing, though.'

Vinnie smiled. 'I said I'd keep an eye on you both. Anyway, I bet that's what's happened. Noreen got called away urgently and in her rush forgot to leave you a note, that's all. She knew I'd tell you anyway. I bet she'll be in touch as soon as she can to let you know what's going on.'

'Oh, what a relief! Let's hope she comes back her normal sunny self.'

Vinnie laughed. 'I'm sure she will.'

Before she shut her door she glanced up and down the street. It was deserted, no sign of Tommy whatsoever. Her annoyance grew. He really was pushing her good nature to the limit.

She had just arrived in the back room when the door knocker pounded again and she rushed to answer it. 'Tommy, thank God! I was . . .' Her voice trailed off at the sight of two solemn-faced policemen looking at her.

'Mrs Lavinia Deakin?' one asked.

Stupefied, she nodded.

'Can we come in?'

'Er . . . yes,' she said, standing aside. As she made to lead them through into the room at the back her face paled alarmingly as the significance of a visit from the police registered. She spun round to face them. 'Oh, God, my daughter,' she cried. 'There's been an accident. She's all right, isn't she?' she beseeched.

The taller of the policemen took off his helmet and eyed her gravely. 'It's not your daughter, Mrs Deakin, it's your husband. He is Thomas Deakin?'

A surge of acute fear filled her. Terrified eyes fixed on him, she slowly nodded.

He took a deep breath. 'There's no easy way of telling you this, Mrs Deakin, but there's been an incident involving your husband. I'm afraid he's dead.'

Chapter Six

'Drink your tea, Mrs Deakin. It'll make you feel better. I've put plenty of sugar in.'

Vinnie's eyes flashed to the person addressing her. Was this policeman mad? He had just informed her that her husband was dead. How on earth was a cup of tea going to make her feel better? He was smiling sympathetically at her and she fought a great urge to reach over and wipe that smile off his face. She didn't need his sympathy. Tommy wasn't dead. A terrible mistake had been made. It was someone else with the same name. Thomas Deakin couldn't be that uncommon. Any minute her Thomas Deakin, worse for wear from his drink with George Collins, silly grin splitting his handsome face, would bang on the door demanding to be let in. Then the police would have to apologise to her. She wouldn't be annoyed with them; after all, mistakes were made, it was human nature. She just pitied the poor woman whose husband was really dead.

She felt a touch on her arm. 'I know what you're

hoping for, Mrs Deakin. That we've made a blunder. But we haven't, I'm so sorry. Apart from his other things, your husband was carrying his union card on him and from that we were able to confirm his identity.'

'It must have been stolen,' she said with conviction.

'The deceased man is definitely your husband, Mrs Deakin.'

She shook her head dismissively. 'You've made a mistake,' she insisted. 'Whoever that man is he's *not* my Tommy. My husband is fetching his case. He'll be back any minute.'

'Fetching his case?' the Sergeant queried.

'Yes. We'd . . . oh, it's very embarrassing really, but we'd had a silly misunderstanding. Couples who have been married as long as we have do, don't they? He'd stopped with a friend for a night which turned into a few days because he pulled a muscle in his back. Such terrible pain he was in, he couldn't walk, poor love. He's fine now, though.'

With great sadness Sergeant Alan Mayhew looked at the deeply shocked woman before him, clearly unwilling to accept what he was telling her. He generally loved his job bringing law and order to the citizens of Leicester but this part of it he detested. There was no easy way to break the terrible news of a loved one's demise, however it was caused. In his experience the bereaved either fainted, quietly sobbed or burst into wails of anguish, kicking and screaming. One had even punched him and almost broken his nose. Never, though, had he seen anyone react quite like this before.

He laid a hand gently on her arm. 'Is there anyone we can fetch to be with you? A relative or close friend? You mentioned a daughter. Would you give the constable your daughter's address and we'll have her collected?'

'What's the point in upsetting my daughter unnecessarily, Sergeant? Can you imagine what this would do to her, being told her father is dead only to find out it's not true? Anyway, she's on her honeymoon. Not due back until late-afternoon Saturday.' She gave a distant smile. 'I hope they've both had a good time, although I expect the weather hasn't been great at this time of year. Have you children, Sergeant?'

Alan Mayhew flashed a worried look at the constable hovering by the fireplace, then back at Vinnie. 'I've three boys, Mrs Deakin. All grown up but still at home, managing to run my wife ragged. Now, you must listen to me. His voice was low, gentle. 'Mr Deakin was attacked. Stabbed in the chest. If it's of any comfort he wouldn't have suffered.' That was a lie but told with the best of intentions. Thomas Deakin would have felt the pain of the knife doing its worst and died looking into the eyes of his murderer.

Vinnie looked at him incredulously. 'Don't be silly. Who'd want to stab my husband?'

Her mind whirled. Why was this man telling her such an outrageous story? Tommy stabbed? What nonsense. She looked across at the clock. It was getting on for twelve. Tommy really had pushed her patience to the limit and she would tell him so as soon as he came in. So much for making up! A sudden chill ran through her then, someone walking over her grave, and she gave a violent shiver. Then a strange sensation overcame her. She seemed to be floating in a grey fuzzy haze. A voice reached her ears. It was close by, a man's. He was shouting at her. Her body suddenly felt heavy, the room began to sway and she had the sensation she was falling. She instinctively reached forward to cushion herself and felt a firm hand clasp her arm, pushing her backwards.

'Are you all right, Mrs Deakin?'

Dazed, she turned her head and looked at the person addressing her. 'I'm fine, thank you,' she snapped, freeing her arm from his grasp. 'Why are you shouting at me?' She frowned, confused. 'Who are you?'

'I'm Sergeant Mayhew, Mrs Deakin. And I wasn't shouting at you. I was concerned because you seemed about to faint.'

She stared at him blankly then slowly nodded. 'Oh, yes, I remember you now. You told me a silly sorry about Tommy being murdered. It is murder, isn't it, when someone stabs another person and kills them? You know, I'm concerned for the poor woman who's waiting for her husband to come home only he won't because he's dead. It's her you should be with, Sergeant, not me.'

He eyed her kindly. 'You were going to tell me the address of a relative?' he coaxed gently.

'Was I? Oh!' Her eyes glazed over. 'I've no living

relatives. My father died when I was young, my mother a few years back. Two brothers in the war. Aunties and uncles gone, too. I've cousins somewhere, we weren't close. Never kept in touch. I can't see how this information is helping you with this other woman, Sergeant?'

'What about your husband?' he asked.

'What about him?'

'Has he any relatives?'

'No, he hasn't either. His parents died before my mother and Tommy's an only child. Like me, all his relatives are gone now. I suppose we're both orphans, Sergeant.'

'What about a friend then?'

She gave an irritated sigh. 'I just wish you'd both go now and leave me alone.'

He smiled patiently at her. 'We will as soon as you tell me what I need to know.'

She clamped her mouth tight. These futile questions were really beginning to annoy her. What was Tommy going to say when he came back and found his house full of policemen? But the Sergeant had said they would leave if she answered his questions. She supposed the sooner she did, the sooner they would go. 'I've not really got a close friend. Never needed one.' That wasn't true. All women needed a close friend, but Noreen had made sure that any friendship Vinnie had begun to forge with anyone else was doused long before it grew into something deep and lasting. But this inability to stand up to her neighbour's domineering ways she felt was none of the policeman's business so all she said was, 'I've everything I need in my family. I've a neighbour but she's away at the moment as her sister's sick.' She looked at him in concern. 'Shouldn't you be off home now? I should think your wife is getting worried about you, and more to the point you really should go to see the poor widow of the real victim.'

Just then a knock resounded on the front door. A bright smile lit her face and she made to rise. 'That'll be my husband. See, I told you that you'd made a mistake.'

'You sit where you are, Mrs Deakin. My constable will do the honours for you.' He motioned to the young man and mouthed, 'That'll be the Inspector. Let him in.'

A middle-aged man entered, accompanied by a younger one. Sergeant Mayhew immediately got up and went over to them.

'How's she taking it?' the older man asked in hushed tones.

Sergeant Mayhew took a deep breath, his face grave. 'She's badly shocked, sir. I'm very worried about her. She's not taking this in at all. Insists we've made a mistake. I'm afraid she might tip over the edge if we don't tread carefully. She's no living relatives, it seems, neither had Mr Deakin apart from a daughter, but apparently she's away on honeymoon, not due back until Saturday afternoon. I'm still trying to get the address of a friend.'

'Have you managed to get any details about her husband out of her?'

'Hardly anything. Only that Thomas Deakin was supposed to be fetching his case.' He repeated what Vinnie had told him.

The Inspector sighed despondently. 'So much for hoping to clear this matter up quickly. Why can't incidents like this happen at the beginning of a shift and not at the end? I should have been off duty hours ago. I was supposed to have taken my wife out for dinner tonight. It's our anniversary.' He noted the expression on the Sergeant's face. 'Don't worry, Mayhew, I'll be as gentle as I can with her. She's insisting it's a misunderstanding, you say? I'll try that tack.'

The Inspector went over to Vinnie and sat down beside her. 'Hello, Mrs Deakin. I'm Detective Inspector Banks and the colleague who came in with me is Detective Piper. We've a few questions we need to ask you so we can clear this . . . er . . . misunderstanding up and then we can be on our way. But you need someone with you when we go. Police procedure, I'm afraid. There must be someone you know well. What about a person you work with?'

'I work with lots of people, Inspector. I suppose I'm closest to Betty. She gave me a lot of good advice this week, so yes, she's a friend.'

'What's Betty's surname and where does she live?'

'Trubshaw. Betty Trubshaw.' She gave him the address. 'But it's a bit late to be calling on her at this time of night. She's not a young woman. I'd really prefer it if you didn't bother her.'

He patted her arm. 'I'm sure she won't mind.' He

glanced across at the constable and mouthed, 'Go outside and radio in for her to be collected – and quick about it.' He then turned his attention back to Vinnie. 'Mrs Deakin, what were you doing between the hours of seven and eight tonight?'

'I can't imagine why you'd want to know but I was making Tommy's dinner. Meat pie. It's in the oven. I wish I hadn't taken so much trouble as it's more than likely ruined now. He'll have to make do with a sandwich when he comes in.'

'Mrs Deakin, have you any idea why your husband would be at a flat on Long Street? Number 18a?'

She replied matter-of-factly, 'He knows lots of people, Inspector. I suggest you ask him that question yourself when he comes home. He shouldn't be long now.'

Banks exhaled sharply then rose and walked out of Vinnie's earshot, motioning Sergeant Mayhew to join him. 'We ain't going to get anything out of her tonight.'

'Is she a suspect, Inspector?'

'The wife is always a prime suspect, Sergeant. But my gut instincts tell me it wasn't her. I personally don't think she's a clue what's been going on. Obviously we've still some checking to do but I'd be very surprised if we ain't already got our murderer in the cells. It all points that way.' He flashed a glance over at Vinnie and gave a heavy sigh. 'Like you, Mayhew, I don't like the way she's acting. I prefer it when they're hysterical, I can cope with that, not this. Let's hope Betty Trubshaw isn't long in coming. And to be on the safe side we'd better get a doctor. Oh, and we'll need Mrs Deakin to make a proper identification but that'll have to wait until tomorrow.'

Chapter Seven

Vinnie woke with a start and sat bolt upright. 'Oh!' she exclaimed, yanking the bedclothes up under her chin. She'd had a terrible dream, so vivid, and now she was awake she thanked God it was just that. She suddenly sensed another presence in the room and a warm glow filled her. Tommy had brought her a cup of tea. She turned her head to thank him, then her mouth dropped wide in shock when she saw who it was hovering by her bed. 'Betty! What . . . what on earth are you doing here?' she asked, easing back to support herself against the headboard. Then she noticed the grave expression on Betty's face, eyes red and swollen from crying. Her own face screwing up worriedly, Vinnie asked, 'What on earth is the matter, Betty?'

The older woman put the cup of tea she was holding on the bedside table, eased herself down on the edge of the mattress and looked at her tenderly. 'Don't yer remember, Vinnie lovey?'

'Remember? Remember what?'

'Oh, dear,' Betty sighed. She took a deep breath, then

reached over and took Vinnie's hands gently in hers. 'The police fetched me last night to be with you. Tommy . . . well . . . he's dead, ducky.'

Her face twisted and she cried, 'No! That was a nightmare, I know it was. I'm still dreaming . . . I must be. You're not really here.'

'Vinnie, now listen ter me.' Betty's voice was firm. 'Yer gonna mek yerself really poorly in the head if yer don't accept what's happened. Tommy's dead. This is no nightmare, lovey.'

The other woman stared at her wildly, face ashen, heart pounding erratically. She faltered, 'It's . . . n . . . not a nightmare I'm having, Betty?'

Solemnly, her friend shook her head. 'No, Vinnie. I'm so, so sorry.'

Her face crumpled. Huge fat tears began to tumble down her cheeks. 'Oh, Tommy, Tommy!' she wailed as racking sobs shook her.

Betty hurriedly released Vinnie's hands, threw her arms around her and pulled her close. 'That's it, ducky,' she said, tenderly patting the back of her head. 'Let it all out. It'll do yer good.'

It seemed to Betty that hours passed before Vinnie's desolate sobs finally subsided and she pulled herself away from the tight embrace to wipe her blotchy face on the edge of the sheet. Bleak eyes rested on Betty. 'Tommy . . . he . . . he was stabbed, wasn't he?' Her voice was so low it was barely a whisper. 'I remember the policeman trying to tell me last night. I kept insisting it wasn't my Tommy. I couldn't accept it, you see.

He was kind, that policeman. He must think me an idiot.'

'I'm sure he doesn't, lovey,' Betty said with conviction. 'Would yer like me to mek yer a fresh cuppa?'

'No, Betty, but thank you. I feel sick.' She swallowed hard to try and rid herself of the huge lump sticking in her throat. 'Who'd want to stab my Tommy, Betty? What sick-minded man would want to take his life? He did no harm to anyone. My Tommy had no enemies.' She paused as a memory struck her and her face contorted in bewilderment. 'I remember the policeman saying something about a flat. Whose flat was he talking about? Why was Tommy there?'

Betty gave a helpless shrug. 'I don't know, lovey. The bobbies wouldn't tell me n'ote other than that Tommy had been fatally injured. I thought he'd been robbed or summat. Look, the detective called in earlier to see how you were. I told him yer were still out cold after what the doctor gave yer. I expect yer don't remember him calling either? Well, never mind. But I asked the Inspector ter call back later. Yer should really try and talk to 'em, Vinnie.' She saw the horror on her friend's face. 'You'll have ter sometime, ducky, so best get it over with. Yer need to know what happened, don't yer?'

Do I? she thought. Her whole body sagged despairingly. The thought of having to listen to the terrible details of Tommy's death filled her with dread.

Betty sensed what she was thinking. 'I'll be with yer, Vinnie. I ain't going nowhere. And I'm staying put here for as long as it teks. I'll square it with work,' she said, despite not knowing at the moment whether she still had a job with Brewin's after her conduct on Thursday. She was waiting to hear her fate after the company's investigation into the incident. 'In the circumstances I know they'll allow me some compassionate leave.' They weren't obliged to do this as Betty was no kin to Vinnie but she hoped that with all her friend had to contend with this wouldn't matter. Vinnie needed someone like Betty around to take charge while she faced the ordeal that lay before her.

Vinnie flashed her a grateful smile. 'You're very kind, Betty.' Then she gnawed her bottom lip anxiously. 'I have to do this, don't I? Talk to the police?'

Betty gravely nodded. 'Yer do. There might be summat you know that will help them nail the bastard what done it.'

Vinnie sighed despairingly. 'I don't know what.' Her eyes glazed over. 'But, yes, I want whoever did this to pay.' They softened again and she looked at Betty gratefully. 'Oh, how can I thank you for being with me?'

'There's no need, ducky. That's what friends are for, ain't it?'

Vinnie's already white face suddenly turned paler. 'Oh, God,' she cried, horrified. 'Julie . . . she needs to know. But how am I going to tell her, Betty? This news about her father will crucify her.'

'Eh, we'll deal with that when the time comes. It's bound to knock her sideways but no more than it has you, Vinnie. Anyway, you need ter deal with one thing at a time. Let's get the police out of the way first. Julie

116

ain't due back 'til about tea-time termorrow, is she? And this ain't summat yer can tell her over the telephone. What's the point of spoiling her honeymoon? One day ain't gonna mek no difference to what that poor gel's gonna go through.'

Vinnie wrung her hands tightly. She knew Betty was right. It would also give her time to prepare herself. The thought of breaking this dreadful news to her own daughter terrified her more than facing the police.

Vinnie gripped the side of the sofa she was sitting on so tightly her knuckles shone white. 'Maxine Upton! It was *her* that killed my husband?'

Inspector Banks nodded. 'In a fit of temper it looks very much like, Mrs Deakin. Though Miss Upton is denying it.'

'Well, she would,' erupted Betty. 'Best liar I've ever met in me life, she is. You ask the gels at work, Inspector. She caused more trouble with her lies than it took Hitler to start World War Two. So why did she do it, Inspector? Vinnie has a right to know. You do, don't you, Vinnie?'

Her mouth clamped tight. Part of her wanted to know what Tommy was doing in Maxine's flat and how she had come to do to him what she had, the other part didn't. She felt a desperate urge to flee, get away from this terrible situation. But what would that achieve? She had to face this sometime and she was very fortunate to have Betty here for support. Reluctantly, she nodded.

Inspector Burns looked at Vinnie for a moment, wondering whether he should divulge all his information at this moment in time, but then thought, what the hell. The poor woman had to know sometime, she would find it all out eventually. Whenever it came, there was no escaping the fact that hearing the truth would completely devastate her.

He took a pack of cigarettes out of his pocket and lit one, then fixed his eyes on Vinnie. 'Apparently Mr Deakin was having an affair with Miss Upton, it had been going on for several months. Miss Upton told us she got fed up of being a secret, his bit on the side as she put it. She gave Mr Deakin an ultimatum. Either he left you, Mrs Deakin, and went to live with her or they were finished. But she did threaten him that if he finished with her he'd better be prepared for you to find out what had been going on. She gave him until the morning of your daughter's wedding. Leave you or she'd spill the beans. She was surprised but delighted when he turned up late last Saturday night at her flat with his belongings, and since then Miss Upton says she was under the impression everything was great between them. Mr Deakin took the week off work claiming he was sick to give himself some breathing space before he told you, Mrs Deakin, what was really going on and asked you for a divorce.

'Yesterday evening Miss Upton swears she got home from work about four-thirty, earlier than usual because of a rumpus there which she said had involved yourself. She said Mr Deakin was out but came back at a quarter to seven. Before she could ask him where he'd been, he informed her he was going back to you. He said he knew about the trouble at work and what Maxine had said but that he had convinced you, Mrs Deakin, it was all a pack of lies and he hadn't been involved with Miss Upton at all. He had got one of his mates to say he had been staying with him during the time he was actually staying with Miss Upton, so there was no point in her trying to blackmail him into staying.

'Miss Upton says she then pleaded with him to stay and give her another chance but he just laughed at her. She said she stormed out then and went for a walk. She came back about forty minutes later, hoping Mr Deakin had thought better of his threat to leave her and was going to stay. She said the front door was ajar and she couldn't hear him moving about so thought the worst, that after all he'd carried out his threat. She got the shock of her life when she entered the kitchen to make herself a cup of coffee and found him on the floor with a knife in his chest. She said he was already dead.

'It was the downstairs neighbour who alerted us. He arrived home from work just after eight and heard Miss Upton screaming. He immediately dashed up and found her hysterical, covered in blood which she says she got through throwing herself on Mr Deakin in the shock of finding him.'

Vinnie listened to this tale dumbstruck, her face screwed up in incredulity. 'Inspector, she's lying!'

Vinnie spoke with utter conviction. 'Tommy wasn't living with her or even having an affair with her. Maxine had been spreading rumours around work that he was, but he *wasn't*,' she said, vehemently shaking her head. 'He'd been staying with George Collins after we'd had a silly misunderstanding, and that was only for the length of time it was because of Tommy hurting his back. After collecting his belongings from George's, Tommy must have decided to go round to see Maxine to warn her to stop spreading her malicious rumours. He told me why she was doing it. It was revenge, Inspector. Maxine had been coming on to Tommy at work. He wanted nothing to do with her and told her so. She threatened him, said he'd regret turning her down.' Her face was dark with horror. 'I don't suppose it crossed Tommy's mind for a minute that she would attack him.'

Banks took a deep breath. 'It was your husband who was lying, Mrs Deakin. For those days he wasn't at home here with you, he *was* living with Miss Upton. We have proof.'

'No!' she cried adamantly. 'He wasn't. It's all lies.'

The detective took a drag from his cigarette and tapped ash into an ashtray. 'It's the truth, Mrs Deakin. Your husband *had* been having an affair with Miss Upton for quite a while. Her neighbours have confirmed this. Your husband was seen regularly going into her flat at all sorts of times, and this week it was apparent he was actually living there with her.'

'No,' she insisted. 'It's not true. Tommy wouldn't do

that to me. We had a good marriage. It's lies, I tell you!'

He solemnly shook his head. 'Mr Collins confirmed that Mr Deakin never stayed with him at all, and also informed us that Mr Deakin went to see him on Friday evening around six-thirty and asked him to cover his story should he be asked by anyone, especially you. Mr Collins only agreed because Mr Deakin said he'd make things difficult at work for him if he didn't. He was Mr Collins' foreman, I understand, and could very well have done what he threatened.'

Frozen with shock at these revelations, Vinnie was staring blindly at him.

'You are sure of yer facts, Inspector?' Betty asked him. She was sitting beside her friend holding her hand protectively and she too was shaken to the core by what she was hearing.

He nodded. 'Positive, Mrs Trubshaw.'

She turned to face Vinnie. 'Oh, lovey, I'm so sorry.'

'But this can't be true,' she uttered, bewildered. 'I'd have known if Tommy was having an affair. But I had no reason, no reason whatsoever, to suspect anything of the sort.'

'With due respect, Mrs Deakin, you'd only have known if your husband was slipshod about it and it looks to us as if he was very adept at covering his tracks.'

'He could have easily,' said Betty, gently squeezing her hand. 'Tommy worked shifts, didn't he? Lots of time to himself when you weren't around. And he used

ter go down the pub a couple of nights a week by
himself. Could yer swear blind he was there every time
he said he was?'

Vinnie looked at her, astounded. 'Whose side are you
on?'

'Yours, Vinnie, yours. I'm as gobsmacked about all
this as you are but you ain't gonna help yer own cause if
you don't accept the truth. These coppers ain't gonna
sit here and spin yer a line. What would be the point in
their doing that, eh, ducky?'

Vinnie's whole body slumped defeatedly. 'I can't
believe it,' she murmured. 'Tommy . . . well, he was so
sincere when he assured me there was no substance to
the rumours Maxine was spreading. Swore to me he
wouldn't touch the malicious little slut with a bargepole. Those were his words, Inspector.' She gripped
Betty's hand so tight the woman winced in pain. 'I
can't believe he'd lie to me bare-faced like that. I never
doubted for a minute what he was saying to me.' She
stared at the policeman for several long moments then
her face became defiant. 'I know my Tommy would
not have done this of his own free will, Inspector,' she
said with conviction. 'You've only Maxine's word on
how things happened. She must have blackmailed him
into doing what he did, I don't know how. Probably
made something up. People do that all the time to get
what they want. Inspector, we were *happy*.' She saw the
look on his face, the pity and disbelief. Then she
realised that what he was telling her was the truth, the
evidence they had gathered too overwhelming for it to

be otherwise. She started to shake. Face crumpling in desolation, she looked at Betty and cried, 'Oh, Betty, what had Maxine to offer him that I hadn't? Yes, I admit she was young and pretty, but we all have to get old and lose our looks. Even Maxine would have eventually. I'm his wife. We've a home, children, roots together. What did I do so wrong that made Tommy have an affair with someone young enough to be his daughter? Someone with a reputation like she had made for herself?'

'Don't, Vinnie,' her friend pleaded. 'Stop punishing yerself. You can't blame yerself for what Tommy did. You're a good woman. You gave him yer all. If that wasn't good enough for him then that was his problem, ducky. I'm just so sorry you've had to find all this out.'

Tears streaming down her face she choked, 'So am I, Betty. So am I.' She wiped her face with her hand then and looked at the Inspector. 'Have you charged Maxine with my husband's murder?'

'We're about to, Mrs Deakin. We just needed to speak to you first to clarify a few things. Our enquiries have traced several passersby who claim they heard a man and a woman arguing loudly in the flat. None of them thought much of it as Miss Upton is renowned for being a trouble-maker. But it does seem to us from the timings the witnesses gave us that there were two separate arguments, not one, and the later one which we are sure resulted in Mr Deakin's death was certainly going on at the time Miss Upton claims she was out. We can find no witnesses at all to prove she left the flat and therefore deduce she is not telling the truth and never went out at all. They must have had an argument, then a second one after a lull. She's claiming she went out to try and shift the blame for what she did on to someone else. We were called to the scene pretty quickly and our doctor was able to ascertain that Mr Deakin died not long before we arrived. All things considered we have no reason to suspect that there is anyone else involved in this terrible tragedy.'

He stubbed out his cigarette. 'We firmly believe that, in a fit of temper, Miss Upton stabbed Mr Deakin when he made it plain he was coming back to you. There'll be an inquest in the next day or so, Mrs Deakin, but that's just a formality. The outcome will be that Mr Deakin was unlawfully killed by Miss Upton. His death certificate will be issued and you can arrange his funeral. Miss Upton will stand trial and you may be called on to give evidence.' He paused and eyed her for a moment. 'I'm sorry but as his wife we'll need you to come to the mortuary to make an official identification.'

Vinnie looked at him, horrified. 'What, now? But I couldn't . . . I can't, Inspector.'

'Tomorrow will be fine, Mrs Deakin,' he said kindly.

'Don't worry, Vinnie, I'll be with yer,' said Betty, putting her arms around Vinnie's shoulders and pulling her close.

He rose and buttoned up his dark brown Crombie

coat. 'We shouldn't need to question you again but should you need us for anything, Mrs Deakin, then please don't hesitate to contact us.'

He looked sadly at Vinnie then at Betty beside her. 'About eleven tomorrow?'

She gave a wan smile. 'We'll be there, Inspector.'

Chapter Eight

'Goodness, Mother, why are you sitting here in the dark?' Julie tutted disdainfully as she flicked on the light switch.

Possessing a figure tailor-made for the skimpy short fashions of the sixties, Julie was today dressed in a maxi-length black coat edged around the collar with fun fur; the blue and green kilt-style skirt she wore underneath finished mid-thigh and a ribbed light blue polo-necked jumper fitted her like a second skin as it was designed to do. Covering her legs were pale green panty hose and knee-length black boots. Her thick flaxen hair had been tinted ash blonde with Hint of A Tint colour shampoo and was cut in the latest Mary Quant geometric bob. Miner's foundation tinted her face with a pale shade, her large sooty eyes heavily edged in black liner and long false lashes. Big round green earrings dangled from her earlobes.

Totally oblivious to the fact that her mother was sitting rigid in an armchair, her face a frozen mask, Julie deposited her black shoulder bag and a carrier bag on the table and took out two parcels. She put the smaller on the table and held the larger lovingly in her hand. 'Dad will love this. It's a real leather wallet. I know the one he's got is falling to bits, and anyway that was only plastic. As soon as I saw this in the shop window, I said to Gary, "That's for my father and I don't care how much it costs." Oh, I hope you like what I got you. It's an imitation mother-of-pearl heart-shaped brooch with Mother across it in gold lettering.

'Anyway, this is just a quick visit to let you know we're back safe and bring you your presents. I've left Gary with the unpacking – hopefully he'll have put the washing in the twin tub and made a start on the tea when I get in.' Her pretty face screwed up with disappointment. 'I was just so looking forward to seeing Dad's face when I gave him his present. Where is he? Gone to the football with Eric?' She picked up her handbag. 'Will you give him my love and tell him me and Gary will be round as soon as we can to see him?'

She made to leave, then halted. 'Oh, by the way, that hotel we stopped in . . . I thought you said that woman at work highly recommended it? Well, I don't think it deserves three stars. I asked for clean towels at least twice before I gave up and collected them myself. Gary said I shouldn't have made such a fuss but I told him straight: my dad and mother paid good money for our week's stay and I expect to get exactly what the brochure told us we would.' She grimaced, disgruntled. 'The weather in Scarborough was foul and there was hardly anything to do. The whole place is filled with old people all moaning about anything they can think of, and everything shuts in winter. And they all stared at me as though I was from another planet or something because of the way I dress. It's like stepping back at least twenty years up there. The girls my age dressed so old-fashioned. And you should have heard the rumpus the old timers caused in the television room when I tuned in the set to watch *Ready Steady Go!* But I stuck it out. As a paying guest I'd as much right to watch what I wanted as they had.' Her eyes suddenly lit up as a thought struck her. 'Oh, did I tell you that Gary's mum is having the photographs mounted in a proper wedding book? Isn't that good of her? I can't wait to see them. I hope she brings them with her toni . . . er . . . er . . . the next time I see her.

'Oh, and that reminds me. I wouldn't recommend those caterers who did the food at our reception. That trout wasn't fresh. I had a bit of an upset tummy the next day and I'm sure the fish was to blame. And just what was in the vol-au-vents? It was supposed to be chicken supreme. Well, I know chicken supreme when I taste it and that was chicken in a tasteless paste.' She abruptly stopped her flow of words and looked hard at her mother. 'You've barely said a word, Mother. I thought you'd be excited to see me. And aren't you usually busy at this time getting on with Dad's tea? It's after five. Come on, Mother, chivvy yourself up. It wouldn't be fair for him to come home and find nothing on the table.'

'Oi, and who are you ter be speaking ter yer mam like that?'

Julie spun around and looked at the stranger framed in the doorway. 'And just exactly who are you?' she retorted.

'Yer mam's friend, that's who I am,' Betty said, bustling breathlessly in. She plonked two brown carriers filled with provisions on to the table and looked hard at Julie. 'I dunno, I pop out for a few minutes to get some shopping in before they shut and come back to find you throwing yer weight around.' She placed her hands on wide hips and stared at the girl crossly. 'Ain't yer noticed there's summat the matter with yer mam? No, I suppose not because you've got yer head so full of what's happening in yer own little world yer tek no notice of anyone else.'

Julie's jaw dropped in shock. 'How dare you speak to me like that?'

'I dare 'cos, as I said, I'm yer mam's friend. I've come ter take care of her for a while. Now I suggest yer sit down as she's summat ter tell yer. I'll go and mash a cuppa tea.'

Julie spun on her heel to face Vinnie. 'Mother, are you going to let this woman speak to me like this? MOTHER?'

Vinnie slowly raised her head and stared at her daughter. How she wished Julie wouldn't address her so coldly. The times she had asked her to say Mum, but she'd adamantly refused. To Vinnie the title Mother, especially the way Julie said it, always sounded so formal, with no warmth to it at all. She took a deep breath to summon up her courage, knowing she would need every ounce. 'Julie, please sit down, dear. I need to speak to you.'

'It'll have to wait,' she snapped tartly, still annoyed at the way Betty had addressed her. 'Surely you appreciate I've just returned from honeymoon and have things to do. Anyway, I'm not staying in this house while that woman is here. I'm surprised Dad allows you to have such a common person in his house. I thought Noreen was bad enough, but *she* is worse. And who is she anyway? And what does she mean, she's come to care for you for a while?'

'Oi, I might be old but I ain't deaf!' Betty snapped, poking her head around the kitchen door. 'Now, yer mam asked yer to sit down 'cos she's summat ter tell yer. So sit,' she ordered.

Julie stared at Betty, taken aback, and before she realised it was perched on the edge of the sofa. She fixed her eyes on Vinnie in agitation. 'It'll have to be quick. What is it you need to tell me so badly?' She ran her eyes over her mother. 'What's wrong? Are you ill?'

Vinnie took another breath to steel herself. 'There's no way to break this to you gently, Julie. I'm so sorry. It's . . . your father.'

'My father?' she said, frowning quizzically. 'What about him?'

Vinnie rose and hurried across to sit next to her daughter. Tenderly she took Julie's hands in hers. 'Oh, Julie dear, I'm so sorry but he's dead.'

Julie wrenched her hands free, her face contemptuous. With the flat of her hands she forcibly pushed her mother away from her. 'Don't be stupid, Mother, of course he's not!' she cried.

Totally unprepared for such a harsh physical response Vinnie fell sideways, hitting her head hard on the arm rest. Heedless of the blow she had received on the side of her temple, she hurriedly righted herself. 'I'm so sorry, Julie. I know this must be a terrible shock . . .'

The girl leaped up, wagging an accusing finger at her. 'My dad isn't dead! You're lying.'

Betty came in then. 'Julie, fer God's sake, listen ter yer mam!'

Julie turned on her. 'This is family business and nothing to do with you.'

'Julie, please don't speak to Betty like that. She's my friend and has been good enough to come and be with me to help me through this. You must listen. Your father is dead. I'm so, so sorry, Julie, really I am.'

Her daughter stared at her, stunned, mouth gaping. Slowly she sank back down on the sofa. 'No,' she uttered, her voice thick with emotion. 'No, not my dad.' She gulped hard and looked at Vinnie. 'When did this happen?'

'Thursday evening.'

'And I'm only finding out now?'

'Julie, please,' Vinnie begged. 'It was an awful shock to me. I couldn't take it in. It was yesterday afternoon before I found out all the details from the police. Oh, how could I have told you over the telephone? We just felt it best . . .'

'We?' the girl demanded.

'Me and Betty.'

'I see. Now you're making all the decisions in this family,' Julie snapped, pointing an accusing finger at Betty. 'How dare you decide to keep this from me? I had every right to know. I am his daughter.'

'Oh, Julie, don't be like this. I wasn't thinking straight and Betty was only trying to help. We were thinking of you.'

Lips clamped tight, Betty tried to hide her growing dislike of this young madam. Unpleasant as she was the poor girl had just received the most terrible shock. 'D'yer take one or two spoons of sugar in yer tea?' she asked kindly.

'None,' hissed Julie. Eyes filled with pain and confusion, she looked at her mother. 'How . . . how did my dad die? An accident, was it, at work?' She scowled darkly. 'Whoever is responsible will suffer for taking my father from me.'

Vinnie inwardly groaned. She had thought that the worst thing she had had to face was identifying her husband in the mortuary this morning. Any last flicker of hope she had harboured that the police had made a dreadful mistake had cruelly faded then as she had stared down at Tommy's lifeless form. If it hadn't been for Betty she would never have come through such a terrible ordeal. And now this. This was worse. How did you tell your daughter, a girl who had worshipped the ground her father walked on, that he hadn't been the person any of them had thought him to be? That he was a liar, and a cheat, and through his own double standards had met a tragic end.

Wringing her hands, distraught, she took a deep breath. 'It was no works accident, Julie. Your father was . . . well, he was stabbed in the chest.' Vinnie looked at her sympathetically and the love she felt for her daughter rose up to choke her. How she wished she could spare her this pain. 'He didn't suffer, Julie, I promise you,' she implored.

'Stabbed?' she cried, her face baffled. 'You mean . . . are you saying he was murdered?'

Her mother slowly nodded. 'Please, Julie, let me tell you the whole story and I would ask you not to interrupt. This is very painful for me. You're not going to like what I have to tell you, but please, please believe me, everything I'm about to say is the truth.'

She was stunned into silence by the tone of her mother's voice. Vinnie had hardly finished her story when Julie leaped up, screaming, 'Do you really think I'd believe that my father had left you and was living with a woman not much older than me, and it was *her* who killed him in a fit of temper? You've been watching too much television, Mother. I don't believe it! I won't, not a word of it.' She rushed across to the door, shouting, 'I'm going to the police. I'm going to find out what really happened.'

'Julie, please wait,' cried Vinnie.

But it was too late, she had gone.

Vinnie leaped up, intending to chase after her daughter, but before she could Betty had her arms around her and was pushing her back down onto the sofa. 'Leave her, lovey. Yer tried yer best.'

'No, Betty, I must go after her. She needs me.'

She made to rise again but Betty stopped her. 'Leave her, Vinnie. Trust me, the mood Julie's in she won't be satisfied until she has heard it from the police herself. Your chasing after her will only make matters worse. She'll come back when she's calmed down. Yer did yer best, ducky.'

Grief-stricken eyes looked at her. 'Oh, I hope so, Betty,' she uttered, bereft. She gave a mournful sob. 'I just wanted to put my arms around her. I desperately wanted to cuddle her. I should have known she'd push me away.' She sniffed hard, her eyes glazing over. 'When she was a child I would ask her to do something for me and she'd ignore it, but she'd only to hear her father's key in the lock and she'd jump up and fetch his slippers. I always had the feeling she resented the fact that he loved me. I felt she wanted him all for herself.' Tears glistened in her eyes. 'If it was me who'd died, Betty, I know she wouldn't be taking it anywhere near so badly.'

'Now that's a silly thing to think and you know it is,' Betty scolded. 'You've admitted yerself that Tommy doted on her and in return Julie got her own way with him, so outwardly it's gonna look like she loved him more than you. But I know deep down that's not the case.' She looked sadly at the desolate woman she was cradling in her arms and ran her hand up and down

Vinnie's back by way of offering a little comfort.

She pulled away from Betty's embrace and wiped her tear-streaked face with a sodden handkerchief. 'I wonder if Julie realises how hurtful she can be? She's brought Tommy a leather wallet back from her honeymoon, and I know she would have taken great pains to choose something nice for her father, but she also knows that his old plastic one is something I bought him for our first wedding anniversary. I had to scrape the money together as I had just given birth to Janie and wasn't at work. Julie knew this very well but just dismissed it as "that old plastic thing".' She sniffed back a sob. 'And I did everything I could to make her wedding day special but all I heard were complaints over things she wasn't happy with. I don't think she appreciates that Tommy and I used practically all our savings to give her a day to remember. I know she resents the fact we couldn't do what Gary's parents did for them. They gave them the deposit on the house, Betty, and helped to furnish it and paid for the extras we couldn't.'

'Julie should count herself lucky she's met a chappy whose parents can afford ter do that,' her friend said harshly. 'My kids had ter make do with a reception at home and whatever token me and their dad could afford to buy 'em at the time. I'm sorry ter say this about yer daughter, Vinnie, but she does come across as a selfish little madam. We'd never have dared speak to our parents or treat them the way some youngsters do these days. My mam would have knocked me into

Kingdom Come if I'd have so much as spoken out of turn to her. Kids these days have no respect for their elders.'

Vinnie sighed. 'Julie wasn't always like that, Betty. She was a lovely little girl. Both my girls were. Do anything I asked them with a smile on their little faces. We all used to be so close. They both loved a cuddle at night after they'd been bathed and were ready for bed. They'd fight over who was going to sit on my knee first and listen to a story. And they were both so helpful too. Loved to stand on a chair at the sink and help me wash up. We did so much together. Then everything changed so suddenly it was like a switch being flicked. Janie became ... well ... very aloof, hardly speaking to either of us unless she had no choice. I'd catch her looking at me like I was a stranger but she was worse with her dad. It was as if she hated him and I could never understand why.

'My mother, bless her, tried to coax Janie into open-ing up to her, but the more she tried the more she went into her shell. And meantime Julie formed this unbreakable bond with her father, became his little shadow. I tried so hard, Betty, to keep things normal between us but there was always this tension bubbling beneath the surface. I just prayed things would improve as the girls grew older. But they never did. Then Janie left home like she did, so unexpectedly with no word as to why or where she was going, and deep down I felt Julie was secretly glad. She was barely fourteen at the time but all she said when it happened was "Oh, good,

136

I'll have the bedroom to myself now," and I had to stop her from throwing out all Janie's bits and pieces she hadn't taken with her. I kept them, though, in a big box in the loft for when she comes back.' She suddenly looked mortified. 'Oh, Betty, Janie should be told about this. Tommy was her father, too, and she needs to know what has happened to him.'

'But how can yer tell her if yer don't know where she is? Come on, Vinnie, lovey, yer torturing yerself again. Don't you think yer going through enough without dredging up the past and blaming yerself for everything?' She held Vinnie at arm's length and smiled at her warmly. 'Listen, I've got us a nice bit of cod fer tea. I gorrit cheap 'cos the 'monger was just closing. What say I poach if fer yer and do cheesy mash?'

'Oh, Betty, thank you,' she said gratefully. 'But I couldn't eat a thing.'

'Yer will,' she scolded kindly. 'If I'm kind enough ter cook it for yer, then you'll bleddy eat every morsel. Yer need ter keep yer strength up, Vinnie, and I knows for a fact you've hardly eaten 'ote for nearly a week. While I'm in the kitchen I'll put the telly on for yer. *Take Your Pick*, or is it *Double Your Money* on around now? And after that usually a variety show. Oh, and later *Rawhide*. I've got quite a fancy for that Rowdy Yates. Anyway, watching a bit of telly will help tek yer mind off things for a while.'

Sometime later Vinnie laid down her knife and fork on the plate that was sitting on the tray on her lap. 'That was lovely, Betty, but I can't manage any more.'

Betty, who was glued to the small black and white television, willing a contestant on *Double Your Money* not to take the money but open the box, prised her eyes away long enough to study the amount of food Vinnie had left. 'Huh, you ain't eaten enough ter keep a cat alive but what you have is better than n'ote, I suppose.' She laid down her cutlery on her own empty plate. 'Delicious if I say it meself.' She noticed Vinnie about to rise. 'Sit where yer are,' she ordered, struggling up. 'Won't tek me a minute to get the pots done and I'll mash yer a fresh cuppa.'

Vinnie smiled at her gratefully. Truth be told, she hadn't the energy or will-power to move herself. She was so grateful for Betty's company, hadn't a clue how she would ever begin to repay her for her kindness. She would never have got through this awful time without her. A vision of Noreen suddenly rose in her mind and it shocked her to realise she hadn't given her neighbour a thought since the police had tried to question her the night before last. She wondered if Eric had telephoned her at her sister's in Blackpool and told her the news.

Tommy's death was going to shock her when she heard how he had died and what lay behind it. Knowing Noreen as she did it wouldn't have surprised Vinnie if Noreen had organised a lynch party to deal with Maxine. In view of all this, maybe it was a good thing she had suddenly been called away to look after her sister.

Vinnie then felt guilty to realise she was grateful it was Betty and not her neighbour who was here with her now. Both women weren't afraid to speak their mind but there was a soft, caring side to Betty that Noreen did not possess and Betty handled situations far less aggressively. Vinnie knew without doubt that Noreen would have been embarrassingly outspoken while the police were interviewing her and would also have charged after Julie and given her a mouthful for the way she had reacted to the news of her father's death, making matters even worse between them, if that were possible. She knew Betty had been right to advise her not to chase after Julie; let her return of her own free will when she was ready to deal with all this rationally.

Vinnie glanced warmly at the older woman as she bustled through carrying a cup of fresh tea. 'Now, 'ote else I can get yer?' she asked Vinnie.

'Nothing, Betty, thank you.'

Just then a knock sounded on the back door. Betty held up a warning hand. 'I'll get it.'

Vinnie heard hushed voices then Betty came back through. 'It's yer son-in-law, Gary. I'll mek meself scarce while yer chat to him.'

'There's no need, Betty, really. Hello, Gary,' she said to the distressed young man who entered.

Three years older than Julie, Gary was not a tall man and neither was he particularly handsome, but attractive enough in a pleasant kind of way. He was stocky in build and like his wife dressed up to the minute in the latest Mod fashions. He wore his carrot red hair in a Beatle-style mop, full fringe falling into startlingly pale blue eyes.

He was a good catch and Vinnie's daughter had known exactly what she was doing when she had pursued the young man vigorously after going to work for his father's very successful importing company where she was employed as office junior. Vinnie suspected Gary hadn't known what had hit him and before he knew it was being manoeuvred into proposing marriage. But, regardless, it was apparent that he loved her daughter and had been a willing accomplice in her snaring of him. Vinnie herself was delighted with the match, couldn't have asked for a better husband for her daughter, and surprisingly, considering his closeness to Julie, Tommy too had wholeheartedly embraced this relationship and treated Gary just like a son.

'Oh, Mrs Deakin,' he blurted out now. 'Julie . . . well, what she's saying . . . is it true that Mr Deakin has been . . . well . . .?' He couldn't bring himself to say the word 'murdered'.

Swallowing hard, she nodded.

'Oh, God, Mrs Deakin,' he groaned, face twisting in utter disbelief as he sank down on the sofa and raked one hand through his hair, making it stick up wildly. 'I was so hoping Julie had somehow got this all wrong. It's so dreadful.' He stared at her, stupefied. 'So what she said about Mr Deakin going off with that woman and her stabbing him to death is right?'

She nodded again. 'Yes, it seems so, Gary,' she said, her voice thick with emotion. 'The police are convinced of their facts, and what else can I do but believe them?'

Her heart sank in despair. This young man had come

to respect his wife's parents, making it clear he felt himself fortunate to have them as his in-laws and seemingly undeterred that the Deakins' financial status could in no way compare with that of his own family. He was just about to have all his illusions about Tommy and herself shattered and she dare not think what shame and humiliation his father-in-law's death would bring Gary or how he would deal with it – and view Vinnie herself in future. She wished she could spare him what she was about to tell him but as her daughter's husband he had a right to know all the sordid details.

When she had finished her terrible tale he looked at her, dumbstruck. 'Oh, God! But what made Mr Deakin do such a thing?' He gazed at Vinnie incredulously. 'I mean, you're such a lovely woman, Mrs Deakin. You always seemed so happy together, and yet he was carrying on behind your back like that. I can't believe it of him, really I can't. He is . . . was . . . such a nice man. He was so good to me.' He suddenly looked ashamed. 'Oh, Mrs Deakin, I'm so shocked about all this I haven't asked after you. How are you?' he asked with genuine sympathy.

She smiled gravely at him. 'To be honest I couldn't describe to anyone how I feel right now. But Julie?' she implored. 'How is she?'

His face flooded with worry. 'She's not good, Mrs Deakin. I'm really bothered about her. She was hysterical. I couldn't calm her down so I called the doctor in. He's given her enough of whatever it is to make her sleep for at least twelve hours and said if she was still the same when she woke up, I was to get him in again. I've seen her in some states, Mrs Deakin, you know how she can be when she throws one of her tantrums, but I've never seen her like this. She idolised her dad, didn't she? Wouldn't hear a bad word said against him.'

Vinnie looked at him anxiously. 'I'll come round in the morning and speak to her. Hopefully she'll have calmed down enough by then at least to listen to me.'

He gulped hard and eyed her worriedly. 'That's just it, Mrs Deakin. Julie . . . well, she said she doesn't want to see you at the moment.' What she had actually screamed was that she never wanted to clap eyes on her mother again, but he could not bring himself to tell that to Vinnie. He shifted uncomfortably in his seat. 'Er . . . I'm sorry to tell you this, Mrs Deakin, but Julie's got it into her head that it's all your fault her father is dead. She said it must have been you treating him badly that drove him into this woman's arms. I'm sure she didn't realise what she was saying. I'm sure she didn't mean it, Mrs Deakin,' he stressed urgently. 'She's just upset which is natural, isn't it? I really didn't want to tell you but I think it best you're warned what she might be like.'

Vinnie fought to hide her hurt. 'Thank you, Gary, you did right in telling me. But it's most important Julie and I talk. I have to explain to her, make her understand that I'm as much in the dark about all this as she is. I won't be able to settle until we've made our peace.' Her eyes filled with acute sadness. 'Then it's her choice whether she has anything to do with me or not. We haven't the best of relationships, Gary, she never has been as close to me as she was to her father, but having what we had is better than nothing to me. I do love her, I just wish she realised how much.' She looked at him gravely. 'I will understand, though, if you don't want to have anything to do with me in future.'

'What! Mrs Deakin, let me assure you this changes nothing as far as I am concerned. Of course I can't speak for my parents ... and at the end of the day Julie has a mind of her own. I could talk to her until the cows come home, she'll still do what she wants. But I'm your son-in-law and I will continue to be that. I'll do whatever I can for you.' He smiled at her affectionately. 'Besides, I happen to like you and I'll always be grateful for how well you've always treated me.'

Her eyes filled with tears. 'Oh, Gary, thank you.'

Vinnie suddenly realised she hadn't introduced Betty to him. Her friend had been sitting quietly on the settee all this time. 'Oh, this is Mrs Trubshaw. She's my friend from work and has been good enough to come and stop with me for a few days.'

He got up and went over to shake Betty's hand. 'Very pleased to meet you,' he said sincerely before sitting down again.

'Nice to meet you too,' she said, thinking to herself that Vinnie's son-in-law wasn't at all what she had expected, judging by his wife. He seemed such a pleasant, well-mannered young man it crossed her mind to wonder how he'd managed to land himself with someone with Julie's self-centred and bossy personality. Love was indeed blind, she thought. 'Would yer like a cuppa?' she asked him.

'Please don't go to any trouble on my account but I wouldn't mind one, actually.'

Betty bustled off into the kitchen.

Despite her problems Vinnie's motherly instincts rose to the fore. 'Have you eaten, Gary?' she asked him.

He shook his head. 'Not since we left Scarborough, and we didn't bother when we got home because of what we had planned for tonight.' He saw Vinnie's quizzical look. 'I suppose you've forgotten with all this going on but we'd invited you and Mr Deakin and my parents round tonight for a family get together so we could tell you all about our honeymoon. My mum said we'd have enough to do with our unpacking and everything and offered to bring the main course with her. Julie said you and Mr Deakin couldn't manage it as you'd something else arranged.'

Her daughter hadn't mentioned the occasion at all and Vinnie knew why. Despite the way she idolised her father she was nevertheless ashamed of the fact that her own parents worked in a factory and lived in a little rented house whereas Gary's ran their own successful business and lived in an imposing four-bedroomed property in Stoneygate. Vinnie didn't begrudge the Cooks their affluent status, they had worked hard for what they had. Regardless of the huge financial differences between them, both sets of parents had made great efforts to forge a good relationship for the sake of their children. Julie was wrong, Vinnie felt, to have the attitude she had, and she was hurt by the non-invitation. She was worried as well, though. How would Gary's parents react to this news of their daughter-in-law's father?

She smiled wanly at him. 'Yes, that's right, unfortunately we had other plans.'

'I've rung my mum and dad up and put them off,' he continued. 'I didn't tell them the reason over the telephone. I couldn't, could I, in case Julie had somehow got it all wrong. I'm on my way round there when I leave. I will have to tell them before they read of it in the papers.'

'Please tell them I'm sorry,' said Vinnie.

He looked at her blankly. 'Why should I give my mum and dad your apologies for something you haven't done? They'll be devastated by what's happened but they won't blame you, Mrs Deakin. How could they?'

'Well, they might,' she said softly. 'They might not want anything to do with me after this.'

'Of course they will,' he said with conviction. 'My mum and dad aren't like that.'

She flashed a wan smile at him. She wasn't so sure. Tragedies of this nature tended to bring out surprising traits in people. Unlike their son, they might feel that being associated with the widow of a murdered man was something they'd rather not do. She hoped Gary was right and that when they got over their shock they'd be sympathetic towards her. 'Your mother and father are lovely people, Gary, but we must let them decide how they want to behave towards me in the future and abide by their decision. Would you like something to eat?' she asked again.

He shook his head. 'I couldn't eat anything at the moment, but thanks for asking. I feel sick to my stomach, I really do.' He paused for a moment. 'This isn't the right time, I know, but I really would like to thank you for what you did towards our wedding. I never got a chance with all that was going on that day. The reception was grand, Mrs Deakin. I know how much effort you put into making it special. Both of you,' he added sadly. 'And the honeymoon. It was so good of you both to give us that. The hotel was smashing and we had a lovely time. The weather wasn't great but then, what else can you expect at this time of year?' His face suddenly filled with shame, knowing he was being thoughtless talking about such a happy event at this dreadful time. 'I apologise, Mrs Deakin, I just wanted to make sure you knew we both appreciated what you did.' He looked at her earnestly. 'Is there anything, anything at all, I can do for you? Anything – you've just got to name it?'

She smiled gratefully at him. 'Just look after Julie for me, Gary. She's going to need you very much now. I'm so sorry for you both – it's not exactly the best start to your marriage, is it, having to deal with something like this?'

'We'll get through it, Mrs Deakin. I love Julie and would do anything for her, you know that.'

'She's very lucky to have you,' Vinnie said emotionally. 'You must get back to her, Gary, just on the off chance the medication the doctor gave her doesn't work for as long as he said it would. I don't like the thought of her waking up and finding no one with her. I'll take my chances over coming tomorrow.' And just pray that my daughter is more receptive than she was today, she thought.

'Oh, Betty,' Vinnie sobbed the next afternoon, distraught. 'How could Julie have said all those things to me? She didn't mean it . . . she couldn't have! She didn't, did she, Betty?' she asked her friend beseechingly.

Every word, I suspect. The spiteful, selfish little cow! Betty thought to herself. She handed Vinnie a tea towel so she could dry her face and wipe away the river of snot that was running from her nose. 'A stiff drink is what you need. I'm gonna pop to the corner shop and get a bottle of summat. I know it's Sunday but I'm sure Mrs Braddock will let me have something, considering the circumstances.' She eased her stiff bones down on the settee beside Vinnie and placed a hand on her arm, giving it a gentle squeeze. 'I did try and warn yer not to go and see her just now, to leave it another day at least. And I did offer ter come with yer for support.'

'I know, Betty,' she blubbered. 'I did appreciate your offer, really I did. I just felt it best to talk to her alone. Oh, Betty, I can't believe she accused me of such things! She can't seriously believe I wasn't a good wife to her father.'

'There, there, lovey. The poor gel's distraught, ain't she? Just lost her dad in horrible circumstances. She's

147

gonna lash out at the closest person to her that's involved in this mess, and unfortunately, Vinnie ducky, that's you.'

'Yes, I suppose.' She sniffed hard and wiped her face again. 'Poor Gary didn't know what to do. I don't think he could quite believe what was coming out of Julie's mouth.' Her bottom lip trembled and she fought hard to stem the renewed flood of tears. 'Julie didn't mean it about never seeing me again, did she, Betty? I couldn't bear it if she did. Losing Janie and now Tommy is bad enough without losing her too.'

''Course she didn't mean it,' Betty soothed, while secretly knowing the girl had meant every rotten word she'd spat at her mother. 'Just give her time, lovey, and she'll be back. After all, you're her mam, ain't yer? She knows damn' well you ain't in no way to blame for what happened. But, as I said before, she's gorra blame someone and at the moment that's you.' Betty's eyes glinted with suppressed anger and she fell silent for a moment as her thoughts whirled. Finally she said, 'Will yer be all right for a moment while I pop to the shops? I really do think a drop of medicinal brandy would do yer good.'

'You don't need to go to all this trouble for me, Betty. You must be tired after everything you've done for me today.'

'It's no trouble, ducky, no trouble at all,' she said, picking up her bag and collecting her coat.

A while later, Betty stood before Gary on his front

doorstep. 'Now I'm sorry about this, lad, but I'm afraid I need to speak to that wife of yours. I won't keep yer long as the taxi meter is ticking over.' In her urgent need to talk some sense into Julie without Vinnie knowing it she had not thought twice about what the ride would cost. Without waiting for Gary's invitation she pushed past him and walked into the little semi-detached house. Julie was prostrate on the settee in the living-room, her face puffed and blotchy from crying. As Betty entered she sat up. When she saw who it was her face darkened contemptuously, but before she could berate the visitor for daring to enter her house unin-vited, Betty wagged a warning finger at her and when she spoke her voice was very firm.

'Now look here, Julie, love, no one is denying that you've suffered a terrible shock, but that don't give yer the right to treat yer mam the way you are. She was a good wife to your father and you know damn' well she was. Yer've no right accusing her of being in any way responsible for what happened to him.'

Julie struggled to sit upright. 'Oh, and you know how things were between my parents better than me, do you?' she hissed, her pretty face contorted with rage. She glared across at her husband hovering in the door-way. 'Are you going to stand there and let this . . . this . . . woman speak to me like this in my own home?'

Betty spun round to face him. 'I've come here to say me piece and I ain't leaving 'til I have,' she warned. She turned back to Julie. 'Now you listen, gel. I've worked alongside your mam for over twelve years and when yer work close with someone you gets to know 'em pretty well. She thought the world of your dad and was a good wife to him. Couldn't have been better. In all the time I've known her I've never heard her say a bad word against him. And nor has she about you, young lady, though by God you've given her more than enough reason ter want ter wring yer neck on occasion.

'You're a spoilt little brat, Julie, there's no other way to describe yer. It's about time you grew up and started treating those who care about yer with respect, else you'll wake up one morning and find you've no one. Your mam is going through the worst thing she's ever had to face, the worst anyone should have to deal with and, by God, your sister's disappearance was bad enough. The least you could do is show her a little compassion. What your dad done was wrong but whether he deserved it or not he's paid a hefty price. Stop blaming yer mother for something she had no hand in. Let me hear you've treated her like that again and, I warn yer, you'll have me ter deal with.'

She paused just long enough to draw breath. 'Now, if you decide never to see your mother after this that's your choice, but whether you like it or not you'll have to one more time: at yer dad's funeral. You'd better watch that tongue of yours then, gel. Your mother'll be upset enough on the day without *you* making it worse. Say or do anything untoward and I'll personally make you very sorry. Understood?'

Betty turned to go, nodding goodbye to Gary as she walked past him on her way out.

A while later she bustled into Vinnie's back room. 'Sorry I was such a time, lovey, there was quite a queue,' she fibbed to cover her long absence. 'Got a little bottle of brandy. A good dollop in hot water will do yer the power of good. Help yer sleep if n'ote else.'

Vinnie, who had been sitting staring blankly at the flickering television screen, lost in her own private thoughts, hadn't any idea how long her friend had been away. She managed a smile. 'Thanks, Betty.'

Just then a knock sounded on the door. 'Now who the bleddy hell can that be calling at this time of a Sunday night?'

Betty bustled off and several minutes later came back. 'It's started. I was wondering when it would.'

Vinnie looked at her, bemused. 'What has, Betty?'

'The nosey masses calling. Well, word's gone round, ain't it, about Tommy? 'Course they're all coming calling now to "express their condolences" – but really it's to get the juicy gossip.'

Vinnie looked mortified. So consumed was she in trying to deal with Tommy's betrayal of her, his grisly end, and the fact that despite everything she was feeling raw grief at his loss, she hadn't thought of other people. She was also trying to cope with her daughter's animosity and her own desire to put things right between them. There hadn't been time to worry about anything else. But, of course, the way Tommy died would be the sensation of the streets. It was natural for people to gossip, to want to know all the gory details. This was something that would bring excitement into their normally mundane lives.

'Oh, Betty,' she murmured, 'how on earth am I going to deal with all this?'

'Yer leave it ter me, that's what yer do, ducky. I'll sort out the genuine sympathisers from the nosey bleeders. Let 'em get what facts they want from the newspapers, and the reporters can get what they want from the police. I ain't gonna let no one near yer, Vinnie, and that's a promise.'

She gave a grateful sigh. 'I keep asking myself what I would do without you, Betty.'

'I'm beginning to wonder meself,' she replied jocularly. 'I shall have ter think about charging yer for me expert services,' she added, tongue in cheek, and leaned over to give Vinnie's arm an affectionate pat. 'Now I'll get yer that brandy.'

Chapter Nine

Vinnie lifted her eyes and gazed skywards. The clouds were thick and heavy and the chill in the air meant snow was a possibility. She gave a shiver as a wintry blast whipped through her black coat and matching jersey shift dress. She felt a hand gently squeeze her arm and heard a voice whisper, 'You all right, gel?'

She gave a smile as bleak as the weather. 'I'm just about managing, thank you, Betty.' She forced herself to look down into the abyss below containing the coffin of her husband. Just over ten days ago she and Tommy had been making final preparations for their daughter's wedding, both worrying that something had been forgotten, both fretting in case anything went wrong. Now here she was burying him, bad enough in itself without having to deal with everything else on top.

Since news of his death and the circumstances surrounding it had become common knowledge, making headlines in local and national newspapers, the callers at the house who had begun in small numbers quickly escalated into a crowd. Betty, true to her word, had somehow managed to sift out those genuinely wanting to offer their support to Vinnie, from those whose intentions were based on nosiness. Thankfully the sensation was over now, and as other events took precedence in people's lives callers were far fewer.

Since she had learned of Tommy's death, apart from that fateful visit to see Julie and try and talk sense to her, today was the first time Vinnie had ventured out of the house. That had been a feat in itself and she had only summoned the courage because of the importance of the occasion. In the future she knew she would have to endure whispers and nudges from insensitive types she happened upon who knew of her association with the man who'd been murdered by his mistress in a jealous rage. She only hoped she could cope with it. Betty had assured her that after Tommy's funeral, interest in her should start to wane and then disappear altogether. She prayed this was right. She needed to be allowed to grieve for the loss of the man she had thought Tommy to be, and come to terms with what he had done to her, then somehow find the will to forge on with her life.

She scanned the mourners gathered by the graveside listening to the vicar say the final prayers over the coffin. She was gratified to see the turn out was a good one. Despite Tommy's betrayal of her, he had been a well-liked man. Though she suspected many people, if not all, privately condemned his actions, some perhaps even feeling he deserved what he'd got, they had at least come to pay their last respects.

There were several of his mates from the pub, and those he'd met through attending football matches; his manager from work, Ralf Kimble, and others he'd known well at Brewin's; many neighbours and other acquaintances. All in all around forty people.

Vinnie's eyes settled for a moment on Eric whose genuine grief at the loss of his friend and neighbour was very apparent. Poor man, she thought. He would miss Tommy. The pair of them had over the years spent a great deal of time together tackling house repairs that the landlord seemed unwilling to do; both of them keen football supporters, they'd gone together to matches when Leicester City had played at home; had usually visited the local pub at least twice a week – and that was on top of the frequent get togethers the friendly neighbours had shared in one another's houses.

Eric looked lost and lonely without his wife by his side. Due to her sister's continued ill health it hadn't been possible for Noreen to attend the funeral but she'd been very upset, so Eric had told Vinnie, to hear what had happened when he managed to get through to her via the guest house's telephone. She had sent her deepest sympathies and was glad to hear Vinnie had a good friend in Betty to help her through such a difficult time. She was only sorry it couldn't be her and just hoped Vinnie understood? Of course she had. Noreen's sister must come first, she was after all family.

From under her lashes she stole a look at Julie, clinging to the arm of a solemn-faced Gary. She didn't know what to think of the fact that his parents hadn't turned up. In fact, she'd had no word of condolence from them. But at this moment it was worry for her daughter that overrode all else. Julie appeared utterly bereft, in severe danger of collapse, and Vinnie's heart went out to her. How she longed to rush over, sweep her protectively into her arms, offer support to her daughter throughout this terrible ordeal. She knew, though, Julie would not welcome that. Since she'd arrived at the house just before the funeral procession had departed, Vinnie's hope of a reconciliation, of even witnessing a flicker of remorse in Julie for what she had said and how she had acted towards her, was cruelly dashed. She hadn't even looked in her mother's direction, making it plain she still blamed her for the part she had played in her father's death.

Julie suddenly seemed to sense Vinnie's scrutiny of her and lifted her head. For a brief moment their eyes locked. Before Vinnie could make a move Julie's face froze and she looked away. So mortified was Vinnie that she clutched her chest and uttered, 'Oh, God.'

'What is it?' whispered a worried Betty.

'It's Julie,' she whispered back. 'She needs me, I know she does, but she's hurting too badly and is too stubborn to admit it.'

Betty patted her hand. She felt it best not to comment.

It seemed an age had passed before the congregation finally said 'Amen' as the last prayer ended. As directed by the vicar Vinnie picked up a handful of earth and, before she scattered it across the coffin, forced herself to look once more into the grave. 'Goodbye, Tommy,' she said, her voice choked.

Betty's grip on her arm tightened. 'Come on, me duck, let's get you back to the car and home.'

'People do know they're invited back to the house if they wish?' she asked her friend.

'They do, so stop worrying.' Hopefully not many, if any, will bother, Betty prayed to herself.

This wouldn't be the normal kind of wake where people mingled discussing the good qualities of the deceased. Tommy had after all been murdered after cheating on his wife. There had been nothing virtuous about his actions when alive or blessed about his death. Mourners would find it impossible not to discuss the subject. It was only human nature. Betty worried that after all Vinnie had gone through, and what she faced in the future, hearing insensitive mourners mulling over the whys and wherefores of Tommy's death was the last thing she needed. Instead she should put all this behind her and forge ahead with a new life for herself.

Betty also worried that the absence of Vinnie's daughter and husband at the funeral wake was bound to be noticed. She knew via Gary, who had taken his chance to have a quick word with her while his distraught wife was being consoled by another mourner, that Julie was still unfairly blaming her mother for the part she had played in Tommy's death, and despite Gary's doing his best to persuade her, they would not be coming back to the house. He'd also told Betty that the fact his parents were not present was not through their choice but after a resolute request from Julie who'd said she wanted to spare them the embarrassment of attending. According to Gary his parents had wanted to offer their support, but after long deliberation had decided it would be wisest to honour their daughter-in-law's wishes. Betty thought it best not to tell Vinnie this information, knowing that her daughter's involvement in Mr and Mrs Cook's non-appearance would upset her more than the fact they themselves had decided not to come.

Before they could make their escape several people came up to Vinnie and expressed their condolences for which she politely thanked them. The mourners had started to disperse before Betty was finally leading Vinnie across the grass towards the waiting funeral car.

She spotted the shabbily dressed woman before Betty. She was partially hidden by a large gravestone, weeping uncontrollably into a worn handkerchief. Vinnie's heart went out to her in sympathy.

'That poor woman,' she remarked to Betty. 'I feel so sorry for her. She's obviously lost someone close judging by how upset she looks.'

As they walked past her Betty took a glance at the woman, whom she herself hadn't noticed until Vinnie had remarked on her. It amazed Betty that despite her own terrible heartache Vinnie could still summon up compassion for others. She was right, the woman did look very upset.

'Do you think we should ask her if we can do

anything for her, Betty? It doesn't look as though she's got anyone with her.'

Betty looked at her in surprise. 'Don't yer think you've enough to contend with at the moment? Anyway, the driver's waiting ter take us back.'

'Yes, I suppose so.' She glanced back at the woman and her concern deepened. 'A bit of charity goes a long way, Betty. You should know that, you've given me enough over the last few days. Surely the driver won't mind waiting a couple of minutes longer, just while we check on her?'

Her friend sighed. 'Oh, come on then.'

They had just made their way up to her when, seemingly from nowhere, a young man of about nineteen, wearing dirty workman's clothes, dashed breathlessly up to the woman. 'There yer are, Mam,' he cried in a relieved voice, protectively taking hold of her arm. 'I thought we'd thrashed this out last night but I might have known you'd still come.'

The woman shuddered violently and gave a loud sniff as she wiped her nose on a sodden piece of cotton. 'I needed to, son. Can't yer understand? It was just something I had to do,' she uttered, her voice thick with emotion.

He shook his head. 'No, I can't understand, Mam. Not at all I can't.' His face softened and he looked at her lovingly. 'But it's done now, ain't it?' The young man suddenly noticed Vinnie and Betty looking on and frowned at them enquiringly. 'Er . . . sorry, I don't know yer, do I?'

159

'No, yer don't,' replied Betty. 'We just happened to be passing and noticed how upset yer mam was. We'd stopped to ask if she needed any help.'

He smiled gratefully at them both. 'That were good of yer, ta very much. But Mam's fine now I'm here.'

'Get her home and a strong cuppa down her. Plenty of sugar,' Betty recommended. 'That'll soon sort her out.'

'I will, and thanks again.'

'And that's the first thing I'm gonna get you when we're back,' said Betty, eyeing Vinnie tenderly. 'Come on, let's hurry. I'm bleddy freezing.'

Betty was relieved to note her prayers had been answered and only a handful of people returned to the house, most of the mourners having to get back to their respective workplaces. Those who did return did not stay very long and not once did she hear any mention of how Tommy had died or the way he had mistreated his wife.

As she lay in bed that night a great sadness enveloped Betty. Now that Tommy's funeral was over the time for her to return to her own home was drawing near. How she would miss Vinnie's company, having her to care for. But her friend needed to get back to normality as soon as possible, and after all so did Betty herself. Regardless, wherever she was, she would still be on hand should Vinnie need her. And they were great friends now, far closer than they had ever been at work.

In a strange way some good had come out of Tommy's tragedy. It had helped to forge this friendship and as far as Betty was concerned the bond between them would last a lifetime. The best part of it was that she knew Vinnie felt the same.

Chapter Ten

'I've been dreading you raising this subject,' said Vinnie over the breakfast table two days later. 'I've got so used to you being here. You've been so good to me, Betty.'

'Despite the circumstances, I've enjoyed being here as well. It's done me good having someone ter care for again. But we both have to get back to normality, Vinnie, and the sooner we do that the better, eh? Let's be honest, I've done all I can. I've seen yer through the worst of it. Yer've still yer grieving ter do but, well, that's gonna tek time.'

She gave a wan smile. 'You're right, I know you are. I don't know how I'm going to manage without you, though.'

'You will, I've no doubt. And after all, I ain't that far away.' Betty gave a despondent sigh. 'And we both have ter think about work too 'cos I don't know about you but I can't live on fresh air.' That's if I still have a job, she inwardly worried. She still had not heard one word about the company's decision after her attack on Maxine. She had a little money put by in her Post Office

162

savings account but it wouldn't last long. She was also concerned that although jobs were plentiful and hosiery companies desperate for people with skills like hers, they might be reluctant to take her on at her age of sixty-one with only four years to retirement.

Vinnie was eyeing her, looking shocked. 'Work! Oh, Good Lord, with all that I've had on my mind I'd forgotten about that. I haven't even sent cards thanking the girls for their flowers and best wishes. How awful of me!' Then a terrible thought struck her. 'Oh, Betty,' she exclaimed, 'after what you and I did, do you think we even have jobs with Brewin's?'

'What do you mean, what *you* and I did? I know what *I* did was most certainly a sackable offence, Vinnie, but *you* didn't do anything.'

'I did. I walked out, remember, without asking permission or telling Doddsie what I was doing. And I haven't been back since because of . . . well . . . I know the firm's aware of what's happened as the police informed them and they needed to question Tommy's workmates, but I haven't received a letter from them telling me how long I can stay off. Well, not to my knowledge. No official letter from Brewin's has arrived for me, has it, Betty?'

She gave a shrug. 'Not that I am aware of. I'd have given it yer if it had.'

'Sorry, yes, I know you would. Usually the company sends a representative from the personnel department in cases of bereavement, offering advice and such like, so I wonder why no one has called on me?' She scraped her hands through her hair and sighed despondently. 'To be honest, Betty, I have to work but right at this minute I couldn't care less whether I've got a job or not, if that makes sense. It's you I'm concerned about. You need your job. They can't sack you, surely they can't, now they know what Maxine is capable of? If we explain that she provoked you by what she said to me, they'll understand, won't they?'

'You'd think they would but I doubt it, ducky. Doddsie's never thought much of me. I speak me mind too much for her liking. She'll use this chance ter get rid of me, I've no doubt of that.'

'But I won't stand by and do nothing, Betty. I'll go and see Mr Hamlin myself and plead your case. I'll demand they don't sack you.'

'I appreciate that, gel, but if they've already decided ter sack me n'ote you say will change their minds. When all's said and done what I did was out of order, provoked or not. You know that as well as I do. It's in the company rules, in't it? Thou shall not thump another workmate no matter what. And . . .'

Her voice trailed off and Vinnie looked at her enquiringly. 'And what, Betty?'

She gave a heavy sigh. 'Well . . . I never exactly asked if I could tek leave from work to help you through all this.'

'What! Oh, Betty . . .'

'Eh, no good meking a fuss, gel. You needed me, and whether they agreed or not I was staying put here 'til I felt you were in a fit enough state ter start managing by yerself. Anyway, I shall soon find out me fate when I get home and see what mail I've got, won't I? Getting het up about summat we ain't even aware of yet won't do us any good. Is there any more tea in that pot?'

Vinnie refreshed her cup. 'I've decided what to do with Tommy's things that the police returned.'

'Oh, yeah, and what's that?'

'I'm going to send them all to the men's hostel. I'm sure they could make good use of everything.'

Betty smiled at her. 'I'm proud of you, gel. That decision took a lot of teking. I know 'cos I remember how hard it was for me to part with Alfred's stuff.' As she took a sip of her tea she eyed Vinnie searchingly. 'Before I start getting me bits and pieces together ready for the off, there's summat I want you ter promise me, Vinnie.'

'Oh? What's that?'

'That you'll start sleeping in your own bed. Kipping on the settee is no good. It plays havoc with yer back. I know you ain't slept decent since all this happened. At least back in yer own bed you'll be more comfortable, whether yer sleep or not. You can't avoid it for ever, Vinnie, so yer might as well get on with it now.'

She gasped, horrified at the very thought. 'Oh, I couldn't move back in there. I just can't bring myself to do it. There'll be that great empty space where he used to sleep. I know I'll still feel him beside me.' Sadness filled her face. 'I know I should hate Tommy for what he did to me, Betty. I've tried, believe me I have, but I just can't seem to.' She glanced around the room. 'It's strange, it's not so bad down here, but somehow the bedroom seems to be where I sense him most. I only have to open the door and I burst into tears.'

'Yes, I had noticed,' Betty said quietly. 'And it's understandable. To you yer marriage was good, yer'd no reason to believe otherwise, and bed is where you and Tommy were closest.' She took a deep breath. 'Well, I hope yer'll forgive me, ducky, but I've been giving this bedroom business some thought and I've come up with a couple of ideas that might help.

'What if we moved everything around, made it a new room so to speak? We could put the bed on the opposite side and move the wardrobes and dressing table around. Even get rid of the wardrobe Tommy used if that would mek a difference, though it's a shame ter waste a good bit of furniture. We could redecorate, if yer like. I'm that not great with a paintbrush but I'll have a go. Or better still change your girls' . . . sorry, I mean Julie's old room, the one I've been using, over with yours. That would be a complete change, wouldn't it? It's not quite as big as your room but it's still a decent size. Fit all your furniture in easily.'

Vinnie looked at her astounded, then tears of gratitude glistened in her eyes. 'Oh, Betty, you're a wonder, you are. Yes, I'll swap bedrooms. I never thought of that idea at all. Anything is worth a try. You're right, I don't sleep well on the sofa. My back aches terribly in the morning.'

'That's the spirit, gel,' said her friend, beaming in

delight. 'Well, hurry up and finish yer breakfast and we'll get cracking.'

'Just shove it, Vinnie. It'll go in, trust me. More ter the left. That's it. One good push should do it. Oh, bleddy hell, I'm stuck!'

Vinnie rushed around to look at her and gawped in shock. Betty was jammed in tightly, her back against the outside wall, her front pressed against the side of the wardrobe. Vinnie had been doubtful the double wardrobe would fit into the recess in the first place but Betty had insisted it would. After inching the heavy object out of the other bedroom, on down the passageway and across to this room they had then painstakingly heaved it little by little into position. Betty had been right. It did fit in the recess very snugly. But not Betty as well.

'How on earth did you come to land up like that?' Vinnie asked, scratching her head, bemused.

'I dunno,' she snapped back. 'It just happened.'

Despite the severity of the situation, Vinnie couldn't help but giggle.

'Eh, although it does me heart good ter see yer laughing, gel, this ain't funny,' Betty scolded. 'Now get me out, will yer? I can't breathe.'

'Oh, God,' groaned Vinnie. 'I don't think I can move the wardrobe by myself.'

'Well, yer'll have ter. I don't plan on staying here much longer. Oh, God, that's just what we need now, someone at the door,' she tutted, having heard a knock.

'They'll have to come back,' Vinnie replied, her thoughts fully occupied by the predicament Betty was in. 'Now, I need to try and get this wardrobe out a bit to allow you to squeeze by, but how on earth I'm going to manage it as it took two of us to get it in . . .'

The front door knocker resounded again. 'Fer God's sake, go and see who it is. It might be urgent. And hurry, Vinnie.'

She couldn't hide her shock to find Keith Hamlin standing on her doorstep. 'Oh!' she exclaimed.

'Hurry up, Vinnie. Me leg's going dead,' Betty's voice boomed out.

'Problems?' Keith asked her.

'Well, er . . . yes, actually. Betty . . . Mrs Trubshaw . . . is wedged between the wardrobe and the wall.'

Not a muscle on his handsome face flickered when he said, 'Well, it looks like I came at the right time then, doesn't it?'

'Pardon?'

'You could obviously do with a strong pair of arms?'

'Oh, yes, very much so, thank you. I'll show you the way.'

A while later Keith Hamlin was thanking Vinnie for the cup of tea she'd given him before she turned back into the kitchen to collect her own and Betty's. He turned his attention to Betty, sitting in the armchair opposite him. 'No worse for your ordeal, I hope, Mrs Trubshaw?'

'Apart from me chest being shoved through me back,

no, I'm fine,' she replied matter-of-factly. A twinkle of amusement sparkled in her eyes. 'I must admit, I never expected the likes of yerself to be me knight in shining armour, Mr Hamlin. Oh, and . . . er . . . thanks fer helping us shift the rest of the furniture.'

'It was the least I could do,' he responded, smiling at her warmly.

'Yer should smile more often, Mr Hamlin,' she said before she could control her tongue. 'Yer ain't bad-looking when yer do.' She ignored the surprised expression on his face and continued, 'Look, if yer've come here ter sack me then let me save yer the bother. I resign.'

Before he could respond Vinnie re-entered with a cup of tea for Betty and a plate of Rich Tea biscuits which she placed on the coffee table. 'Please help yourself, Mr Hamlin,' she said before perching herself on the settee. She stole a look at her boss. She knew why he'd come: to tell her her services were no longer required. What did surprise her was that he had come in person to do the deed.

'I hope it's strong enough for you?'

'Sorry, Mrs Deakin?'

'The tea.'

'Yes, it's fine thank you. Look, Mrs Deakin,' he began, his voice somewhat brusque. 'I . . . we at the factory are very sorry about your troubles. We were all shocked to hear what had happened. I know collections were made in all departments and flowers were sent you but it was felt that what was collected around our own department was far too much just to spend on a wreath so I have been asked to give you this to do with as you feel fit.'

She took the envelope he held out towards her, opened it and let her mouth drop open. 'But there must be . . .'

'Just over twenty pounds,' he finished for her.

'Oh, goodness me!' Vinnie exclaimed.

'People gave generously, Mrs Deakin, and of their own free will. I'm sure you'll find good use for it.'

She was struck speechless by her colleagues' generosity when she knew many needed every penny of their earnings in order to survive. Her immediate thought was that if she was indeed out of a job, this money would be a Godsend.

'Mrs Deakin, you're probably wondering why an official representative from the company's personnel department hasn't called on you?' Mr Hamlin said.

'Well, yes, it had crossed my mind.'

'I'm afraid their non-appearance was down to me. As your immediate manager I took it upon myself to put a stop to the visit.'

Vinnie frowned at him questioningly. 'You did?'

'Yes. I just felt . . . well . . . you'd enough to deal with without added pressure about work. Personnel people are very good at times like these but even they can be insensitive sometimes. I didn't feel them asking if they could be of help in any way, then in another breath informing you that company rules state bereaved employees are allowed only four days off . . .' He shifted position uncomfortably, and all the time he was talking his eyes were looking everywhere but directly at her. 'Well . . . what I'm trying to say is that your situation is not a normal bereavement and four days' compassionate leave seemed inadequate under the circumstances. Thankfully, in view of your long service, the powers that be agreed with me.'

She looked at him in surprise. 'Thank you, Mr Hamlin. I very much appreciate what you did.' Her face was wreathed in shame. 'I must admit, I never gave work a thought. Well, until this morning that is.'

'And that's understandable. But I also appreciate you have to earn your living. So . . . now that I know Mr Deakin's funeral is over I just wanted to come round and tell you in person that we'll be glad to see you back when you're ready. Hopefully Monday?' he added, for the first time meeting her eyes.

ᐟ She was stunned by his request. 'Oh. Er . . . yes, Monday will be fine.'

He turned his attention to Betty. 'You too, Mrs Trubshaw.'

'What! Yer ain't sacking me then?'

'No. You have Miss Dolman to thank for being your champion.'

'What, our Ruby?'

'Yes. She made it abundantly clear how severely provoked you were by Miss Upton over what she apparently said to Mrs Deakin, and in light of what transpired afterwards it was felt that sacking you would not be in Brewin's best interest. You are both respected employees and we wouldn't like to lose either of you unnecessarily.'

Betty's lips pursed in shock. 'Well, I *am* surprised, I must say. Not that I ain't pleased. I'll be back Monday, Mr Hamlin. Eight o'clock sharp.'

'I'm glad that's settled.' He drained his cup and placed it on the table. 'Mrs Deakin, there's something else I would like you to consider. I'm sure you won't mind my talking in front of Mrs Trubshaw?'

She shook her head. 'Not at all. What do you want me to consider?'

'I'm in need of a new forelady and wondered if you would give some thought to taking the position?'

Before Vinnie could respond Betty asked, 'But what about Doddsie . . . I mean, Mrs Dodds?'

He took a breath. 'Mrs Dodds and Brewin's have parted company, Mrs Trubshaw.'

'And about bleddy time!' she erupted, clapping her hands in delight. 'She's gotta be the worst bloody forelady I've ever worked for.'

'Yes, well, you aren't alone in that opinion. So will you give my proposal some consideration, Mrs Deakin?'

'She don't need to. She'll tek it.'

'Betty!'

'But yer will, Vinnie, won't yer?' she pleaded. 'You'd mek a grand forelady. The gels all like yer and yer know the job inside out.'

Keith Hamlin nodded in agreement. 'My thoughts exactly. My only worry is that I am aware you need time to recover from your bereavement. The problem is I need a replacement now and wouldn't like you to miss this opportunity. Please forgive me if you think I'm pushing you but I do need a decision by Monday.' He stood up. 'I'll leave you ladies to finish your removals. Thanks for the tea.'

'Well,' said Betty after he'd gone, 'you could have knocked me down with a feather. I think I've grossly misjudged that man. I honestly thought I'd got the sack. A big bag of chips is coming Ruby's way and she bloody deserves every one of 'em. And warrabout you, eh? I thought you told me you felt Happy Hamlin didn't like yer? Well, he can't not like you all that much to offer you a job where you'd be working so closely with him, can he? Forelady, eh? Who'd 'a' thought it? You're gonna mek a whole lot better forelady than Doddsie ever did. Oh, I'm so glad she's gone and you're teking her place. I can't wait to see all the other gels' faces when they find out.'

'Betty, stop it. I've not had time to think about this. I'm not at all sure about it. I . . . I don't think I'm up to the job.'

Betty stared at her incredulously. 'Don't be daft, 'course yer are. Mr Hamlin wouldn't have asked yer if he didn't think you was. You've gorra give it a try. Anyway if n'ote else, think about the pay rise.'

'No, Betty, you don't understand, I can hardly cope with day-to-day things at the moment. I haven't been able to summon up the courage to go out of the house since all this happened except for the funeral, and only got to that with you supporting me. You're going home today and I'll be on my own then, won't I? I've never been on my own before, Betty. I've got to go back to work on Monday and don't know how I'm going to do it. Having all those people staring at me, whispering behind my back. Inside I'm quaking at the thought. In fact my whole future just seems like . . . well, blackness. I don't know whether I can face this. Oh, Betty, I'm so frightened.' Tears filled her eyes and, putting her hands to her face, she wept.

Betty went over to her and put a hand on her arm. 'Eh, come on, gel. 'Course yer frightened. Bloody hell, yer've just had yer whole world come crashing down around yer, and if yer weren't scared ter death about what the future held I'd think there was summat wrong with yer. But yer gotta stare that fright in the face and meet it head on, that's the only way to deal with it. And give yerself more credit, Vinnie. You're very well liked. Yer've only got to look at all the cards yer received to know that. And all the money collected. Bloody hell, Vinnie, if that don't confirm matters for yer, n'ote will. And look at how yer son-in-law was with yer. He thinks the world of yer, gel. Yer daughter . . . well, she'll come to her senses sooner or later, yer just gotta give her time. And as for those that yer catch staring at yer or whispering behind yer back, well, they're just plain ignorant in my opinion and you've just gotta ignore them. Before yer know it they'll be whispering and giggling about someone else.

'Now yer can shut yerself away and wallow in yer

own self-pity if that's what yer want to do but, believe me, ducky, that ain't gonna get yer nowhere. What's happened to yer has been dreadful, Vinnie, no one's denying that, and I know life seems pointless to yer just now. But it does get better, believe me, and one day you'll look back on this time and marvel at how you got through it. You can do this, Vinnie, or yer ain't the woman I know yer are.'

'Oh, Betty, I wish I could believe that,' she whispered miserably. 'I just feel so worthless.'

'That you bleddy ain't!' her friend snapped crossly. 'If yer were that worthless, Happy Hamlin wouldn't have offered yer the job in the first place. And more ter the point, I wouldn't have just spent the last few days of me precious time helping yer through all this.'

Vinnie sniffed hard. 'No, you wouldn't. But I can't understand why Mr Hamlin wants me for this job when it's obvious he doesn't like me.'

Betty's mouth clamped tight. She had to admit there did appear to be some substance behind Vinnie's assumption. She had noticed herself how ill at ease Keith Hamlin had seemed all the time he was here. 'He was the same with me as he was with you, Vinnie. I think he's just shy around women, which is daft considering he works with so many. But he can't really not like yer or he wouldn't have suggested it. Eh, and have yer thought that having summat new to occupy yer might help yer get through all this?' A spark of mischief glinted in her eyes. 'I mean, we gels are going to give yer hell, ain't we?'

Vinnie gave a small laugh. 'Oh, Betty, I bless the day I met you. You're right, I know you are. I've got to start getting on with things, making some sort of life for myself.' She wiped her eyes and blew her nose. 'This job Mr Hamlin's offered me is a wonderful opportunity to give me something else to concentrate on. I'm still not sure if I'm up to the challenge of it yet but I have until Monday to decide, don't I?' She gave her friend a sudden smile. 'At least we're both still in work and that's the main thing. Because even if I don't take the new job, I've still got my old one, haven't I?'

'Yeah, and so have I, thank God.' Betty eyed Vinnie tenderly. 'Oh, it's good to see you smile, gel.' Then she looked at her seriously. 'I hate to bring this up but you'll have to pull yer horns in, won't yer, now you've only yer own wage coming in?'

Vinnie gave a heavy sigh. 'That's just one of the things that has kept me awake at nights, Betty. Not knowing what was facing me, I didn't spare a penny on Julie's wedding so our savings such as they were took a hefty battering. Tommy's insurance covered his funeral with not much left over. So things aren't that great. I'm not exactly a spendthrift but some of the things I've taken for granted as our money problems eased these past few years, I shall have to learn to do without. Well, I did without before and it didn't do me any harm. Marge tastes just as good as butter if the alternative is dry bread. Anyway, you manage, don't you?'

'After a fashion. It ain't easy but I ain't been evicted yet.'

'Well, I don't plan to be evicted either. As long as I pay my bills and manage to eat I shall think myself lucky. Things could be worse, couldn't they?'

'A lot bleddy worse, Vinnie. Having the means to keep a roof over your head if not much else has gotta beat pushing yer belongings around the streets in a pram, ain't it?'

Vinnie laughed. 'Oh, Betty, you are a tonic.'

She smiled back warmly. 'I'm just that glad ter see yer beginning to think more clearly. Anyway, a' yer fit?'

Vinnie eyed her, non-plussed. 'For what?'

'Finishing off upstairs?'

She took a deep breath. 'Yes, come on. That room is going to look lovely when we've finished.'

'Then me bruised chest was worth it,' said Betty matter-of-factly.

Later that night Vinnie stared at the bed and a feeling of trepidation filled her. Despite all their efforts to make her new bedroom inviting and Betty's wise words, this bed was still the one she had shared all those years with Tommy. Vinnie knew that as soon as she got into it and switched off the light she would feel his presence strongly, as though he was haunting her; regardless of the fresh linen she'd still be able to smell him. If only Betty had stayed just one more night. Knowing she was close by, within calling distance should Vinnie need her, would maybe have helped her to conquer her fears. But Betty was back in her own home, where she belonged, getting back to normal. Vinnie worried her own life would never be normal again.

Pulling the covers off the bed, she made her way down the stairs and arranged them over the sofa. She was just about to switch off the lights when a knock sounded on the back door. Wondering who would be calling at such a late hour she tentatively went to open it and was shocked to find her caller was Betty.

Without a word she pushed past Vinnie. Inside the kitchen she turned to face her. 'Yer couldn't do it, could yer?' she accused.

Vinnie knew what she meant. 'No.'

'I knew it! I knew that as soon as it came to it you'd bottle out. Well, yer going to do it and I'm gonna see that yer do. Come on.'

'Where are you going, Betty?'

'Ter bed. And I don't know about you but I'm knackered. You can sleep in your new room and I'll sleep in yer old. We'll bury your ghosts together. It's just fer tonight, mind, to give yer moral support.' Placing a reassuring hand on Vinnie's arm, she looked at her meaningfully. 'That bed is yours now, lovey, not yours and Tommy's. This house is yours now, not yours and Tommy's. It's not Tommy and Vinnie anymore, it's just Vinnie. You're gonna have to get used to that. But, Vinnie, I know without a doubt you're a woman with a bright future to look forward to. You've already taken yer first steps by dealing with Tommy's belongings and deciding to get back to work. Tek a great leap this time, lovey, by snuggling down in that bed of yours and getting a good night's rest. You'll feel so proud of yerself in the morning, you mark my words.'

Vinnie looked at her for several long moments, then she threw her arms around her and hugged her tightly. 'Oh, Betty, thank you.'

Chapter Eleven

Vinnie hesitated outside the door to Keith Hamlin's office. Through the glass she could see he was immersed in a pile of paperwork and was undecided whether to disturb him or not. She only wanted to inform him of today's progress, it wasn't an urgent matter.

He suddenly sensed her presence, lifted his head and seemed to waver momentarily before beckoning her in.

'What can I do for you, Mrs Deakin?' he asked briskly as she entered.

You could look more pleased to see me, she thought. If only Keith Hamlin knew how much she dreaded coming into his inner sanctum, avoided it as much as she could. Despite the fact he was always cordial to her, she couldn't shake off the feeling he didn't quite like her, was uncomfortable in her company, and this was having an effect on her. He never looked her in the eye longer than was absolutely necessary and she wondered why. It wasn't as though she had been anything other than polite and respectful to him. She handed him a pile of dockets. 'That's the completed work for today, Mr Hamlin.'

He flicked through them. 'That's a fair amount the girls have done. Since you started as forelady .... this is your fourth week, isn't it? . . . the workload has been steadily climbing but this is a good deal above the daily quota when Mrs Dodds was in charge.' He flashed a brief look at her, then settled his gaze on the paperwork in front of him. 'How did you manage that, Mrs Deakin?'

He flashed another brief look at her and, noticing she was looking hesitant, said, 'You can speak freely. I won't bite you, I promise. And . . . er . . . please sit down,' he said, indicating the chair to the front of his desk. 'I do owe you an apology,' he said matter-of-factly, straightening up a sheaf of papers and putting them into a tray on his desk. 'Since you took over as forelady I've been so busy I really haven't had the chance to have a good talk with you. I never seem to get a minute to myself these days. Several times I've tried to find an opportunity to discuss how you feel you're getting on but as soon as I get a minute either someone comes into the office or I'm called into a meeting. I shouldn't be complaining but orders for Brewin's products have suddenly shot through the roof and all departments in the factory are under the same pressure.'

The last thing she wanted was to sit down but as this was a request from her boss she felt obliged to comply, so perched on the edge of the chair ready to spring up and make her escape as soon as an opportunity arose. 'Better that way, Mr Hamlin, than us facing short time.'

'I agree entirely.' He reached over for a pencil and began sharpening it, knocking the shavings into a waste bin at the side of his desk. 'I haven't been so busy I didn't notice the women seem much happier these days,' he said, replacing the sharpener and twiddling the pencil between his fingers. 'So, what miracle did you use to get this much work out of them?'

Vinnie gave a shrug. 'No miracle, Mr Hamlin. It's all down to courtesy and respect for your colleagues. When I decided to have a go at this job, I sat and thought of all the things that used to annoy me.'

He flashed her a look of surprise. 'Annoy you?'

'Well, yes. Like being constantly treated as though I didn't have any idea what I was doing, not being given any kind of encouragement or thanked for a good job done. Apart from those in training the rest of the women are very experienced at what they do, Mr Hamlin, and the last thing they want is their forelady treating them like imbeciles.'

Fixing his eyes on a scenic calendar pinned on the wall behind her, he gave a thoughtful frown. 'And I take it Mrs Dodds did exactly that?'

She hesitated, not feeling comfortable about voicing her opinions of the last forelady. 'Well, yes, she did. She also had her favourites and would make sure the work they got was always the easiest and quickest to do so they could earn extra bonuses. To me that isn't fair, Mr Hamlin, so I make sure all the girls get a fair mixture and have the same chance of earning some extra.'

He looked concerned. 'I knew Mrs Dodds was . . . well . . . a little harsh in her approach, but I didn't know she carried on like that.'

There was another practice that had gone on but she felt it best not to mention it. Cynthia Dodds had accepted payment from her favourites at the end of each week in return for pushing good work their way.

'Well, with due respect, Mr Hamlin, you wouldn't, would you? You trust your forelady to run a happy floor while you get on with managing the department. There were several other practices Mrs Dodds insisted upon which I felt did more harm than good, so I've changed them.'

'Oh?' he said enquiringly.

She gnawed her bottom lip anxiously. 'I should have discussed them with you first, shouldn't I?'

'Not necessarily, Mrs Deakin, unless they were major.'

'Oh, they weren't major, Mr Hamlin,' she insisted. 'But Mrs Dodds wouldn't allow chatting while the girls were working, which of course they did behind her back. I don't think it does them any harm, or singing along with the music either. I feel that if the girls are happy then they'll do a better and quicker job. I want them to enjoy coming to work, Mr Hamlin, not dread it. It costs the company time and money to train people up so the last thing we want is them leaving if we can help it.'

'That's very true. Er ... anything else I should know?'

'No, I don't think so. Oh, just that I've also got a points system in operation and it seems to be working very well.'

'A points system?' he asked quizzically.

She shifted uncomfortably on her seat, wishing she hadn't mentioned it, but then Mr Hamlin had a right to know what she was up to. 'Any garments that are returned faulty, I keep a note of what section examined them and at the end of the week the section with the least points gets a box of chocolates. Only a small Dairy Box, nothing elaborate. It works, Mr Hamlin, the girls are taking much more pride in their work and the number of complaints we're getting back from customers has dropped. It wasn't high before by any means but any return is a slur on our department, isn't it, and there's no point in having an inspection department if we don't inspect the goods properly before they go out. I know mistakes happen, it's human nature, but if we can do anything to tighten things up this end then it's worth it to help maintain the company's good name.'

'It certainly is.' He flicked through some paperwork on his desk. 'There's a memo here somewhere from the factory manager. I haven't had a chance yet to read it properly but I did notice it mentioned something on that subject. Ah, here it is.' He quickly read the note in his hand. 'The fact that the return of faulty garments has been steadily dropping recently has been noticed by the hierarchy and our department has been pinpointed as the one ultimately responsible.' He flashed her a brief look then turned his attention back to the memo in his hand. 'It's you who's to be thanked and I will mention that at the next managers' meeting. Well done, Mrs Deakin, I'm just sorry I was too busy to have noticed myself.'

She lowered her head, embarrassed. 'I'm just doing my job,' she said, and rose. 'I'd better leave you to yours.'

Before he could say another word she had left his office, closing the door behind her.

'I saw yer getting cosy with the boss,' Betty chided, a spark of mischief in her eyes when Vinnie passed by her work bench moments later.

She stopped and looked at her friend crossly. 'I wasn't getting cosy, Betty, we were discussing work.'

Betty shot her a warning look. 'Eh, no need ter be getting on yer high horse with me, Lavinia Deakin. I knew you when yer were wet behind the ears, remember, and they put yer with me to help teach you all you know about inspecting.'

She gave a heavy sigh and looked at her friend, bewildered. 'I'm sorry, I didn't mean to snap at you, it's just what you said about me and Mr Hamlin getting cosy is far from the truth. What on earth it is I've done to that man I have no idea but, regardless, he only deals with me when he has to. When I was in his office just now he hardly looked at me, Betty, and I got the feeling he couldn't wait for me to leave.'

Her friend looked at Vinnie thoughtfully. 'Eh, yer don't reckon he fancies yer, do yer?'

She glanced back, totally appalled. 'Oh, don't be silly,' she scoffed. 'That is the last thing the man feels for me, I can assure you.' And to change the subject she asked, 'How's that order coming along?'

Betty flashed a disdainful look at Ruby working beside her. 'Well, if *she* got a move on then I'd say we've a good chance of getting it clear this afternoon, but as it is I doubt it.'

Vinnie frowned at Ruby worriedly. 'Why, what's wrong with her?' she asked.

'She's in love, that's what. Ain't yer, Ruby?' Betty addressed the girl loudly.

Ruby looked across at her blankly. 'Eh?'

'See, I told yer, Vinnie. In cloud cuckooland and has bin since Warren, the young lad in packing . . .' she leaned forward and mouthed, 'yer know, the skinny lad with them volcano-like spots and wonky eyes,' then straightened up and in her normal voice continued '. . . finally plucked up courage and asked her out this morning. Going ter the flicks ternight, they are.'

A beam of pleasure lit Vinnie's face. 'I think we can excuse Ruby then, don't you, Betty?' She took a look around the room. Everyone seemed to be busy and no one was trying to catch her attention. She stepped around the bench back into her old position. 'I'll give you a hand.'

Betty looked at her, impressed. 'Bleddy Doddsie would never have lowered herself to chip in and help us menials out.' Then she grinned broadly. 'Like old times, ain't it, Vinnie?'

Chapter Twelve

Keith looked appreciatively at the plate of food that was put before him. 'This looks delicious, love, thank you.'

Angela Hamlin put her own plate on the table and sat down opposite him. 'It might not taste as good as it looks.' She eyed him anxiously. 'I was in a rush tonight to get your dinner on the table but if it's not right I can always rustle you up something else.'

He gave a small sigh, fighting to hide his irritation. Angie fussed unnecessarily over him, at times suffocatingly so. 'You shouldn't worry so much. I appreciate you can't always have my dinner on the table the minute I walk in, I've told you that many times.' He forked a mouthful of the oxtail stew she had prepared into his mouth and smiled at her warmly. 'This tastes good to me but then your cooking always does, my dear. So why were you in a rush tonight?'

'We all got called into a last-minute staff meeting. Nothing serious, just the headmaster wanting to go over a few things. But more importantly, how was your day?'

'The same as usual. Busy. Never enough time to get through all I need to.'

As he ate, his mind drifted back to earlier that day when Vinnie had been sitting in his office. The woman had no idea at all of the extent of his feelings for her, something he seemed unable to control and which took him all his will-power to conceal from her – from everyone.

He remembered their first meeting five years before on the morning he had taken up his new position, replacing the retiring Archie Pegg. On being introduced to the staff, his eyes had met hers as he had shaken her hand and that was all it had taken for Keith to fall in love. Many times since he had wondered how something so momentous could have been caused by something so simple. But when their hands had briefly clasped and he had looked into her lovely blue eyes, a surge of something he could only liken to a bolt of lightning had shot through him, mentally knocking him sideways. It was no momentary feeling either. Each time he saw her his heart would somersault, his whole body weaken alarmingly. Something about Lavinia Deakin, everything about Lavinia Deakin, had captured his soul. He had tried everything he could to quash these feelings but try as he might they would not go away. Instead they deepened and the constant battle to hide his emotions was torture to him. As a man who had always prided himself on his high moral standards, he was shocked that the woman he coveted was married and one of his workers.

From under his lashes he stole a glance at Angie. How was it possible, he thought, to love two women as much as he did? One he knew intimately, the other hardly at all, and both in totally different ways. What would Angie say, how would she react, if she were ever to discover his secret? She'd be angry, upset, dreadfully hurt. What else could he expect? She had given up so much for him; her love, loyalty, caring and responsibility towards him she took very seriously. He could never voluntarily subject her to the devastation this would bring her should she find out. His feelings for Lavinia Deakin would remain his secret as he'd managed to keep them all this time.

The trouble was a further trauma faced him now and he wasn't sure how he was going to handle it should it become reality. Due to Vinnie's husband's shocking infidelity and subsequent death, she was now a free woman. Once over her bereavement, it would be possible for her to love again. He wanted so much for that man to be him. He dreaded to think how he would feel should he learn she had taken up with another, but then how could he selfishly expect Vinnie to spend the rest of her life by herself just so his feelings could be spared?

How he wished he had never clapped eyes on her. Better still, that he could flee this situation, move lock, stock and barrel to another town and try to forget her. But was that an option? Leicester was their home town. They had a nice house in a decent area, both had good jobs and friends. But, most importantly, should he even suggest such a thing, Angie would demand to know why. No excuse he could think of sounded a good enough reason apart from the truth, and he could never tell her that.

He realised she was talking to him and raised his head to give her a distracted smile. 'Sorry, dear?'

'I just asked, how is the new forelady getting on?' she repeated, pushing away her empty plate. 'You were worried about promoting her, wondering if she'd cope after what happened to her husband.'

'She's doing very well,' he said lightly. 'I can't begin to imagine the emotional strain she must be under but at work she keeps whatever she is suffering in check.'

'I couldn't be so brave,' responded Angie. 'But I expect being surrounded by friendly faces and having the new job to concentrate on is doing something to help.'

He nodded and as always when conversing on topics that involved Vinnie chose his words carefully. 'I'm quite impressed with her considering she's only been in the job a month. She's already put some really good ideas into practice that have shown promising results. What's good is that I can leave her to it really and get on with what I have to do. I know I made the right choice in appointing her.'

'Well, from what you've told me it's my opinion no one could be worse than that Mrs Dodds. She sounded a right tartar.'

'I think she was worse even than I believed after what Mrs Deakin relayed to me today. Still, she's gone now.

The girls seem so much happier and the daily production is significantly up.'

She smiled at him affectionately. 'And that's the main thing because then it looks good for you.' She rose and began gathering the dirty plates. 'Now what would you like for pudding? I've some leftover apple pie or I can open a tin of rice pudding. Shall I make some custard to go with the pie? I know that's your favourite.'

He patted his stomach. 'To be honest, Angie, I've had enough. That stew was really delicious and very filling.'

'Oh, but you won't have had a proper dinner without having a pudding. I'll get you that pie.'

He hurriedly rose from the table, moved to the side of her and put a hand on her arm. 'Really, my dear, I couldn't do justice to any pudding tonight. Look, I expect you've a pile of books to mark so you go and make a start and I'll clear up in here.'

'You will not. That's my job.' She gave him a gentle push towards the living-room. 'Now you go and relax and leave me to get on with it. The sooner you do, the sooner I can get my marking over with.' She sighed despondently. 'No matter how much I teach them, 3B's English hardly makes easy reading. I set them an essay entitled, "What Did You Do Last Sunday?". I happened to glance at one boy's work when he handed it in and he'd written: "Got up got some bottles of beer for me dad from the offy watched telly had me tea watched telly went to bed." There was no punctuation and six spelling mistakes. What I suspect he omitted to mention was the fact his mother and father had a fight after drinking the beer; that the dinner was more than likely egg and chips he had cooked himself, and that he went out in the evening with his mates and probably made his neighbours' night a misery by playing a transistor far too loudly.' She gave a weak smile. 'At heart, though, they're good kids I teach and I'll do my utmost for them while I do, but what will happen to them after they leave school I dread to think. Now, will you go and put your feet up?'

He smiled at her. 'Well, if you're sure you don't want a hand with the dishes, I've a bit of paperwork I brought home then I'll catch up with the newspaper. I might watch a bit of television too. *Armchair Theatre* is on at nine. I saw a trailer for it and a young actress called . . . er . . . Judi Dench is in it. The story looked quite interesting.'

Angie made an impressed face. 'She's good is Judi Dench. She was in that Shakespeare play I went to see at Stratford last year. Hopefully I can get through my marking by nine and then I'll make us a mug of cocoa and we can watch it together.'

He smiled at her warmly. 'That'll be nice.'

Chapter Thirteen

As Keith was preparing to settle down for the evening, about a mile away, Vinnie was staring in dismay at the letter in her hand. It was informing her of the date of Maxine Upton's trial which was scheduled for two weeks' time. She had already given a detailed statement to the police of Tommy's movements and behaviour prior to his going off to fetch his suitcase and had been warned by them that she would be called to the witness box, but in her efforts to try to come to terms with her traumatic ordeal had felt it best not to dwell on anything that kept the pain fresh so had pushed this thought to the back of her mind.

She had endeavoured to keep herself fully occupied by throwing herself into her job and in the evening taking her time over her chores, mostly doing unnecessary tasks. It was only at night, alone in her bed, that she could not control her thoughts, and when she did find she was dwelling on painful memories she concentrated hard on a little trick that Betty had taught her, something that had worked for her when her own husband had died. 'Think of yourself baking a cake from scratch. Start by imagining yourself buying the ingredients from the shop right through to the icing stage, then cutting a slice and eating it.' It had been hard going at first to stop her thoughts drifting back to matters she was trying to keep them off, but now she'd got to the stage of actually taking the cake out of the oven before she fell asleep. It was far from restful yet, but at least she was managing to rest.

She re-read the contents of the letter. Knowing she had to relive the worst time in her life all over again filled her with dread. But what was worse was having to face all those strangers, to be thoroughly questioned, her and Tommy's intimate life together narrated for all and sundry to listen to and pick over. The thought was unbearable to her. But she had to face it, she had no choice if justice was to be served.

Betty, bless her, had instilled in Vinnie that she would not have to face this alone; that her friend would be with her to support her every step of the way. That fact had warmed Vinnie, but nevertheless Betty could not stand in the witness box with her.

Laying the letter on the table, she walked into the kitchen and absently picked up a newspaper parcel of rubbish that needed to be put into the dustbin. The metal bin was kept beside the back gate and Vinnie tentatively made her way down the dark yard to deposit it. As she put the lid back into place she heard a noise coming from the Adlers' yard. Thinking it was Eric she called out to him, 'Evening, Eric. Any word when Noreen will be back yet?'

There was no response and Vinnie frowned. There was definitely someone in the Adlers' yard. She went across to the wall, and raising herself on tiptoe peered over. Illuminated by a full moon, the sight of Noreen flattened against the outhouse door momentarily stunned her. 'Noreen!' Vinnie finally exclaimed. 'You're back. Your sister is better, I take it? So when did you get here? I bet Eric's glad. He's missed you, I know he has.' She suddenly frowned, Noreen's whole manner puzzling her. 'Whatever's wrong? You're acting like you've seen a ghost.'

Her neighbour peeled herself away from the door. 'N'ote wrong with me, Vin. Yer just gave me a shock, that's all, and I'm tired after me long journey. I got back about four.' She looked all around her then settled her eyes on Vinnie. 'Bit of a shock about Tommy, in't it?'

Her face grave, Vinnie nodded. 'It's been a terrible time, Noreen. Eric told me how upset you were when you heard. I know you'll understand why I didn't manage to keep my promise.'

Noreen eyed her. 'What promise was that?' she asked.

'To look after Eric and Barry while you were away.'

'Oh, yeah, that. Well, in the circumstances that would've bin the last thing on your mind.'

'Yes, it was,' Vinnie said wanly. 'So, how's your sister now?'

'Me sister? Why . . . oh, she's as fit as a fiddle now, thanks. That virus certainly knocked the stuffing out of her. The doc has no idea how she got it. I reckon meself the quacks use the term "virus" 'cos in truth they ain't got a bleeding clue what's up with yer.'

Vinnie nodded. 'I expect you're right.' She paused. Despite Noreen's obviously knowing what had happened to Tommy, from past experience Vinnie knew she would want all the gory details. Although she didn't like that thought one little bit, Vinnie realised she might as well get it over with, saving herself from Noreen's constant badgering until she did. 'Why don't you come round for a cuppa so we can catch up?'

'Not tonight, Vin. Got loads ter do what with just getting back. Another night, eh?'

Vinnie stared at her, taken aback. 'Oh! Yes, all right, I'll look forward to it.'

'Yes, me too. See yer then,' her neighbour said, hurrying away.

Vinnie stared after her. Noreen was acting oddly. Never had Vinnie known her turn down the offer of a cup of tea and a natter, especially when juicy gossip was to be had. Still, Noreen had said she was tired and Vinnie knew she was bound to be after nursing her sick sister for over a month while helping run her guest house.

The contents of the letter she'd received earlier came flooding back and with her thoughts full of all it entailed, Vinnie made her way back inside.

It was a couple of days later when a knock sounded on her back door just after she had finished her evening meal and she opened it to find Eric.

He looked at her apologetically. 'Sorry ter bother yer, Vinnie.'

She smiled at him, standing aside to allow him entry. 'You're never any bother, Eric. Have you come to tell me Noreen's home? If so, I know. I saw her on Tuesday, the evening she returned. She looked tired, I must say. I'm surprised I haven't seen her since but I assume she's resting up after her hectic time.' Then she noticed the look on his face and asked, 'Eric, what's wrong?'

He gave a helpless shrug. 'I dunno, Vinnie. I came round here to see if you'd any idea.'

'Any idea about what? Is something wrong with her, is that what you're saying?'

'Well . . . I can only say that at the moment Noreen's worse than Noreen ever was, if yer get me drift.'

'I'm not sure I do, Eric. I must admit I thought she was acting oddly when I saw her on Tuesday evening but I put that down to her being tired after her journey from Blackpool and the fact she'd looked after her sick sister and the guest house for over six weeks. The work involved in that would knock the stuffing out of anyone, wouldn't it?'

Eric eyed her worriedly. 'Yeah, I grant yer, but it's more than that.'

'What do you mean, Eric?'

'Well . . .' He gave a deep sigh. 'It's like she's in a permanent bad mood, snapping all the time, but even so she's lost her spark, like she's gone dead inside. I know I ain't making much sense but I do know that if she don't calm down soon our Barry will up sticks and I won't be far behind him. Oh, I don't mean that, I'd never leave Noreen, I love her too much, but she is worrying me, Vinnie.'

Her face clouded in concern. 'Have you tried asking her what's wrong?'

'Yeah, and I just got me head bitten off and told to stop being a silly old fool. But I know my wife, Vinnie. There's summat wrong, I'm sure there is.'

'Well, as I haven't seen her for more than a minute I can't say one way or another, Eric. Look, I tell you what, I'll pop round later and have a chat with her. See if I can find out anything. I'm sure you're worrying over nothing and before you know it Noreen will be back to normal and plaguing the life out of you.'

'I hope so, Vinnie, 'cos I'd sooner that than what she's like now. I'd be grateful if you'd mek the time to go and see her.'

She looked at him remorsefully. 'I should have gone before now but it's just that . . .'

'I understand, Vinnie,' he cut in. 'To be honest I can't begin to understand how yer coping with all you've had ter.' He looked at her meaningfully. 'Look, er, yer know if there's 'ote yer need . . .'

She rose and gave him an affectionate pat on his arm. 'I know, Eric, and thanks. I'm managing all right. Keeping myself as busy as I can seems to be helping.'

Just as she closed the door on Eric there was a knock on it and Gary walked in. Vinnie gave him a broad smile of welcome and an affectionate hug. 'Hello, love.' She looked at him meaningfully and the look he gave her back told her all she needed to know. Her daughter remained unrelenting. Gary, though, bless him, and without Julie's knowledge, regularly popped in to see how she was and keep her updated on how her daughter was faring. Vinnie worried that should Julie find out what her husband was doing behind her back all hell would break lose. 'Got time for a cuppa?' she asked, going over to the stove and turning on the electric plate under the kettle.

He unbuttoned his coat and sat down at the table. 'I've just time for a quick one, thanks. You looked a bit worried when I came in?'

'Yes, I am. Noreen's back from Blackpool and it seems she's not her normal self and Eric's worried about her. I'm going round in a bit to have a talk with her.' She poured boiling water into the teapot and set it on the table, then looked at Gary gravely. 'I got a letter from the court today informing me of the trial date. It's just after New Year.'

'Oh!' It was apparent that this news was as much of a shock to him as it had been to Vinnie but his concern was all for her. 'I expect it's upset you. Are you all right, Mrs Deakin?'

'Yes . . . no, well, I knew it was imminent but it still knocked me for six. I suppose I was hoping it would all just go away but I knew it wouldn't. I'm not making much sense, am I, dear, but I know what I mean.' She gave a despondent sigh as she poured out the tea. 'The thought of having to face all this frightens the life out of me, but then I have to and once it's over maybe I can really start to get my life back together.'

'I think you're doing remarkably well as it is, Mrs Deakin.'

She flashed him a smile. 'I'm a good actor then, aren't I? How's Julie?'

'She's fine.'

His reply was just a little too hurried for her liking but she thought better of probing, feeling that as newly marrieds they were bound to have adjustments to make, and also that having to cope with Tommy's terrible secrets and traumatic demise hadn't been exactly the best of starts to a marriage. Besides, she knew Gary to be a very caring young man and one who wouldn't want to add to her own burdens at the moment, so unless events in his and Julie's world were life-threatening he would keep his own counsel. 'And you?' she asked.

'Me too.'

Again his answer was too glib but she declined to comment further.

He took a sip of his tea. 'This . . . er . . . court business . . .'

She held up a warning hand. 'Please don't worry, Gary. I know what a dilemma you're in. The situation between my daughter and me is none of your doing and I know it must be very difficult for you to handle, but your place is beside her. I take it Julie plans to attend?'

He nodded.

'And she has every right to. But, Gary, you will have

to try and prepare her. Sitting through the trial is going to be horrendous. She's going to hear things about her father I'd rather she didn't, but at least she will have you to support her. I won't be on my own, Gary. I'll have Betty with me and I'm sure Noreen too.'

'Oh, Mrs Deakin, I just wish . . .'

'I know, son. Maybe one day Julie will come round and we can all be a happy family again. I just hope that day will be soon.' Vinnie gave a forlorn sigh. 'To be honest, I need my daughter more than ever just now but I can't force her to change her opinion of me. She's hurting, Gary. I wish with all my heart I could take away the pain she's suffering, at least help her through it, but you know how strong-minded she is. However hard it is for me the best thing I can do is wait until she comes to me.'

'I've tried to talk to her, Mrs Deakin.'

'Yes, I know, love, and I appreciate all you've tried to do but my daughter is stubborn and, let's be fair to her, she's had her whole world blown apart. I hardly remember my father but I know how devastated I'd have been if I'd found out he wasn't the man I thought he was. Julie's having difficulty believing all she's found out about Tommy, and it's easier for her to make me entirely responsible for his actions than to admit that the man she idolised for the most part never existed.' She took a sip of her tea and eyed him in concern. 'You know, I do worry your popping in to see me will cause trouble between you should Julie find out. I wouldn't want that, Gary.'

'If Julie does find out then she'll just have to understand that this is something I have to . . . want to . . . do. I couldn't turn my back on you, Mrs Deakin. Julie's entitled to her opinions and so am I.'

She smiled at him warmly. 'You are a lovely young man and my daughter is very lucky to have you.' She took a deep breath. 'Look, I ought to say something about Christmas. It's only a week away now and it's not a day I'm looking forward to or suspect any of us are really. The way Julie is at the moment I don't stand much chance of seeing her on the day unless a miracle happens. Anyway, Betty has asked me to join her . . . well, she gave me no choice, bless her . . . and I agree with her that it's probably a good idea I don't spend it alone in this house. Anyway that will put your mind at rest that I'm not on my own, Gary. I expect you'll both be going to your parents so I know you'll be in good company. I've yet to go Christmas shopping but Betty has volunteered to deliver your presents. Whether Julie will accept hers is up to her but I can't let the day go unmarked.' She could see Gary was too upset to comment so said lightly, 'I'm glad I've cleared that up. Now, hadn't you best get off, dear?'

They both rose and she kissed him affectionately on his cheek. 'Thank you so much for coming. Take care.'

'I'll see you soon, and if you need me for anything meanwhile . . .'

'Yes, I know, I can get a message sent through your

work via that lady in the office who's promised not to breathe a word to Julie. Oh, how I hate all this cloak and dagger business but . . . .'

'Hopefully it won't be for much longer,' he cut in.

She flashed him a brief smile. 'Hopefully.'

Chapter Fourteen

'Noreen, it's me, Vinnie. Open the door.' Vinnie knocked loudly on the door again and stepped back as it was opened just a chink and an eye peeked at her through the gap. Then it was pulled further open and Noreen stood on the threshold.

She folded her arms and glared. 'Oh, it's you. What d'yer want?'

Despite obviously being in a foul mood Noreen looked pale and drawn and if Vinnie wasn't mistaken she had lost some weight. Caring for her sister had clearly taken its toll on her. Vinnie smiled warmly.

'I haven't seen you for a while, I've come to see how you are. Aren't you going to ask me in?'

'Now's not really a good time,' she said offhandedly. 'I was just off to bed.'

'But it's only just gone half-seven.'

'Oh, you're me mother now, a' yer, telling me when I can go ter bed and when I can't?'

'Stop it, Noreen. I don't know what's bothering you but as far as I know I haven't done anything to upset you.'

'Who said anything is bothering me?' she barked.

'Well, you've always been prone to moods, Noreen, but usually there's a reason for them.' Even if that reason isn't what anyone else would think a valid one, she thought. She decided to try a different approach. 'Noreen, I had a letter from the court today informing me of the trial date and . . .'

'And let's hope that little hussy gets all she deserves!' Noreen finished for her.

'Well, yes, I agree with you but it doesn't make me happy to think of her spending the rest of her days in prison.'

'No, hanging would have bin better. Pity it's bin abolished.'

'Noreen!'

She glared back and wagged a finger. 'You telling me, Lavinia Deakin, that you don't want justice served for what *she* was responsible for?'

'Yes, I want justice, I'd be a liar if I said I didn't.'

'Well then,' she snapped, re-folding her arms. 'I hope that little bitch gets life in the harshest prison in the country and lives to a ripe old age to suffer every minute of it.' Her mouth tightened, her eyes were cold. 'She set her cap at Tommy and enticed him with her big tits and short skirts, but *he* was the fool for being stupid enough to fall for someone young enough to be his daughter. It was doomed from the start. And I'd like him to have seen what she'd have looked like in ten years' time after giving birth to a screaming brat and having to put up with his conniving ways . . .' Her eyes narrowed darkly. 'I ain't saying it were nice fer yer, Vinnie, but I think it was a good thing yer found out what Thomas Deakin was really like. If yer want my honest opinion, *he* got what he deserved, the double-crossing liar!'

'Noreen!' Vinnie exclaimed, stunned by her friend's brutal tirade.

'As far as I'm concerned, he did,' Noreen hissed savagely. 'When yer mek promises, Vinnie, yer supposed ter keep 'em.'

'Oh, Noreen, when we made our wedding vows Tommy didn't know that twenty-odd years later he was going to have his head turned by a flirty young woman, did he? I can't say I wasn't devastated about it but we all make mistakes, we wouldn't be human if we didn't. It's having the guts to hold your hand up and admit what you've done that counts. Tommy did. He told me how sorry he was for having his fling and I believed him. How was he supposed to know she would kill him in temper when he told her he was coming back to me?'

Vinnie stopped abruptly, wondering why Noreen was acting almost as though it was herself Tommy had betrayed, then the truth struck her forcibly. Noreen saw him as her friend and was grieving for the loss of him. This was being shown on her part by aggression. Vinnie looked at her with remorse.

'Oh, Noreen, please forgive me. I was so wrapped up in my own grief that I never gave a thought to how our neighbours and friends would be feeling. You and Eric were so very fond of Tommy. It must have come as such a terrible shock to find out what he had been up to. It was behind all our backs really because he would have lied to all of us to cover his tracks. I expect you must have felt dreadful too for not being able to be here to help me through this. But it wasn't your fault your sister was sick.'

Noreen looked at her for several long moments before she said, 'Yeah, well, when sympathy's being dished out no one considers anyone other than the family, do they? Anyway, as I said earlier, yer just caught me going ter bed. So if there's n'ote else?'

'Er . . . no.'

'Right, then I'll say goodnight.'

With that she shut the door.

Betty was waiting at Vinnie's back door when she returned.

'Hello, me duck. Gary popped in to see me earlier and told me you'd had word about the court case and thought yer might need a shoulder to cry on. He's a nice young man, not many of his kind around these days.' She noticed the distressed expression on Vinnie's face. 'Gary was right, wasn't he?'

'Sorry? Oh, yes, receiving the letter has upset me, Betty, but not so much as Noreen's just done.' She flashed her a welcoming smile. 'Thanks for coming. Come in and make yourself comfy while I put the kettle on.'

A short while later, both seated at the table sipping on their tea, Betty eyed Vinnie enquiringly. 'So how come madam next-door has upset yer? What's she done?'

'Taken Tommy's death really badly. I feel awful because I was so wrapped up in myself I never gave Noreen's feelings a thought. I know she's been the bane of my life since the day we moved in and Tommy couldn't stand the sight of her, but then you can't be as close neighbours as we have been for all these years and not be devastated when something terrible happens, can you? And it wasn't like Tommy's death was expected and we were prepared.' Her voice lowered to barely a whisper. 'His death was . . . well . . . so sudden.'

'Eh, stop letting this upset yer, Vinnie. Yer've got enough to deal with as it is without teking on someone else's pain. Noreen was only a neighbour and an interfering one at that. You were his wife so whatever she's feeling won't be anywhere near as bad as you.'

She gave a despondent sigh. 'Oh, Betty, you should have heard the things she said. Really harsh she was. Noreen's always been like that. She says what she thinks before she thinks about what she's saying, and she doesn't care how much she hurts those who are listening. She said Tommy deserved what he got. Oh, Betty, what he did was wrong but he didn't deserve to die.'

Tears of distress welled in her eyes and slid down her cheeks.

Betty reached over and laid a comforting hand on her arm. 'Come on, gel,' she soothed. 'Don't take any notice of her. She's entitled to her opinions even if you don't agree with 'em. It's not really my place to pass comment on the woman as I've never met her but to my mind it's Noreen that's being selfish, not you. Yer see, what she thinks is that Tommy's death has put a stop to all your neighbourly get togethers. They won't happen now, will they, and she won't find it easy with her nature building up a friendship with anyone else as most round here know her reputation and wouldn't entertain her in that capacity.' She paused and eyed Vinnie knowingly. 'I hate to bring this to your attention but lots of things will be different for you now you're a woman on yer own.'

Vinnie looked at her, stunned. 'I suppose they will,' she uttered. 'I haven't given any thought to that side of my life.' She gave a distracted sigh. 'Noreen and Eric frequently came around here for a game of cards or such like on a Saturday night, or we'd go down the pub together. That's the sort of thing couples do together, isn't it? Now I'm not part of a couple anymore, am I?' She gave a deep sigh. 'You're right as far as Noreen is concerned too, Betty. She's always upsetting someone by speaking out of turn. It all goes over Eric's head, bless him. Well, he loves her, doesn't he? I suppose me and Tommy were the nearest they both had to friends. For the most part we never let them see that her attitude bothered us so they stuck to us like glue. I can't say we've always seen eye to eye but I suppose living next-door you're more likely to make an extra effort to get on with someone because you're so close. Especially when your children are young and all playing together. The couple the other side of me, Mr and Mrs Gilbert, well, we pass the time of day but never more than that. Poor Noreen will suffer now our social occasions have come to a halt because I'm on my own. I've no doubt she'll find something to replace them with, though. But really it's Eric that I feel sorry for. He'll have to find another mate to go for a drink or to the football match with.'

'He seems a nice enough bloke to me, Vinnie, so I shouldn't think he'll have that much trouble. As fer Noreen, well, it's my opinion yer better off without her and if I were you I'd just leave her to get on with it. Anyone who can tek pleasure in further upsetting someone that's already suffering don't deserve no one's sympathy. And while we're on the subject, your Julie is doing just what my daughter did when her dad died only Julie's taking it to extremes. I remember when my Alfred died, my eldest daughter was that distraught there was no talking to her for over a week. But her grieving was all for herself because with her dad gone there was no one now to do all the odd jobs for her around her house. Her husband is useless in that department whereas my Alfie was very good with his hands.

'There was never any thought for me from her, for the fact that I'd lost the man I loved, the father of me kids, just for what *she'd* lost. Same goes fer yer daughter. If yer want my opinion that gel should come begging for forgiveness to you on her hands and knees, the way she treated you. I shouldn't have voiced me opinions like that but, well, that's how I feel.'

Betty leaned on the table and eyed Vinnie hard. 'Now, this court case, ducky. You ain't worrying about it, a' yer? Well, yes, I know that's a daft question, but you have to face it and worrying about it won't make it any easier to deal with. Yer know I'll be with yer every step of the way, apart from actually standing in the witness box that is.'

Vinnie looked at her gratefully. 'Thank you, Betty. I really don't know how I'm ever going to repay you for all the kindness and support you've given me throughout all this.'

'Well, actually, there is a way.'

'Oh?' She eyed Betty eagerly. Anything she could do for her would give Vinnie so much pleasure.

What she asked for struck Vinnie speechless.

'Could we catch the end of *Coronation Street*? When I left home Elsie Tanner was having a terrible row with Ena Sharples over something Dennis Tanner had done in the vestry and Albert Tatlock was getting involved and yer know what a gruff old bugger he can be. But it's Jack Walker I feel sorry for, having to live with that stuck-up cow Annie. Their Billy is on his way back from Liverpool for the weekend and I can feel trouble brewing with Deirdre Langton 'cos Billy's got a fancy for her, yer know, and Len Fairclough's got wind of it, and what's the betting he lets it slip to Deirdre's husband Ray when he's had too much to drink at the Rovers? And I'll tell yer summat fer n'ote, Annie's gonna hit the roof when she finds out what her son is up to. Anyway, can we watch it else I'll never get ter sleep ternight for worrying what I've missed?'

Despite her wretchedness Vinnie couldn't help but chuckle. 'Oh, Betty, please be my guest.'

Chapter Fifteen

'Oh, Betty, her screams . . . I can still hear them. "*I'm innocent. I never did this.*" Over and over. Betty, what if . . .'

'Eh, just stop it, Vinnie. She was guilty. Judge and jury found her so. 'Course she was going to scream her innocence. The gel had just been told she was going to spend the rest of her life in prison so she's not exactly going to say, "Oh, thank you, Me Lord," is she?'

Vinnie's whole body sagged despairingly. 'No, I suppose not,' she uttered.

Betty put an arm protectively around her shoulders and pulled her close. 'Don't forget, Maxine Upton took Tommy's life, whether she meant to or not, and she has to pay the price.'

'Yes, I know, but it still seems such a harsh sentence. Such a waste of a young life.'

'Well, she should have thought about that before she picked up the knife and did what she did with it. Now look, Vinnie, yer've got to put all this behind you. It's over now.'

She took a deep shuddering breath. 'This is something I doubt I'll ever fully get over, Betty. What I have to do is my best not to let it blight the rest of my life.' She gave a deep forlorn sigh. 'I just hope . . .' Her voice trailed away and a trickle of tears flowed down her face.

'What, ducky, what do you hope?'

'Oh, just that Julie will find it within herself to forgive me for whatever she thinks I'm guilty of.'

'I'm sure time will do that, lovey, and of course you have a champion on your side in Gary.'

'Yes, and thank God for it. But did you see her, Betty, throughout the trial? Her face was like marble, and when the jury pronounced the guilty verdict she stood up and gave Maxine a murderous look before she walked out of the court.' Vinnie's face filled with utter misery. 'Not once during any of it did she look in my direction. Not once, Betty. It took all my self-control not to rush over to her and, whether she wanted me to or not, just hug her, especially when all the evidence of Tommy's affair with Maxine was being dissected by the prosecutor. They made him sound such a terrible person.'

Betty looked at her, marvelling at the way this woman, who'd just been put through a living hell as the trial of Maxine Upton had progressed, felt concern only for her daughter and her husband's murderer, none for herself. Also she knew, despite Vinnie's not mention- ing the fact, that her eldest daughter Janie was preying heavily on her mind. She was inwardly worrying herself witless, wondering if the young woman actually knew of her father's terrible death, and if so how she was coping. But as no word had been heard from her Betty assumed she either didn't know or else didn't care, and Vinnie's worries over her were wasted.

She took a deep breath. 'It's their job, ducky. They have ter get to the truth and the only way they can do that is to pull people's lives apart so they can get to the bottom of things, then the jury mull over the evidence and decide between 'em what's what. You know as well as I do that in this case their decision was honest and just.

'It was Julie's own wish to attend the trial, but then in fairness to the gel nothing could prepare her for what she was going to face. Still, I don't care what you say, Vinnie, she could have shown you some support regardless of her misguided animosity. I know she idolised her father but you're still her mother when all's said and done. And while we're on the subject, I know yer mind's on your Janie too. Well, if n'ote else this tragedy should have brought her forward. I think you have yer answer to how that gel is feeling about you all as she's not used this situation to make her peace with yer.'

Betty hated herself for voicing this but felt someone had to. She suddenly noticed several reporters descending upon them and grabbed Vinnie's arm. 'Come on, lovey, I'm gonna get you home.'

Keith Hamlin stared blindly across his office. For the last few weeks the woman he adored from afar had been under a terrible strain as she tried to come to terms with what had befallen her. The last three days had been a terrible strain for him also, knowing Vinnie was having to relive her nightmare all over again in court in an effort to see justice served. The fact he could not openly be with her to lend his support had almost crucified Keith.

Angie had noticed how distracted he had become as the date of the trial arrived and had asked him several times if he was sickening for something. He had managed to fob her off with a story about being under extreme pressure at work but if he carried on behaving like he was her suspicions would be aroused that there was far more to this and she'd demand answers to some difficult questions.

He pulled back his cuff and looked at his watch. It was a quarter to four. He had heard through gossip in the canteen at lunchtime that the jury was considering its verdict. Surely they had reached a decision by now and the ordeal of the woman he loved would soon be over.

He was suddenly jerked out of his distracted state by a loud cheer resounding around the main inspection room and through his office window could see the workers outside all cheering and clapping. His heart raced, hoping they were celebrating what he was praying they were. He jumped up and rushed through.

'What's going on, ladies?' he asked.

It was Ruby who answered him. 'We just got word, Mr 'Amlin. The jury's returned and gave a guilty verdict. That trollop's bin sent down fer life and it's no more than she deserves for what she done.'

'Er . . . yes, quite. And . . . er . . . Mrs Deakin? Has anyone heard how she is?' He hoped he sounded no more interested than a boss would in any of his workers.

'Bloody jumping fer joy, I should think, Mr 'Amlin,' one of the crowd cried. 'Well, wouldn't you be, knowing justice had been served? Hooray for British Justice,' she erupted.

They all cheered and clapped again, dancing around hugging each other.

Keith too was relieved it was all over but couldn't show it.

'All right, ladies, that's enough. Maybe the best way we can show Mrs Deakin our support is by the smooth running of this department in her absence.'

Mumbles of agreement were expressed and they all returned to their work stations.

Keith went back to his office, sat down and rubbed his hands wearily over his face. He was glad that now the trial was over Vinnie could hopefully put the past behind her and move forward. In truth, though, he didn't want her to rebuild her life if that meant the possibility of another man winning her affections. His face set. It still greatly confused him that he could have such strong feelings for a woman he only knew through work, and he wondered if he'd ever fathom what it was about her that had done this to him. He already had a woman in his life who was totally committed to him, and unless something happened to change that or unless he abandoned her then he wasn't free to pursue Vinnie or any other woman. Face up to Angie was what he should do but he couldn't, knowing what it would mean to her. Despite everything he did love her so very, very much. He took a deep breath. Deep down he knew the best and only solution was to concentrate on quashing his feelings for Vinnie and getting on with his own life without her in it.

Chapter Sixteen

Vinnie smiled a greeting at Barry as he opened the door to her. He was dressed very loudly in the fashion of the day: a pair of bright green hipster trousers, glaring orange shirt with a long pointed collar and a multi-coloured striped tank top. His hair had grown since the last time she had seen him and was now well past his collar and so full around his face his features were hardly visible. In the background she could hear a record being played. It was one that was high in the charts – she knew this information via the younger members of her work team – and regularly played over the wireless system at work. 'Oh, that's the Swinging Blue Jeans, isn't it?'

Impressed, he eyed her from under his full fringe. 'Fer an old 'un you ain't bad, Mrs D. It's groovy this one, ain't it?' he said, clicking his fingers in time to the beat.

'It certainly is.' And she added, a twinkle of amusement sparkling in her eyes, 'I rather like the Dave Clark Five and Gerry and the Pacemakers.'

'Can't beat the Stones though, can yer? Wadda yer think of them then, Mrs D?'

'Well . . . I think they're a little way out, isn't that what you youngsters say, for my tastes.'

He gave a raucous laugh. 'If yer think *they're* way out, wadda yer make of the Troggs then?'

'The what?'

He laughed again. 'Never mind, Mrs D.'

'Er . . . I suppose it's a silly question, being's you're playing your music so loud . . .'

'Oh, yer not wanting me ter turn it down, a' yer?' he interjected, a worried look spreading across his youthful face.

'No, not at all. You youngsters need to have a way to express yourselves. Though any louder and I would,' she said, giving him a light warning. 'I was going to ask if your mother was in but hearing that music, I doubt she is.'

'No, she ain't, thank God.' He eyed her enquiringly. 'You two had a falling out 'cos I know me mam don't practically live in your house like she used to?'

She gave a shrug. 'If I've upset your mother, Barry, then I'm at a loss to know how.'

He pulled a disapproving face. 'You know as well as I do, Mrs D, that my mam don't need much of a reason for 'ote she does. I reckon she's going doolally in her old age. She's palled up with a woman at work and the pair of 'em are off out most nights, dolled up to the eyeballs and no telling what time she'll be home. Me dad ain't happy but she just tells him that if he

221

don't like it then he knows what he can do. I'll tell me mam yer called.'

You could, she thought, but doubted her visit would be acknowledged by Noreen. 'Yes, please tell her I was asking after her, and your father too.'

Back in her own house Vinnie read again the crude leaflet she had caught hold of as it fluttered down the street outside the factory. It was advertising the services of a painter and decorator, stating his skills were proven and rates extremely competitive. She took a slow look around her living-room. Tommy and she had worked hard to make the room inviting and comfortable, and considering it was over six years since Tommy had painstakingly and with Eric's help decorated it, it was still in a very presentable state apart from the chimney breast which was darker due to the gradual smoke damage. Prompted by the offered services of the decorator, Vinnie wondered if it was time for a change away from the present muted browns and creams to something brighter. She wasn't sure what but maybe the decorator could advise her.

She had no idea what the work would cost but still had the collection from her workmates intact. She had never had good reason before now to excuse spending their hard-earned money but something of such a nature she felt would be putting their gracious gift to good use.

She jumped, realising someone had entered the room, and spun round to face the intruder. 'Oh, hello, Gary dear,' she said, sighing in relief.

'Sorry if I made you jump. You looked very far away,' he commented to her.

'I was. Just deciding whether to get this room brightened up.' She handed him the leaflet. 'What do you think?'

He read it and nodded. 'Wouldn't hurt to get him in and ask for a quote. What about purples and oranges?'

She gave a laugh. 'More you and Julie's taste, I should think. I'll stick to safe pastels.' She paused and looked at him meaningfully. 'How is Julie?' she asked.

'She's fine.'

At his tone she frowned. 'Is everything all right?'

'Yes, everything is fine, thank you.' The look she gave him told him his mother-in-law suspected otherwise and he gave a heavy sigh. 'I don't want to burden you, Mrs Deakin.'

'Gary, please don't think you're a burden in any way. Come through to the kitchen and I'll make us some tea.

'So . . .' she said a few minutes later, pushing a steaming cup to him across the table, 'is there anything I can help you with?'

He gave a shrug. 'I don't know, Mrs Deakin. If Julie was on better terms with you I'd ask you to have a chat with her, try to make her see reason.'

She looked at him in concern. 'About what, Gary?'

'Her spending.' He gave a deep sigh, his face clouding over in bewilderment. 'It's like she can't stop herself, Mrs Deakin. Practically every day she buys something new for the house. Mostly only little things but it adds up to quite a lot by the end of the week. Then of course there's her clothes and whatnot. Julie's got enough clothes in her wardrobe to stock a shop and more pairs of shoes and matching handbags than she can ever use in a lifetime. I keep telling her I earn a wage, not own the company, but she just says it's her money that buys these things. I can't argue with that but in truth we need some of her wage to meet our living expenses. As it is she contributes very little, if anything, most weeks.' He raked his hand despairingly through his thatch of red hair. 'I don't begrudge her her money, Mrs Deakin, after all it's my job to provide for Julie and I don't mind that responsibility . . . Oh, I don't know, I just never realised being married was so expensive even though we don't live like lords.'

Vinnie frowned in thought. If Julie didn't curb her spending then their situation could become very damaging. She didn't like to think ill of the dead but Tommy was to blame for Julie's lackadaisical attitude. She'd only had to pout and Tommy's hand was in his pocket, whether he could actually afford to give her what she wanted or not. Julie obviously thought Gary would act the same with her.

'Could you speak to your mother and ask her to have a word with Julie?' she suggested. Not that she liked doing so. Julie was her daughter and Vinnie felt she should be the one to speak to her on this matter, but as things stood between them Julie wouldn't even acknowledge her if they passed in the street let alone let her in the house for a serious mother-daughter talk.

Gary rubbed his chin, bothered. 'My mum would, I

suppose, but then it would mean I'd have to explain to her what's going on. My mum's lovely, Mrs Deakin, but I can't talk to her in the same way I do you, and without decrying her she's not the best person to deal with something like this. She'd want to settle the bills for us, but then that wouldn't stop the problem, would it? Julie would take that as licence to continue her spending spree at my parents' expense. All it would achieve is them having to bail us out all the time. I have to stand on my own two feet, Mrs Deakin.'

He gave a worried sigh. 'I know Julie sees my mum's kind of lifestyle as the kind she wants but, as I keep telling her, they've worked years to get where they are and when they were young they had to struggle, but she takes no notice of me. She's determined she wants everything now, Mrs Deakin. She isn't prepared to wait. I'm sure our friends are really envious, thinking we're rolling in it, when in truth we're not.'

Vinnie gave a sigh, wishing she could do something, but knew that any intervention from her would only cause trouble between Julie and Gary. 'You'll have to sit Julie down and talk to her. Make her understand she has to curb her spending before you're both in dire straits,' Vinnie advised.

'I have to do something as the soft approach isn't working. I find it very hard to get annoyed with her, though. I love her so much and I hate it when she cries.'

Vinnie smiled at him affectionately. 'I'm glad to hear it, but sometimes loving someone means we have to do things we don't like.'

'Did you and Mr Deakin ever go through anything like this?' he asked.

'Not really.' She suddenly looked at him knowingly. 'But if you think that Mr Deakin and I never had a cross word then you'd be wrong, Gary. Sometimes we'd go for a week hardly seeing each other because of the hours he worked but we had our ups and downs like any other couple, especially when the children were growing up.' She gave a forlorn sigh. 'I like to think it was just a blip in our marriage when Tommy had his fling with Maxine Upton. From what he told me, I believe it was.' She smiled at him sadly. 'Of course, our expectations when we married were far lower than you youngsters' these days. Goodness me, magazines are full of the latest gadgets on the market now, aren't they, and of course the young wives want them and who can blame them if these new inventions make their lot easier? But affording them is another matter. I never dreamed of owning a washing machine, fridge or television. These days they're a must.

'We rented our first television set from Radio Rentals for five shillings a week and I agonised over whether we could afford it. Nineteen fifty-five it was. Tommy said hang the cost, it would keep me company when he was on evening and nightshift, and if we found we were struggling to pay for it then we could always send it back.' She gave a small laugh as a memory surfaced. 'My mother was so proud, telling everyone who would listen that her daughter and son-in-law had a television set. You'd have thought we'd won the pools. She didn't tell people it wasn't actually ours, though. She was funny, my mum, you'd have liked her, Gary. I know what she'd say now about Julie's carryings on.'

'Oh, and what's that?' he asked keenly.

' "Give her a good slap on her backside and a dose of cod liver oil." My mum's remedy for everything was a tablespoon of cod liver oil. Two tablespoons if you were unlucky.'

He pulled a face. 'Yuk!'

'Precisely,' she said, chuckling. 'I don't think a dose of cod liver is what our Julie needs right now or a good slap but she does need a talking to.'

'Yes, I agree. I just don't fancy doing it, but I will.' Gary picked up the leaflet and studied it. 'I hope this man can decorate better than he can spell.' He pushed the leaflet back in her direction. 'He's spelt services with three s's.'

Vinnie cocked an eyebrow at him. 'We can't all be good at everything. Can you decorate?' she asked him.

He shook his head.

'But you *can* spell,' she laughed. 'You and this man would make a good team.' Then she looked at him questioningly. 'Gary, do you think it would be wrong of me to have the living-room repapered?'

He gave a shrug. 'In what way?'

'Well, Tommy did it last time.' She gave a reminiscent smile. 'With lots of swearing and the odd accident.'

'Oh, you think if you redecorate people will think you're starting to eradicate any trace of Mr Deakin from your life?'

She gnawed her bottom lip anxiously. 'Do you think Julie would see it like that?'

'Mrs Deakin, I think she would see anything you did at the moment in that light.'

'Oh, I see. So I should leave it as it is then? If there was any chance of getting the mess between us sorted out I wouldn't want to jeopardise that by making her feel I'm trying to get rid of everything connected with her father.'

'Mrs Deakin, Julie will have to understand that you are only doing your best to get on with your own life. The room would have to be repapered sometime after all. Nothing lasts for ever, does it?'

'Mmm, yes. I suppose it won't hurt to ask for a quote. I still have the money from the collection from work and I'd like to use it wisely.'

He looked at her hesitantly. 'Would you mind if I suggested something, Mrs Deakin?'

'No, of course not.'

'Well, it's just that when you ask this decorator chap to call, I wouldn't give your proper name out.'

She eyed him, bemused. 'Why ever not?'

'Well, I could be wrong so forgive me if I am, I just want to save you any possible problems. You see, Mr Deakin's murder was headline news and . . . well, I'm not saying he will, but this man could have read all about it and realise who you are. Apart from the fact you don't want him coming here out of nosiness, neither do you want him trying to fleece you, a woman on your own and also one who's just been through a very bad time. He might think you're ripe for the picking. To be on the safe side, it's best to let this man think your husband's out at work or something.'

'Oh, yes, Gary, I see what you mean and thank you for the thought. I'll do what you suggest and be on my guard. Betty said that things would change now I'm on my own and she's obviously right.'

Gary drained the last of his tea and stood up to go. 'I'd best get off. I'm going to have that chat with Julie before I lose my nerve.'

She rose also and kissed his cheek. 'Thanks for coming, Gary.'

'Thanks for listening to me,' he responded.

'That's what mothers-in-law are for, isn't it?'

He smiled affectionately at her. 'You're more than a mother-in-law to me, Mrs Deakin. You've become my friend too.'

Tears of gratitude pricked her eyes. 'Oh, Gary, thank you.'

Chapter Seventeen

'Shaun O'Connell, pleased ter meet yer, Mrs Pumpkin.'

As she accepted his proffered hand Vinnie looked at the young man, startled, then she remembered she had taken Gary's advice and given her maiden name when making an appointment for him to call with a very hesitant-sounding woman at the other end of the telephone. 'Actually,' she said, hiding her mirth, 'the name I gave the lady on the telephone was Perkins.'

As he withdrew his hand he looked at her, horrified. 'Oh, I'm so sorry. It's me mother. She hates having to answer the telephone but I told her if she didn't when I was out working then I could lose potential business. I thought it was a funny name when she told me, it just never crossed me mind me mam had got it wrong.'

'That's quite all right,' Vinnie assured him. She looked at him searchingly. He wasn't at all what she had been expecting. He couldn't be much more than twenty. She looked at his face more closely. Strange, but he seemed familiar to her. 'Have we met before?' she asked him.

He shook his head. 'Don't think so, Mrs Perkins. Is this the room you want doing?' he asked, taking a look around.

'Yes, it is. Er . . . you're much younger than I was expecting.'

He turned back to face her. 'I might only be twenty-one, Mrs Perkins, but I know more about the decorating business than some what call themselves professionals and are twice my age. I've bin doing this since I was not much more than a nipper. Me dad is in the trade, yer see, and I used to follow him around like his shadow. I learned everything I know from him. He's a proper craftsman with a real love for his work which rubbed off on me. He got me my apprenticeship with the firm he worked for. Like most places, when my time was up they didn't like the thought of paying me proper rates so got rid of me and took on another apprentice. Until a few months ago I worked for a firm called Wilson's on Gypsy Lane, but to be honest after being taught so well by me dad, I got fed up with working in a gang who drank more tea than they did work. But more than that, I hated having ter cut corners. Customers paying fer good paint and cheap being used, that sorta thing.

'I took a gamble on going out on me own a few months ago. Me mam was worried but I told her that if it didn't work out I could always get a job with another company. Now things are going better than I expected and hopefully in the future I can ask me dad to join me as a partner. If yer do decide to tek me on, Mrs Perkins,

I can give you addresses where I've already done work, so yer can check me work out first. I'll do yer a good job and that's me promise or yer don't pay me.'

She looked at him, impressed. 'That sounds fair to me.'

'How's yer young man shaping up?' Betty asked Vinnie the following Wednesday.

They were both in the busy canteen eating their lunch, surrounded by tables filled with numerous other factory workers and members of the office staff.

Vinnie looked tentatively at a forkful of macaroni cheese. She gave a grimace as she put it into her mouth. It hadn't looked all that appetising in the first place. After tasting it she felt all the praise she could offer was that it was hot. She swallowed it down and responded loudly to make herself heard above the other lunchtime workers. 'Are you referring to the young gentleman I've employed to decorate my living-room?'

'Young gentleman you've employed,' Betty mimicked. 'Oh, excuse me, I fergot yer'd gone up in the world now yer an employer. So, Mrs Deakin, how is your young gentleman getting on?'

Vinnie tutted, hiding a smile. 'He's getting on fine, thank you, Mrs Trubshaw.' Then she grimaced. 'It's funny, but when I first met Shaun I'd a feeling I'd seen him before though for the life of me I can't think where . . . I must be mistaken.'

Betty eyed her in amusement. 'I shouldn't worry too much, ducky, when yer getting old yer memory starts playing tricks on yer. Mind you, young chaps all look the same these days, don't they, with all that hair and their fancy clothes? I bet some mothers can't tell son from friend from a distance, and when their backs are turned I bet some mams even mistake sons for daughters.'

Vinnie laughed. 'I must admit I rather envy the youngsters of today, being able to dress just how they please and in such lovely bright colours. Remember the awful dull shades we had no choice about when we were growing up?'

Betty snorted. 'Don't remind me! I'm older than you so it was even worse for me. It was like we lived in one of them sepia photographs. Brown, brown, and black – if yer were lucky.' She gave a wistful sigh. 'I saw this blouse once in Snelgrove's window. Beautiful it was. Soft pink satin. I'd have given a month's wages for it. I wanted it badly so Alfred could see me looking feminine for a change. But even if I'd had a month's wage ter squander on such a garment, me month's wage wouldn't have paid fer half of it.'

Vinnie's eyes twinkled at her mischievously. 'And them were the days, weren't they, Betty?'

She gave a haughty sniff. 'They had their good points. We might not have had so much spare cash to splash out on frivolities or so much freedom but we never would have back-chatted our parents the way the youngsters do now. We showed respect for our elders or it was a clip around the ear hole. Most of the youngsters these days don't know the meaning of the word respect.' She felt Vinnie herself should know exactly what she was talking about, with the way Julie was acting towards her now, but thought it best not to comment. 'So yer room's coming on fine then, is it?'

'It is, Betty, and I know you're itching to see it. You can as soon as it's finished. If he's not done today, he definitely will be by tomorrow.' Vinnie's attention was suddenly drawn to Ruby sitting next to Betty. She was staring into space looking the picture of misery. 'Er . . . what's wrong with Ruby? She's hardly said a word all dinner break and hasn't touched her food.'

Betty glanced at her. 'She's been funny all morning. I keep asking her what's up but she just sez n'ote is.' She gave Vinnie a knowing grimace. 'Probably having a moody 'cos it's her monthlies.'

Vinnie looked doubtful. 'Ruby isn't prone to moods whatever the time of month.' She looked at the girl in concern. 'Ruby?'

She slowly raised her head and looked at Vinnie blankly. 'Yes, Mrs Deakin?'

'Oh, Ruby,' she lightly scolded. 'We're friends so it's plain old Vinnie off the inspection floor. Excuse me for prying but is there anything wrong, dear?'

'Eh? Oh, no, I'm fine.'

It was obvious she wasn't telling the truth. 'I don't believe you, and neither does Betty. Come on, Ruby love, we're your friends. If there was anything troubling you, you would tell us, surely?'

To Vinnie and Betty's horror, huge tears suddenly spilled down the girl's face and she sobbed, 'It's Warren!

I think he's finished with me.'

Vinnie pulled a clean handkerchief out of the pocket of her forelady's overall and handed it to Ruby. 'Warren?' she queried.

'Spotty Muldoon with the wonky eyes,' Betty mouthed in a whisper to her.

Vinnie gave her a hard nudge in the ribs, annoyed at her reference to the character played by Spike Milligan in The Goons. Warren wasn't a good-looking lad by any means but that taunt was out of order. 'I'm sorry, Ruby, Warren's name had escaped me for the moment. So why do you think he's finished with you? As far as I know, you two were getting on famously.'

'We were,' she blubbered. 'He'd asked me ter marry him.'

'But that's wonderful!' Vinnie exclaimed in delight. Then her face fell in dismay. 'Oh, no, it's not if he's finished with you, is it?'

'So, Ruby, spit it out,' demanded Betty, grimacing as she pushed away her empty plate. 'That cottage pie were bleddy awful. I'm gonna have a word at the next Union meeting about the state of the food this place dishes up.' She looked at Ruby hard. 'Why has the lad proposed then dumped yer? Don't mek sense ter me. Yer didn't turn him down, did yer, and now yer regretting it?'

She shook her head. 'No. I was over the moon when he asked me and said yes straight away. I love him, dun't I?' she uttered, bereft.

Vinnie and Betty looked at each other, bewildered.

'So . . . what's the problem then, Ruby?' Vinnie asked.

She dabbed at her eyes and noisily blew her nose. 'Me mam and dad.'

'Ah, might have known it!' Betty snorted in disgust. 'They don't approve of him, I tek it?'

The girl shook her head. 'No. They said I could do much better fer meself than a packer. Oh, Betty, Vinnie, it were so awful. I told me mam and dad about him and thought they were happy for me 'cos they asked me to invite him round fer tea last night. But as soon as Warren arrived they started on him. Oh, they were so nasty to him I could have died! But he stuck up to them, he did. Told 'em he loved me and wanted ter marry me. He said he'd some money saved for a deposit for the rent. They . . . they . . .'

'Fer God's sake, Ruby, they what?' Betty demanded.

She took a deep breath and, head low, muttered despairingly, 'They asked him what he wanted with a fat ugly thing like me and told him they knew it was 'cos he thought they had money. Then they ordered him out of the house and told him that if they ever found out he was still seeing me they'd get the bobbies on him for pestering me.'

Vinnie's mouth dropped open in shock.

'They what?' Betty roared. 'Right, you go home ternight, Ruby gel, and yer pack yer bags.'

She eyed Betty, bemused. 'Why?'

''Cos yer leaving that hell hole, and not before time,' she hissed.

Ruby looked at her, horrified. 'But I can't. I've nowhere to go. Besides, if I left there'd be no one ter look after me mam and dad.'

'And that's precisely why they've just done what they have. Don't yer see, ducky, it wouldn't matter who yer took home they'd still pick fault. They don't want yer to have anyone else. They want you at home to care for them in their old age. But that ain't gonna happen, ducky, not while I'm living and breathing.'

Vinnie eyed her kindly. 'Betty's right, Ruby love. I know you love them but your parents' aim is to keep you at home. It's very obvious, Ruby.'

'Oh! But if I left where would I go?'

'My house,' said Betty. 'You can stop with me 'til you and Warren get married. I'll happily help yer plan the day and give yer what other help yer need. Be my pleasure it would. And let your parents start on me if they dare 'cos they won't be able to push me around like they do their daughter. Now, the choice is yours, Ruby. Either you stay put and give up any chance of happiness you could hope to have, just stay a drudge fer yer folks, or yer grab this chance to be happy with Warren.'

'But what if he don't want me after what happened? I ain't seen him all morning.'

'If he loves yer, gel, no one, not even yer parents, 'll put him off. Anyway, whether he does or doesn't want yer, yer still coming ter live with me. You've got ter get away from yer folks, Ruby, or yer'll never have any life to speak of and you know it.'

She stared at Betty for several long moments while

what she had been told sank in. Finally she took a deep breath, swallowed hard and said, 'Yer right, I know yer are. Will yer come home with me ternight, Betty, and stay while I pack me stuff?'

Betty grinned. "Course I will. And it'll give me great pleasure to entertain your parents while I'm waiting.'

Just then a tall gangly youth bounded up. 'There yer are, Ruby,' he exclaimed in relief. 'I skived off work this morning and I've bin down the register office. We can get married in three weeks. Yer will still marry me, Ruby?' he begged. 'Please say yer will?'

Betty turned to Vinnie. 'Your new living-room is gonna mek a great venue for an engagement party, ain't it?'

'Why, you've finished!' Vinnie exclaimed that evening as soon as she arrived home from work. She took off her coat and laid it across her arm as she looked around her newly decorated room. Shaun had even put all her furniture back in its place and swept her Hoover Junior across the carpet. 'Oh, it looks lovely, Shaun. You've done me such a wonderful job. It's like a completely different room. The colour of the paper you helped me choose goes perfectly with my suite and carpet. You have such a good eye.'

He wiped his hands on a piece of rag. 'Glad yer like it, Mrs Perkins. There is just one thing I should point out, though.'

She eyed the young man, worried. 'Oh?'

'Well, it's just I had to patch the bit over the door. Yer

can't really tell unless yer get up close and it saved me starting a new roll, which means I only used five and not six. It saved you money.'

'Oh,' she said, relieved. 'Goodness me, I thought you were going to tell me my house was falling down or something.' She gave a warm smile. 'I admire your honesty and I'm sure no one will notice. I wouldn't have myself if you hadn't told me.' She took another look around and beamed in delight. 'Oh, Shaun, I'm so pleased with this job, thank you.'

'My pleasure,' he said, grinning back. 'And if yer decide yer want another room doing then yer know where ter come, and if yer could see yer way ter recommending me to yer friends then I'd appreciate that. I'll just finish packing me tools away, then that's me done.'

A few minutes later she was handing over his payment of twenty pounds: exactly the amount of the collection money. Without checking it, he put it in his pocket. She smiled inwardly. When he got home and counted it out he'd get a nice surprise as she had overpaid him by two pounds in appreciation of his good work. She felt he more than deserved it. As they were making their goodbyes, a sudden knock resounded on the back door and Betty charged in.

'Oh, what a bleddy performance that was,' she breathlessly announced. 'I've left 'em both to it, settling Ruby in my back bedroom, and come round here ter calm meself down. Her parents want bloody locking up, if yer ask me. I've never met such a pair of selfish sods in all me life. That was the right decision, getting her away from them. She's upset at the moment but it won't tek her long ter realise she's done the right thing in coming to me. Oh, hello,' she said to Shaun. 'Vinnie's right. Yer've done a cracking job in here,' she said, looking around admiringly. 'If I ever win the pools I won't hesitate ter get yer in ter see what yer can do with my old place. Anyway,' she said, giving him her full attention, 'how's yer mam? Recovered by now, I hope.'

Vinnie looked at her, surprised. 'Do you know Shaun?'

'Yes . . . well, no, not by name, but you're the young man from the cemetery, ain't yer?' she said to him.

'Oh,' he exclaimed. 'And you're the two ladies who stopped and offered to help me mam. You were right, Mrs Perkins, we had met before. I'm sorry I never recognised you but I was too upset for me mam at the time ter tek much notice of 'ote else.'

'Mrs Perkins?' Betty enquired, looking at her quizzically.

'I'll explain later,' Vinnie whispered back.

'It was good of yer, teking the time to offer to help me mam,' Shaun continued. 'I did appreciate it.'

Betty looked at him sympathetically. 'Just lost yer dad, had yer?'

He frowned at her, surprised. 'How did you know?'

'I didn't. Just guessed by how upset yer mam was that it musta bin someone close. Yer dad was the obvious person.'

His youthful good looks were suddenly replaced by a

scowl. 'You're wrong about him being close, 'cos he wasn't. And by rights me mam should have hated him for what he did to her, but she ain't got a nasty bone in her body.' Then his face filled with remorse. 'I'm sorry, I shouldn't have said that, it's just that that man didn't deserve anyone's sympathy, least of all me mother's.'

'Oh, I see, a blessed release then,' Betty said matter-of-factly.

'I expect it was for his wife.' Shaun looked at Betty and Vinnie, mortified. 'I'm sorry, I never meant ter say that either, only I'm very touchy on the subject of me so-called father.'

'Oh, I see,' said Betty knowingly again. 'He got yer mother in the family way and him already married so she was left on her own?'

'That's about the size of it,' he said gruffly. 'Me mam didn't deserve what he did to her, and if yer ask me she might have had a hard struggle bringing me up but we both agree she had a lucky escape, all things considered. I couldn't understand why she wanted to be at the cemetery when they buried him but she said she just needed to say her goodbyes. Why in God's name I'll never know 'cos that rotter stopped my mother making summat of herself.' He took a deep breath. 'I was loath ter take the job here, Mrs Perkins, but as me mam sez I'm not in any position yet to turn good work away.'

'But why not work here?' Vinnie asked, puzzled.

''Cos he lived around here, that's why, and I didn't want ter bump into any of the family. Well, no point in risking hurt unnecessarily, not to me or to them yer

241

understand, 'cos even if I had come across the family
I'd never had said 'ote, but me mam would have wanted
to know about them out of curiosity and it'd only have
hurt her, dredging up the past.' He looked at them both
uncomfortably. 'Look, I've said more than I meant to, I
do apologise. Yer asked me to do yer decorating, Mrs
Perkins, not listen ter me sordid family history.' Then he
couldn't help but add, 'I do pity his poor wife, 'cos
judging from the newspaper reports he must have led
her a rum life. I'm not saying he deserved ter get himself
murdered but it's my opinion she's better off without
him, like me mother was.'

Vinnie stood staring at him, frozen. Betty too was
looking stunned.

Face a deathly grey, Vinnie asked, 'What was your
father's name, Shaun?'

Betty grabbed her arm and, looking at Shaun, said,
'Excuse us a minute, lad, but I've just remembered
summat urgent I've to tell Mrs D . . . Perkins.' Pulling
Vinnie aside, her face set tight, she warned, 'Leave it,
Vinnie.'

Vinnie shook her head vehemently, pulling her arm
free. 'He's talking about Tommy, I know he is,' she
urgently whispered. 'I need to know, Betty. I have to
know.' She turned her attention back to him and,
taking a very deep breath, asked, 'Are you talking about
Thomas Deakin, Shaun?'

He looked at her for several long moments then
nodded. 'Yer know of him, do yer?'

Heart pounding painfully, she said far more calmly

than she felt, 'I do. As you say, he lived around here.'

He looked at her earnestly. 'As a matter of interest, did his wife know what he was really like?'

'Oh, I think she's beginning to,' was the flat response.

His face twisted in pity. 'I see. His antics are coming to light now he's dead. I tek it she's still finding out things about him, is she?'

'I believe so.'

'She doesn't live around here anymore,' interjected Betty. 'Family moved away after what happened. She was a nice woman,' she said as she placed a warning hand on Vinnie's arm, afraid she might say something she would later regret. 'Up until he died she had no idea what her husband was doing behind her back. It was all such a shock to her. And she certainly had no idea about yer mother or you.'

'How do you know all this?' he insisted.

''Cos I knew Mrs Deakin well and she would have told me. Unlike her husband, Mrs Deakin is an honest, upstanding woman who never did anyone any harm.' Her face became enquiring. 'How . . . er . . . did your mother meet Thomas Deakin?'

Shaun ran his paint-stained hand through thick dark hair as he told the story. 'In a pub where she was working. It was on Walnut Street near the football ground. She'd not long arrived over from Ireland and was paying her own way through college. She was going ter be a top secretary was me mam and she'd 'a' done it too if she hadn't met that man.' He smiled wryly. 'She told me she fell in love with Thomas Deakin the first time she clapped eyes on him over the bar.'

'So it was she who pursued him?' probed Betty.

'Oh, no,' he vehemently insisted. 'It was him that made all the running. My mam was only seventeen and, as she put it, very naïve where men were concerned. Thomas Deakin kept on at her to take a walk with him after her shift was finished. She reminded him he was going to the match. He laughed and said she was worth giving up a football match for. She was flattered by his attentions and finally gave in. As they strolled down by the canal he stopped and without any warning kissed her. She said that sealed her fate. He told her he worked in a factory on twelve-hour shifts which meant he could only see her once or occasionally twice a week, sometimes not even that. Me mam didn't care as long as she saw him. She even swapped her stints at the pub and sometimes missed college too so she wouldn't lose a chance of being with him.' He lowered his voice gruffly. 'She thought she'd met the man of her dreams and would spend the rest of her life with him.'

'And when she told him she was expecting his child, she never saw him again?' guessed Betty.

He looked at her hard. 'How did you know?'

She leaned over and patted his arm. 'It's a classic tale, Shaun lad. Yer mam ain't the first to have fallen unawares for a married man, and she won't be the last.'

He gave a deep sigh. 'No, I expect not. She was terrified. She was alone in a strange country and couldn't go home with this shame on her. She tried desperately to find him, went to the factory where he'd

said he worked but they said they'd never heard of him
and she thought it was her that'd got the name of the
place wrong. For a long time she prayed he'd turn up
with a good excuse for his absence, but when he never
she assumed summat had happened to him, like he'd
had a crippling accident or even a fatal one. It was such
a hard struggle for her, trying to look after me and
work to support us both.

'Then she met Terry, who's bin a great dad to me, and
with his love and care managed to put it all behind her
until she read of Thomas Deakin's murder in the paper.
That brought it all back. Me mam was devastated,
finding out after all these years that he was married
while he was seeing her and that his wife must have
given birth to their first child when she was carrying me.
She said she felt very sorry for his wife, who probably
didn't know what he was getting up to behind her back.
But it was me she felt for most, finding out that the man
who'd fathered me was rotten to the core. I'm just glad I
never met up with him because if I had I'd have told
him exactly what I thought of him.'

Vinnie swallowed hard to rid herself of a huge lump
of distress that was lodged in her throat. 'I'm so sorry,'
she uttered.

He looked at her, bemused. 'Why should you be
sorry, Mrs Perkins? This ain't n'ote ter do with you.'

'No, it ain't,' interjected Betty before Vinnie could
respond. 'But she's a woman and feels fer what yer mam
had to go through.'

He gave a proud smile. 'All credit to me mam, she

managed and I never went without food or a roof
over me head. She's happy with Terry now and he's
good to her and to me too so it's all turned out all
right. Terry doesn't know Mam went to the cemetery
that day and I warned her it's best he doesn't. It
would hurt him so much if he thought for a minute
me mam still had any feelings for the man who
fathered me. But she ain't, as I said earlier, she just
needed to say her goodbyes, for my sake not her own.
I wouldn't go, you see. Well, why should I want to pay
my respects to a man who caused me mam such
misery? Mind you, she's always telling me that her
pain was all worth it because she got me.' He suddenly
paused, looking at them both uncomfortably. 'I've . . .
er . . . never told anyone any of this before. I just tell
them me dad died before I was born. Terry's me dad
as far as I'm concerned.'

Betty smiled kindly at him. 'Best that way, love. Yer
secret's safe with us. We don't see any of the Deakin
family now.'

He flashed her a grateful smile. 'I'd best be off. Me
mam'll be wondering where I am. Nice to have met yer,'
he said to Betty. 'And yer know where ter find me
should you need any more work done, Mrs Perkins.'

'I'll see yer out,' said Betty, accompanying him to the
door.

After shutting the door behind him she returned to
the front room and looked at Vinnie worriedly. She was
still standing where she had been, staring blindly into
space.

'I don't know what ter say, Vinnie lovey, really I don't.'

Vinnie slowly turned her head to look at her friend, face devoid of any expression. 'What else, Betty? What else am I going to find out about Tommy?'

She gave a helpless shrug. 'N'ote, I hope.'

Vinnie walked across to the window and gazed out down the yard. 'I cannot believe that lovely young lad is Tommy's son. He looks nothing like him, does he, except that he's tall like Tommy was. I just hope to God he hasn't inherited any of his other traits. From what I got to know of him he doesn't seem to have, thank goodness.' She took a deep shuddering breath as she turned to face her friend. 'Oh, Betty, what kind of man would leave a woman to fend for herself, knowing she was carrying his child with no one to turn to? How did he sleep at night, knowing he had a child growing up without any knowledge of his own father?'

Betty rushed over and threw her arms around her, pulling her close. 'Some men have no conscience, Vinnie, and it seems your Tommy was one of them. Whether he was just highly sexed or loved the danger of what he was doing, we'll never know. One thing is for certain. If yer've any feelings left for Thomas Deakin then he doesn't deserve 'em,' she hissed. 'He didn't deserve a woman like you, full stop, Vinnie.'

She pulled away from Betty and looked her straight in the eye. 'That's just it, Betty. It's that boy's mother I feel for. For Tommy I feel nothing. Nothing at all. I'm just numb. I should hate him, I suppose. Detest him.

After all he's done to me I should feel something, shouldn't I?'

Face grim, Betty shook her head. 'I think it's a good thing yer don't. You've spent enough time mourning that man. He was what I'd call a Jekyll and Hyde character. You only saw the good side. The other he very cleverly hid.'

Vinnie sighed heavily. 'At least I know that poor woman has fared all right and her son turned into a well-adjusted young man.' She looked at Betty meaningfully. 'Maybe he's done better than he would have if Tommy had been around. I mean, look how my two girls turned out.' Then her face filled with shame. 'Betty, I feel so bad lying to Shaun.'

'It was for the best, Vinnie. What good would it have done him, knowing who you really were or the fact that he had sisters who never even knew about him? Julie took her father's death badly enough, she'd never cope with this on top. Vinnie lovey, this is summat that goes no further than these walls. I'll never breathe a word to anyone and you must do the same.'

She looked at her friend for several long moments, then issued a deep sigh. 'You're right, Betty, I know you are.'

Betty sadly shook her head. 'I just wish I'd never come here ternight and then this wouldn't have come out.' She eyed Vinnie worriedly. 'This ain't gonna set you back, is it?'

'No, I'm determined not to let it. I could tie myself up in knots for the rest of my life, trying to fathom why

Tommy felt the need to live his double life, but what would be the point? He's not here now and I have a few good years left, I hope. I want to make the best of them. What I'm going to concentrate on is finding a way of bringing myself and Julie back together and making sure she finds out nothing about this. Even being on speaking terms with her would be something. You know I never give up hoping Janie will return too. My dream is that we'll all be reunited.' Vinnie took a deep breath and planted a smile on her face. 'Now, I believe we've an engagement party to organise and, as you said, Betty, my new room will make the ideal setting.'

Chapter Eighteen

Vinnie's head was pounding. After swallowing two aspirin she drank down the rest of the water, then leaning back against the sink, placed the cold glass against her aching forehead. She hadn't realised she had drunk so much, but she must have to have such a hangover. Whatever she was suffering this morning, though, it was all worth it.

Ruby and Warren's engagement party had been a huge success. At least forty friends and relatives of the happy couple had gladly accepted their invitation, wanting to express delight at this future union. Vinnie had never seen Ruby so happy as she was last night, and Warren was the person who had brought this about. The young couple were determined to marry with or without Ruby's parents' blessing.

Vinnie's eyes travelled around the small kitchen, taking in the chaos that reigned, knowing that the sitting-room was as bad. Regardless, her cleaning chores would be pleasurable. Her thoughts flew back to the previous evening. The table had been laden with party food, bottles of drink and a keg of beer; the record player boomed out popular music, and good humour prevailed. Vinnie, determined to put the trauma of the last few months behind her, had enjoyed every minute as she laughed and danced along with the rest of the revellers, as sad as they were when the evening had drawn to a close and they all trooped home, she to retire upstairs to her lonely bed. The mess she faced this morning had, she felt, been worth all the time and effort.

Vinnie's only surprise of the evening was that, although asked to come via a note pushed through the letter box, only Eric from the Adler household had shown his face. Barry staying away she could understand as he was young and arrangements with his own friends would take priority, but Noreen was a different matter. She loved a good party, and was usually the last to leave. Eric, somewhat embarrassed, had told Vinnie she had chosen to go out with her friend over attending the party. Secretly Vinnie was relieved. Whenever Noreen was in a crowd an argument erupted and she was the cause of it. Vinnie did feel sorry for Eric, being on his own, but regardless he'd seemed to enjoy himself.

She had just finished straightening the living-room when there was a knock on the back door and Gary walked in. She knew instantly that something was dreadfully wrong. Her heart pounded. Before her stood a broken man.

'What on earth is it?' she demanded, grabbing his arm and sitting him down at the table in the back room.

He looked up at her, dazed, giving a helpless shrug. 'I'm so sorry,' he uttered.

Her worry turned to dread. 'Sorry for what, Gary?' she urged.

Bewildered, he shook his head. 'I can't go on, Mrs Deakin. I love her so much but she's destroying me. This morning was the final straw. I couldn't believe it when I found it, and when I tackled her about it she just laughed and told me not to be so stingy. Me, stingy, Mrs Deakin! Julie's had everything she ever wanted, I'd give her the moon if I could afford it, but someone has to be firm or else where will we be?'

'What did you find, Gary?'

'A letter she'd stuffed at the back of the kitchen drawer, hoping I wouldn't find it. I only did because I'd cut my finger and was looking for a plaster.'

'And why did this letter upset you so much?' she asked, her mind racing frantically. Was it a love letter from another man?

He took a deep breath. 'It was from Lewis's department store, addressed to us both, informing us we could have three hundred pounds' credit.' He issued a despondent sigh. 'Spending all her wages on things she doesn't need isn't enough for her, now she has to spend money we haven't got. After all my talking to her, explaining that if she doesn't cut back we'll end up in terrible financial trouble, she took no notice. She forged my signature on the application papers, Mrs Deakin. That was wrong, she shouldn't have done it, and it was because she knew I'd say no.' He wrung his hands, his head drooping. 'We're not a proper married couple really, Mrs Deakin. Julie does what she wants, when she wants. I might as well not be there apart from the fact that she needs me for the money I bring home.'

Vinnie's face drained the colour of his and inside her temper flared. She dashed across to the door and grabbed her coat. 'Make yourself a cup of tea, or if you prefer there's some drink left from Ruby and Warren's engagement party. I won't be long.'

He eyed her, confused. 'Where are you going?'

'To do something I should have done a long time ago.'

A stony-faced Julie answered the door to her mother. 'You're not welcome here,' she hissed, seeing who her visitor was.

'I don't give a damn,' Vinnie responded icily, pushing past her daughter and on into the living-room where she turned to face Julie who had followed her through. 'Sit down,' she commanded. 'You and I need to talk, and by God, girl, you will listen to me.'

At her tone a visibly shaken Julie immediately sat down.

Vinnie took up position before her. 'Julie, you have pulled some tricks to get your own way but this latest stunt takes some beating. What on earth do you think you're playing at?'

'I don't know what you're talking about!' she snapped defensively.

'Yes, you do,' her mother shot back, wagging her

finger in a warning gesture, face contorted angrily. 'Gary loves you with all his heart. He would give you the world if it was in his power. But I know a man at the end of his tether and that man is now sitting in my kitchen deciding his future. And as things stand, I severely doubt that future includes you in it.' She saw her daughter's face turn ashen. 'That's right, Julie, he's had enough of your treatment of him and loving you isn't enough to excuse this latest trick you've pulled. What on earth made you think he'd stomach landing in the bankruptcy court just because you wanted . . .' She flashed her eyes around the room. 'What exactly was it you were going to squander three hundred pounds on, Julie? Look around you. This house is like a little palace. You've more than most women ever acquire the whole of their married lives. You've more clothes in your wardrobe than you could possibly wear.'

She paused momentarily to draw breath and continued, 'It isn't just your mindless spending, Julie, it's the way you treat him too. You act like he's your personal slave, and when you feel he's done something that you don't agree with, you speak to him like an imbecile. You even blame him for things he couldn't possibly have played a part in. He's your husband, Julie. Someone you promised to honour and respect, not treat like something you've dragged through the house stuck to your shoe. I know how your cutting tongue has hurt me more times than I care to remember, so I dread to think how Gary has felt after one of your childish tantrums.

'Now you listen to me, and if you care one bit for

your husband or the survival of your marriage take notice of what I'm saying. Gary is in my kitchen and if you have any sense at all you'll go to him now and beg his forgiveness, make him believe you'll really change your ways. The first thing you should do is rip up that letter from Lewis's, in front of him too, and tell him that for the foreseeable future you'll hand your wages over to him until he knows he can trust you not to waste them.'

Julie jumped up to stand before her mother, thrusting her face into hers. 'You've no right to talk to me like this when you treated my father the way you did,' she spat. 'It was *your* fault he turned to another woman.' And, arms flailing wildly, she added, 'It's *your* fault he's dead.'

Vinnie's face darkened. 'Whether you believe it or not, I was a good wife to your father in every way. He wanted for nothing from me. I loved him more than life itself. If me giving my all wasn't enough for him then that wasn't my fault but his. I can't tell you why he was like he was because I don't understand it myself.' She paused, her mind whirling, trying to be very careful what she said next. After all, Tommy was Julie's father and she didn't want to blacken his memory more than was necessary. 'Now I know you blame me for your father's death because you cannot accept the fact that he wasn't the perfect man you like to think he was. But, whether you like it or not, your father is mostly responsible for the way you are now. He made it blatantly obvious you were his favourite daughter, he turned his back on Janie and centred all his attention on you. He bought your love by giving in to every demand you made while I had no choice but to stand by and watch him do it. He wanted you to idolise him, Julie, and he achieved that, didn't he? But what he also achieved was turning you into a selfish brat. I was the villain of the piece because I challenged his actions and was firmer with you, but even I gave in to you sometimes because I couldn't stand the atmosphere you created when I didn't. If you're honest with yourself you'll look back and see just how it all was and how it is now.'

Vinnie took a deep breath. 'You've made your feelings for me very clear, but that doesn't stop me from loving you and so much it breaks my heart to see what you've turned into. But it's not too late to put it right. If you're sensible you'll push your misguided feelings for me aside and take notice of what I've said. If you don't do something now, Julie, you risk losing everything. Your husband most certainly. Now, I've said what I came to and I'm going to see Betty. I shan't be home for at least another hour. The rest is up to you.'

'I shouldn't have been so hard on her,' Vinnie said to her friend a short while later.

'Yes, yer should. It's about time that girl had a severe talking to and you're the one to do it, Vinnie, you're her mother. Yer weren't hard enough, if yer want my opinion. She needs a good spanking, treating Gary like that. But ter me it's the way she's treating you that hurts the most. Still, let's hope the gel is sensible and teks heed of what yer said. And it's no good you sitting there worrying yerself witless, yer can't do no more than yer have. The rest is up to Julie now. If Gary wants no more ter do with her then it's her own fault, ducky. But let's hope that's not the case, eh? Now, another cuppa? And if yer lucky,' she added, going over to her pantry and rifling through the items stacked on a shelf, 'I've a packet of ginger nuts somewhere.'

A while later Vinnie hesitantly opened her back door, unsure what she would find, and got the shock of her life to see who was waiting for her.

Her face puffy and blotched from crying, Julie looked at her mother hesitantly as she entered. A stunned Vinnie looked back at her, her mind racing frantically as all sorts of reasons for her daughter's presence and distressed state occurred to her.

It was Julie who spoke first. She came over to her mother, her face wreathed in shame. 'Hello, Mum,' she said softly.

Vinnie was stunned by such a pleasant ordinary greeting and then to her surprise she felt the tears start to flow. Automatically her arms opened wide and she gathered her daughter to her. 'Oh, Julie love, Julie love,' was all she could whisper. The girl wept in her arms. Finally she stopped and, after tenderly kissing her forehead, Vinnie held her at arm's length. The look she gave her daughter then left her in no doubt how much her mother loved her. 'Cup of tea?' Vinnie asked.

Wiping her eyes, Julie nodded. 'Yes, please, but you sit down while I make it.'

Vinnie hoped she managed to hide her shock at such an uncharacteristic offer. Sitting down at the table, she watched in silence as her daughter made the tea. Presently a steaming cup was put before her and Julie sat down opposite.

Taking a sip of her own tea, Julie then cradled the cup in her hands and looked at her mother expectantly. 'How do I begin to tell you how sorry I am for how I've been? Is it too much to ask if you can ever forgive me, Mum?'

Vinnie's heart leaped for joy. 'Mothers are very good at forgiving daughters anything, Julie love. When I came to see you earlier all I was concerned about was you sorting your marriage out. I never dared hope we might sort out our differences too.'

Julie put her cup down and took a deep breath before she spoke. 'I have to be honest, Mum, and say that I was very angry with the way you spoke to me earlier. I just thought, Who does she think she is, using any excuse to have a go at me? I never thought for a minute you were right about Gary. I came around here to give him a piece of my mind and . . . oh, Mum . . .' Renewed tears of distress pricked her eyes. 'I couldn't believe it when he told me our marriage was over, that he couldn't go on living with me like I was any longer. He really went for me, Mum. Tore me to shreds. Told me how selfish I was, and that it was a wonder I had anyone left who cared for me after the way I treated them. He said the only friends I had now were the ones that stuck with me because they hadn't as yet suffered one of my tantrums. I couldn't believe Gary was being so horrible to me. I was shocked. Then everything you'd said came back to me.

'Something happened to me then, Mum. It was so weird. It was as if I was standing outside my own body looking back and seeing myself for the very first time.' She gave a deep shudder. 'I didn't like what I saw, Mum, and I knew then that you and Gary were speaking the truth. I'm a horrible person. I don't know why I feel I can just do what I like and not care about anyone's feelings. I don't know why I spend money like I do. I suppose it makes me feel good somehow, I don't understand it myself. Dad used to tell me I could have anything I ever wanted and he forgave me everything so I just thought Gary should treat me the same. Gary tried to talk to me about it but I wouldn't listen.' Her whole body sagged despairingly. 'I don't deserve anyone's love, let alone the two people who mean everything to me.'

Vinnie looked at her questioningly. 'Is one of those two me?' she whispered.

'Oh, yes,' Julie insisted, and flashed her mother a look of remorse. 'I've always loved you, Mum, I just never showed it. I preferred Dad when I was a kid because he was the one who gave me what I wanted, and the more I showed that it was him I loved best the better he seemed to like it, so that's what I did. I don't know why he preferred me to Janie. She was so much prettier than me and cleverer too. All I know is that he suddenly started giving me all his attention when Janie started having her funny moods, and it just stayed like that.'

She eyed Vinnie earnestly. 'Mum, I know how much you loved Dad but I was jealous of you. You had a part of him that I didn't, and I didn't like it. That's why I was nasty to you. I'm ashamed to say that I liked the fact that what I was doing hurt you. I can't describe how I felt when he died but the worst of it was that he'd been seeing another woman who was practically the same age as me. I was so angry she'd stolen him from me. I blamed you, Mum, because . . . because I wanted it to be your fault, because I couldn't believe my dad would do something like that. But I knew deep down you'd nothing to do with it. You were a good wife to him, I realise that.' She looked at Vinnie and uttered, bereft, 'No matter what he did to us both, I still love him so much, Mum.'

'I know, love,' Vinnie whispered back. 'I do too.'

Julie looked at her incredulously. 'Even now, after you've found out what he was doing behind your back?'

She gave a distant smile. 'I loved the side of your father he allowed me to see. I'll always love that Tommy.' She looked at her daughter tenderly. 'I'm learning to forgive and forget, Julie, and move on, and that's what you must do. What's the saying? Out with the old, in with the new.'

'But what about me, Mum? Can you really still love me after everything I've put you through?' she implored.

Vinnie leaped up from her seat and rushed over to

her, throwing her arms around her in a bear hug. 'Oh, Julie, of course I can. Nobody's perfect, we all make mistakes. When you were born I held you in my arms and promised you I'd be the best mother I possibly could be. Loving you regardless of what you threw at me was part of that promise.'

Julie swallowed back a sob. 'Oh, Mum, you've more than fulfilled your promise to me. Now I have to make a promise to you. I will change, I desperately want to, but I'll need your help.'

'And you'll have it, that's goes without saying, love.'

Julie smiled tenderly at her. 'I want to be a daughter you're proud of.'

'I'm proud of you already.'

'No, you can't be, not the way I've acted. I cringe now when I think of some of the things I've said and done.'

'Forgive and forget, Julie, out with the old, in with the new. Isn't that what we agreed upon?' Mischief glinted in Vinnie's eyes. 'But if I do ever see you slipping back, rest assured I'll tell you.' She took a deep breath and asked something she was desperate to know the answer to. 'Julie, how are things between you and Gary now?'

The girl took a shuddering breath. 'I did what you advised me and, oh, I'm so thankful I did! He's going to give me another chance.'

Vinnie exhaled loudly in relief. 'Oh, I'm so glad.'

'So am I, Mum,' her daughter said with conviction. 'I never realised before just how much I love him. The thought of losing him . . . well, I couldn't bear it. I needed a good kick up the backside, didn't I, Mum? You and Gary between you certainly did that.'

Vinnie smiled tenderly at her. 'Where is he now?'

'He suggested he went home so you and I could talk.'

'He's a very thoughtful man, Julie.'

'Yes. I'm lucky, aren't I, having you both? There are some things it's best to forget but I must never forget that.'

Vinnie stared at her thoughtfully. She was having difficulty believing that this was the same girl who'd given out a tongue lashing and stamped her foot in temper whenever anyone said something she didn't agree with. The shock of possibly losing all that was important to her had certainly done the trick. She watched as Julie rose and put on her coat.

'Come on then, Mum,' she said.

Vinnie eyed her, confused. 'Sorry? Come where?'

Julie looked at her lovingly. 'Gary and I are going to toast our future and we can't do that properly without you being there, can we?'

Feeling that a huge weight had been lifted from her shoulders, Vinnie put on her coat. She sneaked a quick glance at Julie, waiting for her by the door. Maybe, she thought, some good would come from Tommy's death after all.

Chapter Nineteen

'I'm so sorry if this is short notice, Mrs Deakin, but I only got the message myself a few minutes ago. You know what it's like. The bosses organise these things and forget to inform the workers.' Keith Hamlin looked at her most apologetically. 'It should only be for an hour or so, definitely no longer.'

Vinnie gnawed her bottom lip anxiously. She had never been into the boardroom before. Never been personally introduced to the great man or his two sons. Now here she was, being summoned for a glass of sherry by way of thanks for her contribution towards improving standards in the inspection department. Several other people from different departments would be there too. Vinnie knew she should feel pleased the hierarchy were acknowledging their contributions towards the company's overall upsurge in prosperity, but the thought of having to mix with people well above her station terrified her witless.

She realised Keith was waiting for her acceptance and gulped in trepidation.

He sensed why Vinnie was so reluctant. She was unused to occasions like this, to having to make small talk with so-called superiors who in truth were no better than she was. Vinnie was afraid she'd say or do something that would make her look silly. He knew she wouldn't. He had faith Vinnie could carry herself through any occasion. Like her, though, he didn't relish the thought of attending the celebration, but not for the same reasons. For him the prospect of being in a social situation with the woman he purposely did all he could to avoid on a personal level was bothering him greatly. He desperately wanted to rush to her now, cradle her protectively in his arms, allay all her fears, assure her that she was safe with him by her side. He groaned inwardly. If only he could! He just hoped he could get through the next hour without letting himself down.

'It wouldn't look good if you refused, Mrs Deakin,' he forced himself to say. 'If it's any consolation, all the managers of the individual departments concerned have been requested to attend with the staff members commended for their efforts, so I'll be there with you for moral support should you need it.'

That last statement made her feel worse. Never at ease in her manager's company due to his reticence with her, how could she bring herself to ask for his help should she require it? She wished Betty was going with her. She knew, though, that she had no choice about attending. As Keith Hamlin had said, she was expected to accept this invitation. She just wished she was wearing something more suitable underneath her forelady's overall than a simple skirt and blouse, and had taken more trouble with her hair that morning.

'Five o'clock sharp you said, Mr Hamlin?'

He nodded. 'As soon as the hooter blows we're expected to make our way up to the boardroom.'

She flashed him a quick smile. 'I'll make sure I finish on time then.'

'Oh, Vinnie, it's an honour, yer can't get away from that,' Betty said to her minutes later after she had told her friend of her summons to the boardroom. 'It's about time that what us lot on the factory floor do to mek the company successful is recognised.' She looked at Vinnie hard, knowing what was going through her mind. 'Eh, and don't you ever forget that you're as good, if not better than, anyone else who'll be there, so fer God's sake tek that look of doom off yer face.'

'But just look at me, Betty. I'm like a tramp.'

Betty eyed her scornfully. 'Yer not. A bit of lipstick and a brush through yer hair and you'll look fine.'

'But what if I say something I shouldn't and make a fool of myself?'

'Like what?'

She gave a shrug. 'I don't know.'

'God'strewth, Vinnie, yer ain't gonna be introduced ter the Queen. Just 'cos Cyril Brewin inherited this factory don't mek him Lord Muck. His father started the business in a shed at the bottom of his yard, so when it all comes down to it Cyril and his sons are no better than us. Mark my words, it'll be a handshake, glass of sherry and bit a cake if yer lucky, then yer'll be shoved out the boardroom before yer know it so Cyril Brewin can get off to his gentlemen's club.'

'If they do have cake bring us back a bit, Vinnie,' said Ruby, coming up to join them.

Betty shot her a scathing look. 'At the mention of food yer've ears like radar. Cake is off the menu for you for the time being, Ruby. Have you forgotten you've a wedding dress to get into?'

Vinnie smiled at the girl. 'If they have cake and I can possibly smuggle some out for you, I will.' She took a deep breath. 'You're right, Betty. I'm making too much of this. I should enjoy the occasion, shouldn't I?'

'Yer should. It's about time yer got some proper praise fer all the difference yer've made in this department since yer took over. Eh, and don't forget to mention us lot.'

'If I get a chance, of course I will, Betty. I would never be able to do my job properly if it weren't for the support you all give me.'

At five o'clock prompt Vinnie presented herself in Keith Hamlin's office. His immediate thought was how lovely she looked in her crisp white blouse and turquoise skirt, its straight style hugging her shapely hips. He'd opened his mouth to compliment her when he realised it wouldn't do and instead said, 'Ah, there you are, Mrs Deakin.' His tone was stiff. 'I'll be with you in a jiffy.'

She watched him as he took off his factory white coat

and slipped on the suit jacket he kept hanging on the office door. He looked very smart, she thought. Obviously his wife took great care of him judging by his immaculately ironed shirt and pressed suit. The fact that she was wearing her working clothes struck Vinnie forcibly then and she hoped she wouldn't be an embarrassment to him; that the other staff, especially senior management, wouldn't think Keith Hamlin's girls were a slovenly lot.

About thirty people were gathered in the boardroom, milling around in small groups, and as they entered a glass of sherry was pressed into Vinnie's hand by one of the junior secretaries. She immediately noted that most of the factory floor staff were dressed no better than she, several in fact still wearing their overalls, and felt herself relax a little. Taking a sip of her drink, she looked around. This room was starkly different from the white-painted brick room where she worked.

Oak panelling lined the walls and in pride of place hung a huge portrait of the late founder of the company. At the two full-length windows overlooking the small grassy area of the factory courtyard were expensive velvet curtains. In the middle of the thickly carpeted room stood a huge highly polished mahogany table with at least twelve leather chairs positioned around it. At the head of the table a group of smartly suited men she presumed were the owner, his sons and senior management were sipping drinks and talking amongst themselves. She couldn't see any sign of food and knew Ruby was going to be disappointed when she went into work the next morning with no cake.

Vinnie glanced up at her boss. 'What happens now?' she whispered to him.

'We stand around looking as though we're enjoying ourselves. Don't forget to act honoured when Mr Brewin greets you.'

'I hope my knees have stopped knocking by then.'

Without thinking Keith responded, 'If you're nervous picture him sitting on the toilet, it always works for me.'

Vinnie looked at him, astounded. She hadn't realised before that Keith had a sense of humour as he was always so formal with her. What he had said really tickled her and she was having a job not to laugh out loud.

He suddenly eyed her, mortified. 'I'm sorry, Mrs Deakin, I shouldn't have said that.'

She smiled up at him. 'I'm glad you did. I was feeling nervous but you've made me realise that we're all the same underneath so I've nothing to be nervous of, have I? The worst Mr Brewin could do is sack me.'

'What, and lose one of his best assets, Vinnie? I hardly think so.'

She stared at him, taken aback. That was the first time he had ever addressed her by her Christian name and she wondered if he'd realised.

Intermittently several other departmental managers came over to speak to Keith and each time he politely introduced her to them. Vinnie wondered if it was her imagination but each time she felt his manner to be that of someone who was proud she was with him.

Finally Cyril Brewin made his way around to them, accompanied by his middle-aged secretary, a very efficient-looking woman wearing a severe tweed suit and sensible brogue shoes, her greying hair styled in a short straight bob.

Cyril shook Keith's hand. 'Hamlin, how are you?'

'I'm very well, sir, thank you.'

Cyril Brewin withdrew his hand and looked at Vinnie. 'So this is the lady whose praises you've been singing?'

Embarrassment tinged his cheeks. 'Well, Mrs Deakin deserves it after all the difference she's made to the department since she was promoted to forelady.'

'As you have told us on numerous occasions,' he said to Keith, a twinkle of amusement sparkling in his aged eyes. 'You have a champion in your boss,' Cyril Brewin said to Vinnie.

She glanced at Keith, surprised, then settled her attention on the owner of the company. 'I couldn't do my job properly without the support of the people I have working with me, Mr Brewin. They're the ones who deserve the real praise.'

'The results speak for themselves,' said Cyril, smiling at her winningly. 'But I'm a great believer in the fact that a good leader breeds a happy workforce. A few more like you on board, Mrs Deakin, and we'll be giving the bosses at Corah's factory a few sleepless nights.' He turned to his secretary and she handed him an envelope which he then held out towards Vinnie.

'Just a token of our appreciation, Mrs Deakin. Please also pass word to your staff that their hard work has been noticed and their reward will be a bigger share of the half-yearly bonus.'

With that he moved away.

Vinnie looked down at the envelope in her hand with surprise.

'Aren't you going to open it?' suggested Keith.

'Er . . . yes.' She did so and gasped. 'It's a ten-pound note!'

He looked surprised himself. 'Goodness, that's more than half a week's wage!' he exclaimed. 'Business must be even better than I thought. Well, you could buy yourself a nice outfit with that and still have change for something for the house.'

She smiled at him. 'I know exactly what I'm going to do with this, Mr Hamlin.' The girls would love the luxury biscuits and chocolates this money would buy and share them amongst themselves.

He smiled back. 'Obviously something that's going to give you great pleasure, judging by the look on your face.' Oh, such a lovely face, he thought.

At the way he was staring at her, Vinnie felt a tide of embarrassment creeping up her neck and wondered if her boss realised that from where she stood it appeared he was looking at her in an affectionate way. Then she inwardly scolded herself. It was just her imagination caused by a glass of sherry on an empty stomach and the situation they were in. She hurriedly averted her gaze, looking around the room, pretending to take great interest in what was going on. Nothing was really, except for a portly middle-aged man standing by the drinks table who Vinnie didn't recognise – which was not surprising considering the size of the workforce. He was greedily helping himself to glass after glass of sherry. All the others were looking bored, glancing at the clock, and some were discreetly making an exit.

Keith looked at his watch. In fact he was immensely enjoying being in such close proximity to Vinnie in a congenial situation and felt sad that it was about time to go. Maybe it was a good thing, though, because he was having real difficulty keeping a check on his resolve not to be too demonstrative towards her. He was fully aware that he'd already made slips at least twice but hopefully Vinnie hadn't noticed. He was just about to suggest they leave when the portly man was upon them, obviously the worse for his consumption of drink.

'It's just suddenly struck me who you are,' he said, eyeing Vinnie intently through bleary piggy eyes. 'You're Tommy Deakin's wife. You are, ain't yer?' He leeringly looked her up and down. 'I think meself the man musta bin mad, carrying on like he did with summat like you waiting fer him at home.'

'That's enough from you,' Keith ordered him stonily.

Swaying dangerously, he sneered at Keith. 'And who the hell are you ter be ordering me about? You ain't my manager.' He shoved his face close to Vinnie, the alcoholic stench of his breath making her stomach churn. 'How about me and you gerring out of here? I know a quiet pub where we can get friendly.' He looked at her suggestively. 'Tommy's bin gone a while now, ain't he? I bet you're gagging fer a good night out and I'm just the man ter give yer one.'

'I said, that's enough,' hissed Keith, putting a protective arm around Vinnie, aiming to steer her away from this odious man.

But he wasn't going to give up that easily. He grabbed her arm and yanked her to him. 'Let the lady speak for herself. So how about it then?'

Before Vinnie could respond Keith had stepped between them, forcing the man's hand from her arm. 'I said, leave it,' he commanded. 'Now if you know what's good for you, I suggest you go home,' he angrily hissed, giving the other man a push.

The man steadied his stance, looking at them both, and a knowing grin split his podgy face. 'Oh, I see what's going on.' He fixed his eyes on Keith. 'She's already spoken for by you, ain't she?'

A deep anger exploded within him. 'How dare you insult Vin . . . Mrs Deakin like that?' And before he could stop himself he clenched his fist, swung back his arm and was just about to punch the man's chin when a hand gripped his arm. 'Don't, Mr Hamlin. You'll be sacked if you do.'

Eyes dark with fury looked at Vinnie.

'Please, Mr Hamlin, don't,' she begged. 'He's not worth getting into trouble for. Please let's go before anyone else notices what's going on. Please, Mr Hamlin.'

Just then another man arrived next to them. He

addressed the inebriated man in annoyance. 'Potter, you're drunk,' he accused. 'I warned you to behave yourself and you promised me you would. Don't you know the difference between a thank you drink and a booze up?'

Potter looked at him defiantly. 'So I've had a couple, Mr Percival. So what?'

'You've had more than a couple,' the man accused. Mr Percival glanced apologetically at Keith. 'I'm sorry if Potter's made a nuisance of himself. There's always one who takes liberties and it had to be someone from my department.'

'I'd get him home, Brian, if I were you. And an apology is in order to Mrs Deakin here,' Keith said sharply.

'I've n'ote to apologise for,' Potter snarled. 'I was only asking her out for a drink. No law against that, is there?' He thrust his face close to Vinnie again. 'So are we on then?'

Mr Percival grabbed his arm and pulled him aside. 'Enough, man,' he demanded. 'I'll see he apologises to you later, Mrs Deakin.'

Keith gave Potter a murderous look before taking Vinnie's arm and leading her away. They were out in the car park before he stopped and looked at her.

'I'm sorry,' he blurted.

'There's no need for you to be sorry, Mr Hamlin. It was Mr Potter who was out of order.' She smiled at him gratefully. 'Thank you for what you did.'

He cleared his throat, shuffling uncomfortably on his

feet, looking across the car park. 'I'm your boss, Mrs Deakin, it's my duty to . . . er . . . protect my staff.'

Yes, that was true, bosses were supposed to look out for their staff but it suddenly struck Vinnie that Keith Hamlin's whole manner during the Potter incident had been much more than that of a boss protecting one of his female staff members from the insulting behaviour of a drunken man. Keith had acted more like an angry lover or husband . . . no, more than angry, he'd been incensed that Mr Potter had had the audacity to treat her like that. And then there was the familiar way he'd acted towards her during the occasion itself, so unlike his normal behaviour.

She stared at him, bewildered, and suddenly it all became clear. She had got it all wrong. Keith Hamlin didn't dislike her at all. He liked her, and something told her it was more than like! If she was not mistaken Keith was in love with her.

Oh, God, it all made sense now – why he'd always acted uncomfortably when in her company. He was afraid he would let his feelings show. Well, without realising it, tonight he had. But what shocked Vinnie more than the realisation of how Keith felt for her was that she didn't mind, was in fact very flattered he should feel this way. But she didn't like him, did she? Or had she only told herself that because she had thought he didn't like her? Oh, God, she was so confused she couldn't think straight.

'Look, I . . . er . . . must get home,' she blurted.

Go home. That was the last thing he wanted her to do, but in reality it was probably best that she did. 'Er . . . yes. I'll see you tomorrow. Good night then, Mrs Deakin.' He made to rush away towards his car, then male chivalry reasserted itself. 'Mrs Deakin, the least I can do is run you home.'

Oh, no, she couldn't sit in a car with him, not now she suspected what she did. 'Thanks for the offer but I'll be fine. The walk will do me good.'

Common sense told him he shouldn't press the point but he couldn't let Vinnie walk home alone because then he wouldn't be able to rest for worrying that something had happened to her. What if Potter was lurking somewhere? 'But it's dark and by the looks of it it's going to rain any minute. Please let me run you home? It's no trouble really.'

Her response was frenzied. 'No, no,' she cried. 'I . . . get car sick.'

Her excuse was so lame it suddenly struck him that Vinnie didn't want to get in the car with him. Was she afraid to be alone with him for some reason? His mind whirled frantically, wondering what he had done to evoke this fear in her. Then the horrifying truth struck him. There was only one answer to her mystifying behaviour. She had somehow uncovered his secret. She knew, or at least suspected, his feelings for her. He stared at her, mortified. 'You know, don't you, Vinnie?' he uttered. 'How I feel about you?'

She looked at him for several long moments before slowly nodding. 'Yes, I think I do.'

His face crumpled into deep regret. 'I'm so sorry if I've embarrassed you.'

'Embarrassed me? Oh, no, Mr Hamlin, you haven't at all. What I am is . . . well, shocked. I mean, you've always been so . . . so . . .'

'Cool towards you? It's the only way I could handle my feelings.' He gazed at her for several long moments. Well, at least she had said she was not embarrassed by his feelings for her, hadn't run off either. Dare he then hope she could feel something for him in return? Before he could consider the possible dire repercussions he blurted, 'Come out with me, Vinnie, please? For a drink, a meal, whatever you'd like? I'd be so honoured if you'd say yes.'

'Oh!'

'You're shocked?'

'Shocked? Well, yes . . . no . . . I suppose I am. You've certainly surprised me. And I'd always assumed you were spoken for, Mr Hamlin.'

'Spoken for?' A vision of Angie came to mind which he hurriedly quashed. 'No . . . no, I'm not spoken for,' he answered.

'You're not? Oh.' Well, neither was she. Tommy had been gone now for nearly a year and she had long finished her mourning for the man she had loved, one who didn't seem to have existed in real life, only in her imagination. What harm would there be in accepting an invitation from Keith Hamlin, a man who obviously wanted to spend time with her? A night out would do her good. Her face lit up with delight. 'Well, then, yes,

276

I'd like that very much, thank you.'

Her answer made his heart leap in utter joy. 'Tomorrow night? You're free? Shall I pick you up at seven-thirty?'

She nodded.

A broad smile lit his face. 'I'll look forward to it then.' He gave a thoughtful frown. 'Oh, just one thing, Vinnie. We should keep this between ourselves, shouldn't we? Stop gossip at work.'

'Oh, I agree,' she replied wholeheartedly.

'Now will you allow me to run you home?'

She shook her head. 'Thank you, but I'll enjoy the walk.'

She wanted to be alone so she could gather her thoughts on this surprising turn of events.

As she made her way home Vinnie was filled with a mixture of excitement and fear and fretted over whether she had done the right thing in accepting Keith's invitation. But then there was no reason why she shouldn't have and she was so looking forward to an evening out. It amazed her that until only a few hours ago she had seriously believed he was indifferent towards her; now she knew that was not the case at all and the thought made her tingle all over in anticipation.

Keith Hamlin was a smart good-looking man, and as she had found out tonight he'd a sense of humour and was chivalrous too. She had never heard any untoward gossip about him at work, in fact never heard one damning word said against him, and despite her bad judgement in respect of Tommy she knew that unless she wanted to risk growing old alone she would have to trust her instincts which were telling her that Keith Hamlin was a thoroughly decent man.

Dare she hope that this meeting between them would be the first of many?

Chapter Twenty

For the umpteenth time Vinnie checked her appearance in her full-length bedroom mirror. She had tried on every decent outfit in her wardrobe, some several times, in an effort to look just right. Having no idea where Keith would be taking her she wanted neither to be overdressed nor underdressed. Finally she had settled on a simple fitted, sleeveless, boat-necked dress in olive green, the hemline brushing her knees. Vinnie knew she could get away with taking the hem up a little as her legs were good but it was her opinion that today's short styles were aimed at the young and the length she wore was more fitting for a woman of her age.

She scanned her reflection in the mirror again and frowned, bothered. Maybe a skirt and top instead? Her eyes caught sight of the bedroom clock then, on a small table at the side of her bed. It was just after seven. Keith would be collecting her in just under half an hour. She hadn't really time to make another change. A bead of sweat formed on her brow, her heart began to thump, her legs to feel weak. She suddenly felt like a teenager again on her very first date and an overwhelming desire to tear off her clothes, dive under the bedclothes and hide away filled her. Then she mentally scolded herself. She was forty years old, not a teenager. It was silly her feeling like this. But regardless it didn't stop her.

In her nervousness she was just about to examine her appearance again when her ears pricked as she heard her back door opening and then voices. 'Oh, God, no, she inwardly groaned. As much as she loved to see them a visit from Julie and Gary was the last thing she needed tonight. She heard her daughter call to her and took several deep breaths in the hope of composing herself. 'Just coming,' she responded cheerily.

Gary was sitting at the kitchen table when she entered, Julie at the sink filling the kettle. 'Hello, Mum,' Julie called, her back to her. 'We thought we'd come and keep you company for a while.' Kettle in hand, she turned to face her mother and her mouth dropped open, eyes widening in surprise. 'Oh, Mum, you look lovely,' she exclaimed.

Vinnie was still getting used to Julie paying her compliments and this one, said with such sincerity, took her aback. 'Why, thank you, dear.'

Gary too was looking at her admiringly. 'Julie is right, Mrs Deakin. You certainly do.'

'Are you going out, Mum?' her daughter asked.

A great surge of guilt reared up in her and she looked at Julie hesitantly. 'Well . . .'

'You've a date, Mrs Deakin, haven't you?' Gary piped

up, a huge grin splitting his face.

Despite Julie's having made huge efforts to reform her character, the thought of her mother becoming involved with someone else didn't appeal and before she could check herself she blurted, 'Don't be silly, Gary. Mum's too old to have a date. Besides . . .'

Worried that his wife was about to remind her mother that her father had hardly been dead a year and that in her eyes her going out, especially with another man, wasn't right, Gary jumped up to stand beside her, putting an arm around her waist. 'It's about time your mother started going out again, isn't it, Julie?' he said, looking at her meaningfully. 'You don't want her getting old by herself.'

Julie's mouth clamped shut and she stared at Vinnie for several long moments before she took a deep breath and said, 'No, of course I don't.' She put the kettle down on the draining board, rushed across to her mother and gave her a tight hug. 'Gary's right, it's about time you had some fun. Who's the lucky man?'

Vinnie sighed in relief. 'Oh, I don't know whether he's lucky,' she said coyly. 'I've only been asked out for a drink, nothing special.'

'He certainly is lucky if he's taking you out,' Gary said. 'If he doesn't think so himself then he damned well should do. Isn't that right, Julie?'

She nodded. 'Yes, it is.'

'Are you sure you don't mind, Julie?' Vinnie asked her, bothered.

She gave her mother a tender smile. 'Of course I do,

you're my mum and I don't like the thought of sharing you with anyone. But I want you to be happy, Mum, you of all people deserve to be. Gary's right. It's about time you started going out again. So who is the lucky man?'

She took a breath before saying, 'My boss, Mr Hamlin.'

Just then there was a tap on the back door and, without waiting for it to be answered, Betty charged in. She took one look at the gathering and immediately jumped to the wrong conclusion. 'I knew summat was up. What's happened?' she demanded.

'Nothing, Betty,' Vinnie insisted. 'And why should you think that?'

She wagged a finger. ''Cos you, gel, have bin like a cat on hot bricks all day. And yer've bin avoiding me. Yer never came with us to the canteen at lunchtime nor took yer tea breaks with us. Now summat's going on, I know it is.' She suddenly noticed Vinnie's attire. 'Oh, yer all dressed up! Why, yer look lovely, gel.'

Julie started giggling. 'Shall I put her out of her misery or do you want the honour, Mum?'

Oh, God, this was getting worse, Vinnie thought. She took a deep breath and looked Betty in the eye. 'Mr Hamlin asked me to have a drink with him, Betty, and I've accepted.'

Her friend gawped, astounded. 'What! Well, I never. I need ter sit down.' She yanked a chair out from under the table and plonked herself down on it, then looked across at Vinnie knowingly. 'I suspected that man had a notion for yer. I was bleddy right, wasn't I? He's bin acting like that with yer to cover up his feelings. So when did all this happen? Last night, I bet.'

She nodded. 'Yes, that's right, it did. It's nothing special, Betty, just a friendly drink,' she insisted.

'Pull the other one, Vinnie! Yer don't take the trouble you have just fer a friendly drink,' she scoffed and lapsed into thought. 'So, Mr Hamlin ain't married then?' she mused. 'Well, bugger me, I could have sworn he was. He looks too well-kept for a man on his own. Come on then, tell us how it happened.'

Vinnie glanced at the clock, very conscious Keith could arrive at any minute. It was just approaching twenty-five past seven and her heart raced frantically. As much as she loved all three of the people in her kitchen she did not want them around when he arrived. 'There's nothing to tell. He asked me out and I accepted. Look, I don't mean to be rude but I'd really like you all to go.'

'Go!' cried Betty. 'We ain't going nowhere. Well, I ain't anyroad,' she said, folding her arms and settling back in her seat. 'I want to check Keith Hamlin's intentions towards yer are honourable.'

'And embarrass me to hell?' Vinnie shot back at her. 'I don't think so. And please, Julie, don't look at me like that. I'll be perfectly safe with him, trust me.'

Gary took his wife's hand. 'Come on, Julie, your mum's right. And it's not going to look good for her if Mr Hamlin is greeted by the Spanish Inquisition. And you, Mrs Trubshaw,' he ordered, inclining his head towards the back door.

Lips tight, she looked resolutely back at him, then giving a resigned sigh, reluctantly rose. 'I suppose seeing us all here could put the fear of God up him and frighten him off.' She went over and gave Vinnie a hug. 'Be warned, I wanna hear all about it in the morning. You have a lovely time, ducky.'

'I will, Betty, but please, I would like this kept between us for now. I couldn't stand the thought of gossip at work. Anyway, you're all jumping the gun. Tonight might just be a one off.'

Just then a knock resounded on the front door. Everyone jumped.

'That's him,' Vinnie cried. 'Quick, out the back. Come on,' she urged, rushing over to the door and yanking it open.

Shutting it after them all, she took several deep breaths and, hoping she appeared a great deal more calm than she felt, went to answer Keith's knock.

He stared at her admiringly. 'You look lovely, Vinnie.'

And how smart you do, she thought, taking in his immaculate navy blazer and cream trousers, the pale blue shirt that was new if she wasn't mistaken. Obviously he'd taken pains with his appearance and she was glad she had taken so much trouble over hers too. 'Thank you,' she replied. 'Won't you come in?'

He made to then paused, cocking his head. 'Someone is in your entry. I can hear giggling. Would you like me to check . . .'

'Er . . . it's just children,' she said hurriedly, knowing exactly who it was and what she would say to them when she saw them all next. 'Please come inside,' she urged.

As she put on her coat and collected her bag, he said to her, 'If it's all right with you I've heard of a nice little pub in Anstey. It isn't too far. I've had it on good authority they do excellent basket meals. It seems they're all the rage now. Probably saves on the washing up,' he added, chuckling, then looked at her questioningly. 'That's if you haven't eaten already?'

She'd hardly had a morsel all day due to anticipation of this evening. She still didn't know whether she could face anything to eat or not but smiled warmly at him. 'It sounds lovely.'

Keith had just opened the car door for her when Vinnie heard the sound of a scooter roaring down the road towards them. Assuming it was Barry, she turned to wave a greeting and stared bemused as he drew the bike to a screeching halt just behind Keith's car, missing the mudguard by less than an inch. He then jumped off, ran to his front door, rammed his key in the lock, pushed the door open and shouted at the top of his voice, 'Mam?' Receiving no reply, he pulled the door shut with a bang and was just about to jump back on his scooter again when he spotted Vinnie. He ran over to her. 'Did yer see me mam go out, Mrs Deakin?'

She shook her head. 'No, sorry.'

'Oh, hell,' he groaned.

Vinnie knew by his whole manner that something

was wrong. 'What's happened, Barry?' she demanded of him.

'It's me dad. He's had a funny turn in the pub and they called the ambulance to tek him to hospital. The landlord waved me down as I was passing and told me to fetch me mam. I knew she was off out. Well, she's out most nights now, but I was hoping to catch her before she left. I don't know what to do. Should I go down the hospital or look for me mam?'

Keith stepped forward. 'Excuse me for butting in, Vinnie, but would it be a good idea if this young man gets off to the hospital and we find his mother and take her there?'

She looked at him gratefully. 'I think that's a very good idea, thank you, Keith. Barry, is that all right with you, only someone should be with your father.'

'Yeah,' he said, relieved. 'That's great, ta.'

'So where will Noreen be?'

'Eh?' He shook his head and gave a helpless shrug. 'She's a law unto herself is me mam, she could be anywhere. Yer could try the Palais as it's over twenty-one night tonight. I've a feeling she might have gone with her pal from work. I overheard 'em whispering about it last night in the kitchen.'

Vinnie's immediate thought was to wonder if Eric was aware of what his wife did on a Wednesday night. 'All right. But if she's not in the Palais, have you any other ideas?'

'Anywhere that sells drink is a safe bet,' he said blandly.

'Oh, I see. We'll do our best then.'

Vinnie watched worriedly as Barry jumped back on his scooter and rode off. She turned to Keith. 'This has ruined your plans, I'm so sorry.'

He smiled reassuringly at her. 'These things happen, Vinnie, don't worry yourself. I'm only too glad to help in any way I can. Come on, we'd better hurry.'

A short while later Keith pulled his car up outside the premises that housed the *palais-de-danse* on the Humberstone Gate and Vinnie wound down her window so she could get a better look at the people in the long queue waiting to get in. It took her several moments to spy her quarry and when she did she was appalled. Beneath her unbuttoned coat Noreen was wearing a thigh-length skirt that was so tight it looked in danger of bursting at the seams and a very revealing low-cut blouse. She was with a woman of about her own age who was dressed in just as tarty a way. It was readily apparent to Vinnie that even at this early hour in the evening both women had already consumed a large amount of drink.

Informing Keith that she wouldn't be a moment, Vinnie got out of the car and hurried over. Noreen looked most surprised. 'Fancy seeing you here. Wouldn't have thought you'd have liked this kind of thing. Well, we live and learn, don't we?'

'Noreen, I need to speak to you, privately,' Vinnie said sharply.

Her neighbour looked at her, nonplussed. 'A' yer come ter say me house has burned down or summat?'

Vinnie quashed a feeling of irritation. 'Noreen, what I have to tell you is serious . . .'

'N'ote's more serious to me than what I'm doing at the moment,' she cut in, then eyed Vinnie nonchalantly. 'And I s'pose you'll be telling that old man of mine what yer caught me doing? Well, go ahead, I couldn't give a toss. I'm having some fun, summat Eric don't know the meaning of.'

Vinnie took a deep breath. She didn't feel it was right, discussing Noreen's private business in front of others, but could see she had no choice. 'Noreen, Eric's in hospital.'

'Why, what's up with him?' she asked casually. 'Oh, the doors are opening!' she exclaimed excitedly, and grabbing her friend's arm added, 'looks like it'll be a good night, judging from the queue.'

'Noreen, about Eric,' Vinnie reminded her. 'It must be serious for them to ask for you to go.'

'Serious? How serious?'

'Probably just cut his finger, yer know what men are like,' her friend piped up.

Vinnie gave her a disdainful look. 'We can give you a lift,' she said to Noreen.

Her neighbour shot her a look of disgust. 'If yer think I'm getting on the back of Barry's scooter, yer can think again. Besides, I'd bust me skirt open,' she added, guffawing with laughter.

'Barry's already down at the hospital. My friend can give you a lift.' Vinnie pointed across to where Keith sat waiting in the car.

Noreen looked across to where Vinnie was indicating and gawped in astonishment. Then she bent down to get a better look at the man sitting behind the wheel. 'Friend, yer say? He's a looker. Car too. Must be well set up. Mmm,' she mouthed thoughtfully. She straightened up and looked at Vinnie, preoccupied, then after several moments sighed in resignation. 'I suppose I'd better come with yer.' She turned to her friend. 'Sorry, gel, but I'll have ter go. He is me husband after all. Come on then, Vin,' she announced, and without further ado tottered off as quick as her stilettos and tight skirt would allow towards the car. She pulled open the front passenger side door and got in, holding out her hand in greeting to a bemused Keith.

'Hello, I'm Noreen, Vinnie's neighbour. This is really good of yer.' Still gripping Keith's hand, she glanced around the car. 'Very nice. What was it yer said yer did?' she asked, smiling at him winningly.

Vinnie got into the back. 'I take it Noreen has introduced herself,' she said lightly to Keith, fighting to keep her annoyance at the woman's rudeness towards her from showing.

Keith flashed her a smile and, without saying a word, put the car into gear and set off for the hospital.

Barry jumped up from a bench in the busy corridor as soon as he saw them all advancing towards him.

'They found yer, Mam,' he exclaimed, rushing up to her.

'Well, I weren't exactly hiding. So what's the dozy sod done then? Summat and n'ote is my guess.'

Barry looked at her hard. 'Don't speak about me dad like that, Mam,' he snapped. 'I don't know what's up with him yet, the doc was waiting fer you to turn up.'

'How long did the doc say he'd be?' she demanded irritably.

Barry gave a shrug. 'He didn't.'

Just then double doors at the other end of the corridor burst open and an elderly doctor strode purposefully through. 'Mrs Adler?' he addressed the gathering.

'That's me,' Noreen responded, stepping forward, Barry along with her. 'So he's wasted yer time, has he, Doc?'

He came up to her. 'Hardly that, Mrs Adler. Your husband fainted due to the fact that his blood pressure was very high. The amount of alcohol he'd drunk on an empty stomach didn't help either.'

'And what's that mean in plain English?'

'That he needs to be taken better care of.'

'A' you saying I don't?' she accused him.

'No, not at all. But he'll need to take medication until we get his blood pressure evened out again, he needs to eat properly, and I've advised him to cut down on his drink. Apart from that . . .'

'Oh, thank God fer that,' exclaimed Noreen, sounding relieved. 'So yer'll be keeping him in for a week or so until yer get him right? I mean, Doc, I'd look after him meself but I have ter work, see.'

The doctor looked at her knowingly. 'Yes, I do see.'

'What would cause me dad's blood thingy to be like

that?' Barry asked in concern.

The doctor smiled at the young man, glad someone was showing proper concern for his patient. 'Could be due to a number of things but in this case I've a feeling it's down to worry. Do you know if your father has reason to be very worried or upset about anything?'

Barry took a deep breath. 'Can't think,' he said with obvious irony. 'Can you, Mam?' he asked, looking at her hard.

'No, I can't. My husband has the life of Riley, Doctor. Waited on hand and foot he is,' she blatantly lied.

'Well then, he's a lucky man, having such a caring family. You can take him home after we've finished stitching the cut on his head.'

Noreen knew by his tone that he hadn't believed a word she had said but before she could respond the doctor added, 'You will excuse me, won't you?'

As he departed Vinnie, who had been standing a discreet distance away with Keith while the doctor spoke to Noreen and Barry, moved forward to address her friend. 'How is Eric?'

'Bit of blood pressure, that's all. And the daft sod knocked himself out 'cos he'd had too much to drink. We've got to wait while they stitch him up.' She pulled a face. 'The doctor was treating me like it's all my fault.'

'I'm sure he wasn't, Noreen,' she said kindly.

'It bleddy *is* your fault, Mam,' accused Barry. 'Yer not looking after me dad at all. He comes home from work and you can't be bothered ter cook him dinner, and yer out all the time.'

'Yer dad's a grown man and quite capable of getting his own dinner now and again.'

Barry's eyes widened in astonishment. 'Now and again?'

'That's enough from you,' she said, cuffing him hard around his ear. 'When I want your opinion, I'll ask for it.' She glanced hurriedly around. 'Where's yer friend gone?' she asked Vinnie.

'To fetch us all a cup of tea. So can Eric come home?'

Noreen sniffed disdainfully and nodded. 'Seems so. I think they should keep him in, personally. Oh, here's Keith back,' she said, a bright smile lighting up her face as he came around the corner carrying a tray with four cups on it. She rushed to meet him. 'This is very good of you,' she gushed, helping herself to a cup. 'I wish my husband was so thoughtful. You know, I go out for one night and this happens. I think he must have done it on purpose to make me feel guilty.'

Just then Eric appeared through the double doors. He looked astounded to see them all. Noreen rushed across to him, hooking her arm through his. 'There yer are, yer daft bugger,' she proclaimed loudly for them all to hear. 'I dunno, I turn me back fer one night so I can help Rita celebrate her birthday, 'cos otherwise she'd have spent it on her own, and you tek sick on me. Trying to mek me feel bad, was yer, fer going out?'

He looked at her, dazed, but before he could respond she continued, 'Let's get you home and tucked up in bed and in future you'll eat all the meals I cook for yer and I ain't gonna tek no excuses! Fancy meking yerself ill like that, yer gave me a right scare. Now this is Mr Hamlin,' she said, introducing him to Keith. 'He's a friend of Vin's and kindly brought me down here in his car, would yer believe? I expect if we're nice to him he'll run us home an' all,' she said, giving Keith a dazzling smile. 'I hate ter put you on the spot but I think Eric needs ter get home as soon as poss, and yer know, yer can wait ages fer a taxi.'

'It'll be my pleasure,' he replied, and turned and gave Vinnie an apologetic look. 'You don't mind if we take them home?' he murmured.

She smiled up at him. 'Of course I don't. It's good of you to agree to.' She gave Eric a worried look. 'He needs to be in bed and the sooner the better, judging by the look of him. He's obviously suffering from shock.'

'Yes, passing out like that he would be. And he's going to have a nice scar to remind him,' Keith answered gravely.

Vinnie hadn't been referring to the shock of the fall but to the one his wife was giving him now by behaving so attentively towards him. It was good to see her showing her husband some affection but all the same Vinnie wondered why she had so suddenly changed her attitude towards him. Maybe Eric's accident had brought home to her what losing him would mean.

A while later, after seeing Eric and Noreen safely to their door, Vinnie looked at Keith gratefully. 'Thank you for what you did.'

'Think nothing of it, Vinnie. Having a car does have its advantages and I was glad to be of help.' He gave a sigh. 'Although I'm sorry it's ruined our evening.'

'Yes, so am I. Look . . . I know it's after ten but have you time for some tea or coffee?'

He looked at his watch. He had told Angie he was having a drink with a colleague from work, so that wasn't a lie, but he really ought to be home before eleven or he risked her asking him awkward questions. 'Yes, I'd love a quick cup, thanks.'

Vinnie hardly had time to put the kettle on before the door opened and Noreen came in unannounced. Ignoring Vinnie, she smiled winningly at Keith. 'I noticed yer car was still outside and I just had ter come and say me thanks. Oh, tea,' she said to Vinnie. 'Ta, I'd love a cup.'

'But you've already thanked me,' he said.

'The word thanks don't seem enough fer what you did tonight. I need ter repay yer properly.'

'There's no need, really.'

'Oh, there is. In my book one good turn deserves another. Ain't that right, Vinnie?'

'Mmm, I suppose so, yes,' she said, putting the tea things down on the table. 'How's Eric?'

'Oh, he's all right. Went straight to bed. Any biscuits?' she asked expectantly.

Vinnie tightened her lips, hoping to hide her annoyance at this blatant intrusion. She fetched a packet of Garibaldis from the larder and arranged them on a plate which she put in front of Noreen. She looked at them, then fixed her eyes on Keith. 'I rarely touch biscuits, have ter watch me figure,' she said, giggling girlishly. 'But after the shock of tonight I feel the need for a bit of sweetness.' She gave a huge sigh. 'I don't know what I'd have done without your support, really I don't,' she said, giving him a grateful smile.

'As you keep saying,' he responded lightly. 'But please, forget about it, Noreen. Neighbours try to help each other, don't they, especially in circumstances like we had tonight.'

'Oh, yes, neighbours do.' She leaned over and patted his knee. 'I'm glad you count me as one of yours. So how about us all having a night together on Saturday? A drink or two and a game of cards? Be like old times, Vinnie, won't it? And you and I,' she said to Keith, 'can get to know one another better.'

He gulped. 'Oh, er . . .'

'Is Saturday night no good for you?' she hurriedly cut in. 'We could make it another night if that's the case?'

'Well, I would have loved to accept but, you see, I've already asked Vinnie to go out then.'

Vinnie gazed at him in surprise. This was news to her, but pleasing news.

'Oh, Vinnie don't like going out,' Noreen said matter-of-factly. 'She's a home bird. The slippers and telly type.'

'Noreen!' she exclaimed.

'Well, you are.' She rested her elbow on the table and put her chin in her hand, looking at Keith meaningfully. 'Not like me, I love a good night out.'

'I'll . . . er . . . bear that in mind,' he replied evenly.

Fighting to keep her composure, Vinnie put the teapot down on the table. 'Shouldn't you be getting back to Eric?' she suggested.

'No hurry. As I said, he's asleep. So, Keith, we on for Saturday?'

He looked at his watch. 'Er . . . I really ought to be going,' he said, rising.

'Oh, surely not?' said a disappointed Noreen. 'It's only ten-thirty.'

'And I have an early start in the morning. You will excuse me, won't you, Vinnie?'

She tried to hide her own disappointment that he was leaving. 'Yes, of course. I'll see you out.'

Before she opened the front door she paused and looked up at him apologetically. 'I'm sorry about Noreen. She means well. When Tommy was alive we all used to be very close and I know she really enjoyed our get togethers. I expect she's trying to resume them but she's got to realise that those times have gone. I know I should have said something to her but . . .' She gave a deep sigh. 'Our relationship has been strained since Tommy's death, she took it really badly, and I was conscious I could spark bad feeling between us again by saying something she might misconstrue. I didn't want to risk that.'

He smiled warmly at her. 'You're a lovely woman, Lavinia Deakin. Do you happen to be free on Saturday night?'

She nodded.

'Pick you up at eight?'

She nodded again.

An urge to kiss her swamped Keith then. He fought to resist, feeling it was far too soon for such an intimate display on his part. Instead he leaned over and his lips lightly brushed her cheek. 'Goodnight,' he whispered.

She pulled the door open. 'Goodnight.'

Noreen was tucking into the biscuits and slurping her tea when Vinnie returned. 'So I'll bring the booze and you provide the sandwiches but yer could always get a couple of bottles yerself, if yer like. About eight.'

Vinnie was still feeling his lips on her cheek and eyed Noreen blankly. 'Sorry?'

'Oh, fer God's sake, Vinnie, come back into the land of the living! The arrangements fer Saturday night.'

She sat down opposite her neighbour. 'Er . . . not this Saturday, Noreen. Keith and I are going out.'

'What? But we arranged . . .'

'He told you we already had arrangements. Look, Noreen, the last thing I want to do is hurt your feelings but Keith and I are just friends. We're not . . . well . . . a couple as such and things like cards nights are for when you're more established, if you get my meaning.'

'I was only trying to be friendly,' her neighbour said, deeply miffed. 'Keith seemed keen but I suppose he felt he ought to honour your arrangement being's he'd already asked you.'

Vinnie smiled at her. 'Hopefully we will have a cards night sometime in the future, let's see how things go. Anyway, Eric might not be well enough by Saturday. The last thing you must want is for him to have a relapse over-exerting himself. More tea?'

''Ote stronger?'

'Er . . . actually I have some sherry left over from Ruby's engagement do.'

'That'll do, I suppose.' She lapsed into silence for several long moments while Vinnie got her a drink. Noreen took several sips of it then asked, 'So what time is Handsome picking you up on Saturday night?'

'Handsome? Oh, you mean Keith. About eight he said.' Vinnie gave a distant smile. 'He's nice, isn't he, Noreen?'

She nodded. 'He is that. Yes, he's quite a catch, I'd say. The type ter treat a woman right and his word would be his bond.'

Vinnie smiled warmly at her. 'Yes, he strikes me like that too. But, regardless, I'm certainly not going to be rushing into anything. I trusted Tommy implicitly and my judgement was all wrong concerning him. I'm not about to make a mistake like that again. My gut instincts tell me that Keith is a thoroughly good man, but time will tell.'

'Mmm,' Noreen mouthed thoughtfully. She took a deep breath and said distractedly, ''Course, you're a free agent, ain't yer? Free to get someone who's gonna bring some excitement into your life. A man like him ain't gonna get entangled with someone who's already spoken for, is he?'

Vinnie frowned at her, puzzled. 'I'm sorry, I don't know what you're getting at?'

Noreen gave a nonchalant shrug. 'Oh, I was just

thinking out loud. Ignore me.' She reached into her pocket, took out a packet of cigarettes, extracted one and lit it, blowing a plume of smoke into the air. 'Like old times, in't it, us sitting here putting the world to rights?'

More like me sitting listening to your opinions, Vinnie thought to herself. But, regardless, she felt it was better she was on some sort of friendly terms with her neighbour than on bad terms. 'So are we friends again?' she asked, smiling warmly.

Noreen stared at her blankly. 'Well, I never knew we weren't.'

Chapter Twenty-one

When Vinnie knocked on the Adlers' door the following evening straight from work it was Barry who opened it to her.

'Mam's not in yet, Mrs D, but she did say she'd be late as she was going shopping for the dinner on her way home.' He gave her a look of utter amazement. 'She even popped home at lunchtime to check Dad was okay.'

Vinnie smiled. 'I'm glad to hear it, Barry. Actually it's your father I came to see.'

He stood aside. 'I know he's ever so grateful for what you and Mr Hamlin did last night. So am I, Mrs D. I was in a right dilemma, I can tell yer, until you offered to help.'

'There's no need for thanks, really,' she said as she followed him through to the Adlers' living-room. 'It was the least we could do.'

Eric was propped up in his armchair with pillows, and a blanket was tucked around the lower part of his body. The television was blaring out the title music to the children's programme *Blue Peter* as the end credits were rolling up. He smiled, genuinely pleased to see her.

'Hello, Vinnie lovey. Nice of yer ter pop in.' He inclined his head towards the television set and said, laughing, 'I've just learned how ter mek a model of Fireball XL5 out of toilet roll tubes and egg boxes. Might come in useful when me son decides to settle down and bless us with a grandson.' He ignored the look Barry gave him and asked, 'Turn the set down will yer, lad, we can't hear ourselves speak. Cuppa?'

When Vinnie declined Barry left them to it and she sat down in the armchair to the side of Eric, placing her handbag on the floor. 'So how are you?' she asked him.

'Oh, can't grumble. The pills are only just beginning ter kick in but I feel much better now than I have for a while. Doctor gave me a right rocket.'

'Yes, I should imagine he did. And you're going to follow his advice, I hope?'

'Got no choice, have I, unless I wanna be seriously ill. No more chips, and rationed to two pints a night 'til me blood pressure settles. Then after that I've still got ter watch it,' he said, disgruntled, before his face brightened. 'Mind you, what happened to me yesterday seems to have bin a blessing in disguise. It must have gave my Noreen a right jolt. She can't do enough for me. Meking me a shepherd's pie for me tea.' He patted his stomach and licked his lips. 'Can't be bad, eh?'

Vinnie was so glad to hear this news. Eric was a good steady man who as far as she was aware had never caused his wife a moment's worry during all their years of marriage, and it was Vinnie's opinion that it was about time Noreen appreciated just what she did have in him instead of complaining bitterly about what she felt she hadn't got but deserved.

'While I've been sitting here today,' he continued, 'I've bin racking me brains for what I could do to give Noreen a treat. I thought about brightening up the kitchen for her. She noticed you'd had the decorator in to do yer front room and has given me earache about it ever since. Was he dear, Vinnie?'

She froze at the thought of Shaun and his association with her late husband, something she had tried hard to push to the back of her mind in her efforts to move forward. Despite his precarious start in life Shaun was a nice young man, a credit to his mother, but Vinnie didn't like the thought of bumping into him again for fear of the story of his parentage surfacing. But neither did she feel it was right for her to quash any chance of the hard-working young man earning money.

'I thought the charges very reasonable for the excellent job he did, Eric, and I could certainly recommend him. Twenty pounds for the living-room and that included the materials. I should imagine a kitchen wouldn't be quite so much.'

Eric's face fell. 'It's still a lot though, in't it?'

'How about doing it yourself?' she suggested.

'Huh! I know I helped Tommy out a few times doing yours but I'm no expert. The one and only time I decorated in here was when we moved in and Noreen complained non-stop about the mess then the fact that yer could see all the joins in the paper, though I didn't think they were that bad considering I'd never done decorating before. That's why I've never bothered since 'cos I couldn't stand the thought of the slanging I'd get. My life's peaceful at the moment, Vinnie, and I don't wanna risk doing anything that could cause Noreen to get upset and lapse back to her old ways again.' He gave his chin a thoughtful rub. 'No, I'll just have ter think of summat else by way of giving her a treat. I could always tek her to Skeggie for the day. Yeah, that's what I'll do next Bank Holiday Monday.' He eyed Vinnie keenly. 'Anyway, that Mr Hamlin seems a decent sort.' His face clouded over. 'I hate ter bring this up but I still ain't got over the way Tommy really was. Still shocked, I am, ter think I could be so pally with a bloke for so many years and not really know him. I mean, I knew he liked a bit of a flirt with the ladies when you weren't around, and lots of times we'd start off from here together to go down the pub or match and he'd remember he had summat else ter do and leave me to it, but I never gave it that much thought. Now it makes me wonder what he was really up to.' Eric shook his head ruefully. 'I'll never get over the way he treated yer, Vinnie. You of all people didn't deserve that. Still, that's past, ain't it, and time for you to move on. Serious with this bloke, is it?'

She laughed. 'We haven't even got past our first evening out together, Eric, so no, nothing like that.'

'And that were my fault,' he said remorsefully. 'I ruined last night for yer, didn't I?'

'You mustn't think like that. I'm just glad we were

around to be of help.' She picked up her handbag and stood to go. 'I'd best be off. Please tell Noreen I was asking after her, won't you?'

'I will, lovey, and thanks fer dropping by.'

Vinnie had finished clearing up her dinner dishes and was looking forward to a peaceful night settled in her armchair catching up with the local news and watching the television. She'd had a busy day. Several urgent orders that the inspection department had not been informed about previously were thrust upon them. Fitting them in with everything else they had to do took all Vinnie's supervisory skills but she managed by cleverly evening out the work amongst her most skilled operatives and by rolling up her own sleeves and setting to herself.

She'd no time for more than a brief update with Keith on how she proposed to handle the extra work and to allay his concerns that it would be done, but as they parted the look he flashed her and the smile along with it told her all she needed to know. He was looking forward to Saturday evening as much as she was herself.

Betty, of course, had pounced upon Vinnie as soon as she had arrived at work that morning, pulling her unceremoniously out of earshot of any of the others and demanding to know how the previous evening had gone. She had been dismayed to learn of the interruption but agreed that in the circumstances Vinnie and Keith had had no alternative but to act as they had. She was delighted to learn that Keith had asked Vinnie out again and said she'd pray that nothing went wrong for them this time.

As Vinnie beavered away in her old position alongside Betty and Ruby, the girl chattered non-stop about her forthcoming wedding. The original date had been put back a while on Betty's advice to give the young couple more time to save for the basics needed to start their new life together. Ruby and Warren had been very reluctant at first, not wanting to wait, but as Betty had said, now that Ruby was away from the clutches of her overbearing parents they could get on with courting and enjoy themselves – under Betty's own watchful eye. She also made them realise that sitting on orange boxes might sound romantic but in reality it was no fun, just hard on the bum. The wedding was to take place the following April which was seven months away. Vinnie and Betty were both to be guests of honour and were extremely proud of the fact.

Now, as she switched on the television and settled herself into her armchair with the evening newspaper, a thought struck Vinnie. By the time Ruby's wedding came round she wondered if she and Keith would be a proper couple, and if so whether she would be able to invite him to go with her. She hoped she wasn't being too optimistic about their relationship but the thought of Keith there beside her at what would be a joyous occasion would certainly make the day perfect for her.

About twenty minutes later she was so absorbed in reading a news report of a warehouse robbery which had taken place only streets away that she jumped when there was a knock on the back door and she heard it open. Thinking it was likely to be Noreen, she hastily folded the paper and rose to greet her. She was surprised but delighted to see that her caller was in fact Julie but this quickly turned to worry when she witnessed how upset the girl was.

Her daughter immediately threw herself on her, sobbing hysterically. 'Oh, Mum,' she wailed. 'I've been so stupid! I've tried so hard too, I don't know what came over me, really I don't. He won't forgive me this time, I know he won't. He'll leave me, he will.'

Cuddling her protectively, all sorts of things were going through Vinnie's mind. What could be so bad that Julie's marriage was doomed? She had worked very hard at reforming her character and it was rare nowadays for her to show any signs of her former self.

'Julie, just what have you done?' Vinnie quietly asked.

She pulled away from her mother and, sniffing miserably, sat down at the table cradling her head in her hands. 'I . . . I bought two lamps for the bedside tables. A bargain they were, Mum, reduced to less than half price in the British Home Stores sale. I'd not gone in with the intention of buying anything, really I hadn't. I was just taking a short cut back to work after shopping for tonight's dinner. I saw them and I couldn't resist them. They were just the right colour. I . . . I spent the last of my housekeeping on them and now I've not enough left to buy the meat for dinner tomorrow. Gary's going to go mad, I know he is. He'll say I've broken my word and gone back to the way I was before.'

Vinnie sat down too and looked at her daughter encouragingly. 'Julie dear, what you did hasn't broken your promise to Gary.'

She raised her head and frowned. 'It hasn't?'

'No. All you did was what most women would do. You saw some things for the house, that you'd both use and that were affordable, and you bought them with your housekeeping money which really is yours to spend as you feel fit. So you'll have to make do with egg and chips tomorrow night or beans on toast? That won't hurt either of you for one night. Love, Gary isn't trying to dictate everything you spend by making you check it's all right with him first. All he's trying to do is stop you spending huge amounts you haven't got on things you don't need and landing yourselves in financial trouble.'

'But the lamps *are* a luxury, Mum.'

Vinnie laughed. 'Not if you can't see what you're doing when you're getting dressed they're not. All right, I suppose you could say you have the overhead light but, well, a bedroom is a place for creating a soft atmosphere, isn't it, and looked at that way then lamps are essential items. I'm sure Gary will see it that way too.'

'So you think he won't mind when I tell him?'

'I'll be very surprised if he does. What have you done with the lamps?'

Julie gave her a sheepish look. 'I've hidden them in the back of the wardrobe. Gary knows something's wrong, he kept asking me over dinner.'

'He loves you, Julie, and because he does he's bound to notice when something is bothering you, however hard you try to hide it. Now go home and put him out of his misery.'

Julie jumped up from her seat and rushed around the table, launching herself at her mother to give her a tight squeeze. 'Oh, Mum, thanks.'

'I'm glad you turned to me about this, dear. You know, you've done far better sorting yourself out than I thought you would in such a short space of time. You should congratulate yourself. You're a joy to me now, Julie, you really are,' she said with emotion.

'Oh, Mum.' Tears of happiness were pricking Julie's eyes. She reached over, pulled a chair next to her mother's, sat down again and took Vinnie's hands in hers. 'We're just like proper mother and daughter now, aren't we?'

Vinnie nodded. 'You don't know how much it means to me, Julie. I felt I'd lost you for all those years, been denied the chance of being a complete mother to you if you understand what I mean. Oh, I fed you and kept you clean, helped provide for you because I worked as well as your father, but those things we should have shared I felt I lost out on. But now I've found you again and we're sharing those things and it's wonderful for me.'

Julie paused thoughtfully, anxiously gnawing her bottom lip. 'Mum, do you ever think of Janie?'

Her question was so unexpected it took Vinnie by surprise. 'Oh, Julie, of course I do. I might not speak of her but she's constantly in my thoughts.' Her face filled with deep sadness. 'Not many people would understand but when Janie went off like that . . . oh, it's more than words can convey. The loss I feel . . . well . . . it's indescribable.' She eyed her daughter curiously. 'Why do you ask?'

She gave a deep sigh and gulped. 'Because I feel guilty.'

'Guilty? Whatever for?'

Julie's face filled with remorse and she lowered her head. 'Because I know it's my fault she left.'

'Why on earth would you think that?'

She rose from the table, walked across to the sink and rested her back against it. Clasping her hands before her, she took a deep breath and said, 'When Dad used to give me things I bragged to her about them. I was so spiteful, Mum. I made her think Dad only cared about me. I caught her once reading a comic I'd wheedled the money for from Dad and I snatched it off her and ripped it into shreds so she couldn't read it, then I got her into trouble by saying she'd done it when it was me all the time. I got her blamed lots of times for things I'd done. You used to stick up for her but Dad believed me so I made sure it was him I went to with my tales. I used to think it was funny when he punished her. She'd have to go to bed with no dinner. Most of the spankings she got, Mum, she never deserved. It was me who broke your best china cup, and it was me who cut the washing line with all the clean sheets on it so you had to do them all over again. And there are other things, Mum.' She made her way back to the table and sat down again, looking at her mother imploringly. 'I need to put things right between us and tell her I'm sorry. I just pray she'll forgive me.'

Vinnie was looking at her, astounded. 'I suspected lots of times Janie was being punished for things she hadn't done but because she wouldn't open up to me I had no choice but to go along with things. It's my fault as much as yours, Julie, because I failed her as a mother. She should have been able to come to me and tell me the truth about what was going on. I could have stopped it then, couldn't I? You carried on because you weren't being checked. But they were childish tricks, Julie, the sort all sisters play against each other. I can't see such silly things being the reason why she finally left.'

'You can't? Oh, Mum, I can't tell you how relieved I am, but all the same I still want to tell her I'm sorry. Why do you think she left then?'

Vinnie gave a helpless shrug. 'I don't know, dear.' She smiled wanly. 'Several months ago you would never have admitted to such behaviour, it's good that you can now. I just hope you get the opportunity to make your peace with Janie. I live in hope she'll turn up one day, but the more time passes I have to say my hopes are fading.' She looked at her daughter quizzically. 'Anyway, Julie, why admit to all this now, out of the blue?'

She gave a forlorn sigh. 'Because I see how close Gary is to his brother and I envy them. I have a sister I could have been close to but because of my own childish spite I caused a rift between us. I made her hate me, Mum, and I can't blame her if she never talks to me again. By rights she should be here with us now. All of us a family. And . . . well, I just needed to be honest with you.'

Vinnie smiled at her lovingly. 'And I admire you for it.' She patted Julie's hand affectionately. 'It took a lot of guts to tell me what you have and risk me being very angry with you.'

'Are you angry with me?' Julie worriedly asked.

'Of course I'm upset to think that Janie suffered unnecessarily but then . . . well, I am loath to remind you of this but I know you aren't responsible for all your past behaviour. Your father and I have to take some of the blame. The main thing is that you're no longer the horrible child you were but a lovely young woman it's a pleasure to be around. Now, as Betty would say, it's no good crying over spilt milk. I can only hope that in the future we are given the opportunity of putting things right with Janie.'

'I hope so too, Mum.' She rose and gathered her belongings. 'I'd best be off to come clean with Gary.'

Vinnie rose to join her and gave her a goodbye hug. 'Tell him the truth and he'll be fine, you'll see.'

'I will, Mum.' She'd turned to leave when a sudden thought struck and she spun round to face her mother, her expression one of shame. 'Oh, Mum, I've been so wrapped up in my own problems I entirely forgot to ask how your evening out went with Mr Hamlin? I hope you enjoyed yourself.'

Vinnie smiled. 'I think we would have enjoyed each other's company if we'd been given the chance to. Eric next door had a funny turn and Keith and I spent half of the evening looking for Noreen, then the other down the hospital waiting to bring Eric and Noreen back home. Eric will be fine as long as he abides by the doctor's advice.'

'I'm relieved to hear that,' Julie said sincerely. 'I have to say I sided with Dad when it came to Mrs Adler. He made no bones of the fact that he hated her and used to get very angry about how much time she spent in this house interfering, and she never took the hint, did she? But I rather like Mr Adler, he's so different from his wife and he's always been nice to me. It makes me wonder how he stays with her. He must love her, mustn't he, to put up with what he does? But what about you and Mr Hamlin?'

'I'm glad to say he has asked me out again.'

'I'm glad he has too. Let's hope nothing happens to spoil your evening next time.'

'Thank you, dear.'

Vinnie had not long settled herself again when her peace was disturbed a second time by a knock at the back door. Before she could rise to open it Noreen charged in and plonked herself down on the settee. Vinnie could tell by her whole manner she was disgruntled.

'I dunno,' she blurted. 'I can't win, I really can't.'

'In what way?' Vinnie asked, getting up to turn down the sound on the television.

'I thought I'd try a different tack. Be nice to him, see if that made any difference. But did it hell! Yer do yer best and all yer get is complaints. There was n'ote wrong with that pie. Best mince and no lumps in the spuds, but *he* said it tasted funny.'

'Well, you know what youngsters are like, Noreen. They prefer those Wimpy things these days to proper food. It's a fad, isn't it?'

'I ain't talking about Barry.'

'Who then?'

'Eric.'

Vinnie gave her neighbour a surprised look as she sat down again. 'Eric? He complained about his dinner? Well, I'm shocked, I must say.'

'Oh, I don't know why I'm upsetting myself over it really. It's n'ote new to me. I can't remember the last time he ate anything I gave him without making some nasty remark or other.'

Vinnie gawped at her. 'Nasty! Are we talking about the same Eric, Noreen?'

She gave a small laugh. 'This is news to you, ain't it?'

'It certainly is.'

'Well, there's lots you don't know.'

'Such as what, Noreen?'

'Oh, just things,' she said evasively. 'Well, a' yer gonna offer me a cuppa or what?'

'Er . . . yes, in a minute. Noreen, you're worrying me. Why have you never said anything about this before?'

''Cos . . . well . . . yer don't spout all yer business, do yer? And, if yer want ter know, I am ashamed that me own husband treated me like that.' She gave a deep sigh, her face crumpling. 'Oh, I knew I shoulda kept me big trap shut, like I have done all these years. I might have known you'd wheedle it outta me.'

'Wheedle what out of you?'

'How Eric really is. He ain't the man you think, Vinnie.' To her horror she watched Noreen's eyes fill with tears. 'I knew I'd made a mistake as soon as I married him.'

'Well, you've told me that many times. But I didn't think you meant it.'

'Oh, yer don't know how much I did. I knew no one would believe me, see. Good old Eric,' she mimicked sarcastically. 'Such a nice man, wouldn't hurt a fly. Even his son don't know what he's really like. What he does to me is just when we're on our own. No witnesses. He's clever, see.'

Eyes wide in shock, Vinnie uttered, 'Are you saying he hits you, Noreen?'

'He has done, yes. Never hard enough to leave bruises, though. But it's his nastiness what really gets me. You wouldn't believe the vile stuff that comes out of his mouth.' She sniffed miserably. 'I didn't wanna come back from Blackpool, Vinnie. But I came because I hoped he'd changed. He hadn't. In fact, he's worse. Look, I'd better go, I've said too much already. I don't want other people to know. They'll only think I'm lying anyway.'

'You'll stay where you are,' Vinnie insisted. 'Please tell me about it, Noreen. Look, I'm finding this very hard to believe. Eric seems like a lovely man . . .' Her voice trailed off as it struck her that people would have had difficulty believing her if she had known what Tommy was secretly doing and had tried to tell them. To everyone except a handful who must have known or at least suspected what he was up to, Tommy was the perfect husband, father and friend. But Eric being nasty to Noreen, hitting her and being so cunning about his brutality, was very hard to take on board.

'I knew you wouldn't believe me,' Noreen snapped defensively. 'I can tell by yer face yer don't.'

'It's not that I don't believe you, Noreen. What I can't believe is that Eric is such a good actor.'

'Oh, I'm wasting my time, I know I am. But now you know why I go out. It's to get away from him and that's the truth of it. Look, I could sit here and tell you lots I've had ter put up with, but what's the point? And before yer suggest it, it's no use you going to talk to him to check out me story 'cos he'll fool you same as he always has.' She abruptly rose, stepped across to Vinnie and wagged a finger at her. 'I'll just say this, though. Haven't yer ever wondered why Tommy and Eric should have been such great pals, them being so different? Have yer never thought maybe they got on so well because they had certain things in common? Like the way they treated their wives without anyone's knowledge, for instance.'

With that she stormed out, leaving a speechless Vinnie staring after her.

Chapter Twenty-two

'What the hell's up with you?' Betty asked Vinnie next lunchtime. She was sitting beside Betty, absently poking her fork into an unappetising hamburger and chips. 'I'd 'a' thought you'd have bin on top of the world with a date on Saturday evening, not looking like you've the weight of it resting on yer shoulders.'

'Pardon? Oh, I'm sorry, Betty. Not very talkative today, am I?'

'You ain't saying anything at all. What's bothering yer then? Can't you decide what to wear?'

'Wear? For what?'

'On yer flipping date on Saturday,' Betty snapped, irritated.

'Betty, please keep your voice down. People might hear.'

'So what if they do? I ain't mentioned no names. You could be going out with the Shah of Persia for all they know. That pretty flowered dress you've got, that's my advice. Yer look lovely in that. There now, that's sorted.'

She glanced at Vinnie shrewdly. 'What ter wear ain't what's bothering yer, is it?'

'No, it isn't, but I can't really talk about it, Betty, as I'd be gossiping about another person's business.'

'Yeah, but sometimes yer need to get another person's thoughts on a problem so yer better armed to help the person that needs it. It's my guess you need to get mine now. So come on, I won't tell yer've blabbed if you don't.'

'Oh, Betty, you do have a way with you.'

'You might see it as nosiness but I'm only trying to be of help,' she said, a cheeky grin twitching her lips.

'Yes, I know you are, but all the same you're dying to know what it's all about. Where's Ruby?' asked Vinnie, glancing searchingly around the crowded canteen.

'She's gone down that shop that sells bridal dresses so she can get some ideas about what she wants the dressmaker to do to. Don't worry, we won't be interrupted.'

'Ruby's gone without her dinner?' Vinnie exclaimed, surprised.

Betty said proudly, 'Ain't yer noticed she's lost weight since she's bin with me? Food was her life before, Vinnie, but it's not anymore 'cos Warren is. And this bleddy wedding is all she goes on about. You'd think she's organising a state occasion the way she's going on. Mind you, the good thing is Ruby don't realise what I'm doing 'cos her mind's so full of other things, and to see her trimming down is worth all the wedding earache I'm getting.'

'Betty, you've done marvels with her, you really have.'

'Yeah, well, in her way she's done me good an' all. It's given me great pleasure having someone ter look after and I shall miss her when she goes. I was thinking of maybe teking in a lodger, but we'll see. Anyway, this is getting us away from your problem. So come on, two heads are better than one.'

Vinnie put down her fork with a deep sigh. 'It's Noreen . . .'

'Mighta known,' Betty erupted, her face creasing in annoyance. 'What's that flippin' neighbour of yours done ter upset yer now?'

'She hasn't done anything, Betty. It's what she's told me that has.'

Her friend's homely face paled alarmingly. 'Oh, no, Vinnie. N'ote about Tommy, I hope? I thought we'd heard all his devious secrets.'

'It's nothing to do with Tommy. What I've already found out about him was quite enough. I only hope to God there's nothing else. Well . . . I say it's got nothing to do with Tommy, but I'm not sure his influence hasn't something to do with it. Noreen came to see me last night and told me such a tale. Apparently Eric is mistreating her.'

Betty grimaced. 'She did? Really? Well, I don't know, of course, but I've passed the time of day with that husband of hers when I was stopping with yer on several occasions, and I chatted to him at Ruby's engagement do. He seemed a decent enough sort ter me. He was certainly put out 'cos his wife had gone off somewhere and he was at the party on his own. But I didn't press him on that subject 'cos after all their marital state ain't none of my business. But him mistreating her . . . well, he don't seem the type to me. From what you've told me about that Noreen I shoulda thought she was quite capable of standing up fer herself if so. Is she meking it up, I wonder? But then, I hate ter remind yer, Vinnie, there was more to your Tommy than ever met the eye, wasn't there? Anyone meeting him not in the know woulda thought he was a lovely man. So just what is Noreen saying her husband does?'

'That he's nasty and hits her but always when no one else is around. Apparently not even the son knows what goes on.'

Betty pursed her lips. 'Seems far-fetched to me. I mean, the kind of treatment she's talking about, usually the immediate family are in the know. And if they were fighting, you'd hear 'em through the walls, wouldn't yer?'

'That's just it, I do. But usually it's Noreen doing the shouting.' Vinnie gave a loud sigh and added distractedly, 'I always thought it was Eric that was the underdog in that house but according to her it's most definitely the other way around.' Her face clouded. 'Betty, you don't think I've had the wrong end of the stick all this time, do you?'

She pulled a face and gave a helpless shrug. 'I can't comment, can I, 'cos I don't know 'em well enough.'

'I don't know whether I do now. What should I do, Betty?'

'What did Noreen say she was going to do?'

'She didn't. Just told me she didn't know why she'd bothered telling me as it was obvious to her I didn't believe her, and stormed out. It's not that I didn't believe her, Betty, I just can't accept that Eric is the monster she reckons he is. I mean, I'm sure after twenty-two years of being such a close neighbour I would have seen something of his other side. You'd have thought so anyway.'

'But yer weren't looking for it, were yer, Vinnie?'

'No, I wasn't. I can't compare Eric to Tommy either. Tommy never hit me or was nasty.' She gave a deep sigh. 'There's nothing I can do, is there? I can't go and accuse Eric with no concrete evidence, and neither can I help Noreen when I don't know what kind of help she needs or wants.'

'Well, yer've gave yerself yer own answer. Yer didn't need my expert advice after all. So are yer gonna eat yer dinner before it's stone cold?'

Vinnie pushed away her plate. 'No, I'm not hungry. I doubt even Ruby could eat these chips, they're so soggy. I could do with a blow of fresh air. Have we time to catch Ruby up and help her decide on her wedding frock?'

'If we hurry.'

Vinnie had just settled down in her armchair later that evening when she heard raised voices coming through the wall from next door. She laid down her newspaper, wondering if she should do something or not. But what could she do? The shouting grew louder and more ferocious but what bothered Vinnie was that it was only the shrill tones of Noreen's voice she could detect, nothing of Eric's. The shouting abruptly stopped and moments afterwards the front door slammed so hard Vinnie felt the vibration from it in her own house. Jumping up from her seat, she rushed into her front room, tweaked aside the net curtain and, feeling just like a nosey neighbour on *Coronation Street*, peered out. She frowned to see Eric making his way down the street in the direction of the pub. This fact worried her as surely he should still be resting after his bad turn two nights ago. Then there was the sound of the back door opening and shutting and she heard her name being called. It was Noreen. Vinnie rushed back through to the kitchen where her neighbour was waiting for her.

'Oh, hello, Noreen,' she greeted her lightly. 'I was just . . . er . . . tidying the front room. Not that it needed it as it's hardly used much these days except when Julie and Gary come for dinner and usually now we end up sitting at the kitchen table. More cosy, isn't it?' She was babbling and she knew it. 'Er . . . I heard shouting, Noreen. Is everything all right?'

'No, it's not,' she snapped. 'He started on me as soon as Barry went out. I'm worried, Vin. That knock on the head he got when he fainted seems to have made him worse. Look,' she said, pulling up her sleeve. There was a large bruise on the side of her elbow. 'That's where the ashtray hit me.'

Vinnie stared at it, appalled. 'What! Oh, Noreen, are

you saying Eric threw an ashtray at you?'

'Yeah, that bleddy thick glass one that sits on our hearth. Even I was shocked, he's never done that before. I'd done n'ote to warrant it either. I was just sitting having a cuppa after I'd finished me dinner. He's gone down the pub now and he'll be at that bar being pleasant to everyone. He'd be like that with me too if I walked in. "Drink, Noreen love?" ' she mimicked mockingly. 'Oh, Vin,' she groaned despairingly. 'What am I gonna do?'

She gave a helpless sigh. 'Do you think you should take him to see the doctor?'

'And say what? "Any anti-nasty pills, doc? Oh, and while yer at it, something ter stop the bastard from belting me when he feels like it." '

'Oh, Noreen, I am sorry.'

'So am I. I feel I've done twenty-odd years of hard labour and I don't know how much longer I can put up with it.'

Vinnie was staring at her, puzzled. 'Er . . . just now, Noreen, the shouting. It was your voice I heard, not Eric's.'

'Yeah, that's right. That was me bellowing at him fer chucking the ashtray at me. He just sat there laughing at me, that's why you never heard him shouting 'cos he never does. I told you he was clever.'

'Mmm.' Vinnie stared at her thoughtfully. 'Was there a reason he threw it at you in the first place, Noreen?'

'He don't need a reason.' She looked at Vinnie scornfully. 'Huh, I don't know why I'm here. Even with evidence yer don't believe me. Call yerself a neighbour?'

'Don't be like that, Noreen. You have to admit if our roles had been reversed and I'd come to you out of the blue after all the years we'd known each other and told you lurid tales about Tommy, you'd have been surprised. You'd have thought I was mad because you never saw him doing anything he shouldn't. Well, *I've* never seen Eric lose his temper or act nasty with you. Can't you understand why I'm having a job with all this?'

Noreen gave a shrug. 'Yeah, I suppose I can. But I'm telling the truth,' she insisted.

Vinnie stared at her for several long moments, her mind whirling. She couldn't think of any reason why Noreen would want to make up such a story. What else could she do but believe what her neighbour was telling her, as far-fetched as it seemed? But, regardless, she still couldn't quite accept that Eric was the brute Noreen was saying he was. 'All right, Noreen, I believe you,' Vinnie said reluctantly.

'You do?'

She nodded.

'So I can count on you to support me?'

'Support you how?'

'Just be there if I need you.'

'I'll try and help you all I can, Noreen. What are you going to do?'

She gave a shrug. 'I dunno yet. But it's good ter know I've you on me side when and if I do decide to do summat. I'll need someone who knows the ropes.'

Vinnie frowned at her quizzically. 'Knows the ropes?'

'Of being single again. You seem to have coped very well.'

Vinnie ruefully shook her head. 'I wouldn't recommend that unless it's a last resort. You might think the grass is greener, Noreen, but in this case I can tell you it isn't. Managing on one wage takes some juggling and there's lots of other drawbacks to being on your own. It can be very lonely at times.'

'Not with a new bloke keeping you occupied,' she mused. 'Anyway,' she hurriedly added, 'I'm just glad I can count on yer, Vinnie, should it come to it.' Her face flooded with sadness. 'This is all very upsetting for me. I can't believe I'm finally facing up ter things after putting up with it for all these years. Well, I am. Just telling you meks me feel better. Look, I'd better go in case Eric should come back and have a go at me for not clearing up the dinner dishes. On the other hand, a couple of pints might have mellowed his mood or else our Barry might be home, in which case I'll get a bit of peace. Tarra, Vin, I'll see meself out.' She unexpectedly gave Vinnie a peck on her cheek before she left.

A deeply thoughtful Vinnie returned to her armchair. This didn't seem real somehow. Something didn't ring true. But she had witnessed Noreen's deep distress, seen the bruise on her arm, and her story was plausible. Regardless, she still couldn't quite believe that behind the mild-mannered mask Eric was a monster.

Noreen had hardly been gone ten minutes when the back door opened and Gary came in. Vinnie rose to greet him, worried when she remembered last night's conversation with Julie.

'Er . . . nothing wrong I hope, Gary?'

'Wrong? Oh, the lamps business. I think they're rather nice and they look great in the bedroom. I told Julie she'd made a good choice.'

'You're not angry then?'

'No, of course not.' He smiled reassuringly at her. 'She told me all about feeling so guilty and coming to see you. I confirmed to her what you told her. That it wasn't my intention to stop her spending money completely, just to make her far more careful with what she does spend. I think she's doing fine, Mrs Deakin, don't you?'

'I certainly do, Gary. She's a different person, isn't she?'

'She's actually better than the one I married. I loved that girl, but this one I absolutely adore. We have words now and again, but that's only natural, isn't it? Julie never has a mardy tantrum because she can't get her own way. And, Mrs Deakin, it's lovely for me to see you two so close now, and I know it's made such a difference to Julie, being on good terms with her mother.' He looked at her searchingly. 'You look tired.'

'A little. We're really busy at work, and it's been one of those weeks when as soon as I sit down to relax in the evening, I get a visitor. It seems to be one after the other lately. But don't think I'm not pleased to see you because I am. Julie at home, is she?'

'She's popped out to see a friend and I took the

opportunity to come round for a private word with you. I wonder if you've got any plans for her birthday a week on Saturday? You hadn't mentioned anything to me so I was beginning to wonder . . .'

'If it had slipped my mind,' she finished for him. 'And, Gary, you're right, it had.' Vinnie was mortified, clamping a hand to her mouth. 'My daughter will be twenty-one and I hadn't given it a thought. For goodness' sake, don't tell her, will you? Oh, dear, how could I have forgotten? So, no, I haven't made any plans.' She looked at him expectantly. 'Have you anything in mind?'

'I have been saving for a while and wondered what you thought about me getting her a gold necklace?'

'Oh, she would love that, Gary. Something from you to treasure and pass down to her own daughter, should you have one,' she added quickly. 'Oh, yes, most definitely. I planned a long time ago to give her a family heirloom on her twenty-first. It's my mother's eternity ring. My father bought it for her on the day I was born. Very pretty it is, three tiny rubies set into a gold band. As soon as he knew she was expecting my father started saving for it. It took him all the nine months. Bless him, he walked to work so he could build up the pennies. Of course it isn't valuable as such but it has sentimental value.'

'Julie will treasure it,' he said softly.

She smiled, then frowned in thought. 'Of course, I would like to do something myself for her since it's such a special occasion.' Her mind drifted and settled on Janie. Due to her disappearance Vinnie had been denied the opportunity of making her twenty-first birthday special, or any birthday since she had left come to that. How had Janie celebrated that day? she wondered sadly. Had she given any thought to her family, who on that day more than any other had grieved for her loss? Well, her mother certainly had. For Vinnie every day since Janie's abrupt departure had been hard to get through but the day of her twenty-first birthday had been particularly difficult. As she had for her youngest daughter, Vinnie had set aside something, her own mother's engagement ring in this case, and had looked forward to presenting it to her eldest daughter on the day she came of age.

'Are you all right, Mrs Deakin?' Gary asked her.

'Pardon? Oh yes, dear. I . . . er . . . was just thinking what we could do for Julie's birthday,' she fibbed, not wanting to tell him the real reason for her sudden distractedness. 'Have you any ideas at all? Is there anything she has her eye on, do you know? Something for herself.'

He pursed his lips thoughtfully. 'Since she's been a reformed character I never hear her hanker after anything. The only items she's bought since all this came about are those lamps. What about a bracelet to go with the necklace I'm getting her?'

'It's an idea, but to be honest, Gary, I don't want to take the shine off the gift you're giving her by buying her jewellery. I could always get her that at Christmas.' A thought suddenly struck her. 'Oh, what about a surprise party?'

His eyes widened in delight. 'Oh, yes,' he enthused. 'That's a great idea.'

Vinnie's mind whirled as ideas began to flood in. 'We ought to make it something special. I could see about hiring a hall. I'm sure Betty will help me make a cake and I know she'll give me a hand with the food. We'll have to do all the preparations at her house in case Julie just happens to pop in here and see me unannounced. If she catches us in the act the secret will be out. Do you know a good band . . . oh, you youngsters like those record chappies now, don't you?'

He stared at her, non-plussed. 'Oh, you mean a disco. My brother should know of a good DJ . . . er, disc jockey we can hire for the evening.' He paused and eyed her in concern. 'Look, please excuse me for saying so but you've not long had all the expense of the wedding. We don't have to make it a huge occasion, just family and a few friends. I'd like to help with the arrangements as much as I can and I know my parents will offer to contribute. If I can somehow manage to get Julie out of the house for the day we can hold it at our house.'

'That would take some planning, Gary. Julie isn't stupid, she would twig something was going on. Be much easier to have it here.'

'Are you sure? It's a lot of work for you.'

'A lot of pleasure, not work, Gary. Julie is my daughter and this is such a special occasion. Something for her to remember.' Vinnie beamed enthusiastically. 'Oh, this is so exciting. I just hope I watch my tongue and let nothing slip when I see her.'

'Me too,' he said, laughing. 'On the night I could tell her I'm taking her out for dinner and use some excuse to say we have to call in here first.' He rubbed his hands together delightedly. 'This sounds just the job. I thought we'd be racking our brains for hours thinking what to do. Right, I'll get back home before Julie returns and I get the third degree on where I've been and she gets an idea we're up to something.' He gave his mother-in-law an affectionate kiss on her cheek. 'I'm just warning you in case you make other plans meantime but I know Julie is going to ask you to come for Sunday dinner along with my parents, but look surprised when she asks you, won't you?'

'Yes, I promise. I'll look forward to that. Julie's a good cook.'

He smiled at her mischievously. 'Not quite up to your standard yet, Mrs Deakin, but she's getting there. Goodnight.'

'Take care, Gary.'

Across town, Keith yawned as he accepted the cup of cocoa Angie handed to him. 'Thanks, love.'

'Can I get you anything else? A biscuit? Sandwich?'

'No, thanks, love. I'm still full after that lovely meal you cooked earlier.'

She scrutinised him. 'You look tired,' she commented. 'Sit forward and let me plump the cushions up to make you more comfortable.'

'Angie, I'm fine, really,' he snapped. 'I'm quite capable of plumping the cushions myself.'

Her face tightened, hurt. 'I was only trying my best to look after you.'

'Yes, I know, dear,' he said hurriedly, regretting his abrasive manner towards her. 'And a grand job you do too.'

'You mean that?'

'Yes, Angie, of course I mean it.'

She sat down on the sofa, curling her legs comfortably underneath her.

'Mmm, this cocoa is delicious, thank you,' Keith said, taking a sip.

'I put a drop of cream in it. I knew you'd like that,' she said, taking a sip of her own. 'Yes, if I say it myself it is good. Oh, I nearly forgot to tell you that I'm thinking of inviting a couple of my colleagues and their spouses for dinner on Saturday night. I can't remember the last dinner party we had so I thought it was about time we did, but mainly I thought the company would do you good. I'm thinking of doing prawn cocktail for starters, a crown roast with all the trimmings, and to follow fruit salad and a Black Forest gâteau. Sound all right to you?'

Keith was looking at her, astounded. He had made arrangements with Vinnie for Saturday night which he had no intention of cancelling. His breathing became short and he felt himself going all hot under the collar. Oh, how he wished he could find the courage to be honest with Angie, but he dreaded her reaction. He knew, though, that he would have to do it soon or else risk her finding out about his relationship with Vinnie through other sources, and that was too terrible to contemplate.

'Angie, I'm . . . er . . . sorry but I've already arranged to go out on Saturday night. It's . . . it's a meeting of the Sports and Social Club and I don't know how long it's going to go on for,' he lied.

'You never told me.' She looked hurt then glanced at him sharply. 'It's becoming a habit, your going out without telling me beforehand. Anyone would think you had something to hide.'

He sat bolt upright, almost upsetting his cup of cocoa. 'Hide! Of course I haven't, but a man is entitled to go out now and again, isn't he, Angie? Anyway I only found out about the meeting myself today and I'm obliged to go because I'm on the committee.' He sat back in his seat, his mind whirling frantically. This cloak and dagger business was becoming too much. What he was doing was so unfair to Angie. She didn't deserve to have him lying to her like this. He'd got to come clean with her, it was the only way. He'd do it next week. That would give him time to decide the best way to break his news to her, as gently as possible.

She was frowning at him thoughtfully. 'Funny time to have a meeting, on a Saturday night?'

'Pardon? Oh, yes, it is, but a couple of urgent things need discussing and it's the only time all of the committee could get together.'

'Oh, I see. So when are you going to take me to some of these works social events you help to organise?'

'You've never expressed an interest in going before. I

didn't think they'd be your cup of tea.'

'Mmm, I suppose not. Playing bingo doesn't interest me at all. Neither does watching people who've drunk far too much and make fools of themselves by climbing on stage and subjecting the audience to a dreadful rendition of a popular song. How some people see that as fun I've no idea.' She looked at Keith tight-faced and said tartly, 'So since you're otherwise engaged I shall have to organise the dinner party for another night. I trust you haven't another meeting planned for the following Saturday?'

He took a deep breath and sincerely hoped his face didn't reveal the guilt that was racking him. 'Not as far as I know.' He drained his cup and rose. 'If you don't mind, I'm going up.' He stepped across to her and pecked her cheek. 'Goodnight, dear.'

'Goodnight,' she snapped back.

Chapter Twenty-three

Thankfully the rest of the week passed relatively quietly for Vinnie. She was kept busy enough at work but during the evening received no unexpected visitors, except for Julie who called by on her way home from work and only stayed long enough to drink a cup of tea while she asked her mother to dinner on Sunday. Vinnie kept her word to Gary and appeared surprised but genuinely delighted at the invitation, and told Julie she would make one of her special apple pies as a contribution.

Vinnie saw no sight of Noreen or Eric and there were no raging arguments to be heard through the walls. She was unsure what to make of this. Was trouble brewing or a period of peace reigning in the Adler household? She vehemently hoped it was the latter.

As Saturday approached Vinnie's emotions, as they had on her previous ill-fated night out with Keith, were making her feel like a giddy teenager preparing for her first date. Friday evening saw her scrutinising her whole wardrobe again and it came down to a choice between a navy skirt and pale blue twin set or the dress Betty had suggested. She looked equally attractive in both. In the end she chose the dress, and after giving it a fresh press it was hung ready for her to put on the next evening. Her best black court shoes were cleaned and polished and her coat brushed to remove any specks of fluff.

By mid-morning Saturday, in an attempt to keep herself and her mind occupied, she had done her weekly shopping at the local Co-op and cleaned the house from top to bottom. She knew it was very doubtful Betty or Julie and Gary would drop in unexpectedly as they had done before when she was meeting Keith; they'd hopefully remember the severe scolding she had given them all after they'd nearly caused her such embarrassment. Still having several hours to fill until it was time to ready herself, she decided to make the promised apple pie to take with her to Julie's the next day.

The row from next door didn't start low and build gradually to a crescendo, it exploded so unexpectedly and with such magnitude it froze Vinnie rigid. Noreen's shrill screams filled the air, mingled with a slamming of doors so violent Vinnie's own house shook.

Hurriedly wiping her hands, she ran out of the front door and into the street, stunned by the sight that met her. Screaming a string of obscenities, Noreen was throwing all Eric's belongings out of the bedroom window. He himself was standing on the pavement staring up at his wife, his whole demeanour that of a bewildered man. Several passers-by had gathered and nearby neighbours were standing on doorsteps or leaning out of windows, taking a great deal of interest in the performance they were watching.

Vinnie rushed up to Eric. 'What on earth is going on?' she demanded as a pile of clothes landed at their feet.

He turned and looked at her, confused. 'I . . . I dunno, Vin,' he muttered as he bent to scoop up the items and ram them into a canvas holdall. 'She just went berserk.'

'Why?'

He gave a helpless shrug. 'Don't ask me, I ain't a clue.'

Suddenly the front door burst open and Noreen appeared, her arms flailing wildly. 'Now yer can piss off!' she hurled at Eric. 'Go and find someone else stupid enough ter put up with yer ways, 'cos I've had enough. And what are you lot looking at?' she screamed at the onlookers. 'Never seen a woman at the end of her tether before? Well, yer have now.'

Just then Barry roared up on his scooter. He jumped off, stared bewildered at his father then gawped at his mother. 'What the hell's going on?' he demanded.

'I've finally come ter me senses, that's what's going on,' Noreen shouted back at him. 'Yer father's used me as a punch bag for the last time. Look,' she cried, pulling up her sleeve. 'See this,' she screamed, displaying what appeared to be an angry red weal just above her wrist. 'Well, he did that ter me with the iron. Slammed it down on me before I could stop him. I just thank

God it weren't still plugged in.'

Barry looked at his father. 'Did you do that, Dad?'

Eric vehemently shook his head. 'I didn't, son, honest I didn't. I'd never hit any woman, let alone yer mother.'

'I believe her, Dad.' Face set hard Barry looked at her. 'How dare yer say me dad did that to yer? He's never so much as raised his hand to me, and by God there's bin times when even I'll admit I deserved a good pasting. Yer a bleddy liar, Mam, and you know yer are. You've finally flipped, ain't yer?'

'He did do it, I tell yer, and it ain't the first time. Anyway, how the hell would *you* know? Yer never at home. Still, I knew yer'd tek his side,' Noreen shouted at him accusingly. 'Well, you can bleddy go an' all.' She spun on her heel and stepped back inside the house, slamming the door shut behind her and shooting the bolts. Seconds later Barry's belongings were being thrown out of the upstairs window and just in time they all jumped out of the way as flying through the air came his record player. It hit the pavement with a crash. A pile of records quickly followed, smashing into smithereens too as they met the hard ground. As a flood of his other possessions quickly followed it occurred to Vinnie that it seemed like all the items had already been piled beneath the window as they were being thrown out in such rapid succession.

Barry ran over and looked down at his ruined belongings, slapping his hand to his forehead in horror. 'Oh, no,' he uttered, mortified, and stared up at his mother. 'Why did yer do that, Mam? Why?'

''Cos I felt like it,' she spat. 'Now get out of it, the pair of yer. And I don't care if I never clap eyes on either of yer again.'

With that she withdrew her head and yanked down the sash window with such force one of the panes of glass cracked.

They all stood there in shocked silence for several long moments. Finally it was Barry who took charge. 'Come on, Dad,' he urged. 'Help me get this lot into a bag.'

Vinnie, still having trouble believing that this very shaken man standing beside her was responsible for what his wife was accusing him of, addressed her question to Barry. 'Where will you go?'

'Who cares as long as it's far away from her. She's gone mad, saying me dad would do that to her. She wants locking up. Me dad's better off without her and so am I.' He paused for a moment from his packing. 'I'll tek him to me Uncle Harry and Auntie Mabel's.' Barry picked up the bag and slung it across his shoulder, taking his father's arm. 'Come on, Dad.'

Vinnie, numb with shock at all that had transpired, watched silently as Barry helped a dazed Eric astride the back of his scooter, wedged the heavy bag between them, kicked the scooter into action, then precariously drove off down the street, disappearing out of sight around the corner. Taking several deep breaths, she walked down the entry between the two houses and knocked on Noreen's back door.

Bolts were shot back and the mortice unlocked

before Noreen finally opened the door to her. Her face was defiant. 'Well, that'll give all them around here summat ter gossip about, won't it?' she snapped, standing aside to let Vinnie enter.

Vinnie stared at her, mystified. 'What on earth started it, Noreen?'

'N'ote. I told yer, Eric needs no excuses. Yer look as though yer don't believe me?'

'No, it's not that, Noreen, it's just that Eric seemed . . . well, so . . .'

'Shocked? Well, that was because he never expected in a million years I'd do summat like this.'

'So just out of the blue he picked up the iron and hit you with it?'

'I told yer he did. Didn't yer hear me scream out in shock? Yer should have done, it were loud enough. It bloody hurt, I can tell yer. As Barry said, I've finally flipped me lid but not in the way he meant. I've flipped 'cos I couldn't tek no more, Vinnie. Anyway, it's done now and I don't want ter talk about it ever again.'

Vinnie looked at her anxiously. 'If Eric has treated you so badly then . . .'

'IF! He bloody has, I tell you.'

'Well, okay then. Eric deserves what he's got in that case. But what about Barry?'

'What about him?'

'He's your son, Noreen. You can't throw him out too. He hasn't done anything to warrant that, surely?'

'Oh, don't start feeling sorry for *him*. It's about time he left home. He's hardly here anyway, always stopping with some mate or other. Stop concerning yerself, Vinnie. They won't be bleddy homeless. Someone'll feel sorry for 'em and tek 'em in. Eric's brother Harry and his wife have never liked me anyway, and once Eric's convinced 'em with his usual cock and bull that it's *him* that's innocent and *me* that's the nutter he'll have the pair of 'em eating out of his hands.' She scowled. 'Look, it's *me* yer should be bothered about,' she cried, stabbing a finger into her chest. 'You should be concentrating on helping *me* get on with me new life, not worrying about the bully what's bin causing me misery all these years. Now me new life starts this very minute and I'm bleddy well looking forward to it, believe me I am.' Her eyes shone brightly. 'Just think, I'm free ter do what I like when I bleddy like without that bastard breathing down me neck. And I know what I'm gonna do first.'

'What's that?' Vinnie asked.

Noreen gave a sly grin. 'Get meself a bloke that'll look after me like I should be looked after.'

Vinnie raised her eyebrows. Noreen really didn't mean to waste any time. 'And have you one in mind?'

'Oh, yes, and he'll fit the bill very nicely,' she replied cagily. 'Right, I expect yer've things ter be getting on with. I'm off up the town ter get meself a new frock,' she said, giving Vinnie a push towards the door. 'See yer later, yeah?'

Vinnie stared at her blankly. Noreen had just suffered a terrible ordeal yet there was no sign of it at all. She looked positively brimming over with excitement. 'Er . . . yes,' Vinnie answered vaguely.

★ ★ ★

It was ten minutes to eight. Having put earlier events to the back of her mind as the excitement of the coming evening overtook all else, Vinnie, looking radiant, was pacing the kitchen, ear cocked for Keith's arrival. Without warning the back door suddenly burst open and Noreen came in. She was dressed for an evening out and it was apparent to Vinnie that she'd had at least a couple of drinks already if not more judging by the flush to her cheeks which was definitely not caused by makeup. She pulled her coat wide, displaying what she wore underneath. 'What d'yer think then?' she asked Vinnie. 'Knock 'em dead, d'yer reckon?'

Vinnie took in the tight-fitting, short, low-cut red dress. Noreen's breasts were spilling out, in Vinnie's opinion most unsuitably for a woman of that age. 'Oh, er . . .'

'Looks great, dunnit?' Noreen cut in. 'Shows off me best assets, me tits and me legs,' she said, grinning proudly and rebuttoning her coat. 'So where's he teking us then?'

Vinnie stared at her. 'Sorry?'

'Keith, where's he teking us? I hope it's dancing. I fancy a smooch.'

'Oh! Er . . . look, I'm sorry, Noreen, but I think Keith is just expecting to take me out.' Vinnie hoped she sounded diplomatic.

'Oh, he won't mind me coming along. In fact, I'm sure he won't after the way he was with me the other night.' Just then there was a knock at the door and

Noreen beamed with excitement. 'Oh, that'll be him. I'll do the honours.' Before Vinnie could utter a word she had rushed off to let him in.

Keith arrived ahead of Noreen, looking very smart in a navy suit. He gave Vinnie a puzzled frown. 'Noreen's just told me she's joining us.' Then he smiled at her admiringly. 'You look lovely, Vinnie.'

'Thank you,' she responded before looking at him apologetically. 'I hope you don't mind but she seems to have invited herself along?'

Keith did mind, very much so; he wanted Vinnie all to himself, but he was too polite to say so.

Just then Noreen tottered in on her impossibly high stilettos. 'We all set then?' she said, hooking her arm through Keith's. 'So where yer teking us?' she asked, flashing him a winning smile.

Vinnie fought to hide her annoyance at the way Noreen blatantly pushed her aside and sat in the front of the car, leaving her no option but to get in the back. As soon as they arrived at the quiet country pub in Anstey she manipulated the seating arrangements, making sure she sat between Vinnie and Keith, and during the whole of the evening made sure it stayed that way. As soon as he arrived back at the table with the first round of drinks Noreen launched into a detailed account of her miserable years living with her bully of a husband, several times bursting into tears.

She was looking tearfully at Keith as she finally arrived at the episode earlier that day. 'Oh, it were dreadful having to resort to such measures, but there was n'ote else I could do, I'm sure you understand, Keith. It was either put up and shut up or take the bull by the horns. I just couldn't stand it no more so I chucked him out.' She made a great display of dabbing her eyes. 'I was so good to that man. Waited on him hand and foot, like I believe a man should be looked after, but what did I get in return? Nasty comments and a good thumping when no one was about. Clever bastard was my old man though yer wouldn't have known to look at him.' She fluttered her eyelashes. 'Still, that's over now. I'm a free woman and ready to find myself a decent man who knows how to treat a woman proper. Someone like you,' she added shamelessly.

He gave a discreet cough and looked at Vinnie. 'Would you like another drink?'

Before she could respond, Noreen drained the dregs in her glass and held it out to him. 'I'd love one, ta. You're a real gent, you are. Oh, can yer mek mine a double? I need it after the day I've had.' She paused just long enough until Keith was out of earshot before she said to Vinnie, 'He's a bloody good-looking chap,' and gave her a hefty nudge in her ribs. 'Not the type yer'd kick outta bed in a hurry. He's gorra good job an' all, ain't he? I bet his house is really nice. What happened with his wife? Any kids, do yer reckon?'

For the first time that evening she gave Vinnie the courtesy of time to answer a question. 'I really don't know much about his private life, we haven't got around to discussing things of that nature. He's never mentioned children . . .'

'Oh, good,' Noreen cut in. 'N'ote worse than bleddy kids around ter cramp yer style. Oh, shush, he's on the way back. We don't wanna let him think we was gossiping about him. Ta,' she said, accepting her drink from him and taking a large gulp. She patted the seat beside her and, giving Keith her full attention, said, 'Now what was we talking about before yer went off ter the bar?'

For Vinnie the evening was turning into a nightmare. Noreen's conduct was highly embarrassing and made worse by the fact that she obviously had no idea how uncomfortable she was making them both feel. Vinnie had to give Keith his due, though. He was far too polite to make any comment about it. Halfway through the evening, feeling a great need to get away from Noreen's constant shrill chatter, she made her excuses to go to the toilet.

Immediately Vinnie was out of sight and earshot Noreen shuffled herself right next to Keith, making sure she was exposing as much leg as possible, and put her hand on his knee. 'Bit quiet in here, ain't it? I expect a man like you prefers somewhere with a bit of life. I know I do.' Keith opened his mouth to respond but before he could she continued, 'In the light of the fact yer didn't know yer was going ter be graced with my company tonight, I s'pose yer did the gentlemanly thing and chose somewhere Vin would prefer. This place is just up her street,' she said, taking a quick glance around. 'Nice and safe, if yer understand what I mean. Oh, don't get me wrong, Vin's been a good neighbour ter me and she's a decent sort but she does like a quiet life, so if yer fancy a good night out yer know me address. I'm home most nights after six. I'll expect yer, will I?

'Oh, hello, Vin,' she said, hurriedly withdrawing her hand and moving a little away from Keith. 'I'm having a cracking time. Keith was just agreeing with me that it's a shame we didn't go somewhere more lively, but then we knew you wouldn't be keen.' Keith made to open his mouth and Noreen, pre-empting what he was going to say, butted in with, 'I'd love another, thanks,' holding out her empty glass.

Vinnie was relieved when Keith finally looked at his watch and suggested it was time they went home. Noreen was very inebriated by this time and needed a lot of persuading but finally relented. She clung to Keith's arm all the way back to his car and took it upon herself once again to sit in the front.

Back outside their respective houses, Noreen awkwardly clambered out of the car and feigned a stumble at which, as expected, Keith came to her rescue. He saw her safely to her front door. Once there she put her hand on his arm, reached up and kissed his cheek. 'Thanks fer a lovely night. I'll be seeing yer then, will I?'

He flashed a quick smile at her. 'You'll be all right now, will you?'

'Oh, yes,' she replied in a slurred voice as she let herself in.

Fighting back tears, Vinnie was by her own front door, fumbling in her handbag for her key. Thankfully she found it and inserted it into the lock. She realised Keith had joined her. Planting a smile on her face, she turned to face him. 'I don't know what to say to you, Keith.'

'Just say you'll come out with me again another night? But please, Vinnie, just us two.'

She stared at him, shocked. 'You really want to see me again after the fiasco of tonight?'

'More than ever. But promise me, let's make the arrangements and not tell a soul. Maybe that way we have a fighting chance of spending some time alone together.'

'I'd like that,' she whispered.

'Wednesday evening?'

Eyes bright, she nodded happily. 'Best I meet you somewhere, I think.'

He laughed. 'I was going to suggest that. Would you like to go to the pictures?'

She smiled. 'It's years since I've been.'

'Well, it's about time you did then. Outside the Odeon on Belgrave Gate at seven-thirty. All right with you? And I promise I'll see you safely onto your bus back home.'

'I'll look forward to it.'

He leaned over and his lips brushed her cheek. 'Goodnight, Vinnie.'

At his touch a shiver travelled through her body. 'Goodnight, Keith,' she whispered.

Vinnie was still in her dressing gown when Betty called

round the following morning.

'I know it's early, gel, but I couldn't wait ter find out how it all went last night.'

A short while later her friend was gawping at her, stupefied. 'She never! She really chucked them both out, just like that? And in public too?'

'It wasn't very nice. If Eric was treating her like that, and I have no reason to disbelieve her, then he deserved to be dealt with but I did feel sorry for him, Betty. He looked so shocked. Still, maybe that proves Noreen's case, that he's a damned good actor.' She tightened her lips and shook her head thoughtfully. 'I can't believe I lived next-door to him for all these years and hadn't a clue what he was doing to her.'

'There's lots of families with secrets like that, Vinnie,' Betty said quietly, not really liking to remind her of what had gone on in her own marriage that she hadn't had a clue about. 'I stopped being shocked long ago, the things I learned about the goings on in neighbours' houses. My own grandmother on me dad's side raised her husband's illegitimate son 'cos he gave her no choice. Just brought the baby home one night and told her to get on with it. What happened to the mother no one ever found out. What a bully he was! He led my gran a life worse than a dog's. He drank and he beat her. Yet yer know the ironic thing? When he died, within weeks she was dead too 'cos despite it all she loved him. I was lucky with my Alfred, wasn't I?'

Vinnie nodded. 'Yes, you were, Betty. I still don't think Noreen should have thrown her own son out but then maybe she was just at the end of her tether.'

'Maybe she was, but that don't excuse her muscling in on your date with Keith. She's a bleddy cheek if yer ask me.'

'Oh, Betty, don't be so harsh on her. She was upset and I did promise her I'd support her all I could.'

'But to the extent of teking her on a date with yer? Yer want yer head examining.'

'Well, I never exactly invited her, Betty, she invited herself and I hadn't the heart to do anything about it.'

'I would have. I'd have told her to sling her hook. Still, Keith apparently understood what an awkward position Noreen put yer in if he's asked yer to see him again.'

'I was shocked myself, to be honest. I thought he'd run a mile after having to sit through what he did last night.'

'He likes yer, Vinnie, that much is obvious.'

Her face lit up in delight. 'It seems so, doesn't it? And I must admit I like him. What the future holds for us I have no idea. There's so much I have to find out about him on a personal level. He needs to get to know me too, for that matter, but now at least we have the chance. Anyway, to be on the safe side we're meeting in town on Wednesday evening and going to the pictures.'

'A snog in the back row then, is it?' Betty said, a twinkle in her eyes.

'Away with you, Betty. We'll leave the back row for the youngsters.'

'Are yer going to invite Keith to Julie's birthday do?'

'Oh, I don't know. It's a bit early in our relationship for me to be doing things like that. He might think I'm trying to rush him as it's a family occasion.'

'I suppose so, but then it's a great opportunity for him to meet them and them him. See how yer feel nearer the time. Yer've another fortnight to weigh up how things are developing between yer. What about Noreen? Are you going to invite her?'

'I won't have any choice in the matter. As soon as she finds out there's something going on, she'll invite herself. Besides, she's bound to be very upset if I don't as, apart from her living next-door, she's known Julie since she was born.'

'Yeah, well, I'll keep an eye on her and mek sure she behaves herself. Now have yer decided what food we're gonna be preparing to mek this do really special for the gel?'

For the next half an hour they discussed what dishes to make and then, having decided, Vinnie made her excuses and went to get changed for Julie's.

Meanwhile, a very preoccupied Keith walked into the dining-room and looked hard at Angie, poring over the pile of school books she was marking. All night he had tossed and turned, unable to sleep. His conscience wouldn't allow him to go on with this charade any longer. Soon Vinnie would start to ask questions about his home life, which was perfectly natural, and he couldn't expect a woman like her to be happy remaining his secret while he dealt with Angie. It was one thing him having a secret love for a woman, quite another openly seeing her behind Angie's back. She needed to know the truth, whether she liked it or not, and the sooner he got it over with the better.

He took several deep breaths and said, 'I'm sorry to disturb you, dear, but we do need to talk.'

She raised her head and looked at him distractedly. 'Does it have to be right now? I really need to get this lot done and then I've to prepare the dinner and I've all the ironing to do . . .'

'I can see to the dinner,' he offered.

She smiled affectionately at him. 'And risk a burnt offering?'

'Well, at least I can tackle the ironing.'

She looked at him, hurt. 'It's my job to look after you.'

'And you do, wonderfully, but I'm not completely helpless, Angie.'

'I never said you were but ironing and cooking are women's jobs.' She laid her pen down on the table and gave him her full attention. 'All right, I'm all ears. So what do you want to talk to me about?'

Just then the telephone shrilled. 'I'd better answer that first,' he said, inwardly annoyed about the intrusion since he had finally plucked up the courage to do what he knew he had to. Seconds later he returned. 'It's for you, dear. Your headmaster.'

She frowned. 'What on earth is he ringing me for on a Sunday morning?' she said, heading off into the hallway where the telephone was. Several minutes later she returned and she didn't look at all happy.

'Bad news?' Keith asked.

'You might say that. Mr Williams has broken his leg so he can't accompany the children on the school trip and it seems I have no option but to take his place.'

'And you're not keen on that?'

'Keen? Would you be at the thought of spending eleven days with thirty lively fourteen year olds who have never been out of the city of their birth before, and most of that time will be closeted on a coach? I prayed my name wouldn't be drawn out of the hat and was so relieved when it wasn't. Still, I expect this is the price I pay for choosing to work in a school with a progressive headmaster. Whatever happened to five days at a camp in the Derbyshire Dales? It was good enough for me when I was at school.'

'You'll enjoy the opportunity of travelling through Europe to Switzerland, surely?'

'With you maybe, but not while I'm constantly having to keep eyes in the back of my head to check up on those little monsters.' She gave a despondent sigh. 'Oh, I suppose I'm being harsh on them. This trip away is probably the only one they'll ever get and the lucky few's families have found it hard to save the money.' Her attractive face looked strained. 'I have so much to do . . . we leave first thing Wednesday morning and won't be back until a week on Saturday evening, probably into the small hours. Oh, hell, that means our dinner party is off again.' She looked at him aghast.

'Oh, and what about you? How will you manage while I'm away?'

He stepped up to her and put his hands on her shoulders. 'I'll survive, I'm sure.'

'But . . .'

'Angie, stop worrying about me. I can cope without you for a few days.'

Her face was wreathed in anxiety. 'But I really don't like the thought of leaving you to fend for yourself.' Her eyes darted as her brain whirled into action. 'Oh, I could arrange for a temporary agency helper to come in?'

'Angie, really, you'll do no such thing. It's not like I'm an invalid or anything. I'm quite capable of getting myself a meal and tackling anything else that might need doing. Just you concentrate on getting yourself ready for this trip. And, Angie, you might enjoy it.'

She looked at him for several long moments before sighing in resignation. 'I have no choice, I have to go and that's that, but I doubt I'll enjoy it knowing there's no one looking after you while I'm away. But I'll make sure I have the basic shopping in to tide you over and you've enough clean clothes and I'll have a word with Mrs Foster next-door . . .'

'Angie, please, will you stop fussing? I've already told you I have no need of a temporary housekeeper or a neighbour popping in, and certainly not that busybody from next-door.' Keith fought to keep annoyance from showing in his voice. 'Now will you please stop worrying about me and get on with what you have to do.'

She reached up and gave him an affectionate kiss on his cheek. 'Don't ask me ever to stop worrying about you. It's like asking me to stop loving you and I'll never do that. I'll put the meat in the oven and while that's roasting I'll finish marking these books. Oh, you wanted to talk to me about something?'

His mind whirled frantically. What he had to tell her was going to upset her greatly and she had enough to cope with at this moment in time. 'It'll keep until you get back. It was . . . nothing urgent.'

'Are you sure?'

'Positive. I'll go and peel the potatoes while you finish your marking. Trust me to do that?' he said, smiling at her fondly.

As he laboured over his task his mind drifted and settled on Vinnie. Their date the previous evening had turned into a nightmare due to that dreadful woman inviting herself along and was made worse for him by the fact Noreen had so shamelessly thrown herself at him. Still, at least Vinnie had been there, even if he hadn't been able to hold any sort of conversation with her. He had Wednesday to look forward to, and the good thing was that Angie would be away which meant he wouldn't have to make up a reason for going out. On her return he would sort this situation out once and for all and next time nothing would stop him from doing so.

Chapter Twenty-four

Vinnie was humming happily to herself as she put the kettle on for a cup of tea. All the preparations for the surprise party were in place. All that remained now was for the guests to arrive just ahead of Julie and give her a lovely surprise.

The living-room looked very decorative. A colourful twenty-first birthday banner was pinned across the far wall and bunches of assorted balloons were dotted around. As with Ruby and Warren's engagement do, the furniture had been rearranged to allow room for dancing and the dining table had been brought through and placed against the wall underneath the banner, laden with food. Over the last week Vinnie and Betty had taken great trouble to prepare it all, the last-minute touches only done that morning. The cake sat in pride of place in the centre and if Vinnie said it herself a good job had been made of it. The table in the kitchen was filled with bottles of drink and stacks of plastic cups.

Betty came through, wiping her hands on her apron.

'That tea mashed yet?' she asked, parking herself on a chair. 'Oh, me bleddy back's killing me,' she groaned. 'Have yer a couple of aspirins, Vinnie, please?'

She unearthed a bottle from the kitchenette drawer and handed them to Betty. 'I told you you were doing too much. You've moved that table by yourself, haven't you? I warned you to wait for me to help,' she scolded.

Betty gave her a shamed look. 'You were busy mashing the tea. The table just needed squaring. It wasn't quite in the centre of the banner. Anyway,' she said, popping two pills into her mouth and swallowing them back, 'these'll soon sort me out. I might have a little sleep on the settee this afternoon. You will as well if yer have any sense, Vinnie. You've bin up since the crack of dawn, ain't yer, and I bet yer didn't sleep much last night from worrying about all this. A kip on the settee will do yer the world of good,' she advised.

'I'll have a job being's my settee is squashed in the dining-room at this moment. I'm going to have a long soak in the bath instead.' She turned and poured out two cups of tea. Moving a stack of plastic cups aside to make room, she put them on the table and sat down by Betty. Vinnie leaned over and affectionately gave her dear friend's arm a pat. 'You've been a treasure. I could never have managed all this without you.'

'We should go into business,' said Betty, tongue in cheek. 'Getting a dab hand at these dos, ain't we? First Ruby's engagement, now Julie's twenty-first. D'yer reckon we'd mek our fortunes?' she mused.

'I doubt it judging by the amount of food you eat

while preparing it,' Vinnie replied, laughing.

'Well, yer have ter taste it, don't yer? That mashed up corned beef mixed with Heinz tomato sauce in sandwiches is lovely. Who gave yer that idea, Vinnie?'

'My mother. She was always trying out new ways to eke out food and that was just one of many concoctions she came up with. She reckoned mixing boiled eggs with salad cream was another. I've my doubts about that one being her idea but it tasted nice anyway.'

'Well, there's one thing, Vinnie, your Julie won't have no complaints about you scrimping on this do. Yer've done her proud. Mind you, it is a red-letter day when all's said and done.' She eyed Vinnie knowingly. 'And one for you too considering who's coming.'

Vinnie eyed her worriedly. 'Do you think I've done the right thing in asking Keith?'

'He accepted quick enough, didn't he, so you must have. Eh, stop worrying. You've bin out together . . . what . . . three times now, excluding that fiasco when Noreen invited herself along, so it's not like yer first date. I reckon meself it won't be long before a proposal is made. Well, yer both free.'

'Now you *are* jumping the gun.'

'Am I? We'll see. It ain't like yer teenagers, Vinnie, is it? Time's rolling on and you want ter make the most of what yer've got left.'

'I'm not quite forty-one, Betty.'

'And yer a long time dead. So don't you go stalling things just 'cos yer think people might frown on yer. He's a good catch, Vinnie, and if yer don't grab him while yer can there's others that will. Talking of that, you ain't mentioned her next-door for a while.'

'I haven't seen her, that's why.' Vinnie grimaced. 'Well, I say I haven't *seen* her but that's not entirely true. I've called in on her several times since Eric left. Just to check how she was coping on her own and the last time to give her tonight's invitation. She never asked me in and seemed in an awful hurry to get rid of me. I had a feeling that when she saw it was me that was calling she was disappointed.'

Betty folded her arms under her ample bosom and tightened her lips knowingly. 'Expecting a man is my guess.'

Vinnie pursed her own. 'Mmm, you could be right. She did say her plan was to get herself one. I've an awful feeling Noreen will plunge in with the first man she meets, convincing herself he's Mr Right before she gives herself time to get to know him. Despite her saying she was never happy with Eric, she's not used to being on her own and having to cope.'

'She's old enough and ugly enough to make her own mistakes. Talking of Eric, have yer heard any word of him or Barry?'

'Not a dicky, and I daren't ask Noreen in case she goes for my jugular.'

'She's coming tonight, then?'

'I mentioned it to her but she didn't say one way or another. Maybe she's other plans, especially if there's a man lined up. Anyway, you'd better get off home and have that rest. I want you in fine fettle tonight, Betty.'

'Oh, I shall be that. Love a good do, me.' She drained the last of her tea, rose awkwardly and untied her apron which she rolled up into a ball and placed in her large handbag. 'I'll see yer tonight about seven then.'

At seven twenty-five prompt all the partygoers were gathered excitedly waiting for the arrival of the guest of honour. Looking very handsome in a smart sports jacket in dark brown, cream shirt and light-coloured trousers, Keith stood looking across at Vinnie, sipping his light ale. She was engrossed in conversation with Gary's mother and father. He thought she looked stunning in a jade satin straight skirt and sleeveless matching top.

'She looks lovely, don't she?'

He jerked his head around to see who had addressed him. 'Oh, hello, Mrs Trubshaw.' Then he smiled. 'Yes, Vinnie does.'

'Yer can call me Betty, Keith,' she said, a glimmer of amusement in her eyes. 'We ain't at work now, are we, so no need for ceremony. Don't worry, I shan't forget me place when we're back there. If I'm ever lucky enough to be graced by yer presence there it'll be "Mr Hamlin".'

'Are you trying to tell me I don't visit the floor often enough, Mrs . . . Betty?'

'Yer could say that. Don't worry, I know that yer busy. Anyway, that's why yer have a forelady as a gofer, ain't it? And we couldn't have a better one than that lady over there,' she said, nodding her head in Vinnie's direction.

Just then a voice piped up, 'They're here!'

The lights immediately went off and the house fell silent. The sound of the back door opening was heard and a bewildered Julie called out, 'Mum?' Then she was heard to say, 'I can't understand it, Gary. If Mum's out, why is the back door unlocked?' The house was then flooded with light and a loud cheer erupted: 'Surprise!' Julie, by now standing in the back room doorway, stared stunned at the sea of faces smiling at her, then her own face broke into a wide beam of delight. Her husband grabbed her to him and kissed her lips. 'Happy birthday, darling.'

She playfully punched him on his arm. 'Oh, you.' Then she spotted her mother, standing alongside Gary's parents. 'And you lot too,' she cried, wagging a finger at them. 'How did you all manage to keep this to yourselves?' Then she saw Betty. 'And I bet you had a hand in this too! Oh, thank you. Thank you all so much.'

Vinnie rushed up to hug her. 'Happy birthday, dear. There's presents for you stacked by the fireplace.' She handed her daughter a tiny wrapped box. 'This is something special. It was your grandmother's and I thought you'd like to have it.'

'Oh, Mum,' she uttered as she unwrapped it, and when she saw the tiny ring inside the box tears of happiness shone in her eyes. 'It's beautiful. I'll treasure it always. I've been so lucky. Look what Gary gave me,' she said proudly, fingering the thick gold chain around her neck.

Vinnie did not let on that she had already seen it

when he had brought it round the previous day for her approval. 'It's beautiful, Julie.' She leaned forward and gave her a kiss on the cheek. 'Just like you. Before you go and greet your guests there's someone I'd like you to meet.' She took her daughter's hand and led her over to where Keith was standing. Someone had put a record on and over the din Vinnie said loudly, 'Julie, this is my friend Mr Hamlin. Keith, this is my daughter Julie.'

They shook hands warmly.

'Your mother has told me so much about you. She hasn't exaggerated like most mothers do. You're as pretty as she says you are.'

Julie blushed. 'Thank you. I know a little about you too. You're Mum's boss, I know that much, and hopefully we'll get a chance to chat later but you will excuse me now while I go and say hello to everyone, won't you?'

'Of course.' He turned to Vinnie. 'A nice girl you have and her husband seems a presentable young man too.'

'Yes, they are,' she said proudly. It crossed her mind that Keith had never married and she wondered whether he had ever regretted not having children. Vinnie thought he had all the qualities to make a wonderful father. Just then a woman grabbed Vinnie's attention. 'Oh, you've got to tell me what's in these sandwiches, they're just delicious,' she enthused.

She smiled at Keith. 'Excuse me!'

A while later she was pouring out a sherry for Gary's mother when the back door opened and Noreen came in. It was very apparent to Vinnie that her neighbour had already been drinking. 'Hello, Noreen,' she greeted her. 'Glad you could come. I was beginning to think you had something better on when you didn't show.'

Noreen gave a disdainful sniff. 'Well, I thought I might too but it appears not, so I thought I might as well come in here as there's free booze and food in the offing,' she said sulkily.

Vinnie bit her tongue. 'Well, the drink is here as you can see and the food is through in the other room. Please help yourself.'

Noreen did to a large vodka and drop of tonic which she knocked straight back then helped herself to another before making her way to where the party was in full swing. Hovering in the doorway, sipping on her drink, she looked sullenly around. Then she spotted the reason for her misery standing by the table talking to Betty Trubshaw and her whole face lit up. Barging through the throng she rushed straight over to Keith and, completely ignoring Betty's presence, hooked her arm through his, nestling into his side. 'Why, there yer are,' she exclaimed. 'Yer should have called fer me and we could have come together. I've bin waiting for yer to call since that Saturday night but I expect yer've bin busy. Still, we're both here now. Shall we dance?'

Struggling to free his arm from her grip, Keith stood looking at her in embarrassment. 'Er . . . not just now if you don't mind.'

'Oh, no bother,' she replied, gazing up at him in adulation. 'Later, eh? I expect yer want another few drinks ter get yer in the mood.' She gave him a nudge in his ribs, tried to hook her arm through his again and when he resisted, looked at him strangely before taking a large gulp of her drink. 'I suppose it ain't a bad do for a make do and mend effort, is it, but if yer get fed up we can always slip away and find somewhere livelier. Or back to mine, if yer like,' she said, winking at him suggestively. 'As yer know, I'm a free woman now so we'll have the place to ourselves.'

Keith was just about to respond when Betty leaned forward and grabbed her arm, yanking her aside. 'What's your game?' she hissed.

'My game?' cried Noreen, wrenching herself free. 'What d'yer mean by that?'

'You know fine well. He's spoken for already.'

The woman's face screwed up scornfully. 'Yeah, by me, so keep yer eyes off, you old bag!'

'How dare yer speak ter me like that?' Betty snorted indignantly.

'Ladies,' urged Keith. 'Please keep it down, this is a birthday party, remember.' He turned his attention to Noreen but before he could say anything she grabbed his arm and demanded, 'Let's get out of here. Come on.'

'Oh, that's it,' Betty snapped. She grabbed Noreen's other arm and yanked her so forcibly away from Keith that her grip on his arm loosened and she stumbled forward. Betty dragged a protesting Noreen behind her, barged through the crowd and didn't stop until she was down at the bottom of the yard where she abruptly turned to face the other woman, wagging a warning finger at her. 'I told yer, Mr Hamlin is spoken for and not by you. Is that clear?'

'Why, you bitch, yer've made me rip me dress!' Noreen exploded, holding up the torn hem which on a short dress meant she was showing her knickers.

'Call that a dress?' Betty scornfully responded. 'I've seen more material in a five year old's skirt. Don't yer know how ridiculous you look?'

Just then Keith arrived and Noreen appealed to him. 'Tell her,' she demanded.

'Tell her what, Mrs Adler?'

'Mrs Adler? What d'yer mean, Mrs Adler?' she mimicked. 'It wasn't Mrs Adler the other Saturday night when yer was giving me the come on.'

'I can assure you, I wasn't,' he vehemently denied.

'You damned well were,' she accused, stabbing him hard in his chest with her finger. 'Yer fancied me rotten, I could tell.'

'I think it was the amount of drink you had had that was making you believe that. I do not fancy you, as you put it, Mrs Adler. The only woman I'm interested in is Vinnie.'

She looked at him in disbelief. 'Yer telling me yer'd choose *her* over me? You've gotta be joking,' she spat. 'Why, she couldn't keep her own husband happy, let alone a man like you.' She paused and a wicked smile curved her lips as she reached over and ran one hand suggestively up and down the lapel of his jacket. 'Share us then. Vin won't mind, she's used ter sharing. Yer don't even have ter tell her neither 'cos she won't have a clue. She never had a clue what was going on under her nose all those years she was with Tommy, so you've no need ter worry about her finding out about us. I can keep mum.'

'You brazen hussy!' Betty mouthed, astounded. 'If I hadn't heard it with me own ears I'd never have believed it.'

Noreen turned on her. 'And who asked you to join in a private conversation between Keith and me? Now piss off before I land yer one.'

'That's enough,' stormed Keith. 'Betty, please go inside. I'll deal with this.'

'But . . .'

'Please, Betty.'

She reluctantly complied and after she was out of earshot he said, 'Now please listen to me, Mrs Adler. I have no interest in you. I'm very sorry but that's the way of it. If you feel I led you on then it wasn't my intention.'

'You did lead me on,' she erupted. 'What yer saying, that I ain't good enough for yer?'

His look gave her her answer.

Her face contorted darkly. 'You'll be sorry you turned me down.' She pushed her face close to his and hissed, 'You ain't all sweetness and light like yer meking out you are. Got a little situation yerself yer not being honest about, ain't yer?'

'What do you mean by that?' he asked, puzzled. Then his heart pounded painfully. Could this woman possibly know about Angie? But how could she?

Noreen gave a sly grin. 'You know exactly what I mean. I wonder what yer wife's gonna say when she hears what her angel of a husband has been doing behind her back. Yer didn't call on me. Stupid I know now, but I was worried yer weren't well or summat. Well, it's easy ter find out where someone lives, and I saw her. Pretty, ain't she, but obviously not pretty enough to keep you at home. Well, as I told yer, I don't mind sharing – for a while at least 'til yer get rid of the wife. That was what you were planning to do so you could have Vinnie, wasn't it, or have I got it wrong and you were just going to be seeing both of them, hoping neither of 'em found out? Is that what yer up to? I wonder if Vinnie knows she's got another Tommy on her hands.'

He shook his head, horrified.

Just then Vinnie ran up to them. 'I've been told there's a row going on.' She glanced at them both worriedly. 'Is that right?'

Noreen flashed Keith a look before addressing her neighbour. 'Rowing? No, we weren't rowing, were we, Keith? Just having a nice little chat, straightening a few things out. Anyway I'm off. Enjoy the rest of yer party, won't yer?'

Vinnie stared after her, bemused. 'It's not like Noreen to be the first to leave a party. And what did she mean, you were straightening a few things out?'

He shook his head. 'She was talking double Dutch. Far too much to drink, I expect.'

Vinnie heard her name being called. It was Julie.

'Come on, Mum. You're missing a good party.'

She smiled up at Keith. 'Shall we go in?'

He took her arm, highly relieved that her deluded neighbour had left.

'Oh, Mum, that was a terrific do,' Julie said as she hugged and kissed her mother goodbye in the early hours of the morning. Her cheeks were flushed, but despite showing her tiredness Julie's eyes were shining brightly with happiness. 'I couldn't have wished to have spent my birthday in a better way. I really appreciate the hard work you did to put it all together.'

'It was my pleasure, sweetheart,' said Vinnie, hugging and kissing her back affectionately. 'I'm just so glad you enjoyed yourself. But please don't forget my comrades-in-arms Betty and Gary.'

'I've already thanked them.' Julie held her mother at arm's length and looked at her knowingly. 'Keith's a lovely man, I thoroughly approve.'

Vinnie blushed. 'We're just friends, dear, nothing more,' she said coyly.

'He likes you, Mum, and you like him. In fact, I'd go so far as to say it's much more than like for the pair of you if the way you were both looking at each other tonight is anything to go by. Right, where's my husband? Gary!' she called.

'Betty,' Vinnie scolded her friend a while later. 'You've done enough. It's two o'clock in the morning and I don't know about you but I'm ready for my bed.'

Betty stacked a dried dish on the shelf and put her soggy tea towel on the draining board. 'Well, that's practically all done now apart from moving yer furniture back.'

'That can wait until tomorrow when Gary comes round.'

Betty leaned her aching back against the sink and smiled at Vinnie tiredly. 'It was a cracking do. Everyone seemed to enjoy 'emselves and the food couldn't have bin that bad as there's hardly a crumb left.'

'I was worried we'd either done far too much or there wouldn't be enough, so it's good to see we got it just right. Yes, everyone did seem to be having a good time. The main thing is Julie did and that's what really counts. Well . . . I say everybody enjoyed themselves,' she mused thoughtfully. 'Noreen left rather suddenly which isn't like her.'

'Shouldn't worry about it,' Betty snapped, not having any intention of telling Vinnie why her neighbour had left so abruptly. 'It's my opinion she was sozzled before she arrived and it was a good thing she decided to go. She's a trouble-maker that one if ever I've spotted one, and if yer want my honest opinion, Vinnie, you were well shot of her tonight.' She rubbed her hands wearily over her face. 'Well, I suppose I'd better be off meself and see what that pair are up to. They left over an hour ago, didn't they?'

'If they've any sense they'll be tucked up in bed by now.'

Betty pulled a worried face. 'That's what bothers me.'

'Oh, Betty, Ruby and Warren are a sensible pair. A kiss and a cuddle on the settee is about as much as they'll get up to.'

'Yeah, they are. I suppose I'm just being over-protective. I'm really fond of that gel, Vinnie, and Warren ain't a bad lad by any means. Tell yer what, let's have a cuppa before I go. I don't know about you but I could murder one.'

'Good idea. You park your body while I do the honours.' Vinnie filled the kettle and put it on and prepared the teapot and cups.

As she busied herself Betty watched her thoughtfully. 'You enjoyed yerself tonight, didn't yer, Vinnie?' It was not a question but a statement.

She turned and smiled warmly. 'I did, very much so.'

'And dare I say that it was because a certain man was here?'

Vinnie flashed a shy smile. 'Could be.'

'Huh, there's no *could be* about it. You two had eyes only fer each other. If I ain't mistaken yer both well and truly smitten.'

'Oh, I don't know about that, Betty,' she said, putting the two steaming cups on the table. 'I mean, we haven't been out together that many times.'

'Three, six, a dozen. How many times must a couple see each other for their feelings to be known? I fell in love with my Alfred the first time I saw him.' She eyed Vinnie knowingly. 'I recognise a woman in love when I see her, and a man too. You two are in love, there's no getting away from that fact, Vinnie, so don't deny it, especially not ter me. I wouldn't mind placing a bet that the next wedding after Ruby's and Warren's will be yours and Keith's.'

'Oh, Betty, you're running away with yourself.'

'Am I? I don't think so. Be honest, Vinnie, you're in love with Keith Hamlin, ain't yer?'

She gave a sigh and stared intently at the table, tracing a pattern on it with her finger. 'Oh, he's a lovely man. But in love . . .' She raised her head and eyed Betty for several long moments before she nodded. 'Yes, I am, and I can't begin to tell you how it's making me feel. It's like a mixture of giddiness, walking on air, and a fear so great I want to shut myself in a dark cupboard and never come out. Tonight, just before Keith arrived, I felt sick with apprehension and when he walked through the door my heart was pounding that hard I thought everyone would hear it. Then just the way he looked at me made me . . . Betty, I can't explain it but it was like an explosion of joy inside me and suddenly everything was all right and I was safe because he was here.

'Oh, this is so silly at my age! How can I be in love with someone I hardly know anything about? I do wonder why a man like him isn't married, or if he ever has been married . . . Betty, all I know is that if Keith decided not to see me again, I'd be absolutely devastated. If you want the truth I'd fall apart. I loved the Tommy I knew with all my heart but what I feel for Keith . . . well, it's different. I feel so comfortable with him, like we've known each other years. But how can I feel like this after such a short space of time?'

Betty chuckled. 'Mother Nature is the only one who can answer that one, ducky. Sometimes, without warning, she smacks us right between the eyes, and it seems ter me that's just what's happened to you and Keith 'cos I've no doubt he feels the same for you as you do for him.'

'For me it's more like being thumped with a ten-pound sledge hammer,' Vinnie said, grinning. 'And I'm still reeling from it. If you'd said to me a couple of months ago that this would be happening between me and Keith, I'd have thought you were a raving idiot.'

'When yer seeing him again?'

'He's asked me to go out for a meal with him on Tuesday night.'

'Oh, dinner, eh? Maybe he's going to propose,' Betty said excitedly.

'Oh, Betty, stop it,' she scolded. 'If ever he does then that's a long way off.' She drained the dregs in her cup. 'Now are you sure you don't want to sleep here tonight, Betty? The bed is all freshly made up, waiting for you to climb into it.'

'That sounds like pure heaven, but I must get off. My youngest has invited herself and family fer dinner tomorrow. Considerate of her, weren't it, being's she knew I'd have a late one tonight. I know what she's after. Her two youngest need shoes and she's hoping I'll notice the holes in them and offer to buy 'em. If her husband spent less at the bookie's then she wouldn't need ter be sponging off her mam, would she? Still, they're me grandkids, bless 'em, so yer do what yer have ter, don't yer?' She scraped back her chair and rose. 'You have a good sleep, Vinnie, and I'll see yer at work on Monday.'

Chapter Twenty-five

Meantime Keith was smiling to himself as the taxi he'd taken turned into his road. Apart from the incident with Noreen, which as soon as she had left the party he had pushed to the back of his mind, he'd had the most wonderful night. It had been years since he had enjoyed himself so much, felt so relaxed, at ease in his surroundings. This new well-being was all down to the presence in his life of Lavinia Deakin. He knew now without a shadow of a doubt that his future lay with her and the need to tell Angie about her was paramount, as was his intention to marry Vinnie. Tomorrow morning Angie should be well rested after her return from her trip and that would be a good time to sit her down and explain everything. He just prayed she would understand.

He was most surprised to see light blazing from the house when the taxi drew up. Angie was safely back then and he was relieved and pleased, if surprised, she hadn't fallen straight into bed as she must be exhausted.

When he walked in she was standing with her back to the fireplace and he couldn't imagine why she was glaring so stonily at him. 'What time do you call this?' was her greeting.

He looked at her, bemused. 'What do you mean? Look, you're annoyed with me because I wasn't here when you arrived back. I'm sorry I wasn't but you must have seen the note I left just in case you arrived before I did. So how did the trip go?' he asked, taking off his coat. 'Were the children the monsters you predicted or little angels? The latter, I hope.'

She ignored his question. 'Your note said you'd gone to another committee meeting.'

'Yes. Why?'

'They go on rather late, don't they? Had a lot to discuss, did you? You look happy enough so I gather it was a successful meeting.'

He frowned at her, puzzled. 'What's this all about, Angie?'

She folded her arms under her shapely bosom, her pretty face scowling darkly. 'You tell me. I know you lied. There was no committee meeting. And what about the others you've attended recently – were they lies too to cover up for where you've really been?'

He froze. Angie knew. Her whole manner was telling him she did. Without taking his eyes from her he sank down in an armchair then looked at her remorsefully. 'You know, don't you?'

'About your sordid secret, yes, I do.'

He looked at her, shocked. 'Sordid! Oh, Angie, it's anything but.' He stared at her, puzzled. 'How did you find out?'

'I had a visitor.'

'A visitor? Who?'

'Oh, some . . . well, what I would describe as a trashy piece. She was common to say the least, and the language she used . . . well. I'd hardly opened the front door when she blurted out what you were up to behind my back. On the doorstep, too, and loudly enough for all the neighbours to hear. If this woman you're seeing is anything like her . . .' She gave him a look of pure disgust. 'The ironic thing is that that despicable woman who came here tonight thought you were my husband. Well, I took great pleasure in putting her straight on that and it was worth hearing what she told me just to wipe that smug smile off her face and see her slink off with her tail between her legs.'

Keith was in no doubt as to the woman's identity. Noreen Adler certainly was spiteful. He felt mortally sorry that Angie had found out about Vinnie in this way but nevertheless shook his head at her, annoyed. 'I'm not surprised anyone would think you're my wife, Angie, because you certainly act like one. But for Christ's sake, you're my daughter!'

'Yes, I am,' she hurled back. 'And I deserve a damned sight more respect than you're showing me.'

'Oh, Angie, how can you say I don't show you any respect? I love you . . .'

'Like you loved my mother? You seem to have forgotten all about her and the promises you made to her on the day she died. *There will never be anyone else for me, Gemma. I will love you for ever.* That's what you said to her. I was there, remember?'

'And I meant every word. I loved your mother so very much, Angie. I still do. I will never forget her, never.'

'Doesn't look like that to me. But you didn't just make promises to Mum, you also made a promise to me. When Mum drew her last breath we clung together, both sobbing. You said, "It's just you and me now, darling." *You and me*,' she repeated, emphasising the words. ' "We have to be strong for each other and look after each other," that's what you told me. And I promised always to be there for you, Dad. To look after you like Mum did so you wouldn't miss her so much. We vowed it to each other, didn't we? I take it that now this woman has come on the scene what you promised me and Mum means nothing to you?'

'That's not fair, Angie!'

'Isn't it? I've honoured my vows to the letter. I look after you as well as Mum did before she took ill.'

'Yes, you do, and I cannot fault you, my dear.'

'So why do you need another woman when you have me?'

'For the same reason you will one day need a man, Angie.'

'I don't need another man. I have you.'

He looked at her strangely. 'But it's not the same, is it? Don't you ever want someone's arms around you, someone to share things with?'

'I get that from you.'

'Yes, but in a fatherly way. Don't you ever feel the

374

need for . . .' His voice trailed off and he looked at her in embarrassment.

'What? Oh, you mean sex. You can say it, you know. It's the sixties and I do know about the birds and the bees. No, actually, I don't. My life is full enough with my career and looking after you. Since Mum's death you've been my first consideration in everything I've done, and I shall continue to honour that. Or would have. But you don't need me now, do you, not since you've replaced both me and Mum with this other woman.' Huge fat tears welled in her eyes and she wailed, 'After all I've done for you, I don't know how you can treat me like this! Mum will be turning in her grave.'

He stared at her, horrified. 'Your mother was a wonderful woman, Angie, and the last thing she would have wanted would be for the two people she loved most dearly to be grieving for her for ever.' His voice faltered. 'It almost destroyed me when she died. I thought the end of the world had come. The only thing that kept me going was you, Angie. But that was ten years ago.'

'Oh, promises have a life span, do they?' she snapped.

'Don't be sarcastic, Angela.' He looked at her searchingly. 'Don't you think you're taking these promises we made too far?' He gave a bewildered shrug. 'I mean, surely promising we would be each other's first consideration didn't preclude either of us finding other sources of happiness sometime in the future? If I ever married again that would not mean I'd be turning my back on you, Angie, and if you did I would not think for a minute you were abandoning me.'

'So you *are* considering marriage?' she cried, astounded.

'I said *if*, Angie.'

'But you are considering it?'

He didn't look at her for several long moments before saying slowly, 'Yes, I am. Look, I didn't keep this from you without a lot of thought, Angie. I didn't want to upset you unnecessarily because I remembered very well how you reacted when I took a woman out for dinner one night several years ago. I was honest then and told you, explained she was a friend and nothing more, but for days you treated me like I'd betrayed you and your mother and your mood never lightened until I'd absolutely convinced you I wasn't seeing her again. I've not enjoyed going behind your back, haven't enjoyed lying to you about my whereabouts. I've so wanted to tell you, about Vinnie . . . Lavinia Deakin. I . . . think a lot of her, Angie. In fact, I'm very fond of her . . . more than just fond.'

She was gawping at him, stunned. 'Lavinia Deakin? But she's one of your workers. The one you promoted to forelady. Her husband was murdered.' She shook her head incredulously. 'You cannot seriously be considering this woman as a future wife? You can't!' she cried, appalled. 'You do that and I will never speak to you again.'

'What? Oh, Angie . . .'

'I mean it. What will people think of you? I couldn't

bear them gossiping behind your back. How can you even be considering saddling yourself to the widow of a philanderer who got himself murdered by his floozy?'

'Stop it, Angie! Vinnie was in no way responsible for what her husband did or what happened to him. She's a lovely woman and you will like her, I know you will.'

'I won't because I've no intention of meeting her. Don't tell me she has nothing to do with what happened to her husband. Why did he feel the need for another woman in the first place? She must be responsible in some way. She must have treated him badly and that's why he went off. She's fooling you. Well, don't expect me to stand by and watch you make an idiot of yourself because I won't. Remember, I've met her friend. You'll finish with her or I'll never, ever speak to you again.'

'You don't mean that, Angie?' he gasped.

'Oh, but I do. You've already betrayed me by seeing her behind my back. She reduced you to that, I know she did. She's a bad influence already, there's no telling what you'd become if she really got her claws into you. The first thing she'd do is get rid of me and then I wouldn't be around to protect you, would I? It's her or me. Make your choice.'

'You're wrong about everything, Angie.'

'I'm not. She's blinded you. Make your choice.'

'You can't do this to me, Angie. I love you. You know I couldn't bear the thought of never seeing you again.'

'Well, prove it by honouring your promise to me on Mother's deathbed. Promise me you'll tell this woman it's over and that you'll never see her again. If you don't, I've told you what I'll do. You should know by now that *I* honour my promises.'

His face drained and his shoulders sagged. The thought of never again seeing Vinnie was unbearable to him, but then so was the thought of losing his daughter. 'I . . . oh, Angie, I can't! Please don't ask me to choose,' he implored. 'Look, just agree to meet Vinnie, then you'll see that all your fears are unfounded. And my feeling what I do for her makes no difference to my love for you. I'm your father and will always be there for you. You can't have any doubts about that, surely?'

She looked at him darkly before spinning on her heel and marching from the room.

He ran after her. 'Where are you going?' he called as she was halfway up the stairs.

She stopped and turned to face him. 'To pack.'

'Angie, you can't!'

'You've made your choice. I hope you'll not live to regret your decision, Father.'

'Angie, don't, please. Come back down and let's talk this through properly.'

'I've said all I have to say on the matter. I cannot believe you are choosing a murdered man's widow over your own daughter.'

'You're really going?' he uttered, distraught.

She nodded.

His whole body sagged despairingly. 'All right, Angie, you win. I promise to break it off with Vinnie and never see her again.'

Her eyes lit up. 'You will?'

He nodded.

'You'll go and see her first thing tomorrow and tell her?'

He nodded again.

She flew down the stairs and hugged him fiercely. 'I knew you'd see sense! You don't need another woman when you've got me. Go and sit down and I'll make us both a nice cup of tea, and then I'll tell you about my trip. Oh, they were little monsters, believe me, and I can't tell you how good it is to be back here at home with you.'

Chapter Twenty-six

Vinnie was stunned but delighted to find Keith on her doorstep just after eleven the next morning.

'Oh!' she exclaimed, her whole face lighting up with delight. 'Oh, how lovely to see you. Please come in,' she said, standing aside. She was suddenly very conscious of her untidy appearance. 'Please forgive me for looking such a mess,' she said, hurriedly untying her apron and running a hand through her dishevelled hair.

As much as he tried not to show it, the look he gave her was full of longing. 'You look lovely to me, Vinnie,' he said softly.

She flushed. 'You're being kind but thank you. You've just missed Gary. He came about an hour ago to help me replace the furniture. Cup of tea?' It was then she realised how terrible he looked and her smile faded. 'Is anything the matter?' she asked.

He gave a deep sigh and took her hands gently in his. 'I need to talk to you, Vinnie.'

'Oh!' Her heart beat furiously as a terrible feeling of dread filled her. Keith had something awful to tell her,

she knew without a doubt. As she silently led him into
the living-room and watched him sit down, all sorts of
things flashed through her mind. Judging by his face,
his whole persona, it surely had to do with the death of
someone close. She sat down next to him on the settee,
clasped her hands tightly, looked at him and waited. He
was staring down at his hands and it seemed an age to
Vinnie before he slowly raised his head and fixed his
eyes on her.

'I have to end our relationship, Vinnie. I'm so sorry.'

His words stunned her senseless. She had prepared
herself to hear bad news from him but not something
that would rock her to the core of her existence. So
shocked was she, all she was able to utter was, 'I see.'

'It's not something I want to do, Vinnie, I need you to
understand that.'

'Then why?' she asked, bewildered.

She was shocked to see his eyes fill with tears. 'So
that I don't lose my daughter.' He bent his head in
shame. 'You deserve a proper explanation, Vinnie, so
please bear with me.' He took a deep breath. 'Since my
wife died ten years ago, Angela, my daughter, has taken
over the role of caring for me. Until last night I didn't
realise how seriously she took her commitment. Her
mother's death was so unexpected for both of us and
such a shock that we made each other a promise then
that we'd always look after each other. Angie needed
me and I needed her. We were so grieved at the time of
Gemma's death that neither of us thought we'd recover
from it. But time does heal. Slowly, very slowly, I came

to terms with losing my wife and found that I was getting on with my life. I didn't feel so wretched when I woke in the morning. I was beginning to look forward to what the day brought for me instead of dreading it because Gemma wasn't around to share it.

'I thought the same was happening for Angie. I had travelled through this grieving period with her, comforted her, talked to her, then listened helplessly to her sobbing alone in her bed at night. I was so relieved for Angie when those times of darkness seemed to grow less frequent and she seemed whole again, happy within herself. It never struck me that what she had done to compensate for the loss of her mother was to centre her whole life around me, to the extent of excluding anyone else. She's got it into her head that the promises we made to each other on my wife's death bed are cast in stone. She is religiously sticking to every word and expects me to do the same.'

He gave a deep sigh. 'I was aware that should I ever introduce another woman to her then I would have a difficult task on my hands. Several years back I did take a lady out to dinner one night and Angie's reaction was . . . well, hard to deal with. But because the lady in question was just a friend and nothing more, our dinner date a one off, that was it really but it did prepare me for the fact that should anything more serious be on the cards in the future, then winning Angie's approval was not going to be easy. But I never thought to be faced with that situation anyway until you and I got together.'

He looked Vinnie full in her face and if ever she'd

had any doubt about Keith's feelings for her, she had none now. Love for her brimmed unashamedly in his eyes.

'Vinnie, the first time I met you, when Archie Pegg introduced us, I fell in love with you. I don't know how or why but I did. As our eyes met and we briefly shook hands I can only say this incredible feeling shot through me and I felt myself go weak. I was appalled at myself. You were a married woman, seemingly happy, and would never be mine. Worst of all, I was coveting another man's wife. But that didn't seem to make any difference. I loved you, Vinnie. I dealt with it by being aloof with you. Doing that kept my feelings a secret and didn't embarrass either of us. Then suddenly you were free and my dream came true when you agreed to go out with me for a drink. I daren't hope that you'd ever feel for me what I did for you but when it appeared to me that you did, I can't tell you how overjoyed I was. Stupidly, though, I never told Angie, never hinted anything.'

'And now she has found out about me?' Vinnie whispered.

He nodded. 'Yes. How is not important, but she has. She challenged me last night when I arrived home from the party. The upshot is, Vinnie, she has given me an ultimatum: either her or you. It seems I cannot have both. I tried my best to talk to her, explain, reason with her, but she is resolute. Vinnie, I love you so much. The thought of us parting, well . . .' His face crumpled and his eyes welled with tears. 'But I love my daughter too. My conscience won't let me shove her aside for the sake of my own happiness.' He rose abruptly. 'I'd best go.'

Completely dumbstruck by what she had been told and the terrible consequences, Vinnie automatically rose also. He took her hands in his and gently stroked them. She was in no doubt that it was taking all Keith's will-power to keep himself under control. 'I hope you can forgive me,' he uttered, his voice choked with emotion.

With that he dropped her hands and rushed from the house.

It was nearly Sunday teatime when a fraught Betty answered the knock on her back door and almost fell upon Vinnie, her face wreathed in a mixture of relief and delight. 'Well, hello, ducky. What a welcome sight you are. The family's still here and it looks like they plan on stopping fer tea an' all. Eating me out of house and home they are, and the kids are driving me daft. All I want is a bit of shut eye 'cos I'm still tired after the party, but I've no chance, have I? Come on in then,' she said, standing aside.

'I won't, Betty, if you don't mind. I didn't want to disturb you but I need a favour.'

'Anything. Yer know that without asking, gel.' She noticed Vinnie's pallor then. 'God strewth, gel, yer look like death. Oh, no one's died, have they?' she hurriedly asked, hoping she hadn't put her foot straight in it.

'No, Betty.' Vinnie thrust an envelope at her. 'When

you get into work tomorrow, would you please give this to Keith?'

Betty looked at it, bewildered, then raised questioning eyes. 'Why?' she asked, taking it.

'It's my resignation.'

'Yer what?' Grabbing her coat from the peg she pulled the door to behind her, took Vinnie's arm and marched her down to the end of the yard. 'What's going on?' Betty asked, pulling on the coat. 'Why are you looking worse than ever I saw yer when Tommy died?'

'I've just had a shock, Betty. I'm upset, that's all.'

'Bleddy devastated more like it. Well, yer ain't leaving here until her tell me everything,' she demanded. She looked down then, feeling a tug on her skirt, to see a grubby little face looking back at her. 'Get back inside,' she ordered the child. 'Can't yer see Grandma's talking?'

'But I'm hungry, Gramma.'

'What, after all the roast chicken and spuds yer rammed down yer neck at dinnertime? Oh, tell yer mam ter get yer a slice of bread and jam. And tell her ter wash yer face first! Go on, skeddadle,' she said, bending down and turning the child in the direction of the house, giving her a gentle tap on her backside. 'Bleddy lazy bugger is our Karen,' she fumed, straightening up. 'She's sitting on her fat arse with that husband of hers, both of 'em glued to the telly, expecting me to chase after their kids while they're here.' She folded her arms and took a stance. 'Now, yer were saying?'

Vinnie had been hoping to avoid this but might have

known she couldn't. She took a deep breath and told her dear friend what had happened.

When she had finished Betty gawped at her. 'I don't believe it! Well, I'll be blowed. I'm stumped fer words, truly I am. But he can't do this, surely? It ain't right. I'll . . . I'll go and see this daughter of his, mek her see reason. It's criminal, that's what it is, her expecting her father to live the life of a monk just 'cos of some promise they made to each other when they were both so upset.'

'No, Betty, you mustn't,' Vinnie implored. 'Please promise me you'll do no such thing? Keith isn't doing this lightly, believe me, I know he isn't. He's a broken man, Betty. He's suffering as much as I am but he's made his decision and I can do nothing but respect that. Part of me does understand, Betty. I've lost a daughter too, remember? I know the pain it brings. I wouldn't wish that on him. If he had chosen to be with me, Angela would always have been between us. It's best this way.'

Betty was staring at her incredulously. 'I wish I had your compassion, Vinnie.'

'You have, Betty. You just show it in different ways. You know I have to accept this and get on with it.'

'And giving yer resignation in is the best way?'

'I have to, Betty. I couldn't go into work and see him every day, knowing how we feel about each other and that it's impossible for us to be together. It's best I leave. Maybe we stand a fighting chance of getting over each other then. I can get another job easily enough.'

'You'll hate working with strangers. And how are we all going to cope without yer? Yer the best forelady that department's ever had. Besides,' she said, sniffing away tears, 'yer me friend and I'll miss yer.'

'You can see me anytime you like, Betty, it just won't be during working hours. Please, don't make this any harder for me than it is already.'

'I'm sorry, this has just knocked me fer six. I'd me wedding outfit planned, hadn't I? Of course I'll deliver yer resignation letter for yer, Vinnie, and anything else that happens to be in here,' she said knowingly, fingering the bulky envelope between her fingers.

Vinnie patted her arm affectionately and gave her a kiss on the cheek. 'Thank you.'

Betty eyed her gravely. 'A' yer sure yer won't come in for a cuppa?'

She shook her head. 'Thank you for asking but I want to be on my own. You understand, don't you?'

She nodded and watched in deep sadness as Vinnie lifted the latch on the back gate and disappeared from view.

Darkness had fallen by the time she'd turned into her street and was making her way towards her house. It was very cold, the sharp easterly wind bearing the promise of the bitter winter that would rapidly be upon them. But Vinnie was heedless of it, the terrible blow she had received earlier that day occupying all her thoughts.

Noreen, dressed for an evening out in her usual unflattering style, almost knocked her over when she charged out of her front door, banging it shut behind her. 'Oh, it's you,' she snorted disdainfully. 'Yer wanna watch where yer going, yer nearly had me over.' Tilting her head to one side, she looked at Vinnie slyly and asked, 'Where's lover boy ternight then?'

Vinnie looked at her blankly for a moment until it struck her what Noreen was getting at. 'Oh, er . . . me and Keith aren't seeing each other anymore,' she said softly.

A smug smile twitched at Noreen's lips. 'Really? Oh, what a shame.' She paused and looked at her gloatingly. 'So neither of us has ended up with the man we wanted. Maybe we're quits now, Lavinia Deakin.'

Vinnie looked at her, puzzled, but before she could ask Noreen what she had meant the woman was tottering off down the street on her three-inch heels.

Chapter Twenty-seven

'Oh, it were a lovely service. Weren't it a lovely service, Vinnie? And she looks beautiful, doesn't she?'

Vinnie nodded in agreement. 'Warren looks very handsome too,' she commented.

Betty pulled a face. 'Well, as handsome as a lanky thing like him can, I suppose. Most of his spots have had a day off, thank God. I had a fight with him over that suit. Yer should have seen what he wanted ter wear – it were maroon, can yer believe? "Well," I said to him, "you turn up in that, lad, and I'll personally make sure yer bride leaves yer standing." ' She gave a chuckle. 'Good job he believed me, ain't it? Still, yer can't show yer grandkids in fifty years' time photos of their grand-dad looking a right berk in a maroon suit and pink shirt with all fancy frills down the front, even if he did swear blind it were all the fashion. "Fashion be buggered," I said. "This is yer bleddy wedding day, not a fancy dress party." ' She glanced skywards. 'Yer'd never think it were only an April day, would yer? That sun's so hot it's more like June ter me. Lucky with the weather too, what more could they have asked for?' She paused and scrutinised her friend. 'You all right, Vinnie, only yer a bit quiet?'

Vinnie flashed her an astonished look. 'As you have just had an attack of the verbals, can you wonder?'

'Well, I s'pose yer've a point.' She looked at her friend searchingly. 'You shed a few tears, didn't yer?'

'Yes, it was a very moving service.'

'It was, but that ain't the real reason yer were having a quiet weep.' Betty laid her hand on Vinnie's arm and gave it a gentle squeeze. 'You were thinking of him, weren't yer, lovey?'

'You're far too shrewd for your own good sometimes, Betty. Yes, you're right, Keith did cross my mind.'

'Well, he's bound to, it's only natural at a time like this. Teks a while to get over someone you loved. There'll be someone else fer you, ducky.'

Trouble was, Vinnie didn't want anyone else. Time healed, so Keith had told her, but in this case it didn't seem to be easing the heartache over her loss. If anything it was as acute as the day he had told her he had no choice but to end their relationship. She realised Betty was asking her something. 'Sorry, Betty?'

'I just asked if yer'd any regrets about leaving Brewin's? Yer know we all still miss yer summat terrible. The new forelady ain't a patch on you. There ain't a chance yer'd change yer mind and come back, is there? Oh, fergive me, Vinnie, that was selfish of me. Coming back wouldn't be right for you, would it? Keith is still there and it's obvious you ain't over him yet. Still, yer seem happy enough in yer new job.'

Vinnie declined to answer. She detested her new workplace. The job was boring and the girls not at all like the lovely friendly ones she had left behind; the forelady presiding over them made Cynthia Dodds seem a saint in comparison and Vinnie was seriously considering looking for something else. She wished she could tell Betty the truth about how she would love to come back to work at Brewin's as since she had left she had had two jobs, both of which she wasn't at all happy with and still wasn't settled work-wise. She knew this information would only upset her friend, though, so thought it best not to tell her.

Six months had passed since Keith had ended their relationship. Since then she felt she had wandered aimlessly through the days. They seemed empty and meaningless without him, the only thing making her life worthwhile the close relationship she now had with Julie and the support she received from Betty. She desperately wanted to enquire after Keith but what good would that do? Only keep him fresh in her mind, and she needed no extra help in doing that. There were times when she wondered if she would ever get over him. With deep respect for Vinnie's feelings, Betty never usually mentioned him in any way, shape or form.

Vinnie took a look around at the wedding guests, all gathered in groups chatting jovially as they waited for the happy couple to have their formal photographs taken before the family shots. Their bright clothes reminded Vinnie of a huge bouquet of wild summer flowers and she thought it such a pity the black and white photographs would not capture this colourful display. There were family and friends from both sides, almost seventy in number. The only two missing were Ruby's parents, still unrelenting about giving their blessing to this union. Ruby, though, had long since come to terms with her parents' alienation from her because she'd finally refused to do their bidding after all her years of unquestioning service. Betty had become a mother to her now and to her joy Ruby had finally learned what it was like to be looked after, cared for, fussed over and chided in a loving not dictatorial way.

Arm in arm, Julie and Gary strolled over to them. Julie looked stunning in a bright yellow mini-dress, white court shoes and matching shoulder bag, her long blonde hair piled in coils and twists at the back of her head, curling tendrils framing her pretty face. Gary was very handsome and smart in a dark blue Mod-style suit.

'I wondered where you two had got to.' Julie smiled, giving her mother a peck on the cheek. 'Got your confetti ready for when they leave? Is the camera all set, Gary?'

He pulled the camera out of its case and wound the film on until it clicked into place. 'It is now. You three stand together and I'll take a snap of you.'

They posed and he clicked.

'Nice shot that should make,' he said, winding the film on again. 'My three favourite ladies.'

'Shouldn't let yer mam hear yer say that,' Betty said. Just then she spotted the newly marrieds emerging from the side of the church where they had been posing for photographs in the garden. 'Oh, quick,' she excitedly exclaimed. 'Here they are!'

Confetti and camera at the ready, they all charged forward.

At just after six that evening, along with most of the other guests except for a few stragglers, Vinnie, Betty, Julie and Gary came out of the wedding reception at the local church hall.

'I hope the weather holds good for them in Inglemells,' Julie said.

'I don't think the weather will make any difference one way or another to Ruby and Warren, I suspect they'll have more pressing things occupying them,' responded Betty bluntly.

Julie and Gary looked at each other and giggled, both remembering their own honeymoon. 'Well, we'd best be off,' said Julie. 'This old married couple is going to spend the evening curled up in front of the television.'

'And that's about all I'm fit for after such a hectic day,' Gary said, stifling a yawn. 'I just hope no friends decide to call round.'

'No chance of that,' said Julie, smiling at him lovingly. 'I warned everyone we were having a night in tonight.' She nestled against her husband and looked at her mother and Betty. 'I want him all to myself.'

Vinnie smiled at them. These days her daughter and her husband certainly seemed happy and content together.

Betty addressed Vinnie. 'Well, this old 'un has still got some life in her even if these young things ain't. I thought I'd round the day off with a bottle of stout and game of bingo down the club. Gonna join me, Vinnie?'

'Thanks for asking, Betty, but I'm going to take a lead from the kids here and curl up in front of the television. You enjoy yourself, though.'

'Oh, I intend to,' she said, grinning. 'Besides, I've gorra get used ter being on me own again now Ruby is no longer with me. Still, that little house of theirs is hardly a stone's throw away so I expect I shall see more of them than I do me own family who only call when they're after summat. 'Least Ruby appreciates me for me and not what she can get outta me.' She leaned over and gave Vinnie a quick peck on her cheek. 'See yer soon then, lovey.'

'I'll call one night in the week, that's if you haven't called on me first,' she responded. Then she gave her daughter a goodbye kiss and hug, followed by her son-in-law. 'You're sure you both still want me to come for dinner tomorrow? Wouldn't you like the day to yourselves?'

'Mum, the only way I'm going to become as good a cook as you is by practising and having you there to keep me right. Besides, we love having you. So we'll expect you around twelve,' said Julie.

After they'd all said their goodbyes Vinnie made her

way home. The warmth of the spring day had given way to a chilly evening and she was looking forward to changing out of her wedding attire, putting on her cosy dressing gown and curling up in her armchair. She hoped there was something entertaining for her to watch on the television, that's if she managed to keep awake.

Making her way up the back path, she stopped short. In the gloom of the evening she could see the outline of someone hovering by her back door. 'Who is it?' she abruptly called out.

'Vinnie, it's me, Eric,' came the whispered response. 'I was just about ter go, thinking yer were out for the night,' he said, stepping closer and smiling an apology. 'Sorry I'm slinking in the shadows but I didn't want Noreen to catch sight of me in case she caused any trouble.'

Vinnie was staring at him blankly, not knowing how to greet her old friend and neighbour. Was he the monster Noreen proclaimed or the lovely man Vinnie had always thought him to be?

From the look on her face he knew what was going through her mind. 'Vinnie, please, yer've got ter believe me – I ain't never said a bad word ter Noreen, let alone struck her in any way, and there were many times when she really did try me patience. Come on, yer don't believe I could do anything bad to her, do yer? I ain't got it in me, Vinnie.'

She looked at him searchingly for several long moments. 'I have to say, I never quite believed what she said.'

He smiled at her. 'I'm glad of that, Vinnie. It's bin bothering me what people round here think of me, especially you. Noreen said some terrible things. All lies, Vinnie, honest.'

She gave his arm a friendly pat. 'Look, it's a bit chilly out here, do you want to come in?'

A few minutes later they were both seated in her living-room, nursing cups of tea. 'So how have you been, Eric?' she asked him.

He put his cup down on the small table to the side of him, leaned forward, clasped his hands and nodded positively. 'Can't grumble, Vinnie. I s'pose, if yer want the truth, I'm happier than I've ever bin. 'Course, I was shell-shocked for a while. Couldn't believe what had happened. One minute I'm sitting in me chair feeling really good that me wife couldn't do enough for me, and the next she's screaming abuse at me, accusing me of attacking her with the iron and chucking me out. I couldn't tek in what was happening, to be honest. I thought she'd had a brainstorm or summat.' He gave her a helpless look. 'I mean, Vinnie, you musta bin shocked an' all when yer saw what was going on?'

'I was,' she said.

'Luckily Harry and Mabel saw fit ter tek me in. I sat there like a zombie for a couple of days, trying to come ter terms with what had happened. I mean, I'd lost everything and couldn't understand why. It didn't help that Mabel was absolutely convinced it was the best thing that could have happened to me. She claims Noreen's led me a dog's life since the minute we got married.' He gave a sad sigh. 'Maybe that's true, Vinnie, but I loved her, you see. Oh, her temper and her ways got me down sometimes, but that was Noreen. I suppose I used to get a bit miffed that she spent so much time in your house.' He flashed Vinnie a hurt look. 'She only seemed happy when she was here with you and Tommy. But then I thought women need friends, don't they, and tried not to let it bother me. Besides, I felt sure that if she overstayed her welcome you'd soon put her straight.' He gave a deep sigh. 'I did me best for her, Vinnie.'

She smiled at him tenderly. 'I know you did, Eric.'

'But it wasn't enough, was it? Mabel said I could have had Buckingham Palace built for Noreen and she'd have complained it weren't big enough.'

Vinnie shook her head and gave a sigh. 'Some women are never happy with what they've got, Eric. Noreen is one of those women, I'm afraid.'

'Yeah, I know that now. A week after she threw me out I came round to see her, to try and talk to her, hoped she'd come to her senses, but she . . . well, yer know what her language is like, Vinnie. The things she said hurt me more than I can ever tell yer. But one of the things she told me was that she knew she'd made a mistake not long after we married, that she hadn't wanted to be with me for years. Why did she stay with me then? I asked her. She just laughed in me face, Vinnie. Said if I didn't know then I was a bigger fool than ever she'd took me for. Then she slammed the door in me face.'

He gave a deep, sad sigh, his face crumpling with hurt. 'I had to accept me marriage was over,' he said gruffly. 'At the start I struggled ter cope but I managed to get a flat and some bits and pieces of furniture together.' His face brightened and he gave Vinnie a smile. 'If I say it meself, it's quite homely. It's got a decent-sized lounge, a small kitchen and two bedrooms. The toilet is out on the landing and there's no bathroom as such but we manage. Barry, I'm glad to say, has moved in with me. He'd gone to stay with a mate while I was at me brother's. He can't stand Mabel, says she gets on his nerves nearly as much as his mother does. She's not a bad woman, Vinnie, just fusses a lot, never leaves yer alone, that sort. Anyway, Barry seems happier than he's ever done, and we get on fine.' He paused and announced proudly, 'I've got meself a girlfriend. Lovely woman she is. My age. Her husband left her with two kids to raise, so she ain't had it easy. We met down the pub. She ain't a boozer but a friend had persuaded her to go out and she said it were her lucky night 'cos she met me.' He stopped and his face clouded over. 'How is Noreen, Vinnie? That's why I've come here ternight, just to check how she is. I suppose I feel guilty for being so happy. But even so, I did love her and can't help but worry about her still.'

She looked at him for a moment. After all Noreen had put him through he still had feelings for her. How could he be the brute his wife had described? Was it possible Noreen had used this cynical ploy to be rid of him just so she was free to pursue other men, could live the life she felt she was entitled to, the kind of life she couldn't with a husband? Had she not given a thought to the fact that in doing so her husband would lose everything through no fault of his own? Vinnie had already been well aware of Noreen's selfish streak but had never before realised how deep it ran.

She gave a despondent sigh. 'I wish I could tell you, Eric.'

'What do yer mean?'

'Well . . . she doesn't have anything to do with me. I don't know why but she obviously has her reasons.' Vinnie knew from the sounds that filtered through their adjoining wall that Noreen often brought people home from her jaunts out at night. From their muted voices she knew they were male. She didn't want to tell Eric this. What good would it do him to know? 'I catch a glimpse of her now and again and she's still alive, that's about as much as I can tell you. I can only think she's turned her back on all her past life, and that includes me too.'

He gave a deep sigh. 'Seems so, don't it? I blame that pal of hers at work. I think she turned Noreen's head with her tales of going out enjoying herself. She's a divorcee, ain't she? From what I can gather a different bloke every night. If that's what Noreen wants and it meks her happy, then who am I to begrudge her?'

'You're very generous, Eric. Anyone else in your position wouldn't look at it like that. I'm glad you've found some happiness with this new lady of yours.'

'Well, no one knows what the future holds, do they,

Vinnie? But at the moment we're very happy together. Barry likes her, I'm glad ter say, 'cos that fact is very important to me, and her kids seem ter like me. Now I know Noreen's getting on very well without me I shall put in for a divorce. Have ter move forward, Vinnie. No point in hanging on to past things that have no consequence. What's the saying? Out with the old . . .' He picked up his cup and took a sip. 'How are you, anyway?'

'Oh, I'm fine, thank you, Eric. Like you, I can't grumble.'

'Glad ter hear it, gel. You more than most have had yer fair share of trouble. So how are you and that chappy you were seeing before I left? Marriage on the cards, dare I ask?'

'No,' she said, rather more abruptly than she'd meant to. 'Things didn't work out between us, I'm afraid to say.'

'Oh, I am sorry, Vinnie,' he said with genuine remorse. 'Still, yer a fine-looking woman and I should imagine there's plenty out there that'd jump at yer. I always thought Tommy a lucky beggar.' He drained the dregs in his cup and rose. 'I've took enough of yer time up. It were lovely seeing yer again.'

She rose also and laid a hand on his arm. 'Likewise, Eric. I'm so glad things are working out for you. Please keep in touch, won't you?'

'I'd like that, Vinnie. Maybe you could come round and have a bite to eat with me sometime?'

'Yes, I'd love to.'

Seeing Eric again had brought back memories for Vinnie and for a long time after he had left she sat reliving happier times shared with her neighbours when she had been oblivious to Tommy's carryings on behind her back. But those times, like Eric's life with Noreen, were all past now, gone for ever.

Chapter Twenty-eight

Geraldine Parker was looking at Vinnie keenly. 'Well, I have to say that from what you've told me your skills would be very valuable to us. I see you worked for over twenty years at Brewin's. You can't come better qualified than having served your time with the likes of them.' She smiled at Vinnie warmly. 'I won't ask why you decided to leave. We all need a change at some time in our lives. Now, we're only a small firm but pride ourselves on our work. We manage to keep abreast of the big companies by specialising in very select lines for the more upmarket outlets, whereas they make their money on cheaper mass-produced products.' She paused for a moment, sat back in her chair and appraised Vinnie. 'We are very careful who we choose to join our workforce. Not only are we looking for people who possess the best skills, my husband and I like to run a happy ship so we want to know that the person we take on will fit in. Would you like to tell me about yourself?'

Vinnie did and hoped that what she was saying

would interest Geraldine. She was glad she had taken the plunge to try her hand at getting this job. The small advertisement for a qualified inspector in the Hosiery Vacancies column of the *Leicester Mercury* had almost slipped her eye but luckily she had spotted it, thinking that maybe she might be happier in a smaller firm after working for years in the largest kind, especially after her most recent experiences where she had been miserable to say the least and that wasn't all down to her heartache over Keith. The more she had heard Geraldine Parker describe the job they were offering and how the company was run, the more Vinnie liked the sound of it, feeling she would be as happy working here as anywhere.

The total workforce was less than thirty, and it had seemed to Vinnie as she had been led through the small factory into Mrs Parker's office that the atmosphere was indeed relaxed and happy as they all worked away, singing along with the radio, laughing and chatting. Several women had smiled at her encouragingly as she had passed by their work stations.

As Vinnie outlined her experience and aptitudes Geraldine Parker took notes. When Vinnie had finished she consulted them again then sat back satisfied, smiling warmly at her. 'You're more than qualified for the job we're offering, and I consider myself a good judge of character and my instincts tell me you'll fit in just fine. We pay the going rate and, instead of bonuses twice a year, give our staff a percentage of our profits. We find that encourages good working ethics. So if you like the sound of what you hear, I'd like to offer you the post.'

A warm glow filled Vinnie. She was going to be happy working here. 'Thank you,' she said. 'I'd be delighted to accept.' Just then she heard the sound of the outer office door opening and shutting.

'Oh, good,' said Geraldine, 'my little treasure has returned from lunch. I'll introduce you.' She laughed at the confused look on Vinnie's face. 'I call her that because that's just what she is. She came here about seven years ago and persuaded me to give her the job of office junior, despite having no experience. I'm so glad I did because she's worth her weight in gold to me. She makes the office run like clockwork.'

Geraldine pressed a buzzer on her desk and Vinnie heard a young, friendly voice politely ask, 'Yes, Mrs Parker?'

'Come through, dear. I'd like to introduce you to our new Quality Inspector.'

Seconds later the door into Geraldine's office opened and a very attractive, blonde-haired woman of around twenty-three walked in.

Vinnie and the young woman looked at each other and froze. Hands clutched to her chest, Vinnie rose slowly and gasped, 'Janie . . .' She felt the room sway, then everything went black.

She was aware of something icy cold on her brow, something wet being pressed inside her lips, and in the distance a muffled voice calling, 'Mum? Oh, Mum, please, please say you're all right?'

She struggled to clear the fog from her brain, fought to understand where she was. Why was someone trying to get her to drink a sip of water? Who was calling her Mum?

Then, like a bolt of lightning, everything came together and she sat upright, staring wildly at the young girl looking back at her whose pretty face was streaked with tears. A face that was like her sister's yet different. A face Vinnie had never given up hope of seeing again. She had prayed so long for this moment, she couldn't believe it was here. Her hand went to her mouth. 'Janie?' she murmured. 'Oh, Janie, is it really you?'

She nodded. 'Yes, Mum. Yes, it is.' She seemed to waver for a moment before she leaned forward and threw her arms around her mother, hugging her fiercely. 'Oh, Mum, Mum,' she wailed. 'I never thought I'd see you again.'

A discreet cough was heard. Startled, they both looked over to see Geraldine Parker holding out Janie's coat and handbag. 'Jane, why don't you take your mother home? It's obvious you two need to talk. Don't worry about work, I'll cover for you.'

Janie looked at her gratefully. 'Are you sure, Mrs Parker?'

'Positive, my dear. Now off you both go.'

Far too numb with shock to speak, Vinnie picked up her bag and silently followed her daughter out.

The tiny flat Janie took her to was spotless, its odd assortment of furniture, although shabby, nicely arranged. There was an assortment of leafy potted plants on the kitchen windowsill which appeared to be well looked after.

Vinnie was still having trouble believing her dearest dream of being reunited with her daughter had actually come true. There was so much she wanted to say to Janie, so much she wanted to ask her, but all she could manage at this moment was, 'You have your home very nice, dear.' She graciously accepted the cup of tea Janie handed her, eyes riveted on her, watching her daughter's every movement as she sat down next to her on the old settee.

Janie took a deep breath. 'It's where I live, Mum. It's not home to me, though.'

Her mother looked at her, deeply puzzled. 'Then why did you leave your home, Janie?'

Clamping her mouth tight, she clenched her hands and stared down blindly at them. 'It was just best I did. Can we please leave it at that?'

Vinnie put her cup and saucer down on the floor then put her hands on Janie's arms, turned her around to face her and fixed her eyes on hers. 'No, Janie, we can't. You're my daughter. I love you. When you left, I can't tell you how I felt. It was like a part of me had gone too. I know we weren't close. I tried, believe me I tried, but the closer I tried to get to you, the more you pushed me away. But that didn't stop me loving you, Janie. When I came home that night and found you'd taken most of your stuff and gone without a word, I went demented. We searched everywhere, did all we could to find you. Have you any idea what went through my mind when we could find no trace of you? Oh, Janie, I didn't know what to think, it was so terrible. Were you in trouble in some way and couldn't bring yourself to tell us? I even worried you were pregnant. As time passed and you never showed, well . . . there was nothing else I could do but pray you'd come home. We all missed you so much, Janie.'

'Oh, I doubt that,' she said harshly.

Vinnie looked at her, horrified. 'But of course we did. How can you think we didn't?'

'You might have, Mum.' And before she could stop herself she'd blurted, 'But not *him*.'

Vinnie frowned, bewildered. 'Him? Who's that?'

Janie rose, walked across to the fireplace then turned around to look at her mother.

Vinnie was horrified to see a look of utter distress all over her face. She leaped up, rushed over and pulled her daughter into her arms. 'Janie, please tell me who this man is? Was it a boyfriend? Was he plaguing you or something? Please tell me, Janie.'

She looked blankly at her mother for several long moments then, gulping, she said, 'Yes, yes, it was a boyfriend.'

'Well, who was it? What was he doing to you?' Vinnie demanded.

'Mum, please,' she begged. 'It's all past now. Can't we just forget about it?'

'I can't, Janie. I've lost over seven years of your life. What happened must have been terrible for you to resort to leaving the family who loved you.'

She frenziedly shook her head. 'Oh, you loved me, Mum, I was never in doubt of that, but as for *him*. . . '

Vinnie frowned at her, deeply bewildered. The way her daughter kept spitting out the word *him*, whoever this person was it was someone close enough to have affected her badly. Her mind was whirling frantically, thinking of all the close males her daughter could possibly have been connected with then. Her thoughts settled horrifyingly on one person, the only one who could evoke such a response from her. Vinnie was astounded. 'Janie, are you referring to your father?' she asked, desperately hoping she was wrong. 'Was he the one behind all this?'

She looked at her mother for several long moments, then slowly nodded. 'Yes,' she uttered. She took several gulps of air before continuing. 'I so wanted to come and see you when I read about his death in the paper, but I couldn't. I knew if I did I'd have to tell you it all and I couldn't bear you to know. I can't bear it now. I stayed away from you so I wouldn't have to do this. Please, Mum, please don't ask me to tell you,' she implored.

Vinnie gasped, a terrible feeling of foreboding racing through her. She took her distraught daughter's arm and led her back to the settee, sitting her down. Seated next to her, she took her hands. 'Janie, please tell me,' she commanded. 'I want to know what it was your father did that made you feel you had no alternative but to leave like that.'

Her face ashen, Janie vehemently shook her head. 'You don't, Mum, you really don't. Look, it's better you go. Pretend you never found me. It's really better this way. Really, Mum, it is,' she begged.

'What!' Vinnie cried. 'Janie, I'm not going anywhere. You must tell me, I want to know it all.'

Taking several deep breaths, Janie clasped her hands so tightly her knuckles bulged and Vinnie was shocked to see her visibly shaking. When she began to talk her voice was low and thick with emotion. 'The first time it happened, Mum, I'd come home from school one lunchtime. I was about seven. I knew I shouldn't but I'd left my gym kit on the kitchen table that morning and the teacher would have made me do gym in my knickers and I couldn't stand the thought of that. So I sneaked out when the dinner lady wasn't looking. I knew Dad was on nightshift and would be asleep so I was very quiet when I let myself in. I got my kit and was just about to leave when I heard funny noises coming from upstairs. I stood for a moment, listening. I couldn't understand what the noises were. It was like strange groaning sounds. Then I could hear laughing. I wondered why Dad was laughing and why he'd been making those noises. I thought if he was ill or something he'd need help. So I went up to find out what was going on. Your bedroom door was half-open and I peeped inside.'

She stopped and looked at her mother, mortified, her pretty blue eyes filled with pain.

Vinnie knew without a doubt that what she was about to be told was something really dreadful and her heart began to pound so painfully it echoed in her ears. 'Go on, Janie, please,' she urged.

She took another deep breath. 'Oh, Mum, it was so awful. I just froze when I saw them. Even at that age I knew what they were doing. She was in your bed with my dad. I remember so clearly everything they said. It's like it's branded into my memory.'

Frozen in shock, Vinnie was staring blindly at her. 'Who was in my bed with your father, Janie? Who?'

Her face crumpled. '*Her*,' she hissed. 'And Dad was always saying how much he hated her, calling her terrible names and making out it was all your fault her always being in our house. Yet there she was, as bold as brass in your bed, cuddling Dad and giggling. Then she suddenly stopped giggling and said, "When are you going to tell her, Tommy? You promised me you'd do it ages ago. I've waited all this time. We can't keep on like this." Dad looked annoyed at her. He said, "Oh, will you stop going on? I can't leave, not while the kids are so young. You can't ask a man to walk out on his kids. You know I love you, and if you love me you'll wait." She said, "You know I'll wait. That's the trouble with you, Tommy Deakin, you know you've got me wrapped around your little finger." He kissed her then and laughed. "That's because you know I'm worth waiting for," he said.

'It was then they saw me. I must have done something to alert them. I can't describe the looks on their faces. Before I could do anything, Dad had leaped out of bed and grabbed me hard and was shaking me. He was calling me all sorts. He threatened me, Mum, said if I breathed a word to you or anyone he would make sure everyone knew I was lying and get me put away in the naughty children's home where I'd be beaten with a stick and put in a dark cellar and never let out. I'd die down there all alone, he said. I was so frightened, Mum. I can't tell you how much.'

'Oh, Janie,' she mouthed, horrified. 'Oh, Janie, Janie. Why didn't you tell me?'

'I just couldn't,' she cried. 'Mum, I couldn't. I knew what they were doing was bad and I wanted to come to you but I was terrified of what would happen to me if I did. And more than that, I knew how upset you'd be. I couldn't do it to you, Mum.'

'So that's why you suddenly went so quiet and withdrawn?' she whispered.

'Yes. Every time Dad and me came into contact he would give me this warning look and I just got more and more terrified. He made it obvious he hated me for what I knew. He tormented me, Mum, and he made it so plain he preferred Julie to me. Dad encouraged her to be awful to me, I know he did. I didn't understand at the time but now I know that it was his way of constantly reminding me what would happen if I opened my mouth. I just felt it best to keep out of his way. I was safe in my bedroom so as much as possible I spent my time in there.'

She took a deep shuddering breath and her eyes glazed with hatred. 'All those years I was growing up, I knew they were still seeing each other every chance they could get and he was still pretending in front of us he couldn't stand the sight of her. Whenever *she* was in our house, she and Dad were always giving each other those looks. You know, Mum, sort of secret. That's why she was always with us. So she could be with *him*. If we ever went out for the day she'd always make sure she got invited along, and when we had family parties and things she came whether she was invited or not.'

She paused and her face darkened. 'Then I caught them again. I was fifteen, not long started work. I'd been feeling rotten and the forelady sent me home. I never gave a thought to the fact Dad was on nightshift and what I might find. I just wanted to get home and go to bed. As soon as I reached the bottom of the stairs I could hear them even from that distance, every word they were saying. She was shouting at him, telling him that if he didn't tell you about them and leave, she was going to tell you herself. He must have slapped her because I heard the smack and she stopped shouting. He was angry. "Don't ever tell me what to do," he bellowed at her. "I told you I'd leave when the kids got married and not before." She told him he didn't care about his kids, was just using us as an excuse. Then she threatened again that she would tell you. He calmed down then, told her not to be so stupid or she'd ruin everything. He promised her faithfully, "I will leave, I will, but only when the kids have gone."

'I just felt this explosion inside me then, Mum. It was like all those years of hatred for what they were doing behind your back and how they had treated me just blew up inside me. Before I knew what I was doing I rushed up the stairs and dived into the bedroom. I was screaming at them. "I've had enough, I'm going to tell my mum what you're both doing to her." Next thing I knew Dad had me against the wall with his hands around my throat. She was egging him on. "Shut the sneaky little bitch up, Tommy. Shut her up, shut her up!" I really thought Dad was going to kill me. He pushed his face into mine. I could smell his breath. And his eyes . . . Oh, Mum, he hated me for finding him like that. He looked so evil. He said to me, "Pack your bags and get out, and if I ever set eyes on you again I'll make you sorry. You have no right to spy on me. You tell your mother any of this and you'll wish you'd never been born." I couldn't breathe. I felt I was going to die. I was so terrified, Mum. Suddenly he let me go and I dashed from the room, grabbed as much of my stuff as I could and fled. I used Grandma's surname, Perkins, so you'd never find me.' Janie burst into tears then, a great torrent which flowed down her face. 'Oh, Mum,' she wailed, wiping snot from under her nose with the back of her hand. 'I'm so sorry, really I am.'

As she had listened, a deathly white Vinnie, utterly numb with shock at what she was hearing, had gripped her own hands so tightly her nails had dug in and drawn blood. For his own selfish reasons Tommy had robbed his daughter of her childhood. By his mistreatment of her he'd made her life a living hell. How could he do that? Then, after he had sent her away, he'd acted so distraught over her disappearance when in truth he was the cause of it. As for *her* . . . How could Vinnie have been so blind?

Throwing her arms around her daughter, she hugged her so tightly Janie could hardly breathe. 'No, it's me that's sorry. I knew none of this, Janie, really I didn't. Please, please forgive me,' she begged. 'I had no idea. No idea at all.' She pulled away from her beloved daughter and looked at her beseechingly. 'I let you down so badly. I should have known.'

'How could you, Mum? They were so clever, so careful. I only found out because I came home when I shouldn't have. It's not your fault. None of this is your fault. You were a good mother. You tried to find out why I changed but I couldn't tell you. I loved you too much to hurt you, Mum.' Her face contorted with pain. 'When I learned about his death in the paper and read how he had died, I felt nothing, was just glad he was gone and couldn't hurt you anymore. I wanted desperately to come home and comfort you, but how could I? It was bad enough your knowing he'd been carrying on with that woman who murdered him. If I'd come home I would have had to tell you the reason I left. Then you would have had even more pain and suffering, wouldn't you? I couldn't do it to you, Mum. Nor could I come to the funeral and pretend to be upset when I hated him for what he'd done to all of us. You and my sister thought Dad was Mr Wonderful until he died. It was bad enough you thinking he'd had just that one affair which ended in his death, without all the rest of it on top.'

A great wash of tears came pouring down Vinnie's face. 'Oh, Janie,' she sobbed, bereft. 'I can't bear to think of all you've suffered. All these years we've been robbed of because of your father. But then, it wasn't just him, was it? It was *her* too. She lied and connived behind my back for all those years and I never had a clue.'

Vinnie felt a surge of fury building within her, an anger so great it was almost suffocating. She ran a hand tenderly down the side of her daughter's face. 'There is so much we have to talk about, so much catching up to do. Please forgive me, darling, but first I have to go somewhere. Will you be all right? I'll be back to help you pack. You're coming home, Janie, where you belong. I'm never going to lose you again, my darling. Never. I know I cannot make up for what you've gone through, but by God, I'll do my best,' she vowed.

'Where are you going, Mum?'

'I think you know, dear.' Her face darkened. 'Of all the things she has done to me, playing her part in taking my daughter from me is something I cannot forgive.'

Chapter Twenty-nine

The door was banged upon with such force Noreen almost leaped out of her skin. Yanking it open she screamed, 'What the blazes did yer hammer like that for? I ain't effing deaf, yer know.'

Icy eyes glared back at her. 'The mood I'm in, you're lucky I didn't break it down with an axe.'

Vinnie's uncharacteristic harshness struck Noreen momentarily speechless. Gathering her wits she nonchalantly asked, 'What's so bleddy urgent then? Mek it quick, I'm going out.'

Without waiting to be asked in Vinnie pushed past her and on into the back room where she turned to face Noreen who had followed her through. 'I know, Noreen,' she said darkly.

She gave a shrug. 'Know? Know what?'

'About you and Tommy.'

A fleeting look of shock crossed her face, then a wicked grin replaced it. 'Huh. Took yer long enough to find out, didn't it? So what's yer problem? Tommy's dead, so what does it matter now?'

At such a matter-of-fact response all Vinnie's pent-up fury erupted and she fought to control an urge to wipe the smile from Noreen's face with a hefty punch. 'What does it matter?' she cried furiously. 'Not only were you deceiving me, but you made my daughter's life a living hell to cover up what you and Tommy were doing. *That* is something I can never, ever forgive you for, Noreen. Do you know what suffering you caused all those years? Have you any idea what you and Tommy put that child through?'

'Why all the fuss about *her*?' Noreen shrieked back. 'Warra about *me* and what *I* was suffering?' she screamed, stabbing her finger into her chest. 'I was the one he loved and wanted to be with from the minute we set eyes on each other the day we moved in. If *you* hadn't been pregnant I know we'd have gone off together but Tommy wouldn't hear of it, not with you in that condition. Then you fell so quickly for another and trapped him good and proper. He said his conscience wouldn't let him leave his kids. I kept telling him, kids survive whether their dad's there or not, but he wouldn't hear of it. He said we'd have ter wait to be together 'til his kids left home or he couldn't live with himself. I suffered twenty-odd years waiting for him. Living on his promises. So don't you dare talk ter me about fucking suffering.'

'You and Tommy were lovers since we all moved in? Oh, God. How could you deceive us all for so long?' Vinnie gasped. Though her thoughts were reeling from what Noreen was telling her, another more terrible one

417

struck her. 'Barry?' she urged. 'Whose is he, Noreen? Eric's or Tommy's?'

She gave a dismissive shrug. 'How would I know? Well, I had to keep Eric happy while I was waiting for Tommy to leave. Huh, him and his promises. Just as I thought me waiting was about up that little trollop at work made a play for him and took him off me.' She snatched up a bottle of gin from the cluttered table, unscrewed the top and downed a large swig, then wiped her mouth with the back of her hand. 'You've no idea what it was like for me, watching him play Happy Families with you while I had to stay put here with that boring old sod I'd saddled meself with, make out I was happy. Then to find out, after all those years of living on my hopes, that Tommy was deceiving me with that little tart . . .'

A sudden memory struck Vinnie: Noreen peering through the factory railings. She had thought at the time her neighbour was worried about her. But Noreen hadn't been looking for her at all but for Tommy. All her bewildering changes of attitude suddenly fell into place. Vinnie glared at her accusingly. 'When Tommy left me after Julie's wedding, you thought he'd left me for you, didn't you, Noreen? That's why you kept asking me where he was. You thought he'd gone ahead to set up things ready for you to join him, and when he never came to collect you or contacted you, you began to realise something was wrong. You were looking for him that night at the factory, not for me.'

Noreen took another long swig from the bottle of gin. 'All meking sense ter yer now, ain't it, ducky?' She eyed Vinnie mockingly. 'I use ter laugh at you behind yer back. I've never met anyone as trusting as you. Mind you, I have to admit to being a bit stupid meself. I could never understand why a man like Tommy insisted on staying with you. It's only now I realise that it was because he had it cushy. You running after him like a good little wife should, and me seeing to all his extra needs in bed. He got the excitement from me he found lacking in you. A clever bugger our Tommy, weren't he, Vinnie?' Her face darkened thunderously. 'But his big mistake was in thinking he could treat me like he did you,' she cried, stabbing a finger in the air. 'I ain't so gullible as you, far from it. He made promises to me and he shouldn't have broken 'em.'

She took another gulp of gin and gave a bitter laugh as she began pacing the room. She was on a roll now. All her years of pent-up frustration, of biding her time waiting to be with the man she loved, spilled out. 'I warned him,' she snarled. 'I gave him a chance to leave that tart and honour his commitment to me. He laughed at me. Actually laughed.' She stopped her pacing and fixed Vinnie with her eyes. 'He laughed at me and said she was no more of a trollop than I was, and at least she was young and not past it like me. He told me he'd never had any intention of leaving you for me, only promised me that to keep me sweet for all those years. I was just his bit of fun, on tap when he needed me, and I went along with it, convinced he loved me. Love! Huh, he didn't know the meaning of the word.'

Her face contorted as bitter memories surfaced. 'He told me he had no need of me anymore. I didn't excite him, see. Sex with me was boring. He hurt me, Vinnie, hurt me more than I can ever tell yer. After all we'd had together, he could say things like that to me. But still I gave him another chance. I told him if he didn't do what he'd always said he would, I'd tell you everything. I was desperate, couldn't believe he was doing this ter me. He laughed again. Said I could tell you what I liked, you'd never believe me, so go ahead. Then he told me to piss off and stop pestering him. *He* told *me* to stop pestering *him*,' she hissed, incensed, her eyes flashing. 'How dare he? I'd waited to be with that man all those years. I'd let him have his way with me whenever he snapped his fingers, always under the impression that one day we'd be together. Well, if I weren't having him no one was.' A smile split her face and her eyes danced wickedly. 'Tommy certainly got what he deserved for double-crossing me. And that little cow got her just deserts for teking him off me, didn't she? I hope she's rotting in hell where she is. I hope they both are. Wanna drink?' she asked Vinnie, thrusting the bottle in her direction. 'Let's make a toast ter Tommy,' she said, raising the bottle. 'Rest in peace, you BASTARD.'

Face drained bleach white, Vinnie felt her life's blood draining from her as she stared at Noreen, stupefied, the horrible truth striking her forcibly. A sickening bile rose up to burn the back of her throat. 'It was you who killed Tommy, wasn't it?' she uttered, confounded. 'Maxine Upton was telling the truth when she screamed her innocence. There *were* two arguments in her flat that night. One Maxine caused, but the other one the witnesses heard was with you, wasn't it?'

Noreen gave her a malicious smirk. 'Well, congratulate yerself, Vinnie. You've done summat the police never could. You've sussed out the real culprit. Now is that all 'cos if yer don't mind I've ter get meself ready. I've a date tonight.'

'Oh, no, you've not,' she cried with conviction. 'There's a young girl in prison serving a life sentence for a murder she never committed. You're coming with me to the police station where you'll tell them what really happened that night.'

Vinnie made a grab for her but Noreen was too quick, stepping out of her way. She gave a nonchalant snigger. 'Oh, fuck off, Vinnie. What do yer think I'm gonna do, eh? Tell the nice Sergeant what really happened? Grow up! You've no witnesses, yer can't prove anything. No one saw me follow Tommy back to her flat that night after he'd left your house. Not even Tommy knew I was following him. He got the bleddy shock of his life when he saw me standing in the kitchen just after the little madam had stormed out. He got more of a bleddy shock when I grabbed that knife off the draining board after he'd told me ter get lost and stuck it in his chest. I just thank God I was wearing me gloves and left no fingerprints.' She eyed Vinnie mockingly. 'Even if yer did get the police ter listen to yer, I'd tell them you've just found out that me and Tommy were carrying on all those years and it's a vengeance thing you're trying on.

'The only one who knows the truth besides you now is me sister. Well, I had to tell her, didn't I, 'cos we hadn't spoken for years and she wondered why I turned up like that out of the blue and in such a state. She was never ill. When I thought Tommy had finally left you to be with me, I used the excuse of going to look after her to cover me tracks and give me and Tommy a chance ter settle down together before the shit hit the fan. But after I realised what I'd done, I have ter admit I was shit scared and all I could think of was getting away 'til the heat died down. Me sister was the only one I could go to.' She smirked. 'I can assure yer that she's sworn to secrecy and wouldn't dare breathe a word. It's more than her life's worth to betray me. If she does, she knows what will happen to her, I've made sure she understands that.' She took another gulp from the bottle of gin and looked Vinnie straight in the eye. 'I'm not sorry for what I done, so don't think I am. Tommy deserved it. You should be thanking me 'cos I did you a big favour.'

'A favour!' she cried, aghast. 'How on earth do you make that out?'

'Well, I got rid of that bastard for yer. So I am yer friend really after all. What I did freed both of us up to find a decent man.' She gave an ironic laugh. 'And I got rid of Eric. Oh, I can't tell yer what a relief that was. I only kept him dangling around while I waited for

Tommy ter make his move, but when that went down the plug hole I'd no reason to want Eric around any longer, had I?' She gave a snigger. 'The one good thing Tommy did for me was give me the idea how to get rid of my own millstone. I thought if Tommy could fool you all these years, then why shouldn't I make out Eric'd been fooling people too? Yer were right not ter believe me, Vin, 'cos I made all of it up.' Her mouth twisted cruelly. 'That mealy-mouthed excuse for a man wouldn't 'a' dared ever lift a finger to me, 'cos I'd have knocked him ter Kingdom Come if he had. But with Tommy gone he was in my way. I wanted rid of him quick and that's what I done.'

She gave a rueful shake of her head. 'I thought me luck were in when yer kindly brought that Keith ter me doorstep. Just what I was looking for he was. Oh, I was so excited, thinking at long last me knight in shining armour had come ter whisk me away.' She gave a dismissive shrug. 'He's so far up his own arse he couldn't see what he'd got in me. Still, yer can't win 'em all, can yer, Vinnie?' And she added, laughing, 'You weren't good enough for him either.' She looked at Vinnie in a superior fashion. 'Now yer know what that precious husband of yours was really like, and I'm glad I've told yer. Piss off, can't you? I've already told yer, I gorra date ternight and I don't wanna keep him waiting. He ain't n'ote ter shout about but he'll do for now.'

Vinnie stared at her, amazed. 'I don't know how you've the nerve to stand there and admit all this to me and then expect me to go home and carry on like I know nothing. You're sorry for none of it, are you?' she accused. 'You've not a shred of remorse for any of the pain you've caused, you're just bitter and twisted because your life hasn't turned out the way you wanted. Well, I'm sorry for you, Noreen. I suppose that surprises you considering all you've done to me. But I am sorry Tommy led you on all those years. I'm sorry he felt he could treat us all like he did. Regardless, you'd no right to take his life then expect Maxine Upton to rot in jail for something she isn't guilty of.' She took a firm stance, her eyes blazing with conviction. 'I will make the police listen to me. I will scream blue murder if necessary until they agree to reinvestigate Tommy's death. I will tell them all you have told me, and you can say I'm a liar as much as you like but once they start making enquiries they will find something on you. Your sister's maybe not so reliable as you think. I don't know what you threatened her with to keep her quiet but once the police start questioning her it's surprising what she might let slip under pressure. Her doctor for a start will confirm she wasn't sick. That's your first lie disproved. And can you give an alibi for what you were doing at the time of Tommy's death? You can't expect Eric to spin a line for you, not after the way you've treated him.' Vinnie frowned at her. 'There's no point in thinking you can run away either, Noreen. You'll eventually be found. Wanted pictures will be posted everywhere. You certainly can't hide at your sister's because that's the first place the police will look for you, I'll make sure of that.'

Noreen's eyes were darting wildly. She knew by the tone of her voice that Vinnie meant business and was not open to negotiation. But she wasn't about to let Vinnie, a woman whom she'd fooled all these years, get the better of her. She'd come too far, got away with too much, to give up her freedom without a fight. She made a sudden lunge for the bread knife on the table and waved it menacingly at Vinnie. 'We'll see about that,' she snarled.

Anticipating the woman's next move, quick as a flash Vinnie grabbed a chair and held it out protectively in front of her. 'How are you going to explain my death, Noreen? My daughter knows I'm here. You were complacent enough to believe you got away with murder once but you won't get away with it twice.'

Knife raised midair, Noreen glared at her quarry, until the hopelessness of her situation sank in. There was no escape and she knew it. Her heart thumped painfully. She thought she'd been so clever and she had been but her downfall was all her own fault. She shouldn't have opened her mouth to Vinnie and got carried away with all she had told her. Vinnie wasn't her sister, easily made to keep quiet. Noreen glowered in hatred. 'Think you're fucking clever, don't you?' she spat.

'Clever? Not at all, Noreen. At this moment all I am is ashamed to know this was going on under my own nose and I hadn't a clue. Now, do I fetch the police or are you coming to the station with me? The choice is yours.'

★ ★ ★

Nearing midnight that night, Vinnie stared blindly into the cup of hot chocolate Julie had made her before she had returned home with Gary. No one, least of all Vinnie herself, could have guessed how this day would turn out. Little had she known that attending an interview for a job would result in her being reunited with her long-lost daughter and also in a shocking revelation. That in turn had led to even more shocking revelations when Vinnie had tackled Noreen over her terrible treatment of Janie, and then the real truth about Tommy's murder. Everyone was still reeling from the shock of learning it was Noreen who was responsible and not Maxine. Noreen was in police custody now and Vinnie guessed it would only be a matter of time before she went to trial and Maxine was released.

Vinnie was still having trouble coming to terms with what she had learned. It was horrifying, all of it, but to Vinnie nothing was more terrible than the thought of what her daughter had suffered since the tender age of seven. Vinnie knew she could never hope to put that right but she was at last being given the chance to be a proper mother to Janie, and vowed she would be the best mother ever.

A warm glow filled her. Janie was upstairs now, hopefully fast asleep in her old bed. But these would be much happier times for her. No longer was this house overshadowed by her callous father nor his menacing mistress who'd lived next-door. Vinnie smiled tenderly when she remembered Janie and Julie's reunion. The tears as the sisters had wept and hugged each other, and then Julie, supported by her beloved Gary, had listened to Janie's shocking story, and then to Vinnie as she related Noreen's true involvement in all of it. They had all cried then, sobbing in each other's arms until they were exhausted. They had finally made a pact that the past was over and together all of them would look forward to their future as a united family, something previously denied them.

A thought suddenly struck Vinnie. It was ironic but a great good had come from her heartache over Keith. If his own daughter had not been so adamant about fulfilling her mother's deathbed vow then Vinnie herself would still be working at Brewin's and would never have applied for that job today. She knew she would never completely recover from her sadness over the loss of Keith but the joy of Janie's safe return helped to console her.

Chapter Thirty

Angela Hamlin tasted the homemade lemonade and smiled in satisfaction. It was good if she said so herself. But then, only the best was good enough for her dad. If she had felt the slightest thing to be wrong with it she would have started making it all over again. Pouring a measure into a large tumbler, she walked down the garden to where he lay snoozing in a deckchair, surrounded by a tiny copse of trees and shrubs. She noted that the lawn needed cutting, something her father usually tackled regularly in the summer, priding himself on his straight lines and pristine edges. Then she noticed that the shrubs looked straggly. In fact, the whole garden come to that was looking neglected.

She arrived abreast of her father and gazed down at him tenderly. He looked so peaceful she was loath to wake him. She supposed napping in the afternoon was what ageing people did. Her father would be forty-five shortly, hardly young any more, yet he still tackled heavy jobs around the house. She mentally scolded herself. He was too caring towards her and, she suspected, too proud to admit these jobs were too much for him now, knowing she would only take it upon herself to fit them in with everything else she did to make his life comfortable. To save his pride it was up to her to bring up the subject. She could make out that she'd developed a sudden interest in gardening and house maintenance, and in order for her to become as expert as he, could he give her instruction while she did the work? She smiled to herself. That way his pride would remain intact and he could take things far easier with her at the helm. After all, just as her mother had, all Angie wanted was his happiness and well-being. She loved him so much Her mother would be proud to know how her daughter had honoured her vow to care for him.

As she made to put the glass down by the side of the deckchair he roused himself and for a second stared at her, startled. 'Oh, hello, Angie,' he said, giving a yawn. He spotted the glass she was holding. 'That for me? Thank you, dear,' he said, retrieving it from her. 'Oh, this is good,' he said, smiling up at her.

'As good as my mother made?'

'Most definitely.'

'Can I get you anything else?' she asked.

'No, thank you. Just enjoying the sun. I ought to do a spot of weeding but . . .' His voice trailed off. The truth was he couldn't be bothered. Normally he loved to weed, the chore giving him great satisfaction. Trouble was, these days nothing seemed to bring him much joy. He was well aware of the reason for his lethargy.

Vinnie. Despite nearly a year passing since he had so reluctantly told her he had no choice but to give her up, he was still missing her dreadfully. Oh, on the surface he functioned, appeared happy and well, but beneath lay a deep sadness that just would not dissipate. Vinnie was constantly on his mind, in waking hours and sleep. He wondered how she was. What she was doing. Most painful for him, had she found another to love? He gave a deep forlorn sigh.

'Are you all right, Dad?'

His head jerked up. Having lapsed into daydreaming he had forgotten Angie was present. 'Pardon? Oh, yes, yes, I'm fine.'

'Listen, about the weeding. I'd like to take over the garden, Dad.'

He eyed her questioningly. 'Don't you think you do enough already, Angie? I like gardening. Yes, I admit I've let it get a little out of hand this year but . . . well, you know you won't let me lift a finger in the house, so please, my dear, leave me with something.'

'I wasn't trying to take it off you,' she said, hurt. 'I was trying to ease your burdens, that's all. You need to take it easier at your age, Dad.'

He looked at her, startled. 'My age! Angie, for goodness' sake, I'm forty-five, hardly an old crock.'

'No, I know you're not. But I've noticed you've lost interest in many of the things you used to enjoy and I know it's because they've become too much for you.'

He shifted position in his chair and gave her his full attention. 'You think my lack of interest is because I'm getting old, do you, Angie? You don't think there could be any other reason?'

'Such as?' she asked, bewildered.

That I'm miserable without Vinnie and it's all your fault, he wanted to say to her. But couldn't. He had fought long and hard over the past year not to feel resentment against his daughter for forcing him into giving up his happiness with Vinnie, a happiness in truth Angie too could have shared in if she hadn't been so adamant about fulfilling her vow, but he couldn't hurt her by saying so, he loved her too much. He leaned over and patted her arm. 'Oh, nothing, dear. You're right I'm getting old and crotchety.'

'I'll start on the garden tomorrow,' she said happily. 'Now are you sure I can't get you anything else?'

'I'm sure.'

'A newspaper? You haven't done the crossword today. In fact, I can't remember the last time you did it.'

'I'm fine, Angie, really. Please stop fussing.'

'I'm not fussing, I'm trying to look after you properly. I know, a book. I'll fetch you one,' she said, and without waiting for a response set off back to the house.

Keith settled back and sipped his drink, staring into space, lapsing into his daydream again.

Angie looked through all the titles in the bookcase in the hall. Nothing caught her eye that would interest her father. Having until recently been a great reader, he had read all of them at least twice, some of them three times over. She looked at her watch. Had she time to nip down to the local bookshop and buy him one? Then a thought struck her. In his bedroom he kept several books on his favourite topics. Rivers of the world and autobiographies were of particular interest to him. Greek mythology was his favourite subject, or had been. If she got that book for him, maybe she could rekindle his interest. Another thought struck her. She could show an interest in Greek mythology herself. It didn't really appeal to her but it was something they could share together, like her mother would have done. Why hadn't she thought of that before? Maybe she could suggest a holiday in Greece next year where they could explore some of the ancient sites.

Jauntily she set off in search of the book. Normally she would not invade her father's private domain, except to clean and change the bed, but she felt sure he'd have no objection to her looking through his bookcase when he knew her reason. It wasn't as though anything private was kept there. Smiling happily, she found the book almost immediately. Remembering her decision to take an interest in this particular topic she opened it and began to flick through the pages, and as she did so something fell out and fluttered down to her feet. She bent to pick it up and looked at it. It was a letter. A hand-written one. It must be from her mother. It didn't seem to be her mother's writing but it must be. Who else would he treasure a letter from? It had to be from someone very special to be kept safe inside her father's favourite book. She made to replace it then stopped. Natural curiosity made her want to know what her mother had written to her father about.

She sat down on the bed, laid the book to the side of her, opened the letter and began to read.

My dearest Keith,

With this personal letter to you I have asked Betty also to give you my resignation notice. It is best I go, my dear, rather than work alongside you. I cannot bear the thought of seeing you, knowing how much we mean to each other yet not being able to be together.

I cannot deny that the pain of your decision is unbearable to me. I know our time together was only short but for me those times were so special, ones I will always treasure. I do understand why you have to do this. I know that for us to be together would cost you dearly, meaning the loss of your daughter. I have lost a daughter myself and the pain it brings I would not wish on anyone, especially you, my love. I also understand why Angela has acted as she has. She loves you dearly and believes that in being with me you are betraying the memory of her mother, and stopping her from carrying out her vow to care for you. In her desire to do her best by you, she does not recognise that the love of a daughter does not make up for the loss of a wife. She will only realise this when she falls in love herself. Unfortunately, in centring her whole life around you, I fear she could miss her chance of finding that special love we share. Regardless, I know Angela is doing her best for you in the only way she knows how and cannot fault her absolute love and devotion to you. At least I know you will always be cared for.

Please be happy, my love. You will always hold a very special place in my heart and I will never forget you.

Yours always,
Vinnie

Angie slowly folded the letter and raised her head. For several moments she stared blindly around the room as she went over and over in her mind what Vinnie had written. Then she rose and walked across to the window to glance out. She could see her father, still slumped in his deckchair. Suddenly she saw him as he really was. He wasn't getting old as she'd thought but in fact was lonely and very sad. He'd lost his joy in life. Then she realised why. It was her fault. In her eagerness to fulfil her own vow to care for him she was actually suffocating him. He had nothing in his life that she didn't try to be part of. This letter had made her realise it.

Oh, how badly she had misjudged this woman he had found. This was a letter written by a caring person who loved her father enough to let him go rather than risk his losing his daughter. It was such an unselfish act. That was why her father had for the past year been listless and disinterested: he was pining for the woman he loved.

Tears of remorse fell then. She had been so selfish. Had denied her father another chance of happiness.

This woman . . . Vinnie . . . was right about Angela too. In doing what she had, she had forgotten that she had a life of her own to live.

She could only hope it wasn't too late to put these wrongs right.

Vinnie laid down her book in her lap and looked at her daughter in admiration when she bounded in.

'You look beautiful, love,' she said proudly.

'All mothers say that,' Janie replied jocularly as she dashed across, leaned over and gave her a hug. She straightened up and gave a twirl. 'So I'll do then, will I?'

She was dressed in a short red pleated skirt and pale pink fitted shirt with a long pointed collar. Her leather boots were thigh-length; blonde hair styled like the pop singer Cilla Black wore hers.

'You'll more than do. Are you sure it's not a boy you're meeting?'

'Girlfriends, Mum, but you never know. Hopefully I might attract the attention of someone nice tonight.'

'They'd have to be blind not to notice you, my darling,' Vinnie said sincerely. 'Now you'd better hurry or you'll miss your bus.'

As Janie was putting on her coat she said, 'Oh, I forgot to tell you I won't be needing dinner tomorrow night as I'm going straight over to Julie's from work and she's cooking. Gary's having a night out with his mates so we're going to have a girlie night. Do our hair and nails, that sort of thing. Why don't you join us, Mum?'

A flood of warmth rushed through her. It was wonderful for her to witness how well her daughters were getting on. They were as close as any sisters of their age could be and loved and respected each other without question. It was also nice that Vinnie knew without doubt her daughter's invitation for her to join them tomorrow was sincerely meant.

'I'll leave you youngsters to your titivating. Besides, how are you going to discuss this new man you meet tonight with your sister if your mother's there?' she said, smiling. 'I'm quite happy here reading my book. I might watch a bit of television later. Peggy Mount and Sidney James are in a comedy play.'

Janie looked at her searchingly. She saw the deep love her mother had for her shining from her eyes but behind that lay deep sadness. She perched on the arm of the chair and put her arm around her mother's shoulder. 'Mum, I know you're still upset over the fact you were the one who made Noreen give herself up to the police, but you had no choice. If you hadn't made her tell the truth to them, Maxine Upton would still be serving a life sentence for something she never did. You couldn't have kept quiet about this, Mum, you're far too honest. Please stop punishing yourself. What Noreen Adler is facing now is all her own doing.'

Vinnie smiled wanly at her. 'Yes, I know, dear. I know I had no choice. Trouble is, I still find it difficult to believe how your father lied to me so convincingly. I really believed he hated Noreen. Yet all the time they were carrying on. But it was far worse what they did to you. That's what I find it hardest to deal with.'

'It's all in the past, Mum. We're back together now, as close as mother and daughter could ever be, and I thank God every day for that.' She looked at her mother searchingly. 'There's something else upsetting you, isn't there, Mum? I know about Keith Hamlin. Julie has told me. Well, sisters talk, don't they, and especially when it's something to do with the mother they love so much. She told me that for personal reasons Mr Hamlin had to end your relationship. It's so sad for you, Mum. From what Julie told me you loved him a lot. But you can't sit around mourning him for ever. Why don't you go out more with Betty? I know she's much older than you but you two get on so well and you enjoy yourself when you do go to the pub or whatever with her.'

Vinnie smiled at her affectionately. 'It'll please you to know, Janie, that I'm going out with Betty on Saturday night. Apparently there are a couple of good acts on at the social club, a comedian and then a singer, so I shall enjoy myself. Besides, haven't you realised that after a hard day in the factory all I want to do is put my feet up? I'm not so young anymore, you know, dear.'

'Get away with you, Mum,' she scoffed. 'You're forty-one and look at least five years younger. I know for a fact that the chap who comes in to service the machines thinks you're quite a tasty bit of stuff. He doesn't know you're my mother,' she added, laughing merrily. 'I daren't embarrass him by telling him that after he'd expressed such admiration for you.' She paused and looked at her earnestly. 'You do like working for the Parkers, don't you, Mum? You don't regret accepting the job? I only ask because I was so excited about you working where I did that, well, I sort of made it impossible for you to turn it down, didn't I?'

'I'm glad you did persuade me. I love my job.' Vinnie did too. The girls were very friendly, the pay was good and the owners very respectful towards their staff. That didn't stop her, though, missing her old job and the people there, in particular one of them whose memory she was still trying desperately to push to the back of her mind. 'Tell you what, I'll have a good look at this chap the next time he comes in and let you know whether to put in a good word for me or not,' she said, tongue in cheek, to appease her daughter. She didn't mean it, of course. The time was way off yet when she knew she'd be over the loss of Keith sufficiently even to consider the attentions of another man. 'Now off you go,' she ordered Janie. 'Enjoy yourself, eh? And be careful,' she added.

She had just settled down to reading her book again when there was a knock on the front door. On opening it, Vinnie was shocked to see who it was.

Chapter Thirty-one

Vinnie's eyes swept around the restaurant table and a burst of happiness filled her. She was surrounded by all the people most important to her and who she loved most and they were chatting away happily together. There was Julie and Gary; Janie and her fiancé Paul, a lovely man, train driver by trade who absolutely adored her daughter. Then there was Betty, sitting regally, extremely proud of her role as the family's adoptive grandmother. Next to her was Angie and her boyfriend Peter, another teacher she'd met while away on a training course. He was a nice man, rather studious but with a dry sense of humour. The pair seemed well suited to one another and if Vinnie wasn't mistaken an engagement was on the cards sometime in the future.

Beside her sat Keith.

She caught his eye and he smiled, that special smile he kept just for her, and under the table sought her hand and gave it a gentle squeeze. Then unexpectedly he rapped on the table to get their attention. When all eyes were on him he spoke. 'I have asked you here tonight to consult you.' They all looked at him questioningly. He turned and looked at Vinnie lovingly before he focused his attention back on the others. 'I would like your approval before I ask this beautiful lady beside me to be my wife.'

Vinnie's breath caught in her throat. Before anyone could answer she held up her hand in a warning to silence them. She then gave her full attention to Keith.

'Excuse me, but never mind them. *I* give you my full approval. Now, ask me to marry you.'

He took her hand tenderly in his. 'Will you then, Vinnie? Will you please do me the very great honour of becoming my wife?'

'Oh, yes,' she cried ecstatically. 'Yes, I will most certainly.'

The rest of the gathering clapped loudly and cheered their approval.